EVERYMAN'S LIBRARY
EDITED BY ERNEST RHYS

FICTION

TOM JONES BY HENRY FIELDING · INTRODUCTION BY GEORGE SAINTSBURY
VOL. TWO

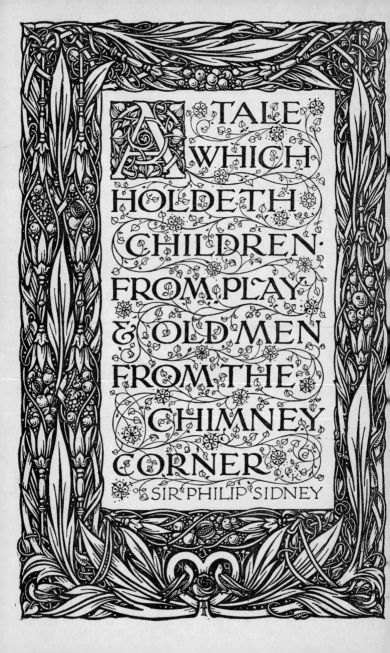

A TALE WHICH HOLDETH CHILDREN FROM PLAY & OLD MEN FROM THE CHIMNEY CORNER

SIR PHILIP SIDNEY

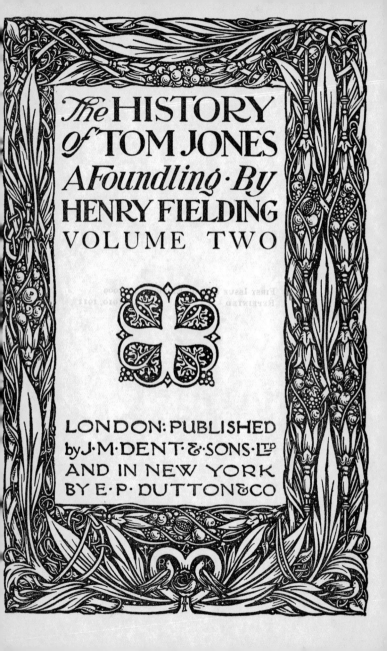

The HISTORY of TOM JONES A Foundling · By HENRY FIELDING
VOLUME TWO

First Issued 1909
Reprinted 1910, 1911

LONDON: PUBLISHED
by J · M · DENT · & · SONS · LTD
AND IN NEW YORK
BY E · P · DUTTON & CO

First Issue of this Edition . 1909
Reprinted 1910, 1912

CONTENTS OF VOL. II

BOOK IX.—*continued.*

CHAPTER V.

PAGE

An apology for all heroes who have good stomachs, with a description of a battle of the amorous kind . . . 1

CHAPTER VI.

A friendly conversation in the kitchen, which had a very common, though not a very friendly, conclusion . . 7

CHAPTER VII.

Containing a fuller account of Mrs Waters, and by what means she came into that distressful situation from which she was rescued by Jones 13

BOOK X.

IN WHICH THE HISTORY GOES FORWARD ABOUT TWELVE HOURS.

CHAPTER I.

Containing instructions very necessary to be perused by modern critics 19

CHAPTER II.

Containing the arrival of an Irish gentleman, with very extraordinary adventures which ensued at the inn . 22

CHAPTER III.   PAGE

A dialogue between the landlady and Susan the chamber-maid, proper to be read by all inn-keepers and their servants; with the arrival, and affable behaviour of a beautiful young lady; which may teach persons of condition how they may acquire the love of the whole world 29

CHAPTER IV.

Containing infallible nostrums for procuring universal dis-esteem and hatred 36

CHAPTER V.

Shewing who the amiable lady, and her unamiable maid, were 39

CHAPTER VI.

Containing, among other things, the ingenuity of Partridge, the madness of Jones, and the folly of Fitzpatrick . . 45

CHAPTER VII.

In which are concluded the adventures that happened at the inn at Upton 50

CHAPTER VIII.

In which the history goes backward 55

CHAPTER IX.

The escape of Sophia 60

BOOK XI.

CONTAINING ABOUT THREE DAYS.

CHAPTER I.

A crust for the critics 70

CHAPTER II.

The adventures which Sophia met with after her leaving Upton 75

Contents

CHAPTER III.
PAGE

A very short chapter, in which however is a sun, a moon, a star, and an angel 84

CHAPTER IV.

The history of Mrs Fitzpatrick 87

CHAPTER V.

In which the history of Mrs Fitzpatrick is continued . . 93

CHAPTER VI.

In which the mistake of the landlord throws Sophia into a dreadful consternation 99

CHAPTER VII.

In which Mrs Fitzpatrick concludes her history . . 104

CHAPTER VIII.

A dreadful alarm in the inn, with the arrival of an unexpected friend of Mrs Fitzpatrick 113

CHAPTER IX.

The morning introduced in some pretty writing. A stage-coach. The civility of chambermaids. The heroic temper of Sophia. Her generosity. The return to it. The departure of the company, and their arrival at London; with some remarks for the use of travellers . 121

CHAPTER X.

Containing a hint or two concerning virtue, and a few more concerning suspicion 126

BOOK XII.

CONTAINING THE SAME INDIVIDUAL TIME WITH THE FORMER.

CHAPTER I.

Showing what is to be deemed plagiarism in a modern author, and what is to be considered as lawful prize . 132

Contents

Chapter II.

PAGE

In which, though the squire doth not find his daughter, something is found which puts an end to his pursuit . . 135

Chapter III.

The departure of Jones from Upton, with what passed between him and Partridge on the road . . . 140

Chapter IV.

The adventure of a beggar-man 146

Chapter V.

Containing more adventures which Mr Jones and his companion met on the road 151

Chapter VI.

From which it may be inferred that the best things are liable to be misunderstood and misinterpreted . . . 156

Chapter VII.

Containing a remark or two of our own, and many more of the good company assembled in the kitchen . . . 160

Chapter VIII.

In which fortune seems to have been in a better humour with Jones than we have hitherto seen her 166

Chapter IX.

Containing little more than a few odd observations . . 171

Chapter X.

In which Mr Jones and Mr Dowling drink a bottle together 175

Chapter XI.

The disasters which befel Jones on his departure for Coventry; with the sage remarks of Partridge . . . 181

Chapter XII.

Relates that Mr Jones continued his journey, contrary to the advice of Partridge, with what happened on that occasion 185

Contents   xi

CHAPTER XIII.

A dialogue between Jones and Partridge 195

CHAPTER XIV.

What happened to Mr Jones in his journey from St Albans 201

BOOK XIII.

CONTAINING THE SPACE OF TWELVE DAYS.

CHAPTER I.

An Invocation 206

CHAPTER II.

What befel Mr Jones on his arrival in London . . 210

CHAPTER III.

A project of Mrs Fitzpatrick, and her visit to Lady Bellaston 216

CHAPTER IV.

Which consists of visiting 220

CHAPTER V.

An adventure which happened to Mr Jones at his lodgings, with some account of a young gentleman who lodged there, and of the mistress of the house, and her two daughters 223

CHAPTER VI.

What arrived while the company were at breakfast, with some hints concerning the government of daughters . 230

CHAPTER VII.

Containing the whole humours of a masquerade . . 237

CHAPTER VIII.

Containing a scene of distress, which will appear very extraordinary to most of our readers . . . 244

CHAPTER IX.

PAGE

Which treats of matters of a very different kind from those in the preceding chapter 250

CHAPTER X.

A chapter which, though short, may draw tears from some eyes 254

CHAPTER XI.

In which the reader will be surprised 258

CHAPTER XII.

In which the thirteenth book is concluded . . . 266

BOOK XIV.

CONTAINING TWO DAYS.

CHAPTER I.

An essay to prove that an author will write the better for having some knowledge of the subject on which he writes 270

CHAPTER II.

Containing letters and other matters which attend amours . 275

CHAPTER III.

Containing various matters 281

CHAPTER IV.

Which we hope will be very attentively perused by young people of both sexes 286

CHAPTER V.

A short account of the history of Mrs Miller . . . 291

Contents   xiii

Chapter VI.
PAGE

Containing a scene which we doubt not will affect all our
readers 295

Chapter VII.

The interview between Mr Jones and Mr Nightingale . 302

Chapter VIII.

What passed between Jones and old Mr Nightingale ; with
the arrival of a person not yet mentioned in this history 308

Chapter IX.

Containing strange matters   316

Chapter X.

A short chapter, which concludes the book .   .   . 321

BOOK XV.

IN WHICH THE HISTORY ADVANCES ABOUT TWO DAYS.

Chapter I.

Too short to need a preface 323

Chapter II.

In which is opened a very black design against Sophia . 325

Chapter III.

A further explanation of the foregoing design .   .   . 331

Chapter IV.

By which it will appear how dangerous an advocate a lady
is when she applies her eloquence to an ill purpose 336

Chapter V.

Containing some matters which may affect, and others which
may surprize, the reader 338

xiv Contents

Chapter VI.
PAGE

By what means the squire came to discover his daughter . 346

Chapter VII.
In which various misfortunes befel poor Jones . . . 352

Chapter VIII.
Short and sweet 360

Chapter IX.
Containing love-letters of several sorts . . . 363

Chapter X.
Consisting partly of facts, and partly of observations upon them 371

Chapter XI.
Containing curious, but not unprecedented matter . . 376

Chapter XII.
A discovery made by Partridge 379

BOOK XVI.

CONTAINING THE SPACE OF FIVE DAYS.

Chapter I.
Of prologues 384

Chapter II.
A whimsical adventure which befel the squire, with the distressed situation of Sophia 386

Contents

Chapter III.

PAGE

What happened to Sophia during her confinement . . 395

Chapter IV.

In which Sophia is delivered from her confinement . . 400

Chapter V.

In which Jones receives a letter from Sophia, and goes to a play with Mrs Miller and Partridge 406

Chapter VI.

In which the history is obliged to look back . . . 414

Chapter VII.

In which Mr Western pays a visit to his sister, in company with Mr Blifil 418

Chapter VIII.

Schemes of Lady Bellaston for the ruin of Jones . . 421

Chapter IX.

In which Jones pays a visit to Mrs Fitzpatrick . . 426

Chapter X.

The consequence of the preceding visit 432

BOOK XVII.

CONTAINING THREE DAYS.

Chapter I.

Containing a portion of introductory writing . . 436

Contents

CHAPTER II.

PAGE

The generous and grateful behaviour of Mrs Miller . . 438

CHAPTER III.

*The arrival of Mr Western, with some matters concerning
the paternal authority* 442

CHAPTER IV.

An extraordinary scene between Sophia and her aunt. . 451

CHAPTER V.

Mrs Miller and Mr Nightingale visit Jones in the prison . 457

CHAPTER VI.

In which Mrs Miller pays a visit to Sophia . . 461

CHAPTER VII.

A pathetic scene between Mr Allworthy and Mrs Miller . 466

CHAPTER VIII.

Containing various matters 469

CHAPTER IX.

What happened to Mr Jones in the prison . . . 477

BOOK XVIII.

CONTAINING ABOUT SIX DAYS.

CHAPTER I.

A farewell to the reader 484

Contents — xvii

Chapter II.

PAGE

Containing a very tragical incident 486

Chapter III.

Allworthy visits old Nightingale ; with a strange discovery that he made on that occasion 492

Chapter IV.

Containing two letters in very different stiles . . . 497

Chapter V.

In which the history is continued 502

Chapter VI.

In which the history is farther continued . . . 509

Chapter VII.

Continuation of the history 514

Chapter VIII.

Further continuation 520

Chapter IX.

A further continuation 530

Chapter X.

Wherein the history begins to draw towards a conclusion . 539

Chapter XI.

The history draws nearer to a conclusion . . . 546

Chapter XII.

Approaching still nearer to the end 554

Chapter the last.

In which the history is concluded 562

The History of Tom Jones,

A FOUNDLING.

BOOK IX.—*continued.*

Chapter v.

An apology for all heroes who have good stomachs, with a description of a battle of the amorous kind.

HEROES, notwithstanding the high ideas which, by the means of flatterers, they may entertain of themselves, or the world may conceive of them, have certainly more of mortal than divine about them. However elevated their minds may be, their bodies at least (which is much the major part of most) are liable to the worst infirmities, and subject to the vilest offices of human nature. Among these latter, the act of eating, which hath by several wise men been considered as extremely mean and derogatory from the philosophic dignity, must be in some measure performed by the greatest prince, heroe, or philosopher upon earth; nay, sometimes Nature hath been so frolicsome as to exact of these dignified characters a much more exorbitant share of this office than she hath obliged those of the lowest order to perform.

To say the truth, as no known inhabitant of this globe is really more than man, so none need be ashamed of submitting to what the necessities of man demand ; but when those great personages I have just mentioned condescend to aim at confining such low offices to themselves—as when, by hoarding or destroying, they seem desirous to prevent any others from eating—then they surely become very low and despicable.

Now, after this short preface, we think it no disparagement to our heroe to mention the immoderate ardour with which he laid about him at this season. Indeed, it may be doubted whether Ulysses, who by the way seems to have had the best stomach of all the heroes in that eating poem of the Odyssey, ever made a better meal. Three pounds at least of that flesh which formerly had contributed to the composition of an ox was now honoured with becoming part of the individual Mr Jones.

This particular we thought ourselves obliged to mention, as it may account for our heroe's temporary neglect of his fair companion, who eat but very little, and was indeed employed in considerations of a very different nature, which passed unobserved by Jones, till he had entirely satisfied that appetite which a fast of twenty-four hours had procured him ; but his dinner was no sooner ended than his attention to other matters revived ; with these matters therefore we shall now proceed to acquaint the reader.

Mr Jones, of whose personal accomplishments we have hitherto said very little, was, in reality, one of the handsomest young fellows in the world. His face, besides being the picture of health, had in it the most apparent marks of sweetness and good-nature. These qualities were indeed so characteristical in his countenance, that, while the spirit and sensibility in his eyes, though they must have been perceived by an accurate observer, might have escaped the notice of the less discerning, so strongly was this good-nature painted in his look, that it was remarked by almost every one who saw him.

It was, perhaps, as much owing to this as to a very fine complexion that his face had a delicacy in it almost inexpressible, and which might have given him an air rather too effeminate, had it not been joined to a most masculine person and mien: which latter had as much in them of the Hercules as the former had of the Adonis. He was besides active, genteel, gay, and good-humoured; and had a flow of animal spirits which enlivened every conversation where he was present.

When the reader hath duly reflected on these many charms which all centered in our heroe, and considers at the same time the fresh obligations which Mrs Waters had to him, it will be a mark more of prudery than candour to entertain a bad opinion of her because she conceived a very good opinion of him.

But, whatever censures may be passed upon her, it is my business to relate matters of fact with veracity. Mrs Waters had, in truth, not only a good opinion of our heroe, but a very great affection for him. To speak out boldly at once, she was in love, according to the present universally-received sense of that phrase, by which love is applied indiscriminately to the desirable objects of all our passions, appetites, and senses, and is understood to be that preference which we give to one kind of food rather than to another.

But though the love to these several objects may possibly be one and the same in all cases, its operations however must be allowed to be different; for, how much soever we may be in love with an excellent sur-loin of beef, or bottle of Burgundy; with a damask rose,

or Cremona fiddle; yet do we never smile, nor ogle,
nor dress, nor flatter, nor endeavour by any other arts
or tricks to gain the affection of the said beef, &c.
Sigh indeed we sometimes may; but it is generally in
the absence, not in the presence, of the beloved object.
For otherwise we might possibly complain of their
ingratitude and deafness, with the same reason as Pasi-
phaë doth of her bull, whom she endeavoured to engage
by all the coquetry practised with good success in the
drawing-room on the much more sensible as well as
tender hearts of the fine gentlemen there.

The contrary happens in that love which operates
between persons of the same species, but of different
sexes. Here we are no sooner in love than it becomes
our principal care to engage the affection of the object
beloved. For what other purpose indeed are our youth
instructed in all the arts of rendering themselves agreeable? If it was not with a view to this love, I question
whether any of those trades which deal in setting off
and adorning the human person would procure a livelihood. Nay, those great polishers of our manners,
who are by some thought to teach what principally
distinguishes us from the brute creation, even dancing-
masters themselves, might possibly find no place in
society. In short, all the graces which young ladies
and young gentlemen too learn from others, and the
many improvements which, by the help of a looking-glass,
they add of their own, are in reality those very *spicula
et faces amoris* so often mentioned by Ovid; or, as they
are sometimes called in our own language, the whole
artillery of love.

Now Mrs Waters and our heroe had no sooner sat
down together than the former began to play this artillery upon the latter. But here, as we are about to
attempt a description hitherto unassayed either in prose
or verse, we think proper to invoke the assistance of

certain aërial beings, who will, we doubt not, come kindly to our aid on this occasion.

" Say then, ye Graces ! you that inhabit the heavenly mansions of Seraphina's countenance ; for you are truly divine, are always in her presence, and well know all the arts of charming ; say, what were the weapons now used to captivate the heart of Mr Jones."

" First, from two lovely blue eyes, whose bright orbs flashed lightning at their discharge, flew forth two pointed ogles ; but, happily for our heroe, hit only a vast piece of beef which he was then conveying into his plate, and harmless spent their force. The fair warrior perceived their miscarriage, and immediately from her fair bosom drew forth a deadly sigh. A sigh which none could have heard unmoved, and which was sufficient at once to have swept off a dozen beaus ; so soft, so sweet, so tender, that the insinuating air must have found its subtle way to the heart of our heroe, had it not luckily been driven from his ears by the coarse bubbling of some bottled ale, which at that time he was pouring forth. Many other weapons did she assay ; but the god of eating (if there be any such deity, for I do not confidently assert it) preserved his votary ; or perhaps it may not be *dignus vindice nodus*, and the present security of Jones may be accounted for by natural means ; for as love frequently preserves from the attacks of hunger, so may hunger possibly, in some cases, defend us against love.

" The fair one, enraged at her frequent disappointments, determined on a short cessation of arms. Which interval she employed in making ready every engine of amorous warfare for the renewing of the attack when dinner should be over.

" No sooner then was the cloth removed than she again began her operations. First, having planted her right eye sidewise against Mr Jones, she shot from its corner

a most penetrating glance ; which, though great part of
its force was spent before it reached our heroe, did not
vent itself absolutely without effect.   This the fair one
perceiving, hastily withdrew her eyes, and levelled them
downwards, as if she was concerned for what she had
done ; though by this means she designed only to draw
him from his guard, and indeed to open his eyes, through
which she intended to surprize his heart.   And now,
gently lifting up those two bright orbs which had already
begun to make an impression on poor Jones, she
discharged a volley of small charms at once from her
whole countenance in a smile.   Not a smile of mirth,
nor of joy ; but a smile of affection, which most ladies
have always ready at their command, and which serves
them to show at once their good-humour, their pretty
dimples, and their white teeth.

"This smile our heroe received full in his eyes, and
was immediately staggered with its force.   He then
began to see the designs of the enemy, and indeed to
feel their success.   A parley now was set on foot between the parties ; during which the artful fair so slily
and imperceptibly carried on her attack, that she had
almost subdued the heart of our heroe before she again
repaired to acts of hostility.   To confess the truth, I
am afraid Mr Jones maintained a kind of Dutch defence, and treacherously delivered up the garrison,
without duly weighing his allegiance to the fair Sophia.
In short, no sooner had the amorous parley ended and
the lady had unmasked the royal battery, by carelessly
letting her handkerchief drop from her neck, than the
heart of Mr Jones was entirely taken, and the fair
conqueror enjoyed the usual fruits of her victory."

Here the Graces think proper to end their description, and here we think proper to end the chapter.

Chapter vi.

*A friendly conversation in the kitchen, which had a very
common, though not very friendly, conclusion.*

WHILE our lovers were entertaining themselves
in the manner which is partly described in the
foregoing chapter, they were likewise furnishing out an entertainment for their good friends in the
kitchen. And this in a double sense, by affording
them matter for their conversation, and, at the same
time, drink to enliven their spirits.

There were now assembled round the kitchen fire,
besides my landlord and landlady, who occasionally
went backward and forward, Mr Partridge, the serjeant, and the coachman who drove the young lady and
her maid.

Partridge having acquainted the company with what
he had learnt from the Man of the Hill concerning the
situation in which Mrs Waters had been found by
Jones, the serjeant proceeded to that part of her history
which was known to him. He said she was the wife
of Mr Waters, who was a captain in their regiment,
and had often been with him at quarters. "Some
folks," says he, "used indeed to doubt whether they
were lawfully married in a church or no. But, for my
part, that's no business of mine : I must own, if I was
put to my corporal oath, I believe she is little better
than one of us ; and I fancy the captain may go to
heaven when the sun shines upon a rainy day. But if
he does, that is neither here nor there ; for he won't
want company. And the lady, to give the devil his
due, is a very good sort of lady, and loves the cloth,
and is always desirous to do strict justice to it ; for she
hath begged off many a poor soldier, and, by her good-
will, would never have any of them punished. But yet,

to be sure, Ensign Northerton and she were very well acquainted together at our last quarters; that is the very right and truth of the matter. But the captain he knows nothing about it; and as long as there is enough for him too, what does it signify? He loves her not a bit the worse, and I am certain would run any man through the body that was to abuse her; therefore I won't abuse her, for my part. I only repeat what other folks say; and, to be certain, what everybody says, there must be some truth in."—"Ay, ay, a great deal of truth, I warrant you," cries Partridge; "*Veritas odium parit.*"—"All a parcel of scandalous stuff," answered the mistress of the house. "I am sure, now she is drest, she looks like a very good sort of lady, and she behaves herself like one; for she gave me a guinea for the use of my cloaths."—"A very good lady indeed!" cries the landlord; "and if you had not been a little too hasty, you would not have quarrelled with her as you did at first."—"You need mention that with my truly!" answered she: "if it had not been for your nonsense, nothing had happened. You must be meddling with what did not belong to you, and throw in your fool's discourse."—"Well, well," answered he; "what's past cannot be mended, so there's an end of the matter."—"Yes," cries she, "for this once; but will it be mended ever the more hereafter? This is not the first time I have suffered for your numscull's pate. I wish you would always hold your tongue in the house, and meddle only in matters without doors, which concern you. Don't you remember what happened about seven years ago?"—"Nay, my dear," returned he, "don't rip up old stories. Come, come, all's well, and I am sorry for what I have done." The landlady was going to reply, but was prevented by the peace-making serjeant, sorely to the displeasure of Partridge, who was a great

lover of what is called fun, and a great promoter of
those harmless quarrels which tend rather to the pro-
duction of comical than tragical incidents.

The serjeant asked Partridge whither he and his
master were travelling? "None of your magisters,"
answered Partridge; "I am no man's servant, I assure
you; for, though I have had misfortunes in the world,
I write gentleman after my name; and, as poor and
simple as I may appear now, I have taught grammar-
school in my time; *sed hei mihi! non sum quod fui.*"—
"No offence, I hope, sir," said the serjeant; "where,
then, if I may venture to be so bold, may you and
your friend be travelling?"—"You have now denominated us right," says Partridge. "*Amici sumus.*
And I promise you my friend is one of the greatest
gentlemen in the kingdom" (at which words both
landlord and landlady pricked up their ears). "He
is the heir of Squire Allworthy."—"What, the squire
who doth so much good all over the country?" cries
my landlady. "Even he," answered Partridge.—
"Then I warrant," says she, "he'll have a swinging
great estate hereafter."—"Most certainly," answered
Partridge.—"Well," replied the landlady, "I thought
the first moment I saw him he looked like a good sort
of gentleman; but my husband here, to be sure, is wiser
than anybody."—"I own, my dear," cries he, "it was
a mistake."—"A mistake, indeed!" answered she;
"but when did you ever know me to make such mistakes?"—"But how comes it, sir," cries the landlord,
"that such a great gentleman walks about the country
afoot?"—"I don't know," returned Partridge; "great
gentlemen have humours sometimes. He hath now a
dozen horses and servants at Gloucester; and nothing
would serve him, but last night, it being very hot
weather, he must cool himself with a walk to yon high
hill, whither I likewise walked with him to bear him

company; but if ever you catch me there again: for I
was never so frightened in all my life. We met with
the strangest man there."—"I'll be hanged," cries the
landlord, "if it was not the Man of the Hill, as they
call him; if indeed he be a man; but I know several
people who believe it is the devil that lives there."—
"Nay, nay, like enough," says Partridge; "and now
you put me in the head of it, I verily and sincerely
believe it was the devil, though I could not perceive
his cloven foot: but perhaps he might have the power
given him to hide that, since evil spirits can appear in
what shapes they please."—"And pray, sir," says the
serjeant, "no offence, I hope; but pray what sort of a
gentleman is the devil? For I have heard some of our
officers say there is no such person; and that it is only
a trick of the parsons, to prevent their being broke;
for, if it was publickly known that there was no devil,
the parsons would be of no more use than we are in
time of peace."—"Those officers," says Partridge,
"are very great scholars, I suppose."—"Not much
of schollards neither," answered the serjeant; "they
have not half your learning, sir, I believe; and, to be
sure, I thought there must be a devil, notwithstanding
what they said, though one of them was a captain;
for methought, thinks I to myself, if there be no devil,
how can wicked people be sent to him? and I have
read all that upon a book."—"Some of your officers,"
quoth the landlord, "will find there is a devil, to their
shame, I believe. I don't question but he'll pay off
some old scores upon my account. Here was one
quartered upon me half a year, who had the conscience
to take up one of my best beds, though he hardly spent
a shilling a day in the house, and suffered his men to
roast cabbages at the kitchen fire, because I would not
give them a dinner on a Sunday. Every good Christian
must desire there should be a devil for the punishment

of such wretches."—"Harkee, landlord," said the serjeant, "don't abuse the cloth, for I won't take it."—"D—n the cloth!" answered the landlord, "I have suffered enough by them."—"Bear witness, gentlemen," says the serjeant, "he curses the king, and that's high treason."—"I curse the king! you villain," said the landlord. "Yes, you did," cries the serjeant; "you cursed the cloth, and that's cursing the king. It's all one and the same; for every man who curses the cloth would curse the king if he durst; so for matter o' that, it's all one and the same thing."—"Excuse me there, Mr Serjeant," quoth Partridge, "that's a *non sequitur*."—"None of your outlandish linguo," answered the serjeant, leaping from his seat; "I will not sit still and hear the cloth abused."—"You mistake me, friend," cries Partridge. "I did not mean to abuse the cloth; I only said your conclusion was a *non sequitur*."*—"You are another," cries the serjeant, "an you come to that. No more a *sequitur* than yourself. You are a pack of rascals, and I'll prove it; for I will fight the best man of you all for twenty pound." This challenge effectually silenced Partridge, whose stomach for drubbing did not so soon return after the hearty meal which he had lately been treated with; but the coachman, whose bones were less sore, and whose appetite for fighting was somewhat sharper, did not so easily brook the affront, of which he conceived some part at least fell to his share. He started therefore from his seat, and, advancing to the serjeant, swore he looked on himself to be as good a man as any in the army, and offered to box for a guinea. The military man accepted the combat, but refused the wager; upon which both immediately stript and engaged,

---

* This word, which the serjeant unhappily mistook for an affront, is a term in logic, and means that the conclusion does not follow from the premises.

till the driver of horses was so well mauled by the leader of men, that he was obliged to exhaust his small remainder of breath in begging for quarter.

The young lady was now desirous to depart, and had given orders for her coach to be prepared : but all in vain, for the coachman was disabled from performing his office for that evening. An antient heathen would perhaps have imputed this disability to the god of drink, no less than to the god of war ; for, in reality, both the combatants had sacrificed as well to the former deity as to the latter. To speak plainly, they were both dead drunk, nor was Partridge in a much better situation. As for my landlord, drinking was his trade ; and the liquor had no more effect on him than it had on any other vessel in his house.

The mistress of the inn, being summoned to attend Mr Jones and his companion at their tea, gave a full relation of the latter part of the foregoing scene ; and at the same time expressed great concern for the young lady, " who," she said, " was under the utmost uneasiness at being prevented from pursuing her journey. She is a sweet pretty creature," added she, " and I am certain I have seen her face before. I fancy she is in love, and running away from her friends. Who knows but some young gentleman or other may be expecting her, with a heart as heavy as her own ? "

Jones fetched a heavy sigh at those words ; of which, though Mrs Waters observed it, she took no notice while the landlady continued in the room ; but, after the departure of that good woman, she could not forbear giving our heroe certain hints on her suspecting some very dangerous rival in his affections. The aukward behaviour of Mr Jones on this occasion convinced her of the truth, without his giving her a direct answer to any of her questions ; but she was not nice enough in her amours to be greatly concerned at the discovery. The beauty of Jones highly charmed her eye; but as she could not see his heart, she gave herself no concern about it. She could feast heartily at the table of love, without reflecting that some other already had been, or hereafter might be, feasted with the same repast. A sentiment which, if it deals but little in refinement, deals, however, much in substance; and is less capricious, and perhaps less ill-natured and selfish, than the desires of those females who can be contented enough to abstain from the possession of their lovers, provided they are sufficiently satisfied that no one else possesses them.

Chapter vii.

Containing a fuller account of Mrs Waters, and by what means she came into that distressful situation from which she was rescued by Jones.

THOUGH Nature hath by no means mixed up an equal share either of curiosity or vanity in every human composition, there is perhaps no individual to whom she hath not allotted such a proportion of both as requires much arts, and pains too, to subdue and keep under;—a conquest, however, absolutely necessary to every one who would in any degree deserve the characters of wisdom or good breeding.

As Jones, therefore, might very justly be called a well-bred man, he had stifled all that curiosity which the extraordinary manner in which he had found Mrs Waters must be supposed to have occasioned. He had, indeed, at first thrown out some few hints to the lady; but, when he perceived her industriously avoiding any explanation, he was contented to remain in ignorance, the rather as he was not without suspicion that there were some circumstances which must have raised her blushes, had she related the whole truth.

Now since it is possible that some of our readers may not so easily acquiesce under the same ignorance, and as we are very desirous to satisfy them all, we have taken uncommon pains to inform ourselves of the real fact, with the relation of which we shall conclude this book.

This lady, then, had lived some years with one Captain Waters, who was a captain in the same regiment to which Mr Northerton belonged. She past for that gentleman's wife, and went by his name; and yet, as the serjeant said, there were some doubts concerning the reality of their marriage, which we shall not at present take upon us to resolve.

Mrs Waters, I am sorry to say it, had for some time contracted an intimacy with the above-mentioned ensign, which did no great credit to her reputation. That she had a remarkable fondness for that young fellow is most certain; but whether she indulged this to any very criminal lengths is not so extremely clear, unless we will suppose that women never grant every favour to a man but one, without granting him that one also.

The division of the regiment to which Captain Waters belonged had two days preceded the march of that company to which Mr Northerton was the ensign; so that the former had reached Worcester the very day after the unfortunate re-encounter between Jones and Northerton which we have before recorded.

Now, it had been agreed between Mrs Waters and the captain that she would accompany him in his march as far as Worcester, where they were to take their leave of each other, and she was thence to return to Bath, where she was to stay till the end of the winter's campaign against the rebels.

With this agreement Mr Northerton was made ac-

quainted. To say the truth, the lady had made him
an assignation at this very place, and promised to stay
at Worcester till his division came thither; with what
view, and for what purpose, must be left to the reader's
divination; for, though we are obliged to relate facts,
we are not obliged to do a violence to our nature by
any comments to the disadvantage of the loveliest part
of the creation.

Northerton no sooner obtained a release from his
captivity, as we have seen, than he hasted away to
overtake Mrs Waters; which, as he was a very active
nimble fellow, he did at the last-mentioned city, some
few hours after Captain Waters had left her. At his
first arrival he made no scruple of acquainting her with
the unfortunate accident; which he made appear very
unfortunate indeed, for he totally extracted every particle
of what could be called fault, at least in a court of
honour, though he left some circumstances which might
be questionable in a court of law.

Women, to their glory be it spoken, are more
generally capable of that violent and apparently disinterested passion of love, which seeks only the good
of its object, than men. Mrs Waters, therefore, was
no sooner apprized of the danger to which her lover
was exposed, than she lost every consideration besides
that of his safety; and this being a matter equally
agreeable to the gentleman, it became the immediate
subject of debate between them.

After much consultation on this matter, it was at
length agreed that the ensign should go across the
country to Hereford, whence he might find some conveyance to one of the sea-ports in Wales, and thence
might make his escape abroad. In all which expedition
Mrs Waters declared she would bear him company;
and for which she was able to furnish him with money,
a very material article to Mr Northerton, she having

then in her pocket three bank-notes to the amount of £90, besides some cash, and a diamond ring of pretty considerable value on her finger. All which she, with the utmost confidence, revealed to this wicked man, little suspecting she should by these means inspire him with a design of robbing her. Now, as they must, by taking horses from Worcester, have furnished any pursuers with the means of hereafter discovering their route, the ensign proposed, and the lady presently agreed, to make their first stage on foot; for which purpose the hardness of the frost was very seasonable.

The main part of the lady's baggage was already at Bath, and she had nothing with her at present besides a very small quantity of linen, which the gallant undertook to carry in his own pockets. All things, therefore, being settled in the evening, they arose early the next morning, and at five o'clock departed from Worcester, it being then above two hours before day, but the moon, which was then at the full, gave them all the light she was capable of affording.

Mrs Waters was not of that delicate race of women who are obliged to the invention of vehicles for the capacity of removing themselves from one place to another, and with whom consequently a coach is reckoned among the necessaries of life. Her limbs were indeed full of strength and agility, and, as her mind was no less animated with spirit, she was perfectly able to keep pace with her nimble lover.

Having travelled on for some miles in a high road, which Northerton said he was informed led to Hereford, they came at the break of day to the side of a large wood, where he suddenly stopped, and, affecting to meditate a moment with himself, expressed some apprehensions from travelling any longer in so public a way. Upon which he easily persuaded his fair companion to strike with him into a path which seemed to lead directly through the wood, and which at length brought them both to the bottom of Mazard Hill.

Whether the execrable scheme which he now attempted to execute was the effect of previous deliberation, or whether it now first came into his head, I cannot determine. But being arrived in this lonely place, where it was very improbable he should meet with any interruption, he suddenly slipped his garter from his leg, and, laying violent hands on the poor woman, endeavoured to perpetrate that dreadful and detestable fact which we have before commemorated, and which the providential appearance of Jones did so fortunately prevent.

Happy was it for Mrs Waters that she was not of the weakest order of females; for no sooner did she perceive, by his tying a knot in his garter, and by his declarations, what his hellish intentions were, than she stood stoutly to her defence, and so strongly struggled with her enemy, screaming all the while for assistance, that she delayed the execution of the villain's purpose several minutes, by which means Mr Jones came to her relief at that very instant when her strength failed and she was totally overpowered, and delivered her from the ruffian's hands, with no other loss than that of her cloaths, which were torn from her back, and of the diamond ring, which during the contention either dropped from her finger, or was wrenched from it by Northerton.

Thus, reader, we have given thee the fruits of a very painful enquiry which for thy satisfaction we have made into this matter. And here we have opened to thee a scene of folly as well as villany, which we could scarce have believed a human creature capable of being guilty of, had we not remembered that this fellow was at that time firmly persuaded that he had already committed a murder, and had forfeited his life to the law.

As he concluded therefore that his only safety lay in flight, he thought the possessing himself of this poor woman's money and ring would make him amends for the additional burthen he was to lay on his conscience.

And here, reader, we must strictly caution thee that thou dost not take any occasion, from the misbehaviour of such a wretch as this, to reflect on so worthy and honourable a body of men as are the officers of our army in general. Thou wilt be pleased to consider that this fellow, as we have already informed thee, had neither the birth nor education of a gentleman, nor was a proper person to be enrolled among the number of such. If, therefore, his baseness can justly reflect on any besides himself, it must be only on those who gave him his commission.

BOOK X.

Chapter i.

*Containing instructions very necessary to be perused
by modern critics.*

READER, it is impossible we should know what
sort of person thou wilt be; for, perhaps, thou
may'st be as learned in human nature as Shakespear himself was, and, perhaps, thou may'st be no
wiser than some of his editors. Now, lest this latter
should be the case, we think proper, before we go any
farther together, to give thee a few wholesome admonitions; that thou may'st not as grossly misunderstand
and misrepresent us, as some of the said editors have
misunderstood and misrepresented their author.

First, then, we warn thee not too hastily to condemn
any of the incidents in this our history as impertinent
and foreign to our main design, because thou dost not
immediately conceive in what manner such incident
may conduce to that design. This work may, indeed,
be considered as a great creation of our own; and
for a little reptile of a critic to presume to find fault
with any of its parts, without knowing the manner in
which the whole is connected, and before he comes

19

to the final catastrophe, is a most presumptuous absurdity. The allusion and metaphor we have here made use of, we must acknowledge to be infinitely too great for our occasion; but there is, indeed, no other, which is at all adequate to express the difference between an author of the first rate and a critic of the lowest.

Another caution we would give thee, my good reptile, is, that thou dost not find out too near a resemblance between certain characters here introduced; as, for instance, between the landlady who appears in the seventh book and her in the ninth. Thou art to know, friend, that there are certain characteristics in which most individuals of every profession and occupation agree. To be able to preserve these characteristics, and at the same time to diversify their operations, is one talent of a good writer. Again, to mark the nice distinction between two persons actuated by the same vice or folly is another; and, as this last talent is found in very few writers, so is the true discernment of it found in as few readers; though, I believe, the observation of this forms a very principal pleasure in those who are capable of the discovery; every person, for instance, can distinguish between Sir Epicure Mammon and Sir Fopling Flutter; but to note the difference between Sir Fopling Flutter and Sir Courtly Nice requires a more exquisite judgment: for want of which, vulgar spectators of plays very often do great injustice in the theatre; where I have sometimes known a poet in danger of being convicted as a thief, upon much worse evidence than the resemblance of hands hath been held to be in the law. In reality, I apprehend every amorous widow on the stage would run the hazard of being condemned as a servile imitation of Dido, but that happily very few of our play-house critics understand enough of Latin to read Virgil.

In the next place, we must admonish thee, my worthy friend (for, perhaps, thy heart may be better than thy head), not to condemn a character as a bad one, because it is not perfectly a good one.   If thou dost delight in these models of perfection, there are books enow written to gratify thy taste; but, as we have not, in the course of our conversation, ever happened to meet with any such person, we have not chosen to introduce any such here.   To say the truth, I a little question whether mere man ever arrived at this consummate degree of excellence, as well as whether there hath ever existed a monster bad enough to verify that

——nulla virtute redemptum
*A vitiis——**

in Juvenal; nor do I, indeed, conceive the good purposes served by inserting characters of such angelic perfection, or such diabolical depravity, in any work of invention; since, from contemplating either, the mind of man is more likely to be overwhelmed with sorrow and shame than to draw any good uses from such patterns; for in the former instance he may be both concerned and ashamed to see a pattern of excellence in his nature, which he may reasonably despair of ever arriving at; and in contemplating the latter he may be no less affected with those uneasy sensations, at seeing the nature of which he is a partaker degraded into so odious and detestable a creature.

In fact, if there be enough of goodness in a character to engage the admiration and affection of a well-disposed mind, though there should appear some of those little blemishes *quas humana parum cavit natura,* they will raise our compassion rather than our abhorrence.   Indeed, nothing can be of more moral use than

* Whose vices are not allayed with a single virtue.

the imperfections which are seen in examples of this kind; since such form a kind of surprize, more apt to affect and dwell upon our minds than the faults of very vicious and wicked persons. The foibles and vices of men, in whom there is great mixture of good, become more glaring objects from the virtues which contrast them and shew their deformity; and when we find such vices attended with their evil consequence to our favourite characters, we are not only taught to shun them for our own sake, but to hate them for the mischiefs they have already brought on those we love.

And now, my friend, having given you these few admonitions, we will, if you please, once more set forward with our history.

Chapter ij.

Containing the arrival of an Irish gentleman, with very extraordinary adventures which ensued at the inn.

NOW the little trembling hare, which the dread of all her numerous enemies, and chiefly of that cunning, cruel, carnivorous animal, man, had confined all the day to her lurking-place, sports wantonly o'er the lawns; now on some hollow tree the owl, shrill chorister of the night, hoots forth notes which might charm the ears of some modern connoisseurs in music; now, in the imagination of the half-drunk clown, as he staggers through the churchyard, or rather charnelyard, to his home, fear paints the bloody hobgoblin; now thieves and ruffians are awake, and honest watchmen fast asleep; in plain English, it was now midnight; and the company at the inn, as well those who have been already mentioned in this history, as some others who arrived in the evening, were all in bed. Only Susan Chambermaid was now stirring, she being obliged to wash the kitchen before she retired to the arms of the fond expecting hostler.

In this posture were affairs at the inn when a gentleman arrived there post. He immediately alighted from his horse, and, coming up to Susan, enquired of her, in a very abrupt and confused manner, being almost out of breath with eagerness, Whether there was any lady in the house? The hour of night, and the behaviour of the man, who stared very wildly all the time, a little surprized Susan, so that she hesitated before she made any answer; upon which the gentleman, with redoubled eagerness, begged her to give him a true information, saying, He had lost his wife, and was come in pursuit of her. "Upon my shoul," cries he, "I have been near catching her already in two or three places, if I had not found her gone just as I came up with her. If she be in the house, do carry me up in the dark and show her to me; and if she be gone away before me, do tell me which way I shall go after her to meet her, and, upon my shoul, I will make you the richest poor woman in the nation." He then pulled out a handful of guineas, a sight which would have bribed persons of much greater consequence than this poor wench to much worse purposes.

Susan, from the account she had received of Mrs Waters, made not the least doubt but that she was the very identical stray whom the right owner pursued. As she concluded, therefore, with great appearance of reason, that she never could get money in an honester way than by restoring a wife to her husband, she made no scruple of assuring the gentleman that the lady he wanted was then in the house; and was presently afterwards prevailed upon (by very liberal promises, and some earnest paid into her hands) to conduct him to the bedchamber of Mrs Waters.

It hath been a custom long established in the polite world, and that upon very solid and substantial reasons, that a husband shall never enter his wife's apartment without first knocking at the door. The many excellent uses of this custom need scarce be hinted to a reader who hath any knowledge of the world; for by this means the lady hath time to adjust herself, or to remove any disagreeable object out of the way; for there are some situations in which nice and delicate women would not be discovered by their husbands.

To say the truth, there are several ceremonies instituted among the polished part of mankind, which, though they may, to coarser judgments, appear as matters of mere form, are found to have much of substance in them, by the more discerning; and lucky would it have been had the custom above mentioned been observed by our gentleman in the present instance. Knock, indeed, he did at the door, but not with one of those gentle raps which is usual on such occasions. On the contrary, when he found the door locked, he flew at it with such violence, that the lock immediately gave way, the door burst open, and he fell headlong into the room.

He had no sooner recovered his legs than forth from the bed, upon his legs likewise, appeared—with shame and sorrow are we obliged to proceed—our heroe himself, who, with a menacing voice, demanded of the gentleman who he was, and what he meant by daring to burst open his chamber in that outrageous manner.

The gentleman at first thought he had committed a mistake, and was going to ask pardon and retreat, when, on a sudden, as the moon shone very bright, he cast his eyes on stays, gowns, petticoats, caps, ribbons, stockings, garters, shoes, clogs, &c., all which lay in a disordered manner on the floor. All these, operating on the natural jealousy of his temper, so enraged him, that he lost all power of speech; and, without returning any answer to Jones, he endeavoured to approach the bed.

Jones immediately interposing, a fierce contention arose, which soon proceeded to blows on both sides. And now Mrs Waters (for we must confess she was in the same bed), being, I suppose, awakened from her sleep, and seeing two men fighting in her bedchamber, began to scream in the most violent manner, crying out murder! robbery! and more frequently rape! which last, some, perhaps, may wonder she should mention, who do not consider that these words of exclamation are used by ladies in a fright, as fa, la, la, ra, da, &c., are in music, only as the vehicles of sound, and without any fixed ideas.

Next to the lady's chamber was deposited the body of an Irish gentleman who arrived too late at the inn to have been mentioned before. This gentleman was one of those whom the Irish call a calabalaro, or cavalier. He was a younger brother of a good family, and, having no fortune at home, was obliged to look abroad in order to get one; for which purpose he was proceeding to the Bath, to try his luck with cards and the women.

This young fellow lay in bed reading one of Mrs Behn's novels; for he had been instructed by a friend that he would find no more effectual method of recommending himself to the ladies than the improving his understanding, and filling his mind with good literature. He no sooner, therefore, heard the violent uproar in the next room, than he leapt from his bolster, and, taking his sword in one hand, and the candle which burnt by him in the other, he went directly to Mrs Waters's chamber.

If the sight of another man in his shirt at first added

some shock to the decency of the lady, it made her presently amends by considerably abating her fears; for no sooner had the calabalaro entered the room than he cried out, "Mr Fitzpatrick, what the devil is the maning of this?" Upon which the other immediately answered, "O, Mr Maclachlan! I am rejoiced you are here.—This villain hath debauched my wife, and is got into bed with her."—"What wife?" cries Maclachlan; "do not I know Mrs Fitzpatrick very well, and don't I see that the lady, whom the gentleman who stands here in his shirt is lying in bed with, is none of her?"

Fitzpatrick, now perceiving, as well by the glimpse he had of the lady, as by her voice, which might have been distinguished at a greater distance than he now stood from her, that he had made a very unfortunate mistake, began to ask many pardons of the lady; and then, turning to Jones, he said, "I would have you take notice I do not ask your pardon, for you have bate me; for which I am resolved to have your blood in the morning."

Jones treated this menace with much contempt; and Mr Maclachlan answered, "Indeed, Mr Fitzpatrick, you may be ashamed of your own self, to disturb people at this time of night; if all the people in the inn were not asleep, you would have awakened them as you have me. The gentleman has served you very rightly. Upon my conscience, though I have no wife, if you had treated her so, I would have cut your throat."

Jones was so confounded with his fears for his lady's reputation, that he knew neither what to say or do; but the invention of women is, as hath been observed, much readier than that of men. She recollected that there was a communication between her chamber and that of Mr Jones; relying, therefore, on his honour and her own assurance, she answered, "I know not what

you mean, villains! I am wife to none of you. Help!
Rape! Murder! Rape!"—And now, the landlady
coming into the room, Mrs Waters fell upon her with
the utmost virulence, saying, "She thought herself in a
sober inn, and not in a bawdy-house; but that a set of
villains had broke into her room, with an intent upon
her honour, if not upon her life; and both, she said,
were equally dear to her."

The landlady now began to roar as loudly as the
poor woman in bed had done before. She cried, "She
was undone, and that the reputation of her house, which
was never blown upon before, was utterly destroyed."
Then, turning to the men, she cried, "What, in the
devil's name, is the reason of all this disturbance in the
lady's room?" Fitzpatrick, hanging down his head,
repeated, "That he had committed a mistake, for which
he heartily asked pardon," and then retired with his
countryman. Jones, who was too ingenious to have
missed the hint given him by his fair one, boldly
asserted, "That he had run to her assistance upon
hearing the door broke open, with what design he
could not conceive, unless of robbing the lady; which,
if they intended, he said, he had the good fortune to
prevent." "I never had a robbery committed in my
house since I have kept it," cries the landlady; "I
would have you to know, sir, I harbour no highwaymen
here; I scorn the word, thof I say it. None but
honest, good gentlefolks, are welcome to my house;
and, I thank good luck, I have always had enow
of such customers; indeed as many as I could entertain. Here hath been my lord—," and then she
repeated over a catalogue of names and titles, many of
which we might, perhaps, be guilty of a breach of
privilege by inserting.

Jones, after much patience, at length interrupted her,
by making an apology to Mrs Waters, for having

appeared before her in his shirt, assuring her "That nothing but a concern for her safety could have prevailed on him to do it." The reader may inform himself of her answer, and, indeed, of her whole behaviour to the end of the scene, by considering the situation which she affected, it being that of a modest lady, who was awakened out of her sleep by three strange men in her chamber. This was the part which she undertook to perform; and, indeed, she executed it so well, that none of our theatrical actresses could exceed her, in any of their performances, either on or off the stage.

And hence, I think, we may very fairly draw an argument, to prove how extremely natural virtue is to the fair sex; for, though there is not, perhaps, one in ten thousand who is capable of making a good actress, and even among these we rarely see two who are equally able to personate the same character, yet this of virtue they can all admirably well put on; and as well those individuals who have it not, as those who possess it, can all act it to the utmost degree of perfection.

When the men were all departed, Mrs Waters, recovering from her fear, recovered likewise from her anger, and spoke in much gentler accents to the land-lady, who did not so readily quit her concern for the reputation of the house, in favour of which she began again to number the many great persons who had slept under her roof; but the lady stopt her short, and having absolutely acquitted her of having had any share in the past disturbance, begged to be left to her repose, which, she said, she hoped to enjoy unmolested during the remainder of the night. Upon which the landlady, after much civility and many courtsies, took her leave.

Chapter iii.

A dialogue between the landlady and Susan the chamber-maid, proper to be read by all inn-keepers and their servants ; with the arrival, and affable behaviour of a beautiful young lady ; which may teach persons of condition how they may acquire the love of the whole world.

THE landlady, remembering that Susan had been the only person out of bed when the door was burst open, resorted presently to her, to enquire into the first occasion of the disturbance, as well as who the strange gentleman was, and when and how he arrived.

Susan related the whole story which the reader knows already, varying the truth only in some circumstances, as she saw convenient, and totally concealing the money which she had received. But whereas her mistress had, in the preface to her enquiry, spoken much in compassion for the fright which the lady had been in concerning any intended depredations on her virtue, Susan could not help endeavouring to quiet the concern which her mistress seemed to be under on that account, by swearing heartily she saw Jones leap out from her bed.

The landlady fell into a violent rage at these words. "A likely story, truly," cried she, "that a woman should cry out, and endeavour to expose herself, if that was the case ! I desire to know what better proof any lady can give of her virtue than her crying out, which, I believe, twenty people can witness for her she did ? I beg, madam, you would spread no such scandal of any of my guests ; for it will not only reflect on them, but upon the house ; and I am sure no vagabonds, nor wicked beggarly people, come here."

"Well," says Susan, "then I must not believe my own eyes." "No, indeed, must you not always," answered her mistress; "I would not have believed my own eyes against such good gentlefolks. I have not had a better supper ordered this half-year than they ordered last night; and so easy and good-humoured were they, that they found no fault with my Worcestershire perry, which I sold them for champagne; and to be sure it is as well tasted and as wholesome as the best champagne in the kingdom, otherwise I would scorn to give it 'em; and they drank me two bottles. No, no, I will never believe any harm of such sober good sort of people."

Susan being thus silenced, her mistress proceeded to other matters. "And so you tell me," continued she, "that the strange gentleman came post, and there is a footman without with the horses; why, then, he is certainly some of your great gentlefolks too. Why did not you ask him whether he'd have any supper? I think he is in the other gentleman's room; go up and ask whether he called. Perhaps he'll order something when he finds anybody stirring in the house to dress it. Now don't commit any of your usual blunders, by telling him the fire's out, and the fowls alive. And if he should order mutton, don't blab out that we have none. The butcher, I know, killed a sheep just before I went to bed, and he never refuses to cut it up warm when I desire it. Go, remember there's all sorts of mutton and fowls; go, open the door with, Gentlemen, d'ye call? and if they say nothing, ask what his honour will be pleased to have for supper? Don't forget his honour. Go; if you don't mind all these matters better, you'll never come to anything."

Susan departed, and soon returned with an account that the two gentlemen were got both into the same bed. "Two gentlemen," says the landlady, "in the same bed! that's impossible; they are two arrant scrubs, I warrant them; and I believe young Squire Allworthy guessed right, that the fellow intended to rob her ladyship; for, if he had broke open the lady's door with any of the wicked designs of a gentleman, he would never have sneaked away to another room to save the expense of a supper and a bed to himself. They are certainly thieves, and their searching after a wife is nothing but a pretence."

In these censures my landlady did Mr Fitzpatrick great injustice; for he was really born a gentleman, though not worth a groat; and though, perhaps, he had some few blemishes in his heart as well as in his head, yet being a sneaking or a niggardly fellow was not one of them. In reality, he was so generous a man, that, whereas he had received a very handsome fortune with his wife, he had now spent every penny of it, except some little pittance which was settled upon her; and, in order to possess himself of this, he had used her with such cruelty, that, together with his jealousy, which was of the bitterest kind, it had forced the poor woman to run away from him.

This gentleman then being well tired with his long journey from Chester in one day, with which, and some good dry blows he had received in the scuffle, his bones were so sore, that, added to the soreness of his mind, it had quite deprived him of any appetite for eating. And being now so violently disappointed in the woman whom, at the maid's instance, he had mistaken for his wife, it never once entered into his head that she might nevertheless be in the house, though he had erred in the first person he had attacked. He therefore yielded to the dissuasions of his friend from searching any farther after her that night, and accepted the kind offer of part of his bed.

The footman and post-boy were in a different dis-

position. They were more ready to order than the
landlady was to provide; however, after being pretty
well satisfied by them of the real truth of the case, and
that Mr Fitzpatrick was no thief, she was at length
prevailed on to set some cold meat before them, which
they were devouring with great greediness, when Partridge came into the kitchen. He had been first awaked
by the hurry which we have before seen; and while he
was endeavouring to compose himself again on his pillow,
a screech-owl had given him such a serenade at his
window, that he leapt in a most horrible affright from
his bed, and, huddling on his cloaths with great expedition, ran down to the protection of the company, whom
he heard talking below in the kitchen.

His arrival detained my landlady from returning to
her rest; for she was just about to leave the other two
guests to the care of Susan; but the friend of young
Squire Allworthy was not to be so neglected, especially
as he called for a pint of wine to be mulled. She
immediately obeyed, by putting the same quantity of
perry to the fire; for this readily answered to the name
of every kind of wine.

The Irish footman was retired to bed, and the post-
boy was going to follow; but Partridge invited him to
stay and partake of his wine, which the lad very thankfully accepted. The schoolmaster was indeed afraid
to return to bed by himself; and as he did not know
how soon he might lose the company of my landlady,
he was resolved to secure that of the boy, in whose
presence he apprehended no danger from the devil or
any of his adherents.

And now arrived another post-boy at the gate; upon
which Susan, being ordered out, returned, introducing
two young women in riding habits, one of which was
so very richly laced, that Partridge and the post-boy
instantly started from their chairs, and my landlady

fell to her courtsies, and her ladyships, with great eagerness.

The lady in the rich habit said, with a smile of great condescension, "If you will give me leave, madam, I will warm myself a few minutes at your kitchen fire, for it is really very cold; but I must insist on disturbing no one from his seat." This was spoken on account of Partridge, who had retreated to the other end of the room, struck with the utmost awe and astonishment at the splendor of the lady's dress. Indeed, she had a much better title to respect than this; for she was one of the most beautiful creatures in the world.

The lady earnestly desired Partridge to return to his seat; but could not prevail. She then pulled off her gloves, and displayed to the fire two hands, which had every property of snow in them, except that of melting. Her companion, who was indeed her maid, likewise pulled off her gloves, and discovered what bore an exact resemblance, in cold and colour, to a piece of frozen beef.

"I wish, madam," quoth the latter, "your ladyship would not think of going any farther to-night. I am terribly afraid your ladyship will not be able to bear the fatigue."

"Why sure," cries the landlady, "her ladyship's honour can never intend it. O, bless me! farther to-night, indeed! let me beseech your ladyship not to think on't——But, to be sure, your ladyship can't. What will your honour be pleased to have for supper? I have mutton of all kinds, and some nice chicken."

"I think, madam," said the lady, "it would be rather breakfast than supper; but I can't eat anything; and, if I stay, shall only lie down for an hour or two. However, if you please, madam, you may get me a little sack whey, made very small and thin."

"Yes, madam," cries the mistress of the house, "I

have some excellent white wine."—"You have no sack, then?" says the lady. "Yes, an't please your honour, I have; I may challenge the country for that —but let me beg your ladyship to eat something."

"Upon my word, I can't eat a morsel," answered the lady; "and I shall be much obliged to you if you will please to get my apartment ready as soon as possible; for I am resolved to be on horseback again in three hours."

"Why, Susan," cries the landlady, "is there a fire lit yet in the Wild-goose? I am sorry, madam, all my best rooms are full. Several people of the first quality are now in bed. Here's a great young squire, and many other great gentlefolks of quality." Susan answered, "That the Irish gentlemen were got into the Wild-goose."

"Was ever anything like it?" says the mistress; "why the devil would you not keep some of the best rooms for the quality, when you know scarce a day passes without some calling here?——If they be gentlemen, I am certain, when they know it is for her ladyship, they will get up again."

"Not upon my account," says the lady; "I will have no person disturbed for me. If you have a room that is commonly decent, it will serve me very well, though it be never so plain. I beg, madam, you will not give yourself so much trouble on my account." "O, madam!" cries the other, "I have several very good rooms for that matter, but none good enough for your honour's ladyship. However, as you are so condescending to take up with the best I have, do, Susan, get a fire in the Rose this minute. Will your ladyship be pleased to go up now, or stay till the fire is lighted?" "I think I have sufficiently warmed myself," answered the lady; "so, if you please, I will go now; I am afraid I have kept people, and particularly that gentleman (meaning Partridge), too long in the cold already. Indeed, I cannot bear to think of keeping any person from the fire this dreadful weather."—She then departed with her maid, the landlady marching with two lighted candles before her.

When that good woman returned, the conversation in the kitchen was all upon the charms of the young lady. There is indeed in perfect beauty a power which none almost can withstand; for my landlady, though she was not pleased at the negative given to the supper, declared she had never seen so lovely a creature. Partridge ran out into the most extravagant encomiums on her face, though he could not refrain from paying some compliments to the gold lace on her habit; the post-boy sung forth the praises of her goodness, which were likewise echoed by the other post-boy, who was now come in. "She's a true good lady, I warrant her," says he; "for she hath mercy upon dumb creatures; for she asked me every now and tan upon the journey, if I did not think she should hurt the horses by riding too fast? and when she came in she charged me to give them as much corn as ever they would eat."

Such charms are there in affability, and so sure is it to attract the praises of all kinds of people. It may indeed be compared to the celebrated Mrs Hussey.* It is equally sure to set off every female perfection to the highest advantage, and to palliate and conceal every defect. A short reflection, which we could not forbear making in this place, where my reader hath seen the loveliness of an affable deportment; and truth will now oblige us to contrast it, by showing the reverse.

* A celebrated mantua-maker in the Strand, famous for setting off the shapes of women.

Chapter iv.

Containing infallible nostrums for procuring universal disesteem and hatred.

THE lady had no sooner laid herself on her pillow than the waiting-woman returned to the kitchen to regale with some of those dainties which her mistress had refused.

The company, at her entrance, shewed her the same respect which they had before paid to her mistress, by rising; but she forgot to imitate her, by desiring them to sit down again. Indeed, it was scarce possible they should have done so, for she placed her chair in such a posture as to occupy almost the whole fire. She then ordered a chicken to be broiled that instant, declaring, if it was not ready in a quarter of an hour, she would not stay for it. Now, though the said chicken was then at roost in the stable, and required the several ceremonies of catching, killing, and picking, before it was brought to the gridiron, my landlady would nevertheless have undertaken to do all within the time; but the guest, being unfortunately admitted behind the scenes, must have been witness to the *fourberie*; the poor woman was therefore obliged to confess that she had none in the house; "but, madam," said she, "I can get any kind of mutton in an instant from the butcher's."

"Do you think, then," answered the waiting-gentlewoman, "that I have the stomach of a horse, to eat mutton at this time of night? Sure you people that keep inns imagine your betters are like yourselves. Indeed, I expected to get nothing at this wretched place. I wonder my lady would stop at it. I suppose none but tradesmen and grasiers ever call here." The landlady fired at this indignity offered to her house;

however, she suppressed her temper, and contented
herself with saying, "Very good quality frequented
it, she thanked heaven!" "Don't tell me," cries
the other, "of quality! I believe I know more of
people of quality than such as you.—But, prithee,
without troubling me with any of your impertinence,
do tell me what I can have for supper; for, though
I cannot eat horse-flesh, I am really hungry." "Why,
truly, madam," answered the landlady, "you could
not take me again at such a disadvantage; for I must
confess I have nothing in the house, unless a cold
piece of beef, which indeed a gentleman's footman
and the post-boy have almost cleared to the bone."
"Woman," said Mrs Abigail (so for shortness we
will call her), "I entreat you not to make me sick.
If I had fasted a month, I could not eat what had
been touched by the fingers of such fellows. Is there
nothing neat or decent to be had in this horrid place?"
"What think you of some eggs and bacon, madam?"
said the landlady. "Are your eggs new laid? are
you certain they were laid to-day? and let me have
the bacon cut very nice and thin; for I can't endure
anything that's gross.—Prithee try if you can do a
little tolerably for once, and don't think you have a
farmer's wife, or some of those creatures, in the house."
—The landlady began then to handle her knife; but
the other stopt her, saying, "Good woman, I must
insist upon your first washing your hands; for I am
extremely nice, and have been always used from my
cradle to have everything in the most elegant manner."

The landlady, who governed herself with much
difficulty, began now the necessary preparations; for as
to Susan, she was utterly rejected, and with such disdain,
that the poor wench was as hard put to it to restrain
her hands from violence as her mistress had been to
hold her tongue. This indeed Susan did not entirely;

for, though she literally kept it within her teeth, yet there it muttered many "marry-come-ups, as good flesh and blood as yourself;" with other such indignant phrases.

While the supper was preparing, Mrs Abigail began to lament she had not ordered a fire in the parlour; but, she said, that was now too late. "However," said she, "I have novelty to recommend a kitchen; for I do not believe I ever eat in one before." Then, turning to the post-boys, she asked them, "Why they were not in the stable with their horses? If I must eat my hard fare here, madam," cries she to the landlady, "I beg the kitchen may be kept clear, that I may not be surrounded with all the blackguards in town: as for you, sir," says she to Partridge, "you look somewhat like a gentleman, and may sit still if you please; I don't desire to disturb anybody but mob."

"Yes, yes, madam," cries Partridge, "I am a gentleman, I do assure you, and I am not so easily to be disturbed. *Non semper vox casualis est verbo nominativus.*" This Latin she took to be some affront, and answered, "You may be a gentleman, sir; but you don't show yourself as one to talk Latin to a woman." Partridge made a gentle reply, and concluded with more Latin; upon which she tossed up her nose, and contented herself by abusing him with the name of a great scholar.

The supper being now on the table, Mrs Abigail eat very heartily for so delicate a person; and, while a second course of the same was by her order preparing, she said, "And so, madam, you tell me your house is frequented by people of great quality?"

The landlady answered in the affirmative, saying, "There were a great many very good quality and gentlefolks in it now. There's young Squire All-worthy, as that gentleman there knows."

"And pray who is this young gentleman of quality, this young Squire Allworthy?" said Abigail.

"Who should he be," answered Partridge, "but the son and heir of the great Squire Allworthy, of Somersetshire!"

"Upon my word," said she, "you tell me strange news; for I know Mr Allworthy of Somersetshire very well, and I know he hath no son alive."

The landlady pricked up her ears at this, and Partridge looked a little confounded. However, after a short hesitation, he answered, "Indeed, madam, it is true, everybody doth not know him to be Squire Allworthy's son; for he was never married to his mother; but his son he certainly is, and will be his heir too, as certainly as his name is Jones." At that word, Abigail let drop the bacon which she was conveying to her mouth, and cried out, "You surprize me, sir! Is it possible Mr Jones should be now in the house?" "*Quare non?*" answered Partridge, "it is possible, and it is certain."

Abigail now made haste to finish the remainder of her meal, and then repaired back to her mistress, when the conversation passed which may be read in the next chapter.

Chapter v.

Showing who the amiable lady, and her unamiable maid, were.

AS in the month of June, the damask rose, which chance hath planted among the lilies, with their candid hue mixes his vermilion; or as some playsome heifer in the pleasant month of May diffuses her odoriferous breath over the flowery meadows; or as, in the blooming month of April, the gentle, constant dove, perched on some fair bough, sits meditating on her mate; so, looking a hundred charms and breathing as many sweets, her thoughts being fixed on her Tommy, with a heart as good and innocent as her face was beautiful, Sophia (for it was she herself) lay reclining her lovely head on her hand, when her maid entered the room, and, running directly to the bed, cried, "Madam—madam—who doth your ladyship think is in the house?" Sophia, starting up, cried, "I hope my father hath not overtaken us." "No, madam, it is one worth a hundred fathers; Mr Jones himself is here at this very instant." "Mr Jones!" says Sophia, "it is impossible! I cannot be so fortunate." Her maid averred the fact, and was presently detached by her mistress to order him to be called; for she said she was resolved to see him immediately.

Mrs Honour had no sooner left the kitchen in the manner we have before seen than the landlady fell severely upon her. The poor woman had indeed been loading her heart with foul language for some time, and now it scoured out of her mouth, as filth doth from a mud-cart, when the board which confines it is removed. Partridge likewise shovelled in his share of calumny, and (what may surprize the reader) not only bespattered the maid, but attempted to sully the lily-white character of Sophia herself. "Never a barrel the better herring," cries he, "*Noscitur à socio*, is a true saying. It must be confessed, indeed, that the lady in the fine garments is the civiller of the two; but I warrant neither of them are a bit better than they should be. A couple of Bath trulls, I'll answer for them; your quality don't ride about at this time o' night without servants." "Sbodlikins, and that's true," cries the landlady, "you have certainly hit upon the very matter; for quality don't come into a house without bespeaking a supper, whether they eat or no."

While they were thus discoursing, Mrs Honour returned and discharged her commission, by bidding the landlady immediately wake Mr Jones, and tell him a lady wanted to speak with him. The landlady referred her to Partridge, saying, "he was the squire's friend: but, for her part, she never called men-folks, especially gentlemen," and then walked sullenly out of the kitchen. Honour applied herself to Partridge; but he refused, "for my friend," cries he, "went to bed very late, and he would be very angry to be disturbed so soon." Mrs Honour insisted still to have him called, saying, "she was sure, instead of being angry, that he would be to the highest degree delighted when he knew the occasion." "Another time, perhaps, he might," cries Partridge; "but *non omnia possumus omnes*. One woman is enough at once for a reasonable man." "What do you mean by one woman, fellow?" cries Honour. "None of your fellow," answered Partridge. He then proceeded to inform her plainly that Jones was in bed with a wench, and made use of an expression too indelicate to be here inserted; which so enraged Mrs Honour, that she called him jackanapes, and returned in a violent hurry to her mistress, whom she acquainted with the success of her errand, and with the account she had received; which, if possible, she exaggerated, being as angry with Jones as if he had pronounced all the words that came from the mouth of Partridge. She discharged a torrent of abuse on the master, and advised her mistress to quit all thoughts of a man who had never shown himself deserving of her. She then ripped up the story of Molly Seagrim, and gave the most malicious turn to his formerly quitting Sophia herself; which, I must confess, the present incident not a little countenanced.

The spirits of Sophia were too much dissipated by

concern to enable her to stop the torrent of her maid. At last, however, she interrupted her, saying, " I never can believe this ; some villain hath belied him. You say you had it from his friend ; but surely it is not the office of a friend to betray such secrets." " I suppose," cries Honour, " the fellow is his pimp ; for I never saw so ill-looked a villain. Besides, such profligate rakes as Mr Jones are never ashamed of these matters."

To say the truth, this behaviour of Partridge was a little inexcusable ; but he had not slept off the effect of the dose which he swallowed the evening before ; which had, in the morning, received the addition of above a pint of wine, or indeed rather of malt spirits ; for the perry was by no means pure. Now, that part of his head which Nature designed for the reservoir of drink being very shallow, a small quantity of liquor overflowed it, and opened the sluices of his heart ; so that all the secrets there deposited run out. These sluices were indeed, naturally, very ill-secured. To give the best-natured turn we can to his disposition, he was a very honest man ; for, as he was the most inquisitive of mortals, and eternally prying into the secrets of others, so he very faithfully paid them by communicating, in return, everything within his know-ledge.

While Sophia, tormented with anxiety, knew not what to believe, nor what resolution to take, Susan arrived with the sack-whey. Mrs Honour immediately advised her mistress, in a whisper, to pump this wench, who probably could inform her of the truth. Sophia approved it, and began as follows : " Come hither, child ; now answer me truly what I am going to ask you, and I promise you I will very well reward you. Is there a young gentleman in this house, a handsome young gentleman, that———." Here Sophia blushed and was confounded. "A young gentleman," cries Honour, "that came hither in company with that saucy rascal who is now in the kitchen?" Susan answered, "There was."—"Do you know anything of any lady?" continues Sophia, "any lady? I don't ask you whether she is handsome or no; perhaps she is not; that's nothing to the purpose; but do you know of any lady?" "La, madam," cries Honour, "you will make a very bad examiner. Hark'ee, child," says she, "is not that very young gentleman now in bed with some nasty trull or other?" Here Susan smiled, and was silent. "Answer the question, child," says Sophia, "and here's a guinea for you."— "A guinea! madam," cries Susan; "la, what's a guinea? If my mistress should know it I shall certainly lose my place that very instant." "Here's another for you," says Sophia, "and I promise you faithfully your mistress shall never know it." Susan, after a very short hesitation, took the money, and told the whole story, concluding with saying, "If you have any great curiosity, madam, I can steal softly into his room, and see whether he be in his own bed or no." She accordingly did this by Sophia's desire, and returned with an answer in the negative.

Sophia now trembled and turned pale. Mrs Honour begged her to be comforted, and not to think any more of so worthless a fellow. "Why there," says Susan, "I hope, madam, your ladyship won't be offended; but pray, madam, is not your ladyship's name Madam Sophia Western?" "How is it possible you should know me?" answered Sophia. "Why that man, that the gentlewoman spoke of, who is in the kitchen, told about you last night. But I hope your ladyship is not angry with me." "Indeed, child," said she, "I am not; pray tell me all, and I promise you I'll reward you." "Why, madam," continued Susan, "that man told us all in the kitchen that Madam Sophia Western—indeed I don't know how to bring it out."—Here she stopt, till, having received encouragement from Sophia, and being vehemently pressed by Mrs Honour, she proceeded thus:—"He told us, madam, though to be sure it is all a lie, that your ladyship was dying for love of the young squire, and that he was going to the wars to get rid of you. I thought to myself then he was a false-hearted wretch; but, now, to see such a fine, rich, beautiful lady as you be, forsaken for such an ordinary woman; for to be sure so she is, and another man's wife into the bargain. It is such a strange unnatural thing, in a manner."

Sophia gave her a third guinea, and, telling her she would certainly be her friend if she mentioned nothing of what had passed, nor informed any one who she was, dismissed the girl, with orders to the post-boy to get the horses ready immediately.

Being now left alone with her maid, she told her trusty waiting-woman, "That she never was more easy than at present. I am now convinced," said she, "he is not only a villain, but a low despicable wretch. I can forgive all rather than his exposing my name in so barbarous a manner. That renders him the object of my contempt. Yes, Honour, I am now easy; I am indeed; I am very easy;" and then she burst into a violent flood of tears.

After a short interval spent by Sophia, chiefly in crying, and assuring her maid that she was perfectly easy, Susan arrived with an account that the horses were ready, when a very extraordinary thought suggested itself to our young heroine, by which Mr Jones would be acquainted with her having been at the inn, in a way which, if any sparks of affection for her remained in him, would be at least some punishment for his faults.

The reader will be pleased to remember a little muff, which hath had the honour of being more than once remembered already in this history. This muff, ever since the departure of Mr Jones, had been the constant companion of Sophia by day, and her bedfellow by night; and this muff she had at this very instant upon her arm; whence she took it off with great indignation, and, having writ her name with her pencil upon a piece of paper which she pinned to it, she bribed the maid to convey it into the empty bed of Mr Jones, in which, if he did not find it, she charged her to take some method of conveying it before his eyes in the morning.

Then, having paid for what Mrs Honour had eaten, in which bill was included an account for what she herself might have eaten, she mounted her horse, and, once more assuring her companion that she was perfectly easy, continued her journey

Chapter vi.

Containing, among other things, the ingenuity of Partridge, the madness of Jones, and the folly of Fitzpatrick.

IT was now past five in the morning, and other company began to rise and come to the kitchen, among whom were the serjeant and the coachman, who, being thoroughly reconciled, made a libation, or, in the English phrase, drank a hearty cup together.

In this drinking nothing more remarkable happened than the behaviour of Partridge, who, when the serjeant drank a health to King George, repeated only the word King; nor could he be brought to utter more; for though he was going to fight against his own cause, yet he could not be prevailed upon to drink against it.

Mr Jones, being now returned to his own bed (but from whence he returned we must beg to be excused from relating), summoned Partridge from this agreeable company, who, after a ceremonious preface, having obtained leave to offer his advice, delivered himself as follows :—

"It is, sir, an old saying, and a true one, that a wise man may sometimes learn counsel from a fool; I wish, therefore, I might be so bold as to offer you my advice, which is to return home again, and leave these *horrida bella*, these bloody wars, to fellows who are contented to swallow gunpowder, because they have nothing else to eat. Now, everybody knows your honour wants for nothing at home; when that's the case, why should any man travel abroad?"

"Partridge," cries Jones, "thou art certainly a coward; I wish, therefore, thou wouldst return home thyself, and trouble me no more."

"I ask your honour's pardon," cries Partridge; "I spoke on your account more than my own; for as to me, Heaven knows my circumstances are bad enough, and I am so far from being afraid, that I value a pistol, or a blunderbuss, or any such thing, no more than a pop-gun. Every man must die once, and what signifies the manner how? besides, perhaps I may come off with the loss only of an arm or a leg. I assure you, sir, I was never less afraid in my life; and so, if your honour is resolved to go on, I am resolved to follow you. But, in that case, I wish I might give my opinion. To be sure, it is a scandalous way of travelling, for a great gentleman like you to walk afoot. Now here are two or three good horses in the stable, which the landlord will certainly make no scruple of trusting you with; but, if he should, I can easily contrive to take them; and, let the worst come to the worst, the king would certainly pardon you, as you are going to fight in his cause."

Now, as the honesty of Partridge was equal to his understanding, and both dealt only in small matters, he would never have attempted a roguery of this kind, had he not imagined it altogether safe; for he was one of those who have more consideration of the gallows than of the fitness of things; but, in reality, he thought he might have committed this felony without any danger; for, besides that he doubted not but the name of Mr Allworthy would sufficiently quiet the landlord, he conceived they should be altogether safe, whatever turn affairs might take; as Jones, he imagined, would have friends enough on one side, and as his friends would as well secure him on the other.

When Mr Jones found that Partridge was in earnest in this proposal, he very severely rebuked him, and that in such bitter terms, that the other attempted to laugh it off, and presently turned the discourse to other matters; saying, he believed they were then in a bawdy house, and that he had with much ado prevented two wenches from disturbing his honour in the middle of the night. "Heyday!" says he, "I believe they got into your chamber whether I would or no; for here lies the muff of one of them on the ground." Indeed, as Jones returned to his bed in the dark, he had never perceived the muff on the quilt, and, in leaping into his bed, he had tumbled it on the floor. This Partridge now took up, and was going to put into his pocket, when Jones desired to see it. The muff was so very remarkable, that our heroe might possibly have recollected it without the information annexed. But his memory was not put to that hard office; for at the same instant he saw and read the words Sophia Western upon the paper which was pinned to it. His looks now grew frantic in a moment, and he eagerly cried out, "Oh Heavens! how came this muff here?" "I know no more than your honour," cried Partridge;

"but I saw it upon the arm of one of the women who would have disturbed you, if I would have suffered them." "Where are they?" cries Jones, jumping out of bed, and laying hold of his cloaths. "Many miles off, I believe, by this time," said Partridge. And now Jones, upon further enquiry, was sufficiently assured that the bearer of this muff was no other than the lovely Sophia herself.

The behaviour of Jones on this occasion, his thoughts, his looks, his words, his actions, were such as beggar all description. After many bitter execrations on Partridge, and not fewer on himself, he ordered the poor fellow, who was frightened out of his wits, to run down and hire him horses at any rate; and a very few minutes afterwards, having shuffled on his clothes, he hastened down-stairs to execute the orders himself, which he had just before given.

But before we proceed to what passed on his arrival in the kitchen, it will be necessary to recur to what had there happened since Partridge had first left it on his master's summons.

The serjeant was just marched off with his party, when the two Irish gentlemen arose, and came down-stairs; both complaining that they had been so often waked by the noises in the inn, that they had never once been able to close their eyes all night.

The coach which had brought the young lady and her maid, and which, perhaps, the reader may have hitherto concluded was her own, was, indeed, a returned coach belonging to Mr King, of Bath, one of the worthiest and honestest men that ever dealt in horse-flesh, and whose coaches we heartily recommend to all our readers who travel that road. By which means they may, perhaps, have the pleasure of riding in the very coach, and being driven by the very coachman, that is recorded in this history.

The coachman, having but two passengers, and hearing Mr Maclachlan was going to Bath, offered to carry him thither at a very moderate price. He was induced to this by the report of the hostler, who said that the horse which Mr Maclachlan had hired from Worcester would be much more pleased with returning to his friends there than to prosecute a long journey; for that the said horse was rather a two-legged than a four-legged animal.

Mr Maclachlan immediately closed with the proposal of the coachman, and, at the same time, persuaded his friend Fitzpatrick to accept of the fourth place in the coach. This conveyance the soreness of his bones made more agreeable to him than a horse; and, being well assured of meeting with his wife at Bath, he thought a little delay would be of no consequence.

Maclachlan, who was much the sharper man of the two, no sooner heard that this lady came from Chester, with the other circumstances which he learned from the hostler, than it came into his head that she might possibly be his friend's wife; and presently acquainted him with this suspicion, which had never once occurred to Fitzpatrick himself. To say the truth, he was one of those compositions which nature makes up in too great a hurry, and forgets to put any brains into their head.

Now it happens to this sort of men, as to bad hounds, who never hit off a fault themselves; but no sooner doth a dog of sagacity open his mouth than they immediately do the same, and, without the guidance of any scent, run directly forwards as fast as they are able. In the same manner, the very moment Mr Maclachlan had mentioned his apprehension, Mr Fitzpatrick instantly concurred, and flew directly up-stairs, to surprize his wife, before he knew where she was; and unluckily (as Fortune loves to play tricks with those gentlemen

who put themselves entirely under her conduct) ran his
head against several doors and posts to no purpose.
Much kinder was she to me, when she suggested that
simile of the hounds, just before inserted; since the
poor wife may, on these occasions, be so justly compared to a hunted hare. Like that little wretched
animal, she pricks up her ears to listen after the voice
of her pursuer; like her, flies away trembling when
she hears it; and, like her, is generally overtaken and
destroyed in the end.

This was not however the case at present; for after
a long fruitless search, Mr Fitzpatrick returned to the
kitchen, where, as if this had been a real chace, entered
a gentleman hallowing as hunters do when the hounds
are at a fault. He was just alighted from his horse,
and had many attendants at his heels.

Here, reader, it may be necessary to acquaint thee
with some matters, which, if thou dost know already,
thou art wiser than I take thee to be. And this information thou shalt receive in the next chapter.

Chapter vij.

In which are concluded the adventures that happened at the inn at Upton.

IN the first place, then, this gentleman just arrived was
no other person than Squire Western himself, who
was come hither in pursuit of his daughter; and,
had he fortunately been two hours earlier, he had not
only found her, but his niece into the bargain; for such
was the wife of Mr Fitzpatrick, who had run away
with her five years before, out of the custody of that
sage lady, Madam Western.

Now this lady had departed from the inn much

about the same time with Sophia; for, having been waked by the voice of her husband, she had sent up for the landlady, and being by her apprized of the matter, had bribed the good woman, at an extravagant price, to furnish her with horses for her escape. Such prevalence had money in this family; and though the mistress would have turned away her maid for a corrupt hussy, if she had known as much as the reader, yet she was no more proof against corruption herself than poor Susan had been.

Mr Western and his nephew were not known to one another; nor indeed would the former have taken any notice of the latter if he had known him; for, this being a stolen match, and consequently an unnatural one in the opinion of the good squire, he had, from the time of her committing it, abandoned the poor young creature, who was then no more than eighteen, as a monster, and had never since suffered her to be named in his presence.

The kitchen was now a scene of universal confusion, Western enquiring after his daughter, and Fitzpatrick as eagerly after his wife, when Jones entered the room, unfortunately having Sophia's muff in his hand.

As soon as Western saw Jones, he set up the same holla as is used by sportsmen when their game is in view. He then immediately run up and laid hold of Jones, crying, "We have got the dog fox, I warrant the bitch is not far off." The jargon which followed for some minutes, where many spoke different things at the same time, as it would be very difficult to describe, so would it be no less unpleasant to read.

Jones having, at length, shaken Mr Western off, and some of the company having interfered between them, our heroe protested his innocence as to knowing anything of the lady; when Parson Supple stepped up, and said, "It is folly to deny it; for why, the marks of guilt are in thy hands. I will myself asseverate and bind it by an oath, that the muff thou bearest in thy hand belongeth unto Madam Sophia; for I have frequently observed her, of later days, to bear it about her." "My daughter's muff!" cries the squire in a rage. "Hath he got my daughter's muff? bear witness the goods are found upon him. I'll have him before a justice of peace this instant. Where is my daughter, villain?" "Sir," said Jones, "I beg you would be pacified. The muff, I acknowledge, is the young lady's; but, upon my honour, I have never seen her." At these words Western lost all patience, and grew inarticulate with rage.

Some of the servants had acquainted Fitzpatrick who Mr Western was. The good Irishman, therefore, thinking he had now an opportunity to do an act of service to his uncle, and by that means might possibly obtain his favour, stept up to Jones, and cried out, "Upon my conscience, sir, you may be ashamed of denying your having seen the gentleman's daughter before my face, when you know I found you there upon the bed together." Then, turning to Western, he offered to conduct him immediately to the room where his daughter was; which offer being accepted, he, the squire, the parson, and some others, ascended directly to Mrs Waters's chamber, which they entered with no less violence than Mr Fitzpatrick had done before.

The poor lady started from her sleep with as much amazement as terror, and beheld at her bedside a figure which might very well be supposed to have escaped out of Bedlam. Such wildness and confusion were in the looks of Mr Western; who no sooner saw the lady than he started back, shewing sufficiently by his manner, before he spoke, that this was not the person sought after.

So much more tenderly do women value their reputation than their persons, that, though the latter seemed now in more danger than before, yet, as the former was secure, the lady screamed not with such violence as she had done on the other occasion. However, she no sooner found herself alone than she abandoned all thoughts of further repose; and, as she had sufficient reason to be dissatisfied with her present lodging, she dressed herself with all possible expedition.

Mr Western now proceeded to search the whole house, but to as little purpose as he had disturbed poor Mrs Waters. He then returned disconsolate into the kitchen, where he found Jones in the custody of his servants.

This violent uproar had raised all the people in the house, though it was yet scarcely daylight. Among these was a grave gentleman, who had the honour to be in the commission of the peace for the county of Worcester. Of which Mr Western was no sooner informed than he offered to lay his complaint before him. The justice declined executing his office, as he said he had no clerk present, nor no book about justice business; and that he could not carry all the law in his head about stealing away daughters, and such sort of things.

Here Mr Fitzpatrick offered to lend him his assistance, informing the company that he had been himself bred to the law. (And indeed he had served three years as clerk to an attorney in the north of Ireland, when, chusing a genteeler walk in life, he quitted his master, came over to England, and set up that business which requires no apprenticeship, namely, that of a gentleman, in which he had succeeded, as hath been already partly mentioned.)

Mr Fitzpatrick declared that the law concerning daughters was out of the present case; that stealing a muff was undoubtedly felony, and the goods being found upon the person, were sufficient evidence of the fact.

The magistrate, upon the encouragement of so learned a coadjutor, and upon the violent intercession of the squire, was at length prevailed upon to seat himself in the chair of justice, where being placed, upon viewing the muff which Jones still held in his hand, and upon the parson's swearing it to be the property of Mr Western, he desired Mr Fitzpatrick to draw up a commitment, which he said he would sign.

Jones now desired to be heard, which was at last, with difficulty, granted him. He then produced the evidence of Mr Partridge, as to the finding it; but, what was still more, Susan deposed that Sophia herself had delivered the muff to her, and had ordered her to convey it into the chamber where Mr Jones had found it.

Whether a natural love of justice, or the extraordinary comeliness of Jones, had wrought on Susan to make the discovery, I will not determine; but such were the effects of her evidence, that the magistrate, throwing himself back in his chair, declared that the matter was now altogether as clear on the side of the prisoner as it had before been against him: with which the parson concurred, saying, the Lord forbid he should be instrumental in committing an innocent person to durance. The justice then arose, acquitted the prisoner, and broke up the court.

Mr Western now gave every one present a hearty curse, and, immediately ordering his horses, departed in pursuit of his daughter, without taking the least notice of his nephew Fitzpatrick, or returning any answer to his claim of kindred, notwithstanding all the obligations he had just received from that gentleman. In the violence, moreover, of his hurry, and of his passion, he luckily forgot to demand the muff of Jones: I say luckily; for he would have died on the spot rather than have parted with it.

Jones likewise, with his friend Partridge, set forward

the moment he had paid his reckoning, in quest of his lovely Sophia, whom he now resolved never more to abandon the pursuit of. Nor could he bring himself even to take leave of Mrs Waters; of whom he detested the very thoughts, as she had been, though not designedly, the occasion of his missing the happiest interview with Sophia, to whom he now vowed eternal constancy.

As for Mrs Waters, she took the opportunity of the coach which was going to Bath; for which place she set out in company with the two Irish gentlemen, the landlady kindly lending her her cloaths; in return for which she was contented only to receive about double their value, as a recompence for the loan. Upon the road she was perfectly reconciled to Mr Fitzpatrick, who was a very handsome fellow, and indeed did all she could to console him in the absence of his wife.

Thus ended the many odd adventures which Mr Jones encountered at his inn at Upton, where they talk, to this day, of the beauty and lovely behaviour of the charming Sophia, by the name of the Somersetshire angel.

Chapter viij.

In which the history goes backward.

BEFORE we proceed any farther in our history, it may be proper to look a little back, in order to account for the extraordinary appearance of Sophia and her father at the inn at Upton.

The reader may be pleased to remember that, in the ninth chapter of the seventh book of our history, we left Sophia, after a long debate between love and duty, deciding the cause, as it usually, I believe, happens, in favour of the former.

This debate had arisen, as we have there shown, from a visit which her father had just before made her, in order to force her consent to a marriage with Blifil; and which he had understood to be fully implied in her acknowledgment "that she neither must nor could refuse any absolute command of his."

Now from this visit the squire retired to his evening potation, overjoyed at the success he had gained with his daughter; and, as he was of a social disposition, and willing to have partakers in his happiness, the beer was ordered to flow very liberally into the kitchen; so that before eleven in the evening there was not a single person sober in the house except only Mrs Western herself and the charming Sophia.

Early in the morning a messenger was despatched to summon Mr Blifil; for, though the squire imagined that young gentleman had been much less acquainted than he really was with the former aversion of his daughter, as he had not, however, yet received her consent, he longed impatiently to communicate it to him, not doubting but that the intended bride herself would confirm it with her lips. As to the wedding, it had the evening before been fixed, by the male parties, to be celebrated on the next morning save one.

Breakfast was now set forth in the parlour, where Mr Blifil attended, and where the squire and his sister likewise were assembled; and now Sophia was ordered to be called.

O, Shakespear! had I thy pen! O, Hogarth! had I thy pencil! then would I draw the picture of the poor serving-man, who, with pale countenance, staring eyes, chattering teeth, faultering tongue, and trembling limbs,

(E'en such a man, so faint, so spiritless,
So dull, so dead in look, so woe-begone,
Drew Priam's curtains in the dead of night,
And would have told him, half his Troy was burn'd)

entered the room, and declared—That Madam Sophia was not to be found.

"Not to be found!" cries the squire, starting from his chair; "Zounds and d—nation! Blood and fury! Where, when, how, what—Not to be found! Where?"

"La! brother," said Mrs Western, with true political coldness, "you are always throwing yourself into such violent passions for nothing. My niece, I suppose, is only walked out into the garden. I protest you are grown so unreasonable, that it is impossible to live in the house with you."

"Nay, nay," answered the squire, returning as suddenly to himself, as he had gone from himself; "if that be all the matter, it signifies not much; but, upon my soul, my mind misgave me when the fellow said she was not to be found." He then gave orders for the bell to be rung in the garden, and sat himself contentedly down.

No two things could be more the reverse of each other than were the brother and sister in most instances; particularly in this, That as the brother never foresaw anything at a distance, but was most sagacious in immediately seeing everything the moment it had happened; so the sister eternally foresaw at a distance, but was not so quick-sighted to objects before her eyes. Of both these the reader may have observed examples: and, indeed, both their several talents were excessive; for, as the sister often foresaw what never came to pass, so the brother often saw much more than was actually the truth.

This was not however the case at present. The same report was brought from the garden as before had been brought from the chamber, that Madam Sophia was not to be found.

The squire himself now sallied forth, and began to

roar forth the name of Sophia as loudly, and in as hoarse a voice, as whilome did Hercules that of Hylas; and, as the poet tells us that the whole shore echoed back the name of that beautiful youth, so did the house, the garden, and all the neighbouring fields resound nothing but the name of Sophia, in the hoarse voices of the men, and in the shrill pipes of the women; while echo seemed so pleased to repeat the beloved sound, that, if there is really such a person, I believe Ovid hath belied her sex.

Nothing reigned for a long time but confusion; till at last the squire, having sufficiently spent his breath, returned to the parlour, where he found Mrs Western and Mr Blifil, and threw himself, with the utmost dejection in his countenance, into a great chair.

Here Mrs Western began to apply the following consolation:

"Brother, I am sorry for what hath happened; and that my niece should have behaved herself in a manner so unbecoming her family; but it is all your own doings, and you have nobody to thank but yourself. You know she hath been educated always in a manner directly contrary to my advice, and now you see the consequence. Have I not a thousand times argued with you about giving my niece her own will? But you know I never could prevail upon you; and when I had taken so much pains to eradicate her headstrong opinions, and to rectify your errors in policy, you know she was taken out of my hands; so that I have nothing to answer for. Had I been trusted entirely with the care of her education, no such accident as this had ever befallen you; so that you must comfort yourself by thinking it was all your own doing; and, indeed, what else could be expected from such indulgence?"——

"Zounds! sister," answered he, "you are enough to make one mad. Have I indulged her? Have I

given her her will?——It was no longer ago than last
night that I threatened, if she disobeyed me, to confine
her to her chamber upon bread and water as long as she
lived.—You would provoke the patience of Job."

"Did ever mortal hear the like?" replied she.
"Brother, if I had not the patience of fifty Jobs, you
would make me forget all decency and decorum.
Why would you interfere? Did I not beg you, did
I not intreat you, to leave the whole conduct to me?
You have defeated all the operations of the campaign
by one false step. Would any man in his senses have
provoked a daughter by such threats as these? How
often have I told you that English women are not to
be treated like Ciracessian* slaves. We have the
protection of the world; we are to be won by gentle
means only, and not to be hectored, and bullied, and
beat into compliance. I thank Heaven no Salique law
governs here. Brother, you have a roughness in your
manner which no woman but myself would bear. I
do not wonder my niece was frightened and terrified
into taking this measure; and, to speak honestly, I
think my niece will be justified to the world for what
she hath done. I repeat it to you again, brother, you
must comfort yourself by rememb'ring that it is all
your own fault. How often have I advised——" Here
Western rose hastily from his chair, and, venting two
or three horrid imprecations, ran out of the room.

When he was departed, his sister expressed more
bitterness (if possible) against him than she had done
while he was present; for the truth of which she appealed to Mr Blifil, who, with great complacence,
acquiesced entirely in all she said; but excused all the
faults of Mr Western, "as they must be considered,"
he said, "to have proceeded from the too inordinate
fondness of a father, which must be allowed the name

* Possibly Circassian.

of an amiable weakness." "So much the more inexcuseable," answered the lady; "for whom doth he ruin by his fondness but his own child?" To which Blifil immediately agreed.

Mrs Western then began to express great confusion on the account of Mr Blifil, and of the usage which he had received from a family to which he intended so much honour. On this subject she treated the folly of her niece with great severity; but concluded with throwing the whole on her brother, who, she said, was inexcuseable to have proceeded so far without better assurances of his daughter's consent: "But he was (says she) always of a violent, headstrong temper; and I can scarce forgive myself for all the advice I have thrown away upon him."

After much of this kind of conversation, which, perhaps, would not greatly entertain the reader, was it here particularly related, Mr Blifil took his leave and returned home, not highly pleased with his disappointment: which, however, the philosophy which he had acquired from Square, and the religion infused into him by Thwackum, together with somewhat else, taught him to bear rather better than more passionate lovers bear these kinds of evils.

Chapter ix.

The escape of Sophia.

IT is now time to look after Sophia; whom the reader, if he loves her half so well as I do, will rejoice to find escaped from the clutches of her passionate father, and from those of her dispassionate lover.

Twelve times did the iron register of time beat on

the sonorous bell-metal, summoning the ghosts to rise and walk their nightly round.———In plainer language, it was twelve o'clock, and all the family, as we have said, lay buried in drink and sleep, except only Mrs Western, who was deeply engaged in reading a political pamphlet, and except our heroine, who now softly stole down-stairs, and, having unbarred and unlocked one of the house-doors, sallied forth, and hastened to the place of appointment.

Notwithstanding the many pretty arts which ladies sometimes practise, to display their fears on every little occasion (almost as many as the other sex uses to conceal theirs), certainly there is a degree of courage which not only becomes a woman, but is often necessary to enable her to discharge her duty. It is, indeed, the idea of fierceness, and not of bravery, which destroys the female character; for who can read the story of the justly celebrated Arria without conceiving as high an opinion of her gentleness and tenderness as of her fortitude? At the same time, perhaps, many a woman who shrieks at a mouse, or a rat, may be capable of poisoning a husband; or, what is worse, of driving him to poison himself.

Sophia, with all the gentleness which a woman can have, had all the spirit which she ought to have. When, therefore, she came to the place of appointment, and, instead of meeting her maid, as was agreed, saw a man ride directly up to her, she neither screamed out nor fainted away: not that her pulse then beat with its usual regularity; for she was, at first, under some surprize and apprehension: but these were relieved almost as soon as raised, when the man, pulling off his hat, asked her, in a very submissive manner, " If her ladyship did not expect to meet another lady?" and then proceeded to inform her that he was sent to conduct her to that lady.

Sophia could have no possible suspicion of any false-hood in this account : she therefore mounted resolutely behind the fellow, who conveyed her safe to a town about five miles distant, where she had the satisfaction of finding the good Mrs Honour : for, as the soul of the waiting-woman was wrapt up in those very habili-ments which used to enwrap her body, she could by no means bring herself to trust them out of her sight. Upon these, therefore, she kept guard in person, while she detached the aforesaid fellow after her mistress, having given him all proper instructions.

They now debated what course to take, in order to avoid the pursuit of Mr Western, who they knew would send after them in a few hours. The London road had such charms for Honour, that she was desirous of going on directly ; alleging that, as Sophia could not be missed till eight or nine the next morning, her pursuers would not be able to overtake her, even though they knew which way she had gone. But Sophia had too much at stake to venture anything to chance ; nor did she dare trust too much to her tender limbs, in a contest which was to be decided only by swiftness. She resolved, therefore, to travel across the country, for at least twenty or thirty miles, and then to take the direct road to London. So, having hired horses to go twenty miles one way, when she intended to go twenty miles the other, she set forward with the same guide behind whom she had ridden from her father's house ; the guide having now taken up behind him, in the room of Sophia, a much heavier, as well as much less lovely burden ; being, indeed, a huge portmanteau, well stuffed with those outside ornaments, by means of which the fair Honour hoped to gain many conquests, and, finally, to make her fortune in London city.

When they had gone about two hundred paces from the inn on the London road, Sophia rode up to the guide, and, with a voice much fuller of honey than was ever that of Plato, though his mouth is supposed to have been a bee-hive, begged him to take the first turning which led towards Bristol.

Reader, I am not superstitious, nor any great believer of modern miracles. I do not, therefore, deliver the following as a certain truth; for, indeed, I can scarce credit it myself: but the fidelity of an historian obliges me to relate what hath been confidently asserted. The horse, then, on which the guide rode, is reported to have been so charmed by Sophia's voice, that he made a full stop, and expressed an unwillingness to proceed any farther.

Perhaps, however, the fact may be true, and less miraculous than it hath been represented; since the natural cause seems adequate to the effect: for, as the guide at that moment desisted from a constant application of his armed right heel (for, like Hudibras, he wore but one spur), it is more than possible that this omission alone might occasion the beast to stop, especially as this was very frequent with him at other times.

But if the voice of Sophia had really an effect on the horse, it had very little on the rider. He answered somewhat surlily, "That measter had ordered him to go a different way, and that he should lose his place if he went any other than that he was ordered."

Sophia, finding all her persuasions had no effect, began now to add irresistible charms to her voice; charms which, according to the proverb, makes the old mare trot, instead of standing still; charms! to which modern ages have attributed all that irresistible force which the antients imputed to perfect oratory. In a word, she promised she would reward him to his utmost expectation.

The lad was not totally deaf to these promises; but

he disliked their being indefinite; for, though perhaps he had never heard that word, yet that, in fact, was his objection. He said, "Gentlevolks did not consider the case of poor volks; that he had like to have been turned away the other day, for riding about the country with a gentleman from Squire Allworthy's, who did not reward him as he should have done."

"With whom?" says Sophia eagerly. "With a gentleman from Squire Allworthy's," repeated the lad; "the squire's son, I think they call 'un."—"Whither? which way did he go?" says Sophia.—"Why, a little o' one side o' Bristol, about twenty miles off," answered the lad.—"Guide me," says Sophia, "to the same place, and I'll give thee a guinea, or two, if one is not sufficient."—"To be certain," said the boy, "it is honestly worth two, when your ladyship considers what a risk I run; but, however, if your ladyship will promise me the two guineas, I'll e'en venture: to be certain it is a sinful thing to ride about my measter's horses; but one comfort is, I can only be turned away, and two guineas will partly make me amends."

The bargain being thus struck, the lad turned aside into the Bristol road, and Sophia set forward in pursuit of Jones, highly contrary to the remonstrances of Mrs Honour, who had much more desire to see London than to see Mr Jones: for indeed she was not his friend with her mistress, as he had been guilty of some neglect in certain pecuniary civilities, which are by custom due to the waiting-gentlewoman in all love affairs, and more especially in those of a clandestine kind. This we impute rather to the carelessness of his temper than to any want of generosity; but perhaps she derived it from the latter motive. Certain it is that she hated him very bitterly on that account, and resolved to take every opportunity of injuring him with her mistress. It was therefore highly unlucky for her, that she had gone to the very same town and inn whence Jones had started, and still more unlucky was she in having stumbled on the same guide, and on this accidental discovery which Sophia had made.

Our travellers arrived at Hambrook* at the break of day, where Honour was against her will charged to enquire the route which Mr Jones had taken. Of this, indeed, the guide himself could have informed them; but Sophia, I know not for what reason, never asked him the question.

When Mrs Honour had made her report from the landlord, Sophia, with much difficulty, procured some indifferent horses, which brought her to the inn where Jones had been confined rather by the misfortune of meeting with a surgeon than by having met with a broken head.

Here Honour, being again charged with a commission of enquiry, had no sooner applied herself to the land-lady, and had described the person of Mr Jones, than that sagacious woman began, in the vulgar phrase, to smell a rat. When Sophia therefore entered the room, instead of answering the maid, the landlady, addressing herself to the mistress, began the following speech: " Good lack-a-day! why there now, who would have thought it ? I protest the loveliest couple that ever eye beheld. I-fackins, madam, it is no wonder the squire run on so about your ladyship. He told me indeed you was the finest lady in the world, and to be sure so you be. Mercy on him, poor heart! I bepitied him, so I did, when he used to hug his pillow, and call it his dear Madam Sophia. I did all I could to dissuade him from going to the wars : I told him there were men enow that were good for nothing else but to be killed, that had not the love of such fine ladies."

* This was the village where Jones met the Quaker.

"Sure," says Sophia, "the good woman is distracted."
"No, no," cries the landlady, "I am not distracted.
What, doth your ladyship think I don't know then?
I assure you he told me all." "What saucy fellow,"
cries Honour, "told you anything of my lady?" "No
saucy fellow," answered the landlady, "but the young
gentleman you enquired after, and a very pretty young
gentleman he is, and he loves Madam Sophia Western
to the bottom of his soul." "He love my lady! I'd
have you to know, woman, she is meat for his master."
—"Nay, Honour," said Sophia, interrupting her, "don't
be angry with the good woman; she intends no harm."
"No, marry, don't I," answered the landlady, emboldened by the soft accents of Sophia; and then
launched into a long narrative too tedious to be here
set down, in which some passages dropt that gave a
little offence to Sophia, and much more to her waiting-
woman, who hence took occasion to abuse poor Jones
to her mistress the moment they were alone together,
saying, "that he must be a very pitiful fellow, and
could have no love for a lady, whose name he would
thus prostitute in an ale-house."

Sophia did not see his behaviour in so very disadvantageous a light, and was perhaps more pleased
with the violent raptures of his love (which the landlady exaggerated as much as she had done every other
circumstance) than she was offended with the rest; and
indeed she imputed the whole to the extravagance, or
rather ebullience, of his passion, and to the openness of
his heart.

This incident, however, being afterwards revived in
her mind, and placed in the most odious colours by
Honour, served to heighten and give credit to those
unlucky occurrences at Upton, and assisted the waiting-
woman in her endeavours to make her mistress depart
from that inn without seeing Jones.

The landlady finding Sophia intended to stay no longer than till her horses were ready, and that without either eating or drinking, soon withdrew; when Honour began to take her mistress to task (for indeed she used great freedom), and after a long harangue, in which she reminded her of her intention to go to London, and gave frequent hints of the impropriety of pursuing a young fellow, she at last concluded with this serious exhortation: "For heaven's sake, madam, consider what you are about, and whither you are going."

This advice to a lady who had already rode near forty miles, and in no very agreeable season, may seem foolish enough. It may be supposed she had well considered and resolved this already; nay, Mrs Honour, by the hints she threw out, seemed to think so; and this I doubt not is the opinion of many readers, who have, I make no doubt, been long since well convinced of the purpose of our heroine, and have heartily condemned her for it as a wanton baggage.

But in reality this was not the case. Sophia had been lately so distracted between hope and fear, her duty and love to her father, her hatred to Blifil, her compassion, and (why should we not confess the truth?) her love for Jones; which last the behaviour of her father, of her aunt, of every one else, and more particularly of Jones himself, had blown into a flame, that her mind was in that confused state which may be truly said to make us ignorant of what we do, or whither we go, or rather, indeed, indifferent as to the consequence of either.

The prudent and sage advice of her maid produced, however, some cool reflection; and she at length determined to go to Gloucester, and thence to proceed directly to London.

But, unluckily, a few miles before she entered that town, she met the hack-attorney, who, as is before mentioned, had dined there with Mr Jones. This fellow, being well known to Mrs Honour, stopt and spoke to her; of which Sophia at that time took little notice, more than to enquire who he was.

But, having had a more particular account from Honour of this man afterwards at Gloucester, and hearing of the great expedition he usually made in travelling, for which (as hath been before observed) he was particularly famous; recollecting, likewise, that she had overheard Mrs Honour inform him that they were going to Gloucester, she began to fear lest her father might, by this fellow's means, be able to trace her to that city; wherefore, if she should there strike into the London road, she apprehended he would certainly be able to overtake her. She therefore altered her resolution; and, having hired horses to go a week's journey a way which she did not intend to travel, she again set forward after a light refreshment, contrary to the desire and earnest entreaties of her maid, and to the no less vehement remonstrances of Mrs Whitefield, who, from good breeding, or perhaps from good nature (for the poor young lady appeared much fatigued), pressed her very heartily to stay that evening at Gloucester.

Having refreshed herself only with some tea, and with lying about two hours on the bed, while her horses were getting ready, she resolutely left Mrs Whitefield's about eleven at night, and, striking directly into the Worcester road, within less than four hours arrived at that very inn where we last saw her.

Having thus traced our heroine very particularly back from her departure, till her arrival at Upton, we shall in a very few words bring her father to the same place; who, having received the first scent from the post-boy, who conducted his daughter to Hambrook, very easily traced her afterwards to Gloucester; whence he pursued her to Upton, as he had learned Mr Jones had taken that route (for Partridge, to use the squire's expression, left everywhere a strong scent behind him), and he doubted not in the least but Sophia travelled, or, as he phrased it, ran, the same way. He used indeed a very coarse expression, which need not be here inserted; as fox-hunters, who alone will understand it, will easily suggest it to themselves.

BOOK XI.

CONTAINING ABOUT THREE DAYS.

Chapter i.

A crust for the critics.

IN our last initial chapter we may be supposed to have treated that formidable set of men who are called critics with more freedom than becomes us; since they exact, and indeed generally receive, great condescension from authors. We shall in this, therefore, give the reasons of our conduct to this august body; and here we shall, perhaps, place them in a light in which they have not hitherto been seen.

This word critic is of Greek derivation, and signifies judgment. Hence I presume some persons who have not understood the original, and have seen the English translation of the primitive, have concluded that it meant judgment in the legal sense, in which it is frequently used as equivalent to condemnation.

I am the rather inclined to be of that opinion, as the greatest number of critics hath of late years been found amongst the lawyers. Many of these gentlemen, from despair, perhaps, of ever rising to the bench in Westminster-hall, have placed themselves on the benches at the playhouse, where they have exerted their judicial capacity, and have given judgment, *i.e.*, condemned without mercy.

The gentlemen would, perhaps, be well enough pleased, if we were to leave them thus compared to one of the most important and honourable offices in the commonwealth, and, if we intended to apply to their favour, we would do so; but, as we design to deal very sincerely and plainly too with them, we must remind them of another officer of justice of a much lower rank; to whom, as they not only pronounce, but execute, their own judgment, they bear likewise some remote resemblance.

But in reality there is another light, in which these modern critics may, with great justice and propriety, be seen; and this is that of a common slanderer. If a person who prys into the characters of others, with no other design but to discover their faults, and to publish them to the world, deserves the title of a slanderer of the reputations of men, why should not a critic, who reads with the same malevolent view, be as properly stiled the slanderer of the reputation of books?

Vice hath not, I believe, a more abject slave; society produces not a more odious vermin; nor can the devil receive a guest more worthy of him, nor possibly more welcome to him, than a slanderer. The world, I am afraid, regards not this monster with half the abhorrence which he deserves; and I am more afraid to assign the reason of this criminal lenity shown towards him; yet it is certain that the thief looks innocent in the comparison; nay, the murderer himself can seldom stand in competition with his guilt: for slander is a more cruel weapon than a sword, as the wounds which the former gives are always incurable. One method, indeed, there is of killing, and that the basest and most execrable of all, which bears an exact analogy to

the vice here disclaimed against, and that is poison :
a means of revenge so base, and yet so horrible, that it
was once wisely distinguished by our laws from all other
murders, in the peculiar severity of the punishment.

Besides the dreadful mischiefs done by slander, and
the baseness of the means by which they are effected,
there are other circumstances that highly aggravate its
atrocious quality ; for it often proceeds from no provocation, and seldom promises itself any reward, unless
some black and infernal mind may propose a reward in
the thoughts of having procured the ruin and misery of
another.

Shakespear hath nobly touched this vice, when he
says—

> "Who steals my purse steals trash ; 'tis something, nothing ;
> 'Twas mine, 'tis his, and hath been slave to thousands :
> But he that filches from me my good name
> Robs me of that WHICH NOT ENRICHES HIM,
> BUT MAKES ME POOR INDEED."

With all this my good reader will doubtless agree ;
but much of it will probably seem too severe, when
applied to the slanderer of books. But let it here be
considered that both proceed from the same wicked
disposition of mind, and are alike void of the excuse
of temptation. Nor shall we conclude the injury done
this way to be very slight, when we consider a book
as the author's offspring, and indeed as the child of
his brain.

The reader who hath suffered his muse to continue
hitherto in a virgin state can have but a very inadequate
idea of this kind of paternal fondness. To such we
may parody the tender exclamation of Macduff, "Alas !
Thou hast written no book." But the author whose
muse hath brought forth will feel the pathetic strain,
perhaps will accompany me with tears (especially if his
darling be already no more), while I mention the un-

easiness with which the big muse bears about her burden, the painful labour with which she produces it, and, lastly, the care, the fondness, with which the tender father nourishes his favourite, till it be brought to maturity, and produced into the world.

Nor is there any paternal fondness which seems less to savour of absolute instinct, and which may so well be reconciled to worldly wisdom, as this. These children may most truly be called the riches of their father; and many of them have with true filial piety fed their parent in his old age: so that not only the affection, but the interest, of the author may be highly injured by these slanderers, whose poisonous breath brings his book to an untimely end.

Lastly, the slander of a book is, in truth, the slander of the author: for, as no one can call another bastard, without calling the mother a whore, so neither can any one give the names of sad stuff, horrid nonsense, &c., to a book, without calling the author a blockhead; which, though in a moral sense it is a preferable appellation to that of villain, is perhaps rather more injurious to his worldly interest.

Now, however ludicrous all this may appear to some, others, I doubt not, will feel and acknowledge the truth of it; nay, may, perhaps, think I have not treated the subject with decent solemnity; but surely a man may speak truth with a smiling countenance. In reality, to depreciate a book maliciously, or even wantonly, is at least a very ill-natured office; and a morose snarling critic may, I believe, be suspected to be a bad man.

I will therefore endeavour, in the remaining part of this chapter, to explain the marks of this character, and to show what criticism I here intend to obviate: for I can never be understood, unless by the very persons here meant, to insinuate that there are no proper judges of writing, or to endeavour to exclude from the common-wealth of literature any of those noble critics to whose labours the learned world are so greatly indebted. Such were Aristotle, Horace, and Longinus, among the antients, Dacier and Bossu among the French, and some perhaps among us; who have certainly been duly authorised to execute at least a judicial authority *in foro literario.*

But without ascertaining all the proper qualifications of a critic, which I have touched on elsewhere, I think I may very boldly object to the censures of any one past upon works which he hath not himself read. Such censurers as these, whether they speak from their own guess or suspicion, or from the report and opinion of others, may properly be said to slander the reputation of the book they condemn.

Such may likewise be suspected of deserving this character, who, without assigning any particular faults, condemn the whole in general defamatory terms; such as vile, dull, d—d stuff, &c., and particularly by the use of the monosyllable low; a word which becomes the mouth of no critic who is not Right Honourable.

Again, though there may be some faults justly assigned in the work, yet, if those are not in the most essential parts, or if they are compensated by greater beauties, it will savour rather of the malice of a slanderer than of the judgment of a true critic to pass a severe sentence upon the whole, merely on account of some vicious part. This is directly contrary to the senti-ments of Horace:

> *Verum ubi plura nitent in carmine, non ego paucis*
> *Offendor maculis, quas aut incuria fudit,*
> *Aut humana parum cavit natura——*

> But where the beauties, more in number, shine,
> I am not angry, when a casual line
> (That with some trivial faults unequal flows)
> A careless hand or human frailty shows.—Mr Francis.

For, as Martial says, *Aliter non fit, Avite, liber.* No book can be otherwise composed. All beauty of character, as well as of countenance, and indeed of everything human, is to be tried in this manner. Cruel indeed would it be if such a work as this history, which hath employed some thousands of hours in the composing, should be liable to be condemned, because some particular chapter, or perhaps chapters, may be obnoxious to very just and sensible objections. And yet nothing is more common than the most rigorous sentence upon books supported by such objections, which, if they were rightly taken (and that they are not always), do by no means go to the merit of the whole. In the theatre especially, a single expression which doth not coincide with the taste of the audience, or with any individual critic of that audience, is sure to be hissed ; and one scene which should be disapproved would hazard the whole piece. To write within such severe rules as these is as impossible as to live up to some splenetic opinions : and if we judge according to the sentiments of some critics, and of some Christians, no author will be saved in this world, and no man in the next.

Chapter ij.

The adventures which Sophia met with after her leaving Upton.

OUR history, just before it was obliged to turn about and travel backwards, had mentioned the departure of Sophia and her maid from the inn ; we shall now therefore pursue the steps of that lovely creature, and leave her unworthy lover a little longer to bemoan his ill-luck, or rather his ill-conduct. Sophia having directed her guide ·to travel through bye-roads, across the country, they now passed the Severn, and had scarce got a mile from the inn, when the young lady, looking behind her, saw several horses coming after on full speed. This greatly alarmed her fears, and she called to the guide to put on as fast as possible.

He immediately obeyed her, and away they rode a full gallop. But the faster they went, the faster were they followed; and as the horses behind were somewhat swifter than those before, so the former were at length overtaken. A happy circumstance for poor Sophia; whose fears, joined to her fatigue, had almost overpowered her spirits; but she was now instantly relieved by a female voice, that greeted her in the softest manner, and with the utmost civility. This greeting Sophia, as soon as she could recover her breath, with like civility, and with the highest satisfaction to herself, returned.

The travellers who joined Sophia, and who had given her such terror, consisted, like her own company, of two females and a guide. The two parties proceeded three full miles together before any one offered again to open their mouths; when our heroine, having pretty well got the better of her fear (but yet being somewhat surprized that the other still continued to attend her, as she pursued no great road, and had already passed through several turnings), accosted the strange lady in a most obliging tone, and said, "She was very happy to find they were both travelling the same way." The other, who, like a ghost, only wanted to be spoke to, readily answered, "That the happiness was entirely hers; that she was a perfect stranger in that country, and was so overjoyed at meeting a companion of her own sex, that she had perhaps been guilty of an impertinence, which required great apology, in keeping pace with her." More civilities passed between these two ladies; for Mrs Honour had now given place to the fine habit of the stranger, and had fallen into the rear. But, though Sophia had great curiosity to know why the other lady continued to travel on through the same bye-roads with herself, nay, though this gave her some uneasiness, yet fear, or modesty, or some other consideration, restrained her from asking the question.

The strange lady now laboured under a difficulty which appears almost below the dignity of history to mention. Her bonnet had been blown from her head not less than five times within the last mile; nor could she come at any ribbon or handkerchief to tie it under her chin. When Sophia was informed of this, she immediately supplied her with a handkerchief for this purpose; which while she was pulling from her pocket, she perhaps too much neglected the management of her horse, for the beast, now unluckily making a false step, fell upon his fore-legs, and threw his fair rider from his back.

Though Sophia came head foremost to the ground, she happily received not the least damage: and the same circumstances which had perhaps contributed to her fall now preserved her from confusion; for the lane which they were then passing was narrow, and very much overgrown with trees, so that the moon could here afford very little light, and was moreover, at present, so obscured in a cloud, that it was almost perfectly dark. By these means the young lady's modesty, which was extremely delicate, escaped as free from injury as her limbs, and she was once more reinstated in her saddle, having received no other harm than a little fright by her fall.

Daylight at length appeared in its full lustre; and now the two ladies, who were riding over a common side by side, looking stedfastly at each other, at the same moment both their eyes became fixed; both their horses stopt, and, both speaking together, with equal joy pronounced, the one the name of Sophia, the other that of Harriet.

This unexpected encounter surprized the ladies much more than I believe it will the sagacious reader, who must have imagined that the strange lady could be no other than Mrs Fitzpatrick, the cousin of Miss Western, whom we before mentioned to have sallied from the inn a few minutes after her.

So great was the surprize and joy which these two cousins conceived at this meeting (for they had formerly been most intimate acquaintance and friends, and had long lived together with their aunt Western), that it is impossible to recount half the congratulations which passed between them, before either asked a very natural question of the other, namely, whither she was going?

This at last, however, came first from Mrs Fitzpatrick; but, easy and natural as the question may seem, Sophia found it difficult to give it a very ready and certain answer. She begged her cousin therefore to suspend all curiosity till they arrived at some inn, "which I suppose," says she, "can hardly be far distant; and, believe me, Harriet, I suspend as much curiosity on my side; for, indeed, I believe our astonishment is pretty equal."

The conversation which passed between these ladies on the road was, I apprehend, little worth relating; and less certainly was that between the two waiting-women; for they likewise began to pay their compliments to each other. As for the guides, they were debarred from the pleasure of discourse, the one being placed in the van, and the other obliged to bring up the rear.

In this posture they travelled many hours, till they came into a wide and well-beaten road, which, as they turned to the right, soon brought them to a very fair promising inn, where they all alighted: but so fatigued was Sophia, that as she had sat her horse during the last five or six miles with great difficulty, so was she now incapable of dismounting from him without assistance. This the landlord, who had hold of her horse, presently perceiving, offered to lift her in his arms from her saddle; and she too readily accepted the tender of his service. Indeed fortune seems to have resolved to put Sophia to the blush that day, and the second malicious attempt succeeded better than the first; for my landlord had no sooner received the young lady in his arms, than his feet, which the gout had lately very severely handled, gave way, and down he tumbled; but, at the same time, with no less dexterity than gallantry, contrived to throw himself under his charming burden, so that he alone received any bruise from the fall; for the great injury which happened to Sophia was a violent shock given to her modesty by an immoderate grin, which, at her rising from the ground, she observed in the countenances of most of the bye-standers. This made her suspect what had really happened, and what we shall not here relate for the indulgence of those readers who are capable of laughing at the offence given to a young lady's delicacy. Accidents of this kind we have never regarded in a comical light; nor will we scruple to say that he must have a very inadequate idea of the modesty of a beautiful young woman, who would wish to sacrifice it to so paltry a satisfaction as can arise from laughter.

This fright and shock, joined to the violent fatigue which both her mind and body had undergone, almost overcame the excellent constitution of Sophia, and she had scarce strength sufficient to totter into the inn, leaning on the arm of her maid. Here she was no sooner seated than she called for a glass of water; but Mrs Honour, very judiciously, in my opinion, changed it into a glass of wine.

Mrs Fitzpatrick, hearing from Mrs Honour that

Sophia had not been in bed during the two last nights, and observing her to look very pale and wan with her fatigue, earnestly entreated her to refresh herself with some sleep. She was yet a stranger to her history, or her apprehensions; but, had she known both, she would have given the same advice; for rest was visibly necessary for her; and their long journey through bye-roads so entirely removed all danger of pursuit, that she was herself perfectly easy on that account.

Sophia was easily prevailed on to follow the counsel of her friend, which was heartily seconded by her maid. Mrs Fitzpatrick likewise offered to bear her cousin company, which Sophia, with much complacence, accepted.

The mistress was no sooner in bed than the maid prepared to follow her example. She began to make many apologies to her sister Abigail for leaving her alone in so horrid a place as an inn; but the other stopt her short, being as well inclined to a nap as herself, and desired the honour of being her bedfellow. Sophia's maid agreed to give her a share of her bed, but put in her claim to all the honour. So, after many courtsies and compliments, to bed together went the waiting-women, as their mistresses had done before them.

It was usual with my landlord (as indeed it is with the whole fraternity) to enquire particularly of all coachmen, footmen, postboys, and others, into the names of all his guests; what their estate was, and where it lay. It cannot therefore be wondered at that the many particular circumstances which attended our travellers, and especially their retiring all to sleep at so extraordinary and unusual an hour as ten in the morning, should excite his curiosity. As soon, therefore, as the guides entered the kitchen, he began to examine who the ladies were, and whence they came; but the guides, though they faithfully related all they knew, gave him very little satisfaction. On the contrary, they rather enflamed his curiosity than extinguished it.

This landlord had the character, among all his neighbours, of being a very sagacious fellow. He was thought to see farther and deeper into things than any man in the parish, the parson himself not excepted. Perhaps his look had contributed not a little to procure him this reputation; for there was in this something wonderfully wise and significant, especially when he had a pipe in his mouth; which, indeed, he seldom was without. His behaviour, likewise, greatly assisted in promoting the opinion of his wisdom. In his deportment he was solemn, if not sullen; and when he spoke, which was seldom, he always delivered himself in a slow voice; and, though his sentences were short, they were still interrupted with many hums and ha's, ay ays, and other expletives: so that, though he accompanied his words with certain explanatory gestures, such as shaking or nodding the head, or pointing with his fore-finger, he generally left his hearers to understand more than he expressed; nay, he commonly gave them a hint that he knew much more than he thought proper to disclose. This last circumstance alone may, indeed, very well account for his character of wisdom; since men are strangely inclined to worship what they do not understand. A grand secret, upon which several imposers on mankind have totally relied for the success of their frauds.

This polite person, now taking his wife aside, asked her "what she thought of the ladies lately arrived?" "Think of them?" said the wife, "why, what should I think of them?" "I know," answered he, "what I think. The guides tell strange stories. One pretends to be come from Gloucester, and the other from Upton; and neither of them, for what I can find, can tell whither they are going. But what people ever travel across the

country from Upton hither, especially to London?
And one of the maid-servants, before she alighted from
her horse, asked if this was not the London road?
Now I have put all these circumstances together, and
whom do you think I have found them out to be?"
"Nay," answered she, "you know I never pretend to
guess at your discoveries."——"It is a good girl,"
replied he, chucking her under the chin; "I must
own you have always submitted to my knowledge of
these matters. Why, then, depend upon it; mind
what I say——depend upon it, they are certainly some
of the rebel ladies, who, they say, travel with the young
Chevalier; and have taken a roundabout way to escape
the duke's army."

"Husband," quoth the wife, "you have certainly
hit it; for one of them is dressed as fine as any
princess; and, to be sure, she looks for all the world
like one.——But yet, when I consider one thing"——
"When you consider," cries the landlord contemp-
tuously——"Come, pray let's hear what you consider."
——"Why, it is," answered the wife, "that she is
too humble to be any very great lady: for, while our
Betty was warming the bed, she called her nothing but
child, and my dear, and sweetheart; and, when Betty
offered to pull off her shoes and stockings, she would
not suffer her, saying, she would not give her the
trouble."

"Pugh!" answered the husband, "that is nothing.
Dost think, because you have seen some great ladies
rude and uncivil to persons below them, that none of
them know how to behave themselves when they come
before their inferiors? I think I know people of fashion
when I see them—I think I do. Did not she call for
a glass of water when she came in? Another sort of
women would have called for a dram; you know they
would. If she be not a woman of very great quality,

sell me for a fool; and, I believe, those who buy me
will have a bad bargain. Now, would a woman of her
quality travel without a footman, unless upon some such
extraordinary occasion?" "Nay, to be sure, husband,"
cries she, "you know these matters better than I, or
most folk." "I think I do know something," said
he. "To be sure," answered the wife, "the poor
little heart looked so piteous, when she sat down in the
chair, I protest I could not help having a compassion
for her almost as much as if she had been a poor body.
But what's to be done, husband? If an she be a rebel,
I suppose you intend to betray her up to the court.
Well, she's a sweet-tempered, good-humoured lady,
be she what she will, and I shall hardly refrain from
crying when I hear she is hanged or beheaded."
"Pooh!" answered the husband.——"But, as to
what's to be done, it is not so easy a matter to determine. I hope, before she goes away, we shall have the
news of a battle; for, if the Chevalier should get the
better, she may gain us interest at court, and make our
fortunes without betraying her." "Why, that's true,"
replied the wife; "and I heartily hope she will have
it in her power. Certainly she's a sweet good lady;
it would go horribly against me to have her come to
any harm." "Pooh!" cries the landlord, "women
are always so tender-hearted. Why, you would not
harbour rebels, would you?" "No, certainly,"
answered the wife; "and as for betraying her, come
what will on't, nobody can blame us. It is what anybody would do in our case."

While our politic landlord, who had not, we see,
undeservedly the reputation of great wisdom among
his neighbours, was engaged in debating this matter
with himself (for he paid little attention to the opinion
of his wife), news arrived that the rebels had given
the duke the slip, and had got a day's march towards

London; and soon after arrived a famous Jacobite squire, who, with great joy in his countenance, shook the landlord by the hand, saying, "All's our own, boy, ten thousand honest Frenchmen are landed in Suffolk. Old England for ever! ten thousand French, my brave lad! I am going to tap away directly."

This news determined the opinion of the wise man, and he resolved to make his court to the young lady when she arose; for he had now (he said) discovered that she was no other than Madam Jenny Cameron herself.

Chapter iij.

A very short chapter, in which however is a sun, a moon, a star, and an angel.

THE sun (for he keeps very good hours at this time of the year) had been some time retired to rest when Sophia arose greatly refreshed by her sleep; which, short as it was, nothing but her extreme fatigue could have occasioned; for, though she had told her maid, and perhaps herself too, that she was perfectly easy when she left Upton, yet it is certain her mind was a little affected with that malady which is attended with all the restless symptoms of a fever, and is perhaps the very distemper which physicians mean (if they mean anything) by the fever on the spirits.

Mrs Fitzpatrick likewise left her bed at the same time; and, having summoned her maid, immediately dressed herself. She was really a very pretty woman, and, had she been in any other company but that of Sophia, might have been thought beautiful; but when Mrs Honour of her own accord attended (for her mistress would not suffer her to be waked), and had equipped our heroine, the charms of Mrs Fitzpatrick, who had performed the office of the morning-star, and had preceded greater glories, shared the fate of that star, and were totally eclipsed the moment those glories shone forth.

Perhaps Sophia never looked more beautiful than she did at this instant. We ought not, therefore, to condemn the maid of the inn for her hyperbole, who, when she descended, after having lighted the fire, declared, and ratified it with an oath, that if ever there was an angel upon earth, she was now above-stairs.

Sophia had acquainted her cousin with her design to go to London; and Mrs Fitzpatrick had agreed to accompany her; for the arrival of her husband at Upton had put an end to her design of going to Bath, or to her aunt Western. They had therefore no sooner finished their tea than Sophia proposed to set out, the moon then shining extremely bright, and as for the frost she defied it; nor had she any of those apprehensions which many young ladies would have felt at travelling by night; for she had, as we have before observed, some little degree of natural courage; and this, her present sensations, which bordered somewhat on despair, greatly encreased. Besides, as she had already travelled twice with safety by the light of the moon, she was the better emboldened to trust to it a third time.

The disposition of Mrs Fitzpatrick was more timorous; for, though the greater terrors had conquered the less, and the presence of her husband had driven her away at so unseasonable an hour from Upton, yet, being now arrived at a place where she thought herself safe from his pursuit, these lesser terrors of I know not what operated so strongly, that she earnestly entreated her cousin to stay till the next morning, and not expose herself to the dangers of travelling by night.

Sophia, who was yielding to an excess, when she could neither laugh nor reason her cousin out of these apprehensions, at last gave way to them. Perhaps, indeed, had she known of her father's arrival at Upton, it might have been more difficult to have persuaded her; for as to Jones, she had, I am afraid, no great horror at the thoughts of being overtaken by him; nay, to confess the truth, I believe she rather wished than feared it; though I might honestly enough have concealed this wish from the reader, as it was one of those secret spontaneous emotions of the soul to which the reason is often a stranger.

When our young ladies had determined to remain all that evening in their inn they were attended by the landlady, who desired to know what their ladyships would be pleased to eat. Such charms were there in the voice, in the manner, and in the affable deportment of Sophia, that she ravished the landlady to the highest degree; and that good woman, concluding that she had attended Jenny Cameron, became in a moment a stanch Jacobite, and wished heartily well to the young Pretender's cause, from the great sweetness and affability with which she had been treated by his supposed mistress.

The two cousins began now to impart to each other their reciprocal curiosity to know what extraordinary accidents on both sides occasioned this so strange and unexpected meeting. At last Mrs Fitzpatrick, having obtained of Sophia a promise of communicating likewise in her turn, began to relate what the reader, if he is desirous to know her history, may read in the ensuing chapter.

Chapter iv.

The history of Mrs Fitzpatrick.

MRS FITZPATRICK, after a silence of a few moments, fetching a deep sigh, thus began:

"It is natural to the unhappy to feel a secret concern in recollecting those periods of their lives which have been most delightful to them. The remembrance of past pleasures affects us with a kind of tender grief, like what we suffer for departed friends; and the ideas of both may be said to haunt our imaginations.

"For this reason, I never reflect without sorrow on those days (the happiest far of my life) which we spent together when both were under the care of my aunt Western. Alas! why are Miss Graveairs and Miss Giddy no more? You remember, I am sure, when we knew each other by no other names. Indeed, you gave the latter appellation with too much cause. I have since experienced how much I deserved it. You, my Sophia, was always my superior in everything, and I heartily hope you will be so in your fortune. I shall never forget the wise and matronly advice you once gave me, when I lamented being disappointed of a ball, though you could not be then fourteen years old.——O my Sophy, how blest must have been my situation, when I could think such a disappointment a misfortune; and when indeed it was the greatest I had ever known!"

"And yet, my dear Harriet," answered Sophia, "it was then a serious matter with you. Comfort yourself therefore with thinking, that whatever you now lament may hereafter appear as trifling and contemptible as a ball would at this time."

"Alas, my Sophia," replied the other lady, "you

yourself will think otherwise of my present situation; for greatly must that tender heart be altered if my misfortunes do not draw many a sigh, nay, many a tear, from you. The knowledge of this should perhaps deter me from relating what I am convinced will so much affect you." Here Mrs Fitzpatrick stopt, till, at the repeated entreaties of Sophia, she thus proceeded:

"Though you must have heard much of my marriage; yet, as matters may probably have been misrepresented, I will set out from the very commencement of my unfortunate acquaintance with my present husband; which was at Bath, soon after you left my aunt, and returned home to your father.

"Among the gay young fellows who were at this season at Bath, Mr Fitzpatrick was one. He was handsome, *dégagé*, extremely gallant, and in his dress exceeded most others. In short, my dear, if you was unluckily to see him now, I could describe him no better than by telling you he was the very reverse of everything which he is: for he hath rusticated himself so long, that he is become an absolute wild Irishman. But to proceed in my story: the qualifications which he then possessed so well recommended him, that, though the people of quality at that time lived separate from the rest of the company, and excluded them from all their parties, Mr Fitzpatrick found means to gain admittance. It was perhaps no easy matter to avoid him; for he required very little or no invitation; and as, being handsome and genteel, he found it no very difficult matter to ingratiate himself with the ladies, so, he having frequently drawn his sword, the men did not care publickly to affront him. Had it not been for some such reason, I believe he would have been soon expelled by his own sex; for surely he had no strict title to be preferred to the English gentry; nor did they seem inclined to show him any extraordinary favour. They all abused him behind his back, which might probably proceed from envy; for by the women he was well received, and very particularly distinguished by them.

"My aunt, though no person of quality herself, as she had always lived about the court, was enrolled in that party; for, by whatever means you get into the polite circle, when you are once there, it is sufficient merit for you that you are there. This observation, young as you was, you could scarce avoid making from my aunt, who was free, or reserved, with all people, just as they had more or less of this merit.

"And this merit, I believe, it was, which principally recommended Mr Fitzpatrick to her favour. In which he so well succeeded, that he was always one of her private parties. Nor was he backward in returning such distinction; for he soon grew so very particular in his behaviour to her, that the scandal club first began to take notice of it, and the better-disposed persons made a match between them. For my own part, I confess, I made no doubt but that his designs were strictly honourable, as the phrase is; that is, to rob a lady of her fortune by way of marriage. My aunt was, I conceived, neither young enough nor handsome enough to attract much wicked inclination; but she had matrimonial charms in great abundance.

"I was the more confirmed in this opinion from the extraordinary respect which he showed to myself from the first moment of our acquaintance. This I understood as an attempt to lessen, if possible, that disinclination which my interest might be supposed to give me towards the match; and I know not but in some measure it had that effect; for, as I was well contented with my own fortune, and of all people the least a slave to interested views, so I could not be violently the enemy of a man with whose behaviour to me I was greatly pleased; and the more so, as I was the only object of such respect; for he behaved at the same time to many women of quality without any respect at all.

"Agreeable as this was to me, he soon changed it into another kind of behaviour, which was perhaps more so. He now put on much softness and tenderness, and languished and sighed abundantly. At times, indeed, whether from art or nature I will not determine, he gave his usual loose to gaiety and mirth; but this was always in general company, and with other women; for even in a country-dance, when he was not my partner, he became grave, and put on the softest look imaginable the moment he approached me. Indeed he was in all things so very particular towards me, that I must have been blind not to have discovered it. And, and, and——" "And you was more pleased still, my dear Harriet," cries Sophia; "you need not be ashamed," added she, sighing; "for sure there are irresistible charms in tenderness, which too many men are able to affect." "True," answered her cousin; "men, who in all other instances want common sense, are very Machiavels in the art of loving. I wish I did not know an instance.—Well, scandal now began to be as busy with me as it had before been with my aunt; and some good ladies did not scruple to affirm that Mr Fitzpatrick had an intrigue with us both.

"But, what may seem astonishing, my aunt never saw, nor in the least seemed to suspect, that which was visible enough, I believe, from both our behaviours. One would indeed think that love quite puts out the eyes of an old woman. In fact, they so greedily swallow the addresses which are made to them, that, like an outrageous glutton, they are not at leisure to observe what passes amongst others at the same table.

This I have observed in more cases than my own; and this was so strongly verified by my aunt, that, though she often found us together at her return from the pump, the least canting word of his, pretending impatience at her absence, effectually smothered all suspicion. One artifice succeeded with her to admiration. This was his treating me like a little child, and never calling me by any other name in her presence but that of pretty miss. This indeed did him some disservice with your humble servant; but I soon saw through it, especially as in her absence he behaved to me, as I have said, in a different manner. However, if I was not greatly disobliged by a conduct of which I had discovered the design, I smarted very severely for it; for my aunt really conceived me to be what her lover (as she thought him) called me, and treated me in all respects as a perfect infant. To say the truth, I wonder she had not insisted on my again wearing leading-strings.

"At last, my lover (for so he was) thought proper, in a most solemn manner, to disclose a secret which I had known long before. He now placed all the love which he had pretended to my aunt to my account. He lamented, in very pathetic terms, the encouragement she had given him, and made a high merit of the tedious hours in which he had undergone her conversation.—What shall I tell you, my dear Sophia?—Then I will confess the truth. I was pleased with my man. I was pleased with my conquest. To rival my aunt delighted me; to rival so many other women charmed me. In short, I am afraid I did not behave as I should do, even upon the very first declaration—I wish I did not almost give him positive encouragement before we parted.

"The Bath now talked loudly—I might almost say, roared against me. Several young women affected to shun my acquaintance, not so much, perhaps, from any real suspicion, as from a desire of banishing me from a

company in which I too much engrossed their favourite
man. And here I cannot omit expressing my gratitude
to the kindness intended me by Mr Nash, who took me
one day aside, and gave me advice, which if I had
followed, I had been a happy woman. 'Child,' says
he, 'I am sorry to see the familiarity which subsists
between you and a fellow who is altogether unworthy
of you, and I am afraid will prove your ruin. As for
your old stinking aunt, if it was to be no injury to you
and my pretty Sophy Western (I assure you I repeat
his words), I should be heartily glad that the fellow
was in possession of all that belongs to her. I never
advise old women: for, if they take it into their heads
to go to the devil, it is no more possible than worth
while to keep them from him. Innocence and youth
and beauty are worthy a better fate, and I would save
them from his clutches. Let me advise you therefore,
dear child, never suffer this fellow to be particular with
you again.' Many more things he said to me, which I
have now forgotten, and indeed I attended very little to
them at that time; for inclination contradicted all he
said; and, besides, I could not be persuaded that women
of quality would condescend to familiarity with such a
person as he described.

"But I am afraid, my dear, I shall tire you with a
detail of so many minute circumstances. To be con-
cise, therefore, imagine me married; imagine me with
my husband, at the feet of my aunt; and then imagine
the maddest woman in Bedlam, in a raving fit, and
your imagination will suggest to you no more than what
really happened.

"The very next day my aunt left the place, partly
to avoid seeing Mr Fitzpatrick or myself, and as much
perhaps to avoid seeing any one else; for, though I am
told she hath since denied everything stoutly, I believe
she was then a little confounded at her disappointment.

Since that time, I have written to her many letters, but
never could obtain an answer, which I must own sits
somewhat the heavier, as she herself was, though un-
designedly, the occasion of all my sufferings : for, had
it not been under the colour of paying his addresses to
her, Mr Fitzpatrick would never have found sufficient
opportunities to have engaged my heart, which, in other
circumstances, I still flatter myself would not have been
an easy conquest to such a person.   Indeed, I believe
I should not have erred so grossly in my choice if I
had relied on my own judgment ; but I trusted totally
to the opinion of others, and very foolishly took the
merit of a man for granted whom I saw so universally
well received by the women.   What is the reason, my
dear, that we, who have understandings equal to the
wisest and greatest of the other sex, so often make choice
of the silliest fellows for companions and favourites ?   It
raises my indignation to the highest pitch to reflect on
the numbers of women of sense who have been undone
by fools."   Here she paused a moment ; but, Sophia
making no answer, she proceeded as in the next
chapter.

Chapter v.

In which the history of Mrs Fitzpatrick is continued.

"WE remained at Bath no longer than a fortnight
after our wedding ; for as to any reconciliation with my aunt, there were no hopes ;
and of my fortune not one farthing could be touched
till I was of age, of which I now wanted more than
two years.   My husband therefore was resolved to set
out for Ireland ; against which I remonstrated very
earnestly, and insisted on a promise which he had made
me before our marriage that I should never take this

journey against my consent; and indeed I never intended to consent to it; nor will anybody, I believe, blame me for that resolution; but this, however, I never mentioned to my husband, and petitioned only for the reprieve of a month; but he had fixed the day, and to that day he obstinately adhered.

"The evening before our departure, as we were disputing this point with great eagerness on both sides, he started suddenly from his chair, and left me abruptly, saying he was going to the rooms. He was hardly out of the house when I saw a paper lying on the floor, which, I suppose, he had carelessly pulled from his pocket, together with his handkerchief. This paper I took up, and, finding it to be a letter, I made no scruple to open and read it; and indeed I read it so often that I can repeat it to you almost word for word. This then was the letter:

'To Mr Brian Fitzpatrick.

'Sir,

'Yours received, and am surprized you should use me in this manner, as have never seen any of your cash, unless for one linsey-woolsey coat, and your bill now is upwards of £150. Consider, sir, how often you have fobbed me off with your being shortly to be married to this lady and t'other lady; but I can neither live on hopes or promises, nor will my woollen-draper take any such in payment. You tell me you are secure of having either the aunt or the niece, and that you might have married the aunt before this, whose jointure you say is immense, but that you prefer the niece on account of her ready money. Pray, sir, take a fool's advice for once, and marry the first you can get. You will pardon my offering my advice, as you know I sincerely wish you well. Shall draw on you per next post, in favour

of Messieurs John Drugget and company, at fourteen
days, which doubt not your honouring, and am,

'Sir, your humble servant,

'SAM. COSGRAVE.'

"This was the letter, word for word. Guess, my
dear girl—guess how this letter affected me. You
prefer the niece on account of her ready money! If
every one of these words had been a dagger, I could
with pleasure have stabbed them into his heart; but I
will not recount my frantic behaviour on the occasion.
I had pretty well spent my tears before his return
home; but sufficient remains of them appeared in my
swollen eyes. He threw himself sullenly into his chair,
and for a long time we were both silent. At length,
in a haughty tone, he said, 'I hope, madam, your
servants have packed up all your things; for the coach
will be ready by six in the morning.' My patience
was totally subdued by this provocation, and I answered,
'No, sir, there is a letter still remains unpacked;' and
then throwing it on the table I fell to upbraiding him
with the most bitter language I could invent.

"Whether guilt, or shame, or prudence, restrained
him I cannot say; but, though he is the most passionate of men, he exerted no rage on this occasion. He
endeavoured, on the contrary, to pacify me by the most
gentle means. He swore the phrase in the letter to
which I principally objected was not his, nor had he
ever written any such. He owned, indeed, the having
mentioned his marriage, and that preference which he
had given to myself, but denied with many oaths the
having assigned any such reason. And he excused the
having mentioned any such matter at all on account of
the straits he was in for money, arising, he said, from
his having too long neglected his estate in Ireland.
And this, he said, which he could not bear to discover

to me, was the only reason of his having so strenuously insisted on our journey. He then used several very endearing expressions, and concluded by a very fond caress, and many violent protestations of love.

"There was one circumstance which, though he did not appeal to it, had much weight with me in his favour, and that was the word jointure in the taylor's letter, whereas my aunt never had been married, and this Mr Fitzpatrick well knew.——As I imagined, therefore, that the fellow must have inserted this of his own head, or from hearsay, I persuaded myself he might have ventured likewise on that odious line on no better authority. What reasoning was this, my dear? was I not an advocate rather than a judge?—— But why do I mention such a circumstance as this, or appeal to it for the justification of my forgiveness?—— In short, had he been guilty of twenty times as much, half the tenderness and fondness which he used would have prevailed on me to have forgiven him. I now made no farther objections to our setting out, which we did the next morning, and in a little more than a week arrived at the seat of Mr Fitzpatrick.

"Your curiosity will excuse me from relating any occurrences which past during our journey; for it would indeed be highly disagreeable to travel it over again, and no less so to you to travel it over with me.

"This seat, then, is an ancient mansion-house: if I was in one of those merry humours in which you have so often seen me, I could describe it to you ridiculously enough. It looked as if it had been formerly inhabited by a gentleman. Here was room enough, and not the less room on account of the furniture; for indeed there was very little in it. An old woman, who seemed coeval with the building, and greatly resembled her whom Chamont mentions in the Orphan, received us at the gate, and in a howl scarce human, and to me unintelligible, welcomed her master home. In short, the whole scene was so gloomy and melancholy, that it threw my spirits into the lowest dejection; which my husband discerning, instead of relieving, encreased by two or three malicious observations. 'There are good houses, madam,' says he, 'as you find, in other places besides England; but perhaps you had rather be in a dirty lodgings at Bath.'

"Happy, my dear, is the woman who, in any state of life, hath a cheerful good-natured companion to support and comfort her! But why do I reflect on happy situations only to aggravate my own misery? my companion, far from clearing up the gloom of solitude, soon convinced me that I must have been wretched with him in any place, and in any condition. In a word, he was a surly fellow, a character perhaps you have never seen; for, indeed, no woman ever sees it exemplified but in a father, a brother, or a husband; and, though you have a father, he is not of that character. This surly fellow had formerly appeared to me the very reverse, and so he did still to every other person. Good heaven! how is it possible for a man to maintain a constant lie in his appearance abroad and in company, and to content himself with shewing disagreeable truth only at home? Here, my dear, they make themselves amends for the uneasy restraint which they put on their tempers in the world; for I have observed, the more merry and gay and good-humoured my husband hath at any time been in company, the more sullen and morose he was sure to become at our next private meeting. How shall I describe his barbarity? To my fondness he was cold and insensible. My little comical ways, which you, my Sophy, and which others, have called so agreeable, he treated with contempt. In my most serious moments he sung and whistled; and whenever I was thoroughly dejected and miserable he was angry, and abused me : for, though he was never pleased with my good-humour, nor ascribed it to my satisfaction in him, yet my low spirits always offended him, and those he imputed to my repentance of having (as he said) married an Irishman.

"You will easily conceive, my dear Graveairs (I ask your pardon, I really forgot myself), that, when a woman makes an imprudent match in the sense of the world, that is, when she is not an arrant prostitute to pecuniary interest, she must necessarily have some inclination and affection for her man.   You will as easily believe that this affection may possibly be lessened ; nay, I do assure you, contempt will wholly eradicate it.   This contempt I now began to entertain for my husband, whom I now discovered to be—I must use the expression—an arrant blockhead.   Perhaps you will wonder I did not make this discovery long before ; but women will suggest a thousand excuses to themselves for the folly of those they like : besides, give me leave to tell you, it requires a most penetrating eye to discern a fool through the disguises of gaiety and good breeding.

"It will be easily imagined that, when I once despised my husband, as I confess to you I soon did, I must consequently dislike his company ; and indeed I had the happiness of being very little troubled with it ; for our house was now most elegantly furnished, our cellars well stocked, and dogs and horses provided in great abundance.   As my gentleman therefore entertained his neighbours with great hospitality, so his neighbours resorted to him with great alacrity ; and sports and drinking consumed so much of his time, that a small part of his conversation, that is to say, of his ill-humours, fell to my share.

"Happy would it have been for me if I could as easily have avoided all other disagreeable company; but, alas! I was confined to some which constantly tormented me; and the more, as I saw no prospect of being relieved from them. These companions were my own racking thoughts, which plagued and in a manner haunted me night and day. In this situation I past through a scene, the horrors of which can neither be painted nor imagined. Think, my dear, figure, if you can, to yourself, what I must have undergone. I became a mother by the man I scorned, hated, and detested. I went through all the agonies and miseries of a lying-in (ten times more painful in such a circumstance than the worst labour can be when one endures it for a man one loves) in a desert, or rather, indeed, a scene of riot and revel, without a friend, without a companion, or without any of those agreeable circumstances which often alleviate, and perhaps sometimes more than compensate, the sufferings of our sex at that season."

Chapter vi.

In which the mistake of the landlord throws Sophia into a dreadful consternation.

MRS FITZPATRICK was proceeding in her narrative when she was interrupted by the entrance of dinner, greatly to the concern of Sophia; for the misfortunes of her friend had raised her anxiety, and left her no appetite but what Mrs Fitzpatrick was to satisfy by her relation.

The landlord now attended with a plate under his arm, and with the same respect in his countenance and address which he would have put on had the ladies arrived in a coach and six.

The married lady seemed less affected with her own misfortunes than was her cousin; for the former eat

very heartily, whereas the latter could hardly swallow
a morsel. Sophia likewise showed more concern and
sorrow in her countenance than appeared in the other
lady; who, having observed these symptoms in her
friend, begged her to be comforted, saying, "Perhaps
all may yet end better than either you or I expect."

Our landlord thought he had now an opportunity to
open his mouth, and was resolved not to omit it. "I
am sorry, madam," cries he, "that your ladyship can't
eat; for to be sure you must be hungry after so long
fasting. I hope your ladyship is not uneasy at anything,
for, as madam there says, all may end better than anybody expects. A gentleman who was here just now
brought excellent news; and perhaps some folks who
have given other folks the slip may get to London
before they are overtaken; and if they do, I make no
doubt but they will find people who will be very ready
to receive them."

All persons under the apprehension of danger convert
whatever they see and hear into the objects of that
apprehension. Sophia therefore immediately concluded,
from the foregoing speech, that she was known, and
pursued by her father. She was now struck with the
utmost consternation, and for a few minutes deprived of
the power of speech; which she no sooner recovered
than she desired the landlord to send his servants out
of the room, and then, addressing herself to him, said,
"I perceive, sir, you know who we are; but I beseech
you—nay, I am convinced, if you have any compassion
or goodness, you will not betray us."

"I betray your ladyship!" quoth the landlord;
"no (and then he swore several very hearty oaths); I
would sooner be cut into ten thousand pieces. I hate
all treachery. I! I never betrayed any one in my
life yet, and I am sure I shall not begin with so sweet
a lady as your ladyship. All the world would very

much blame me if I should, since it will be in your ladyship's power so shortly to reward me. My wife can witness for me, I knew your ladyship the moment you came into the house: I said it was your honour, before I lifted you from your horse, and I shall carry the bruises I got in your ladyship's service to the grave; but what signified that, as long as I saved your ladyship? To be sure some people this morning would have thought of getting a reward; but no such thought ever entered into my head. I would sooner starve than take any reward for betraying your ladyship."

"I promise you, sir," says Sophia, "if it be ever in my power to reward you, you shall not lose by your generosity."

"Alack-a-day, madam!" answered the landlord; "in your ladyship's power! Heaven put it as much into your will! I am only afraid your honour will forget such a poor man as an innkeeper; but, if your ladyship should not, I hope you will remember what reward I refused—refused! that is, I would have refused, and to be sure it may be called refusing, for I might have had it certainly; and to be sure you might have been in some houses;—but, for my part, would not methinks for the world have your ladyship wrong me so much as to imagine I ever thought of betraying you, even before I heard the good news."

"What news, pray?" says Sophia, something eagerly.

"Hath not your ladyship heard it, then?" cries the landlord; "nay, like enough, for I heard it only a few minutes ago; and if I had never heard it, may the devil fly away with me this instant if I would have betrayed your honour! no, if I would, may I—" Here he subjoined several dreadful imprecations, which Sophia at last interrupted, and begged to know what he meant by the news.—He was going to answer, when Mrs Honour came running into the room, all pale and breathless, and cried out, "Madam, we are all undone, all ruined, they are come, they are come!" These words almost froze up the blood of Sophia; but Mrs Fitzpatrick asked Honour who were come? —"Who?" answered she, "why, the French; several hundred thousands of them are landed, and we shall be all murdered and ravished."

As a miser, who hath, in some well-built city, a cottage, value twenty shillings, when at a distance he is alarmed with the news of a fire, turns pale and trembles at his loss; but when he finds the beautiful palaces only are burnt, and his own cottage remains safe, he comes instantly to himself, and smiles at his good fortunes: or as (for we dislike something in the former simile) the tender mother, when terrified with the apprehension that her darling boy is drowned, is struck senseless and almost dead with consternation; but when she is told that little master is safe, and the Victory only, with twelve hundred brave men, gone to the bottom, life and sense again return, maternal fondness enjoys the sudden relief from all its fears, and the general benevolence which at another time would have deeply felt the dreadful catastrophe, lies fast asleep in her mind;—so Sophia, than whom none was more capable of tenderly feeling the general calamity of her country, found such immediate satisfaction from the relief of those terrors she had of being overtaken by her father, that the arrival of the French scarce made any impression on her. She gently chid her maid for the fright into which she had thrown her, and said "she was glad it was no worse; for that she had feared somebody else was come."

"Ay, ay," quoth the landlord, smiling, "her ladyship knows better things; she knows the French are our very best friends, and come over hither only for our good. They are the people who are to make Old England flourish again. I warrant her honour thought the duke was coming; and that was enough to put her into a fright. I was going to tell your ladyship the news.——His honour's majesty, Heaven bless him, hath given the duke the slip, and is marching as fast as he can to London, and ten thousand French are landed to join him on the road."

Sophia was not greatly pleased with this news, nor with the gentleman who related it; but, as she still imagined he knew her (for she could not possibly have any suspicion of the real truth), she durst not show any dislike. And now the landlord, having removed the cloth from the table, withdrew; but at his departure frequently repeated his hopes of being remembered hereafter.

The mind of Sophia was not at all easy under the supposition of being known at this house; for she still applied to herself many things which the landlord had addressed to Jenny Cameron; she therefore ordered her maid to pump out of him by what means he had become acquainted with her person, and who had offered him the reward for betraying her; she likewise ordered the horses to be in readiness by four in the morning, at which hour Mrs Fitzpatrick promised to bear her company; and then, composing herself as well as she could, she desired that lady to continue her story.

Chapter vii.

In which Mrs Fitzpatrick concludes her history.

WHILE Mrs Honour, in pursuance of the commands of her mistress, ordered a bowl of
punch, and invited my landlord and landlady
to partake of it, Mrs Fitzpatrick thus went on with her
relation.

"Most of the officers who were quartered at a town
in our neighbourhood were of my husband's acquaintance. Among these there was a lieutenant, a very
pretty sort of man, and who was married to a woman,
so agreeable both in her temper and conversation, that
from our first knowing each other, which was soon
after my lying-in, we were almost inseparable companions; for I had the good rortune to make myself
equally agreeable to her.

"The lieutenant, who was neither a sot nor a sportsman, was frequently of our parties; indeed he was very
little with my husband, and no more than good breeding constrained him to be, as he lived almost constantly
at our house. My husband often expressed much dissatisfaction at the lieutenant's preferring my company to his;
he was very angry with me on that account, and gave
me many a hearty curse for drawing away his companions; saying, 'I ought to be d——n'd for having
spoiled one of the prettiest fellows in the world, by
making a milksop of him.'

"You will be mistaken, my dear Sophia, if you
imagine that the anger of my husband arose from my
depriving him of a companion; for the lieutenant was
not a person with whose society a fool could be pleased;
and, if I should admit the possibility of this, so little
right had my husband to place the loss of his companion
to me, that I am convinced it was my conversation

alone which induced him ever to come to the house. No, child, it was envy, the worst and most rancorous kind of envy, the envy of superiority of understanding. The wretch could not bear to see my conversation preferred to his, by a man of whom he could not entertain the least jealousy. O my dear Sophy, you are a woman of sense; if you marry a man, as is most probable you will, of less capacity than yourself, make frequent trials of his temper before marriage, and see whether he can bear to submit to such a superiority.—Promise me, Sophy, you will take this advice; for you will hereafter find its importance." "It is very likely I shall never marry at all," answered Sophia; "I think, at least, I shall never marry a man in whose understanding I see any defects before marriage; and I promise you I would rather give up my own than see any such afterwards." "Give up your understanding!" replied Mrs Fitzpatrick; "oh, fie, child! I will not believe so meanly of you. Everything else I might myself be brought to give up; but never this. Nature would not have allotted this superiority to the wife in so many instances, if she had intended we should all of us have surrendered it to the husband. This, indeed, men of sense never expect of us; of which the lieutenant I have just mentioned was one notable example; for though he had a very good understanding, he always acknowledged (as was really true) that his wife had a better. And this, perhaps, was one reason of the hatred my tyrant bore her.

"Before he would be so governed by a wife, he said, especially such an ugly b—— (for, indeed, she was not a regular beauty, but very agreeable and extremely genteel), he would see all the women upon earth at the devil, which was a very usual phrase with him. He said, he wondered what I could see in her to be so charmed with her company: since this woman, says he, hath come among us, there is an end of your beloved reading, which you pretended to like so much, that you could not afford time to return the visits of the ladies in this country ; and I must confess I had been guilty of a little rudeness this way ; for the ladies there are at least no better than the mere country ladies here ; and I think I need make no other excuse to you for declining any intimacy with them.

"This correspondence, however, continued a whole year, even all the while the lieutenant was quartered in that town ; for which I was contented to pay the tax of being constantly abused in the manner above mentioned by my husband ; I mean when he was at home ; for he was frequently absent a month at a time at Dublin, and once made a journey of two months to London : in all which journeys I thought it a very singular happiness that he never once desired my company ; nay, by his frequent censures on men who could not travel, as he phrased it, without a wife tied up to their tail, he sufficiently intimated that, had I been never so desirous of accompanying him, my wishes would have been in vain ; but, Heaven knows, such wishes were very far from my thoughts.

"At length my friend was removed from me, and I was again left to my solitude, to the tormenting conversation with my own reflections, and to apply to books for my only comfort. I now read almost all day long.—How many books do you think I read in three months ?" "I can't guess, indeed, cousin," answered Sophia. "Perhaps half a score." "Half a score! half a thousand, child!" answered the other. "I read a good deal in Daniel's English History of France ; a great deal in Plutarch's Lives, the Atalantis, Pope's Homer, Dryden's Plays, Chillingworth, the Countess D'Aulnois, and Locke's Human Understanding.

"During this interval I wrote three very supplicating, and, I thought, moving letters to my aunt; but, as I received no answer to any of them, my disdain would not suffer me to continue my application." Here she stopt, and, looking earnestly at Sophia, said, "Methinks, my dear, I read something in your eyes which reproaches me of a neglect in another place, where I should have met with a kinder return." "Indeed, dear Harriet," answered Sophia, "your story is an apology for any neglect; but, indeed, I feel that I have been guilty of a remissness, without so good an excuse.—Yet pray proceed; for I long, though I tremble, to hear the end."

Thus, then, Mrs Fitzpatrick resumed her narrative:—"My husband now took a second journey to England, where he continued upwards of three months; during the greater part of this time I led a life which nothing but having led a worse could make me think tolerable; for perfect solitude can never be reconciled to a social mind, like mine, but when it relieves you from the company of those you hate. What added to my wretchedness was the loss of my little infant: not that I pretend to have had for it that extravagant tenderness of which I believe I might have been capable under other circumstances; but I resolved, in every instance, to discharge the duty of the tenderest mother; and this care prevented me from feeling the weight of that heaviest of all things, when it can be at all said to lie heavy on our hands.

"I had spent full ten weeks almost entirely by myself, having seen nobody all that time, except my servants and a very few visitors, when a young lady, a relation to my husband, came from a distant part of Ireland to visit me. She had staid once before a week at my house, and then I gave her a pressing invitation to return; for she was a very agreeable woman, and had improved good natural parts by a proper education. Indeed, she was to me a welcome guest.

"A few days after her arrival, perceiving me in very low spirits, without enquiring the cause, which, indeed, she very well knew, the young lady fell to compassionating my case. She said, 'Though politeness had prevented me from complaining to my husband's relations of his behaviour, yet they all were very sensible of it, and felt great concern upon that account; but none more than herself.' And after some more general discourse on this head, which I own I could not forbear countenancing, at last, after much previous precaution and enjoined concealment, she communicated to me, as a profound secret—that my husband kept a mistress.

"You will certainly imagine I heard this news with the utmost insensibility—Upon my word, if you do, your imagination will mislead you. Contempt had not so kept down my anger to my husband, but that hatred rose again on this occasion. What can be the reason of this? Are we so abominably selfish, that we can be concerned at others having possession even of what we despise? or are we not rather abominably vain, and is not this the greatest injury done to our vanity? What think you, Sophia?"

"I don't know, indeed," answered Sophia; "I have never troubled myself with any of these deep contemplations; but I think the lady did very ill in communicating to you such a secret."

"And yet, my dear, this conduct is natural," replied Mrs Fitzpatrick; "and, when you have seen and read as much as myself, you will acknowledge it to be so."

"I am sorry to hear it is natural," returned Sophia; "for I want neither reading nor experience to convince me that it is very dishonourable and very ill-natured:

nay, it is surely as ill-bred to tell a husband or wife of
the faults of each other as to tell them of their own."

"Well," continued Mrs Fitzpatrick, "my husband
at last returned; and, if I am thoroughly acquainted
with my own thoughts, I hated him now more than
ever; but I despised him rather less: for certainly
nothing so much weakens our contempt, as an injury
done to our pride or our vanity.

"He now assumed a carriage to me so very different
from what he had lately worn, and so nearly resembling
his behaviour the first week of our marriage, that, had
I now had any spark of love remaining, he might,
possibly, have rekindled my fondness for him. But,
though hatred may succeed to contempt, and may perhaps get the better of it, love, I believe, cannot. The
truth is, the passion of love is too restless to remain
contented without the gratification which it receives
from its object; and one can no more be inclined to
love without loving than we can have eyes without
seeing. When a husband, therefore, ceases to be the
object of this passion, it is most probable some other
man—I say, my dear, if your husband grows indifferent
to you—if you once come to despise him—I say—that
is—if you have the passion of love in you—Lud! I
have bewildered myself so—but one is apt, in these
abstracted considerations, to lose the concatenation of
ideas, as Mr Locke says:—in short, the truth is—in
short, I scarce know what it is; but, as I was saying,
my husband returned, and his behaviour, at first, greatly
surprized me; but he soon acquainted me with the
motive, and taught me to account for it. In a word,
then, he had spent and lost all the ready money of my
fortune; and, as he could mortgage his own estate no
deeper, he was now desirous to supply himself with
cash for his extravagance, by selling a little estate of
mine, which he could not do without my assistance;

and to obtain this favour was the whole and sole motive of all the fondness which he now put on.

" With this I peremptorily refused to comply. I told him, and I told him truly, that, had I been possessed of the Indies at our first marriage, he might have commanded it all; for it had been a constant maxim with me, that where a woman disposes of her heart, she should always deposit her fortune; but, as he had been so kind, long ago, to restore the former into my possession, I was resolved likewise to retain what little remained of the latter.

" I will not describe to you the passion into which these words, and the resolute air in which they were spoken, threw him: nor will I trouble you with the whole scene which succeeded between us. Out came, you may be well assured, the story of the mistress; and out it did come, with all the embellishments which anger and disdain could bestow upon it.

" Mr Fitzpatrick seemed a little thunderstruck with this, and more confused than I had seen him, though his ideas are always confused enough, heaven knows. He did not, however, endeavour to exculpate himself; but took a method which almost equally confounded me. What was this but recrimination? He affected to be jealous:——he may, for aught I know, be inclined enough to jealousy in his natural temper: nay, he must have had it from nature, or the devil must have put it into his head; for I defy all the world to cast a just aspersion on my character: nay, the most scandalous tongues have never dared censure my reputation. My fame, I thank heaven, hath been always as spotless as my life; and let falsehood itself accuse that if it dare. No, my dear Graveairs, however provoked, however ill-treated, however injured in my love, I have firmly resolved never to give the least room for censure on this account.——And yet, my dear, there are some people

so malicious, some tongues so venomous, that no innocence can escape them. The most undesigned word,
the most accidental look, the least familiarity, the most
innocent freedom, will be misconstrued, and magnified
into I know not what, by some people. But I despise,
my dear Graveairs, I despise all such slander. No
such malice, I assure you, ever gave me an uneasy
moment. No, no, I promise you I am above all that.
—But where was I? O let me see, I told you my
husband was jealous—And of whom, I pray?—Why,
of whom but the lieutenant I mentioned to you before!
He was obliged to resort above a year and more back
to find any object for this unaccountable passion, if,
indeed, he really felt any such, and was not an arrant
counterfeit in order to abuse me.

"But I have tired you already with too many
particulars. I will now bring my story to a very speedy
conclusion. In short, then, after many scenes very
unworthy to be repeated, in which my cousin engaged
so heartily on my side, that Mr Fitzpatrick at last
turned her out of doors; when he found I was neither
to be soothed nor bullied into compliance, he took a
very violent method indeed. Perhaps you will conclude
he beat me; but this, though he hath approached very
near to it, he never actually did. He confined me to
my room, without suffering me to have either pen, ink,
paper, or book: and a servant every day made my bed,
and brought me my food.

"When I had remained a week under this imprisonment, he made me a visit, and, with the voice of a
schoolmaster, or, what is often much the same, of a
tyrant, asked me, 'If I would yet comply?' I
answered, very stoutly, 'That I would die first.'
'Then so you shall, and be d—nd!' cries he; 'for
you shall never go alive out of this room.'

"Here I remained a fortnight longer; and, to say

the truth, my constancy was almost subdued, and I began to think of submission; when, one day, in the absence of my husband, who was gone abroad for some short time, by the greatest good fortune in the world, an accident happened.—I—at a time when I began to give way to the utmost despair——everything would be excusable at such a time—at that very time I received ——But it would take up an hour to tell you all particulars.—In one word, then (for I will not tire you with circumstances), gold, the common key to all padlocks, opened my door, and set me at liberty.

"I now made haste to Dublin, where I immediately procured a passage to England; and was proceeding to Bath, in order to throw myself into the protection of my aunt, or of your father, or of any relation who would afford it me. My husband overtook me last night at the inn where I lay, and which you left a few minutes before me; but I had the good luck to escape him, and to follow you.

"And thus, my dear, ends my history: a tragical one, I am sure, it is to myself; but, perhaps, I ought rather to apologize to you for its dulness."

Sophia heaved a deep sigh, and answered, "Indeed, Harriet, I pity you from my soul!——But what could you expect? Why, why, would you marry an Irishman?"

"Upon my word," replied her cousin, "your censure is unjust. There are, among the Irish, men of as much worth and honour as any among the English: nay, to speak the truth, generosity of spirit is rather more common among them. I have known some examples there, too, of good husbands; and I believe these are not very plenty in England. Ask me, rather, what I could expect when I married a fool; and I will tell you a solemn truth; I did not know him to be so."— "Can no man," said Sophia, in a very low and altered voice, "do you think, make a bad husband, who is not a fool?" "That," answered the other, "is too general a negative; but none, I believe, is so likely as a fool to prove so. Among my acquaintance, the silliest fellows are the worst husbands; and I will venture to assert, as a fact, that a man of sense rarely behaves very ill to a wife who deserves very well."

Chapter viii.

A dreadful alarm in the inn, with the arrival of an unexpected friend of Mrs Fitzpatrick.

SOPHIA now, at the desire of her cousin, related —not what follows, but what hath gone before in this history: for which reason the reader will, I suppose, excuse me for not repeating it over again.

One remark, however, I cannot forbear making on her narrative, namely, that she made no more mention of Jones, from the beginning to the end, than if there had been no such person alive. This I will neither endeavour to account for nor to excuse. Indeed, if this may be called a kind of dishonesty, it seems the more inexcusable, from the apparent openness and explicit sincerity of the other lady.—But so it was.

Just as Sophia arrived at the conclusion of her story, there arrived in the room where the two ladies were sitting a noise, not unlike, in loudness, to that of a pack of hounds just let out from their kennel; nor, in shrillness, to cats, when caterwauling; or to screech owls; or, indeed, more like (for what animal can resemble a human voice?) to those sounds which, in the pleasant mansions of that gate which seems to derive its name from a duplicity of tongues, issue from the mouths, and sometimes from the nostrils, of those fair **river** nymphs, ycleped of old the Naïades; in the vulgar tongue translated oyster-wenches; for when, instead of the antient libations of milk and honey and oil, the rich distillation from the juniper-berry, or, perhaps, from malt, hath, by the early devotion of their votaries, been poured forth in great abundance, should any daring tongue with unhallowed license prophane, *i.e.*, depreciate, the delicate fat Milton oyster, the plaice sound and firm, the flounder as much alive as when in the water, the shrimp as big as a prawn, the fine cod alive but a few hours ago, or any other of the various treasures which those water-deities who fish the sea and rivers have committed to the care of the nymphs, the angry Naïades lift up their immortal voices, and the prophane wretch is struck deaf for his impiety.

Such was the noise which now burst from one of the rooms below; and soon the thunder, which long had rattled at a distance, began to approach nearer and nearer, till, having ascended by degrees upstairs, it at last entered the apartment where the ladies were. In short, to drop all metaphor and figure, Mrs Honour, having scolded violently below-stairs, and continued the same all the way up, came in to her mistress in a most outrageous passion, crying out, "What doth your ladyship think? Would you imagine that this impudent villain, the master of this house, hath had the impudence to tell me, nay, to stand it out to my face, that your ladyship is that nasty, stinking wh——re (Jenny Cameron they call her), that runs about the country with the Pretender? Nay, the lying, saucy villain had the assurance to tell me that your ladyship had owned yourself to be so; but I have clawed the rascal; I have left the marks of my nails in his impudent face. My lady! says I, you saucy scoundrel; my lady is meat for no pretenders. She is a young lady of as good fashion, and family, and fortune, as any in Somersetshire.

Did you never hear of the great Squire Western, sirrah?
She is his only daughter; she is——, and heiress to all
his great estate. My lady to be called a nasty Scotch
wh——re by such a varlet!——To be sure I wish I had
knocked his brains out with the punch-bowl."

The principal uneasiness with which Sophia was
affected on this occasion Honour had herself caused, by
having in her passion discovered who she was.   However, as this mistake of the landlord sufficiently accounted
for those passages which Sophia had before mistaken,
she acquired some ease on that account; nor could she,
upon the whole, forbear smiling. This enraged Honour,
and she cried, " Indeed, madam, I did not think your
ladyship would have made a laughing matter of it.   To
be called whore by such an impudent low rascal. Your
ladyship may be angry with me, for aught I know, for
taking your part, since proffered service, they say, stinks;
but to be sure I could never bear to hear a lady of mine
called whore.——Nor will I bear it. I am sure your
ladyship is as virtuous a lady as ever sat foot on English
ground, and I will claw any villain's eyes out who dares
for to offer to presume for to say the least word to the
contrary. Nobody ever could say the least ill of the
character of any lady that ever I waited upon."

Hinc illæ lachrymæ ; in plain truth, Honour had as
much love for her mistress as most servants have, that
is to say——But besides this, her pride obliged her to
support the character of the lady she waited on; for
she thought her own was in a very close manner connected with it.   In proportion as the character of her
mistress was raised, hers likewise, as she conceived, was
raised with it; and, on the contrary, she thought the
one could not be lowered without the other.

On this subject, reader, I must stop a moment, to
tell thee a story. " The famous Nell Gwynn, stepping
one day, from a house where she had made a short

visit, into her coach, saw a great mob assembled, and her footman all bloody and dirty; the fellow, being asked by his mistress the reason of his being in that condition, answered, 'I have been fighting, madam, with an impudent rascal who called your ladyship a wh—re.' 'You blockhead,' replied Mrs Gwynn, 'at this rate you must fight every day of your life; why, you fool, all the world knows it.' 'Do they?' cries the fellow, in a muttering voice, after he had shut the coach-door, 'they shan't call me a whore's footman for all that.'"

Thus the passion of Mrs Honour appears natural enough, even if it were to be no otherwise accounted for; but, in reality, there was another cause of her anger; for which we must beg leave to remind our reader of a circumstance mentioned in the above simile. There are indeed certain liquors, which, being applied to our passions, or to fire, produce effects the very reverse of those produced by water, as they serve to kindle and inflame, rather than to extinguish. Among these, the generous liquor called punch is one. It was not, therefore, without reason, that the learned Dr Cheney used to call drinking punch pouring liquid fire down your throat.

Now, Mrs Honour had unluckily poured so much of this liquid fire down her throat, that the smoke of it began to ascend into her pericranium and blinded the eyes of Reason, which is there supposed to keep her residence, while the fire itself from the stomach easily reached the heart, and there inflamed the noble passion of pride. So that, upon the whole, we shall cease to wonder at the violent rage of the waiting-woman; though at first sight we must confess the cause seems inadequate to the effect.

Sophia and her cousin both did all in their power to extinguish these flames which had roared so loudly all over the house. They at length prevailed; or, to carry the metaphor one step farther, the fire, having consumed all the fuel which the language affords, to wit, every reproachful term in it, at last went out of its own accord.

But, though tranquillity was restored above-stairs, it was not so below; where my landlady, highly resenting the injury done to the beauty of her husband by the flesh-spades of Mrs Honour, called aloud for revenge and justice. As to the poor man, who had principally suffered in the engagement, he was perfectly quiet. Perhaps the blood which he lost might have cooled his anger: for the enemy had not only applied her nails to his cheeks, but likewise her fist to his nostrils, which lamented the blow with tears of blood in great abundance. To this we may add reflections on his mistake; but indeed nothing so effectually silenced his resentment as the manner in which he now discovered his error; for as to the behaviour of Mrs Honour, it had the more confirmed him in his opinion; but he was now assured by a person of great figure, and who was attended by a great equipage, that one of the ladies was a woman of fashion, and his intimate acquaintance.

By the orders of this person, the landlord now ascended, and acquainted our fair travellers that a great gentleman below desired to do them the honour of waiting on them. Sophia turned pale and trembled at this message, though the reader will conclude it was too civil, notwithstanding the landlord's blunder, to have come from her father; but fear hath the common fault of a justice of peace, and is apt to conclude hastily from every slight circumstance, without examining the evidence on both sides.

To ease the reader's curiosity, therefore, rather than his apprehensions, we proceed to inform him that an Irish peer had arrived very late that evening at the inn, in his way to London. This nobleman, having sallied from his supper at the hurricane before commemorated, had seen the attendant of Mrs Fitzpatrick, and upon a short enquiry, was informed that her lady, with whom he was very particularly acquainted, was above. This information he had no sooner received than he addressed himself to the landlord, pacified him, and sent him up-stairs with compliments rather civiller than those which were delivered.

It may perhaps be wondered at that the waiting-woman herself was not the messenger employed on this occasion; but we are sorry to say she was not at present qualified for that, or indeed for any other office. The rum (for so the landlord chose to call the distillation from malt) had basely taken the advantage of the fatigue which the poor woman had undergone, and had made terrible depredations on her noble faculties, at a time when they were very unable to resist the attack.

We shall not describe this tragical scene too fully; but we thought ourselves obliged, by that historic integrity which we profess, shortly to hint a matter which we would otherwise have been glad to have spared. Many historians, indeed, for want of this integrity, or of dili-gence, to say no worse, often leave the reader to find out these little circumstances in the dark, and sometimes to his great confusion and perplexity.

Sophia was very soon eased of her causeless fright by the entry of the noble peer, who was not only an intimate acquaintance of Mrs Fitzpatrick, but in reality a very particular friend of that lady. To say truth, it was by his assistance that she had been enabled to escape from her husband; for this nobleman had the same gallant disposition with those renowned knights of whom we read in heroic story, and had delivered many an imprisoned nymph from durance. He was indeed as bitter an enemy to the savage authority too often exercised by husbands and fathers, over the young and lovely of the other sex, as ever knight-errant was to the barbarous power of enchanters; nay, to say truth, I have often suspected that those very enchanters with which romance everywhere abounds were in reality no other than the husbands of those days; and matrimony itself was, perhaps, the enchanted castle in which the nymphs were said to be confined.

This nobleman had an estate in the neighbourhood of Fitzpatrick, and had been for some time acquainted with the lady. No sooner, therefore, did he hear of her confinement, than he earnestly applied himself to procure her liberty; which he presently effected, not by storming the castle, according to the example of antient heroes, but by corrupting the governor, in conformity with the modern art of war, in which craft is held to be preferable to valour, and gold is found to be more irresistible than either lead or steel.

This circumstance, however, as the lady did not think it material enough to relate to her friend, we would not at that time impart it to the reader. We rather chose to leave him a while under a supposition that she had found, or coined, or by some very extra-ordinary, perhaps supernatural means, had possessed herself of the money with which she had bribed her keeper, than to interrupt her narrative by giving a hint of what seemed to her of too little importance to be mentioned.

The peer, after a short conversation, could not for-bear expressing some surprize at meeting the lady in that place; nor could he refrain from telling her he imagined she had been gone to Bath. Mrs Fitzpatrick very freely answered, "That she had been prevented in her purpose by the arrival of a person she need not mention. In short," says she, "I was overtaken by my husband (for I need not affect to conceal what the world knows too well already). I had the good fortune to escape in a most surprizing manner, and am now going to London with this young lady, who is a near relation of mine, and who hath escaped from as great a tyrant as my own."

His lordship, concluding that this tyrant was likewise a husband, made a speech full of compliments to both the ladies, and as full of invectives against his own sex; nor indeed did he avoid some oblique glances at the matrimonial institution itself, and at the unjust powers given by it to man over the more sensible and more meritorious part of the species. He ended his oration with an offer of his protection, and of his coach and six, which was instantly accepted by Mrs Fitzpatrick, and at last, upon her persuasions, by Sophia.

Matters being thus adjusted, his lordship took his leave, and the ladies retired to rest, where Mrs Fitzpatrick entertained her cousin with many high encomiums on the character of the noble peer, and enlarged very particularly on his great fondness for his wife; saying, she believed he was almost the only person of high rank who was entirely constant to the marriage bed. "Indeed," added she, "my dear Sophy, that is a very rare virtue amongst men of condition. Never expect it when you marry; for, believe me, if you do, you will certainly be deceived."

A gentle sigh stole from Sophia at these words, which perhaps contributed to form a dream of no very pleasant kind; but, as she never revealed this dream to any one, so the reader cannot expect to see it related here.

Chapter ix.

The morning introduced in some pretty writing. A stage-coach. The civility of chambermaids. The heroic temper of Sophia. Her generosity. The return to it. The departure of the company, and their arrival at London; with some remarks for the use of travellers.

THOSE members of society who are born to furnish the blessings of life now began to light their candles, in order to pursue their daily labours for the use of those who are born to enjoy these blessings. The sturdy hind now attends the levee of his fellow-labourer the ox; the cunning artificer, the diligent mechanic, spring from their hard mattress; and now the bonny housemaid begins to repair the disordered drum-room, while the riotous authors of that disorder, in broken interrupted slumbers, tumble and toss, as if the hardness of down disquieted their repose.

In simple phrase, the clock had no sooner struck seven than the ladies were ready for their journey; and, at their desire, his lordship and his equipage were prepared to attend them.

And now a matter of some difficulty arose; and this was how his lordship himself should be conveyed; for though in stage-coaches, where passengers are properly considered as so much luggage, the ingenious coachman stows half a dozen with perfect ease into the place of four; for well he contrives that the fat hostess, or well-fed alderman, may take up no more room than the slim miss, or taper master; it being the nature of guts, when well squeezed, to give way, and to lie in a narrow compass; yet in these vehicles, which are called, for distinction's sake, gentlemen's coaches, though they are often larger than the others, this method of packing is never attempted.

His lordship would have put a short end to the difficulty, by very gallantly desiring to mount his horse; but Mrs Fitzpatrick would by no means consent to it. It was therefore concluded that the Abigails should, by turns, relieve each other on one of his lordship's horses, which was presently equipped with a side-saddle for that purpose.

Everything being settled at the inn, the ladies discharged their former guides, and Sophia made a present to the landlord, partly to repair the bruise which he had received under herself, and partly on account of what he had suffered under the hands of her enraged waiting-woman. And now Sophia first discovered a loss which gave her some uneasiness; and this was of the hundred-pound bank-bill which her father had given her at their last meeting; and which, within a very inconsiderable trifle, was all the treasure she was at present worth. She searched everywhere, and shook and tumbled all her things to no purpose, the bill was not to be found: and she was at last fully persuaded that she had lost it from her pocket when she had the misfortune of tumbling from her horse in the dark lane, as before recorded: a fact that seemed the more probable, as she now recollected some discomposure in her pockets which had happened at that time, and the great difficulty with which she had drawn forth her handkerchief the very instant before her fall, in order to relieve the distress of Mrs Fitzpatrick.

Misfortunes of this kind, whatever inconveniencies they may be attended with, are incapable of subduing a mind in which there is any strength, without the assistance of avarice. Sophia, therefore, though nothing could be worse timed than this accident at such a season, immediately got the better of her concern, and,

with her wonted serenity and cheerfulness of countenance, returned to her company.   His lordship conducted the ladies into the vehicle, as he did likewise
Mrs Honour, who, after many civilities, and more dear
madams, at last yielded to the well-bred importunities
of her sister Abigail, and submitted to be complimented
with the first ride in the coach; in which indeed she
would afterwards have been contented to have pursued
her whole journey, had not her mistress, after several
fruitless intimations, at length forced her to take her
turn on horseback.

The coach, now having received its company, began
to move forwards, attended by many servants, and led
by two captains, who had before rode with his lordship,
and who would have been dismissed from the vehicle
upon a much less worthy occasion than was this of
accommodating two ladies.   In this they acted only as
gentlemen; but they were ready at any time to have
performed the office of a footman, or indeed would
have condescended lower, for the honour of his lordship's company, and for the convenience of his table.

My landlord was so pleased with the present he had
received from Sophia, that he rather rejoiced in than
regretted his bruise or his scratches.   The reader will
perhaps be curious to know the *quantum* of this present;
but we cannot satisfy his curiosity.   Whatever it was,
it satisfied the landlord for his bodily hurt; but he
lamented he had not known before how little the lady
valued her money; "For to be sure," says he, "one
might have charged every article double, and she would
have made no cavil at the reckoning."

His wife, however, was far from drawing this conclusion; whether she really felt any injury done to
her husband more than he did himself, I will not
say: certain it is, she was much less satisfied with
the generosity of Sophia.   "Indeed," cries she, "my

dear, the lady knows better how to dispose of her money than you imagine. She might very well think we should not put up such a business without some satisfaction, and the law would have cost her an infinite deal more than this poor little matter, which I wonder you would take." "You are always so bloodily wise," quoth the husband: "it would have cost her more, would it? dost fancy I don't know that as well as thee? but would any of that more, or so much, have come into our pockets? Indeed, if son Tom the lawyer had been alive, I could have been glad to have put such a pretty business into his hands. He would have got a good picking out of it; but I have no relation now who is a lawyer, and why should I go to law for the benefit of strangers?" "Nay, to be sure," answered she, "you must know best." "I believe I do," replied he. "I fancy, when money is to be got, I can smell it out as well as another. Everybody, let me tell you, would not have talked people out of this. Mind that, I say; everybody would not have cajoled this out of her, mind that." The wife then joined in the applause of her husband's sagacity; and thus ended the short dialogue between them on this occasion.

We will therefore take our leave of these good people, and attend his lordship and his fair companions, who made such good expedition that they performed a journey of ninety miles in two days, and on the second evening arrived in London, without having encountered any one adventure on the road worthy the dignity of this history to relate. Our pen, therefore, shall imitate the expedition which it describes, and our history shall keep pace with the travellers who are its subject. Good writers will, indeed, do well to imitate the ingenious traveller in this instance, who always proportions his stay at any place to the beauties, elegancies, and curiosities which it affords. At Eshur, at Stowe, at Wilton, at Eastbury, and at Prior's Park, days are too short for the ravished imagination; while we admire the wondrous power of art in improving nature. In some of these, art chiefly engages our admiration; in others, nature and art contend for our applause; but, in the last, the former seems to triumph. Here Nature appears in her richest attire, and Art, dressed with the modestest simplicity, attends her benignant mistress. Here Nature indeed pours forth the choicest treasures which she hath lavished on this world; and here human nature presents you with an object which can be exceeded only in the other.

The same taste, the same imagination, which luxuriously riots in these elegant scenes, can be amused with objects of far inferior note. The woods, the rivers, the lawns of Devon and of Dorset, attract the eye of the ingenious traveller, and retard his pace, which delay he afterwards compensates by swiftly scouring over the gloomy heath of Bagshot, or that pleasant plain which extends itself westward from Stockbridge, where no other object than one single tree only in sixteen miles presents itself to the view, unless the clouds, in compassion to our tired spirits, kindly open their variegated mansions to our prospect.

Not so travels the money-meditating tradesman, the sagacious justice, the dignified doctor, the warm-clad grazier, with all the numerous offspring of wealth and dulness. On they jog, with equal pace, through the verdant meadows or over the barren heath, their horses measuring four miles and a half per hour with the utmost exactness; the eyes of the beast and of his master being alike directed forwards, and employed in contemplating the same objects in the same manner. With equal rapture the good rider surveys the proudest boasts of the architect, and those fair buildings with which some unknown name hath adorned the rich cloathing town; where heaps of bricks are piled up as a kind of monument to show that heaps of money have been piled there before.

And now, reader, as we are in haste to attend our heroine, we will leave to thy sagacity to apply all this to the Bœotian writers, and to those authors who are their opposites. This thou wilt be abundantly able to perform without our aid. Bestir thyself therefore on this occasion; for, though we will always lend thee proper assistance in difficult places, as we do not, like some others, expect thee to use the arts of divination to discover our meaning, yet we shall not indulge thy laziness where nothing but thy own attention is required; for thou art highly mistaken if thou dost imagine that we intended, when we began this great work, to leave thy sagacity nothing to do; or that, without sometimes exercising this talent, thou wilt be able to travel through our pages with any pleasure or profit to thyself.

Chapter x.

Containing a hint or two concerning virtue, and a few more concerning suspicion.

OUR company, being arrived at London, were set down at his lordship's house, where, while they refreshed themselves after the fatigue of their journey, servants were despatched to provide a lodging for the two ladies; for, as her ladyship was not then in town, Mrs Fitzpatrick would by no means consent to accept a bed in the mansion of the peer.

Some readers will, perhaps, condemn this extraordinary delicacy, as I may call it, of virtue, as too nice and scrupulous; but we must make allowances for her situation, which must be owned to have been very ticklish; and, when we consider the malice of censorious tongues, we must allow, if it was a fault, the fault was an excess on the right side, and which every woman who is in the self-same situation will do well to imitate. The most formal appearance of virtue, when it is only an appearance, may, perhaps, in very abstracted considerations, seem to be rather less commendable than virtue itself without this formality; but it will, however, be always more commended; and this, I believe, will be granted by all, that it is necessary, unless in some very particular cases, for every woman to support either the one or the other.

A lodging being prepared, Sophia accompanied her cousin for that evening; but resolved early in the morning to enquire after the lady into whose protection, as we have formerly mentioned, she had determined to throw herself when she quitted her father's house. And this she was the more eager in doing from some observations she had made during her journey in the coach.

Now, as we would by no means fix the odious character of suspicion on Sophia, we are almost afraid to open to our reader the conceits which filled her mind concerning Mrs Fitzpatrick; of whom she certainly entertained at present some doubts; which, as they are very apt to enter into the bosoms of the worst of people, we think proper not to mention more plainly till we have first suggested a word or two to our reader touching suspicion in general.

Of this there have always appeared to me to be two degrees. The first of these I chuse to derive from the heart, as the extreme velocity of its discernment seems to denote some previous inward impulse, and the rather as this superlative degree often forms its own objects; sees what is not, and always more than really exists. This is that quick-sighted penetration whose hawk's eyes no symptom of evil can escape; which observes not only upon the actions, but upon the words and looks, of men; and, as it proceeds from the heart of the observer, so it dives into the heart of the observed, and there espies evil, as it were, in the first embryo; nay, sometimes before it can be said to be conceived. An admirable faculty, if it were infallible; but, as this degree of perfection is not even claimed by more than one mortal being; so from the fallibility of such acute discernment have arisen many sad mischiefs and most grievous heart-aches to innocence and virtue. I cannot help, therefore, regarding this vast quick-sightedness into evil as a vicious excess, and as a very pernicious evil in itself. And I am the more inclined to this opinion, as I am afraid it always proceeds from a bad heart, for the reasons I have above mentioned, and for one more, namely, because I never knew it the property of a good one. Now, from this degree of suspicion I entirely and absolutely acquit Sophia.

A second degree of this quality seems to arise from the head. This is, indeed, no other than the faculty of seeing what is before your eyes, and of drawing conclusions from what you see. The former of these is unavoidable by those who have any eyes, and the latter is perhaps no less certain and necessary a consequence of our having any brains. This is altogether as bitter an enemy to guilt as the former is to innocence: nor can I see it in an unamiable light, even though, through human fallibility, it should be sometimes mistaken. For instance, if a husband should accidentally surprize his wife in the lap or in the embraces of some of those pretty young gentlemen who profess the art of cuckold-making, I should not highly, I think, blame him for concluding something more than what he saw, from the familiarities which he really had seen, and which we are at least favourable enough to when we call them innocent freedoms. The reader will easily suggest great plenty of instances to himself; I shall add but one more, which, however unchristian it may be thought by some, I cannot help esteeming to be strictly justifiable; and this is a suspicion that a man is capable of doing what he hath done already, and that it is possible for one who hath been a villain once to act the same part again. And, to confess the truth, of this degree of suspicion I believe Sophia was guilty. From this degree of suspicion she had, in fact, conceived an opinion that her cousin was really not better than she should be.

The case, it seems, was this: Mrs Fitzpatrick wisely considered that the virtue of a young lady is, in the world, in the same situation with a poor hare, which is certain, whenever it ventures abroad, to meet its enemies; for it can hardly meet any other. No sooner therefore was she determined to take the first opportunity of quitting the protection of her husband, than she resolved to cast herself under the protection of some other man; and whom could she so properly choose to be her guardian as a person of quality, of fortune, of honour; and who, besides a gallant disposition which inclines men to knight-errantry, that is, to be the champions of ladies in distress, had often declared a violent attachment to herself, and had already given her all the instances of it in his power?

But, as the law hath foolishly omitted this office of vice-husband, or guardian to an eloped lady, and as malice is apt to denominate him by a more disagreeable appellation, it was concluded that his lordship should perform all such kind offices to the lady in secret, and without publickly assuming the character of her protector. Nay, to prevent any other person from seeing him in this light, it was agreed that the lady should proceed directly to Bath, and that his lordship should first go to London, and thence should go down to that place by the advice of his physicians.

Now all this Sophia very plainly understood, not from the lips or behaviour of Mrs Fitzpatrick, but from the peer, who was infinitely less expert at retaining a secret than was the good lady; and perhaps the exact secrecy which Mrs Fitzpatrick had observed on this head in her narrative served not a little to heighten those suspicions which were now risen in the mind of her cousin.

Sophia very easily found out the lady she sought; for indeed there was not a chairman in town to whom her house was not perfectly well known; and, as she received, in return of her first message, a most pressing invitation, she immediately accepted it. Mrs Fitzpatrick, indeed, did not desire her cousin to stay with her with more earnestness than civility required. Whether she had discerned and resented the suspicion above-mentioned, or from what other motive it arose, I cannot say; but certain it is, she was full as desirous of parting with Sophia as Sophia herself could be of going.

The young lady, when she came to take leave of her cousin, could not avoid giving her a short hint of advice. She begged her, for heaven's sake, to take care of herself, and to consider in how dangerous a situation she stood; adding, she hoped some method would be found of reconciling her to her husband. "You must remember, my dear," says she, "the maxim which my aunt Western hath so often repeated to us both; That whenever the matrimonial alliance is broke, and war declared between husband and wife, she can hardly make a disadvantageous peace for herself on any conditions. These are my aunt's very words, and she

hath had a great deal of experience in the world."
Mrs Fitzpatrick answered, with a contemptuous smile,
"Never fear me, child, take care of yourself; for you
are younger than I. I will come and visit you in a
few days; but, dear Sophy, let me give you one piece
of advice: leave the character of Graveairs in the
country, for, believe me, it will sit very awkwardly
upon you in this town."

Thus the two cousins parted, and Sophia repaired
directly to Lady Bellaston, where she found a most
hearty, as well as a most polite, welcome. The lady
had taken a great fancy to her when she had seen her
formerly with her aunt Western. She was indeed extremely glad to see her, and was no sooner acquainted
with the reasons which induced her to leave the squire
and to fly to London than she highly applauded her
sense and resolution; and after expressing the highest
satisfaction in the opinion which Sophia had declared
she entertained of her ladyship, by chusing her house
for an asylum, she promised her all the protection which
it was in her power to give.

As we have now brought Sophia into safe hands,
the reader will, I apprehend, be contented to deposit
her there a while, and to look a little after other personages, and particularly poor Jones, whom we have
left long enough to do penance for his past offences,
which, as is the nature of vice, brought sufficient punishment upon him themselves.

BOOK XII.

CONTAINING THE SAME INDIVIDUAL TIME WITH THE FORMER.

Chapter i.

Showing what is to be deemed plagiarism in a modern author, and what is to be considered as lawful prize.

THE learned reader must have observed that in the course of this mighty work, I have often translated passages out of the best antient authors, without quoting the original, or without taking the least notice of the book from whence they were borrowed.

This conduct in writing is placed in a very proper light by the ingenious Abbé Bannier, in his preface to his Mythology, a work of great erudition and of equal judgment. "It will be easy," says he, "for the reader to observe that I have frequently had greater regard to him than to my own reputation: for an author certainly pays him a considerable compliment, when, for his sake, he suppresses learned quotations that come in his way, and which would have cost him but the bare trouble of transcribing."

To fill up a work with these scraps may, indeed, be

considered as a downright cheat on the learned world, who are by such means imposed upon to buy a second time, in fragments and by retail, what they have already in gross, if not in their memories, upon their shelves; and it is still more cruel upon the illiterate, who are drawn in to pay for what is of no manner of use to them. A writer who intermixes great quantity of Greek and Latin with his works, deals by the ladies and fine gentlemen in the same paultry manner with which they are treated by the auctioneers, who often endeavour so to confound and mix up their lots, that, in order to purchase the commodity you want, you are obliged at the same time to purchase that which will do you no service.

And yet, as there is no conduct so fair and disinterested but that it may be misunderstood by ignorance, and misrepresented by malice, I have been sometimes tempted to preserve my own reputation at the expense of my reader, and to transcribe the original, or at least to quote chapter and verse, whenever I have made use either of the thought or expression of another. I am, indeed, in some doubt that I have often suffered by the contrary method; and that, by suppressing the original author's name, I have been rather suspected of plagiarism than reputed to act from the amiable motive assigned by that justly celebrated Frenchman.

Now, to obviate all such imputations for the future, I do here confess and justify the fact. The antients may be considered as a rich common, where every person who hath the smallest tenement in Parnassus hath a free right to fatten his muse. Or, to place it in a clearer light, we moderns are to the antients what the poor are to the rich. By the poor here I mean that large and venerable body which, in English, we call the mob. Now, whoever hath had the honour to be admitted to any degree of intimacy with this mob, must well know that it is one of their established maxims to plunder and pillage their rich neighbours without any reluctance; and that this is held to be neither sin nor shame among them.   And so constantly do they abide and act by this maxim, that, in every parish almost in the kingdom, there is a kind of confederacy ever carrying on against a certain person of opulence called the squire, whose property is considered as free-booty by all his poor neighbours; who, as they conclude that there is no manner of guilt in such depredations, look upon it as a point of honour and moral obligation to conceal, and to preserve each other from punishment on all such occasions.

In like manner are the antients, such as Homer, Virgil, Horace, Cicero, and the rest, to be esteemed among us writers, as so many wealthy squires, from whom we, the poor of Parnassus, claim an immemorial custom of taking whatever we can come at.   This liberty I demand, and this I am as ready to allow again to my poor neighbours in their turn.   All I profess, and all I require of my brethren, is to maintain the same strict honesty among ourselves which the mob show to one another.   To steal from one another is indeed highly criminal and indecent; for this may be strictly stiled defrauding the poor (sometimes perhaps those who are poorer than ourselves), or, to set it under the most opprobrious colours, robbing the spittal.

Since, therefore, upon the strictest examination, my own conscience cannot lay any such pitiful theft to my charge, I am contented to plead guilty to the former accusation; nor shall I ever scruple to take to myself any passage which I shall find in an antient author to my purpose, without setting down the name of the author from whence it was taken. Nay, I absolutely claim a property in all such sentiments the moment they are transcribed into my writings, and I expect all readers henceforwards to regard them as purely and entirely my own. This claim, however, I desire to be allowed me only on condition that I preserve strict honesty towards my poor brethren, from whom, if ever I borrow any of that little of which they are possessed, I shall never fail to put their mark upon it, that it may be at all times ready to be restored to the right owner.

The omission of this was highly blameable in one Mr Moore, who, having formerly borrowed some lines of Pope and company, took the liberty to transcribe six of them into his play of the Rival Modes. Mr Pope, however, very luckily found them in the said play, and, laying violent hands on his own property, transferred it back again into his own works; and, for a further punishment, imprisoned the said Moore in the loathsome dungeon of the Dunciad, where his unhappy memory now remains, and eternally will remain, as a proper punishment for such his unjust dealings in the poetical trade.

Chapter ij.

In which, though the squire doth not find his daughter, something is found which puts an end to his pursuit.

THE history now returns to the inn at Upton, whence we shall first trace the footsteps of Squire Western; for, as he will soon arrive at an end of his journey, we shall have then full leisure to attend our heroe.

The reader may be pleased to remember that the said squire departed from the inn in great fury, and in that fury he pursued his daughter. The hostler having informed him that she had crossed the Severn, he likewise past that river with his equipage, and rode full speed, vowing the utmost vengeance against poor Sophia, if he should but overtake her.

He had not gone far before he arrived at a crossway. Here he called a short council of war, in which, after hearing different opinions, he at last gave the direction of his pursuit to fortune, and struck directly into the Worcester road.

In this road he proceeded about two miles, when he began to bemoan himself most bitterly, frequently crying out, "What pity is it! Sure never was so unlucky a dog as myself!" And then burst forth a volley of oaths and execrations.

The parson attempted to administer comfort to him on this occasion. "Sorrow not, sir," says he, "like those without hope. Howbeit we have not yet been able to overtake young madam, we may account it some good fortune that we have hitherto traced her course aright. Peradventure she will soon be fatigated with her journey, and will tarry in some inn, in order to renovate her corporeal functions; and in that case, in all moral certainty, you will very briefly be *compos voti.*"

"Pogh! d—n the slut!" answered the squire, "I am lamenting the loss of so fine a morning for hunting. It is confounded hard to lose one of the best scenting days, in all appearance, which hath been this season, and especially after so long a frost."

Whether Fortune, who now and then shows some compassion in her wantonest tricks, might not take pity of the squire; and, as she had determined not to let him overtake his daughter, might not resolve to make him amends some other way, I will not assert; but he had hardly uttered the words just before commemorated, and two or three oaths at their heels, when a pack of hounds began to open their melodious throats at a small

distance from them, which the squire's horse and his
rider both perceiving, both immediately pricked up their
ears, and the squire, crying, "She's gone, she's gone!
Damn me if she is not gone!" instantly clapped spurs
to the beast, who little needed it, having indeed the
same inclination with his master; and now the whole
company, crossing into a corn-field, rode directly towards the hounds, with much hallowing and whooping,
while the poor parson, blessing himself, brought up the
rear.

Thus fable reports that the fair Grimalkin, whom
Venus, at the desire of a passionate lover, converted
from a cat into a fine woman, no sooner perceived a
mouse than, mindful of her former sport, and still
retaining her pristine nature, she leaped from the bed
of her husband to pursue the little animal.

What are we to understand by this? Not that the
bride was displeased with the embraces of her amorous
bridegroom; for, though some have remarked that cats
are subject to ingratitude, yet women and cats too will
be pleased and purr on certain occasions. The truth
is, as the sagacious Sir Roger L'Estrange observes, in
his deep reflections, that, "if we shut Nature out at
the door, she will come in at the window; and that
puss, though a madam, will be a mouser still." In
the same manner we are not to arraign the squire of
any want of love for his daughter; for in reality he
had a great deal; we are only to consider that he was
a squire and a sportsman, and then we may apply the
fable to him, and the judicious reflections likewise.

The hounds ran very hard, as it is called, and the
squire pursued over hedge and ditch, with all his usual
vociferation and alacrity, and with all his usual pleasure;
nor did the thoughts of Sophia ever once intrude themselves to allay the satisfaction he enjoyed in the chace,
which, he said, was one of the finest he ever saw, and

which he swore was very well worth going fifty miles
for.   As the squire forgot his daughter, the servants,
we may easily believe, forgot their mistress; and the
parson, after having expressed much astonishment, in
Latin, to himself, at length likewise abandoned all
farther thoughts of the young lady, and, jogging on at
a distance behind, began to meditate a portion of doctrine for the ensuing Sunday.

The squire who owned the hounds was highly pleased
with the arrival of his brother squire and sportsman:
for all men approve merit in their own way, and no
man was more expert in the field than Mr Western,
nor did any other better know how to encourage the
dogs with his voice, and to animate the hunt with his
holla.

Sportsmen, in the warmth of a chace, are too much
engaged to attend to any manner of ceremony, nay, even
to the offices of humanity: for, if any of them meet
with an accident by tumbling into a ditch, or into a
river, the rest pass on regardless, and generally leave
him to his fate: during this time, therefore, the two
squires, though often close to each other, interchanged
not a single word.   The master of the hunt, however,
often saw and approved the great judgment of the
stranger in drawing the dogs when they were at a fault,
and hence conceived a very high opinion of his understanding, as the number of his attendants inspired no
small reverence to his quality.   As soon, therefore, as
the sport was ended by the death of the little animal
which had occasioned it, the two squires met, and in
all squire-like greeting saluted each other.

The conversation was entertaining enough, and what
we may perhaps relate in an appendix, or on some other
occasion; but as it nowise concerns this history, we
cannot prevail on ourselves to give it a place here.   It
concluded with a second chace, and that with an invita-

tion to dinner. This being accepted, was followed by a hearty bout of drinking, which ended in as hearty a nap on the part of Squire Western.

Our squire was by no means a match either for his host, or for parson Supple, at his cups that evening; for which the violent fatigue of mind as well as body that he had undergone, may very well account, without the least derogation from his honour. He was indeed, according to the vulgar phrase, whistle drunk; for before he had swallowed the third bottle, he became so entirely overpowered that though he was not carried off to bed till long after, the parson considered him as absent, and having acquainted the other squire with all relating to Sophia, he obtained his promise of seconding those arguments which he intended to urge the next morning for Mr Western's return.

No sooner, therefore, had the good squire shaken off his evening, and began to call for his morning draught, and to summon his horses in order to renew his pursuit, than Mr Supple began his dissuasives, which the host so strongly seconded, that they at length prevailed, and Mr Western agreed to return home; being principally moved by one argument, viz., that he knew not which way to go, and might probably be riding farther from his daughter instead of towards her. He then took leave of his brother sportsman, and expressing great joy that the frost was broken (which might perhaps be no small motive to his hastening home), set forwards, or rather backwards, for Somersetshire; but not before he had first despatched part of his retinue in quest of his daughter, after whom he likewise sent a volley of the most bitter execrations which he could invent.

Chapter iij.

The departure of Jones from Upton, with what passed between him and Partridge on the road.

AT length we are once more come to our heroe; and, to say truth, we have been obliged to part with him so long, that, considering the condition in which we left him, I apprehend many of our readers have concluded we intended to abandon him for ever; he being at present in that situation in which prudent people usually desist from enquiring any farther after their friends, lest they should be shocked by hearing such friends had hanged themselves.

But, in reality, if we have not all the virtues, I will boldly say, neither have we all the vices of a prudent character; and though it is not easy to conceive circumstances much more miserable than those of poor Jones at present, we shall return to him, and attend upon him with the same diligence as if he was wantoning in the brightest beams of fortune.

Mr Jones, then, and his companion Partridge, left the inn a few minutes after the departure of Squire Western, and pursued the same road on foot, for the hostler told them that no horses were by any means to be at that time procured at Upton. On they marched with heavy hearts; for though their disquiet proceeded from very different reasons, yet displeased they were both; and if Jones sighed bitterly, Partridge grunted altogether as sadly at every step.

When they came to the cross-roads where the squire had stopt to take counsel, Jones stopt likewise, and turning to Partridge, asked his opinion which track they should pursue. "Ah, sir," answered Partridge, "I wish your honour would follow my advice." "Why should I not?" replied Jones; "for it is now indifferent to me whither I go, or what becomes of me." "My advice, then," said Partridge, "is, that you immediately face about and return home; for who that hath such a home to return to as your honour, would travel thus about the country like a vagabond? I ask pardon, *sed vox ea sola reperta est.*"

"Alas!" cries Jones, "I have no home to return to;—but if my friend, my father, would receive me, could I bear the country from which Sophia is flown? Cruel Sophia! Cruel! No; let me blame myself!— No; let me blame thee. D—nation seize thee—fool —blockhead! thou hast undone me, and I will tear thy soul from thy body."—At which words he laid violent hands on the collar of poor Partridge, and shook him more heartily than an ague-fit, or his own fears had ever done before.

Partridge fell trembling on his knees, and begged for mercy, vowing he had meant no harm—when Jones, after staring wildly on him for a moment, quitted his hold, and discharged a rage on himself, that, had it fallen on the other, would certainly have put an end to his being, which indeed the very apprehension of it had almost effected.

We would bestow some pains here in minutely describing all the mad pranks which Jones played on this occasion, could we be well assured that the reader would take the same pains in perusing them; but as we are apprehensive that, after all the labour which we should employ in painting this scene, the said reader would be very apt to skip it entirely over, we have saved ourselves that trouble. To say the truth, we have, from this reason alone, often done great violence to the luxuriance of our genius, and have left many excellent descriptions out of our work, which would otherwise have been in it. And this suspicion, to be honest, arises, as is generally the case, from our own wicked heart; for we have, ourselves, been very often most horridly given to jumping, as we have run through the pages of voluminous historians.

Suffice it then simply to say, that Jones, after having played the part of a madman for many minutes, came, by degrees, to himself; which no sooner happened, than, turning to Partridge, he very earnestly begged his pardon for the attack he had made on him in the violence of his passion; but concluded, by desiring him never to mention his return again; for he was resolved never to see that country any more.

Partridge easily forgave, and faithfully promised to obey the injunction now laid upon him. And then Jones very briskly cried out, " Since it is absolutely impossible for me to pursue any farther the steps of my angel—I will pursue those of glory. Come on, my brave lad, now for the army:—it is a glorious cause, and I would willingly sacrifice my life in it, even though it was worth my preserving." And so saying, he immediately struck into the different road from that which the squire had taken, and, by mere chance, pursued the very same through which Sophia had before passed.

Our travellers now marched a full mile, without speaking a syllable to each other, though Jones, indeed, muttered many things to himself. As to Partridge, he was profoundly silent; for he was not, perhaps, perfectly recovered from his former fright; besides, he had apprehensions of provoking his friend to a second fit of wrath, especially as he now began to entertain a conceit, which may not, perhaps, create any great wonder in the reader. In short, he began now to suspect that Jones was absolutely out of his senses.

At length, Jones, being weary of soliloquy, addressed himself to his companion, and blamed him for his taciturnity; for which the poor man very honestly accounted, from his fear of giving offence. And now this fear being pretty well removed, by the most absolute promises of indemnity, Partridge again took the bridle from his tongue ; which, perhaps, rejoiced no less at regaining its liberty, than a young colt, when the bridle is slipt from his neck, and he is turned loose into the pastures.

As Partridge was inhibited from that topic which would have first suggested itself, he fell upon that which was next uppermost in his mind, namely, the Man of the Hill. "Certainly, sir," says he, "that could never be a man, who dresses himself and lives after such a strange manner, and so unlike other folks. Besides, his diet, as the old woman told me, is chiefly upon herbs, which is a fitter food for a horse than a Christian : nay, landlord at Upton says that the neighbours thereabouts have very fearful notions about him. It runs strangely in my head that it must have been some spirit, who, perhaps, might be sent to forewarn us : and who knows but all that matter which he told us, of his going to fight, and of his being taken prisoner, and of the great danger he was in of being hanged, might be intended as a warning to us, considering what we are going about ? besides, I dreamt of nothing all last night but of fighting ; and methought the blood ran out of my nose, as liquor out of a tap. Indeed, sir, *infandum, regina, jubes renovare dolorem.*"

"Thy story, Partridge," answered Jones, "is almost as ill applied as thy Latin. Nothing can be more likely to happen than death to men who go into battle. Perhaps we shall both fall in it—and what then ?" "What then ?" replied Partridge ; "why then there is an end of us, is there not ? when I am gone, all is over with me. What matters the cause to me, or who gets the victory, if I am killed ? I shall never enjoy any advantage from it. What are all the ringing of bells, and bonfires, to one that is six foot under ground? there will be an end of poor Partridge." "And an end of poor Partridge," cries Jones, "there must be, one time or other. If you love Latin, I will repeat you some fine lines out of Horace, which would inspire courage into a coward.

> ' *Dulce et decorum est pro patria mori*
> *Mors et fugacem persequitur virum*
> *Nec parcit imbellis juventæ*
> *Poplitibus, timidoque tergo.*' "

"I wish you would construe them," cries Partridge; "for Horace is a hard author, and I cannot understand as you repeat them."

"I will repeat you a bad imitation, or rather paraphrase, of my own," said Jones; "for I am but an indifferent poet:

> ' Who would not die in his dear country's cause?
> Since, if base fear his dastard step withdraws,
> From death he cannot fly:—One common grave
> Receives, at last, the coward and the brave.' "

"That's very certain," cries Partridge. "Ay, sure, *Mors omnibus communis :* but there is a great difference between dying in one's bed a great many years hence, like a good Christian, with all our friends crying about us, and being shot to-day or to-morrow, like a mad dog; or, perhaps, hacked in twenty pieces with the sword, and that too before we have repented of all our sins. O Lord, have mercy upon us! to be sure the soldiers are a wicked kind of people. I never loved to have anything to do with them. I could hardly bring myself ever to look upon them as Christians. There is nothing but cursing and swearing among them. I wish your honour would repent: I heartily wish you would repent before it is too late; and not think of going among them.—Evil communication corrupts good manners. That is my principal reason. For as for that matter, I am no more afraid than another man, not I; as to matter of that. I know all human flesh must die; but yet a man may live many years, for all that. Why, I am a middle-aged man now, and yet I may live a great number of years. I have read of several who have lived to be above a hundred, and some a great deal above a hundred. Not that I hope, I mean that I promise myself, to live to any such age as that, neither.—But if it be only to eighty or ninety. Heaven be praised, that is a great ways off yet; and I am not afraid of dying then, no more than another man; but, surely, to tempt death before a man's time is come seems to me downright wickedness and presumption. Besides, if it was to do any good indeed; but, let the cause be what it will, what mighty matter of good can two people do? and, for my part, I understand nothing of it. I never fired off a gun above ten times in my life; and then it was not charged with bullets. And for the sword, I never learned to fence, and know nothing of the matter. And then there are those cannons, which certainly it must be thought the highest presumption to go in the way of; and nobody but a madman—I ask pardon; upon my soul I meant no harm; I beg I may not throw your honour into another passion."

"Be under no apprehension, Partridge," cries Jones; "I am now so well convinced of thy cowardice, that thou couldst not provoke me on any account." "Your honour," answered he, "may call me coward, or any-thing else you please. If loving to sleep in a whole skin makes a man a coward, *non immunes ab illis malis sumus.* I never read in my grammar that a man can't be a good man without fighting. *Vir bonus est quis?
Qui consulta patrum, qui leges juraque servat.* Not a word of fighting; and I am sure the scripture is so

much against it, that a man shall never persuade me he is a good Christian while he sheds Christian blood."

Chapter iv.

The adventure of a beggar-man.

JUST as Partridge had uttered that good and pious doctrine, with which the last chapter concluded, they arrived at another cross-way, when a lame fellow in rags asked them for alms; upon which Partridge gave him a severe rebuke, saying, "Every parish ought to keep their own poor." Jones then fell a-laughing, and asked Partridge, "if he was not ashamed, with so much charity in his mouth, to have no charity in his heart. Your religion," says he, "serves you only for an excuse for your faults, but is no incentive to your virtue. Can any man who is really a Christian abstain from relieving one of his brethren in such a miserable condition?" And at the same time, putting his hand in his pocket, he gave the poor object a shilling.

"Master," cries the fellow, after thanking him, "I have a curious thing here in my pocket, which I found about two miles off, if your worship will please to buy it. I should not venture to pull it out to every one; but, as you are so good a gentleman, and so kind to the poor, you won't suspect a man of being a thief only because he is poor." He then pulled out a little gilt pocket-book, and delivered it into the hands of Jones.

Jones presently opened it, and (guess, reader, what he felt) saw in the first page the words Sophia Western, written by her own fair hand. He no sooner read the name than he prest it close to his lips; nor could he avoid falling into some very frantic raptures, notwithstanding his company ; but, perhaps, these very raptures made him forget he was not alone.

While Jones was kissing and mumbling the book, as if he had an excellent brown buttered crust in his mouth or as if he had really been a book-worm, or an author who had nothing to eat but his own works, a piece of paper fell from its leaves to the ground, which Partridge took up, and delivered to Jones, who presently perceived it to be a bank-bill. It was, indeed, the very bill which Western had given his daughter the night before her departure ; and a Jew would have jumped to purchase it at five shillings less than £100.

The eyes of Partridge sparkled at this news, which Jones now proclaimed aloud ; and so did (though with somewhat a different aspect) those of the poor fellow who had found the book ; and who (I hope from a principle of honesty) had never opened it : but we should not deal honestly by the reader if we omitted to inform him of a circumstance which may be here a little material, viz. that the fellow could not read.

Jones, who had felt nothing but pure joy and transport from the finding the book, was affected with a mixture of concern at this new discovery ; for his imagination instantly suggested to him that the owner of the bill might possibly want it before he should be able to convey it to her. He then acquainted the finder that he knew the lady to whom the book belonged, and would endeavour to find her out as soon as possible, and return it her.

The pocket-book was a late present from Mrs Western to her niece ; it had cost five-and-twenty shillings, having been bought of a celebrated toyman ; but the real value of the silver which it contained in its clasp was about eighteen-pence ; and that price the said toyman, as it was altogether as good as when it

first issued from his shop, would now have given for
it. A prudent person would, however, have taken
proper advantage of the ignorance of this fellow, and
would not have offered more than a shilling, or perhaps
sixpence, for it; nay, some perhaps would have given
nothing, and left the fellow to his action of trover,
which some learned serjeants may doubt whether he
could, under these circumstances, have maintained.

Jones, on the contrary, whose character was on the
outside of generosity, and may perhaps not very unjustly have been suspected of extravagance, without
any hesitation gave a guinea in exchange for the book.
The poor man, who had not for a long time before
been possessed of so much treasure, gave Mr Jones
a thousand thanks, and discovered little less of transport
in his muscles than Jones had before shown when he
had first read the name of Sophia Western.

The fellow very readily agreed to attend our travellers
to the place where he had found the pocket-book. Together, therefore, they proceeded directly thither; but
not so fast as Mr Jones desired; for his guide unfortunately happened to be lame, and could not possibly
travel faster than a mile an hour. As this place, therefore, was at above three miles' distance, though the fellow
had said otherwise, the reader need not be acquainted
how long they were in walking it.

Jones opened the book a hundred times during their
walk, kissed it as often, talked much to himself, and
very little to his companions. At all which the guide
exprest some signs of astonishment to Partridge; who
more than once shook his head, and cryed, Poor gentleman! *orandum est ut sit mens sana in corpore sano.*

At length they arrived at the very spot where Sophia
unhappily dropt the pocket-book, and where the fellow
had as happily found it. Here Jones offered to take
leave of his guide, and to improve his pace; but the

fellow, in whom that violent surprize and joy which the first receipt of the guinea had occasioned was now considerably abated, and who had now had sufficient time to recollect himself, put on a discontented look, and, scratching his head, said, " He hoped his worship would give him something more. Your worship," said he, " will, I hope, take it into your consideration that if I had not been honest I might have kept the whole." And, indeed, this the reader must confess to have been true. " If the paper there," said he, " be worth £100, I am sure the finding it deserves more than a guinea. Besides, suppose your worship should never see the lady, nor give it her—and, though your worship looks and talks very much like a gentleman, yet I have only your worship's bare word ; and, certainly, if the right owner ben't to be found, it all belongs to the first finder. I hope your worship will consider of all these matters : I am but a poor man, and therefore don't desire to have all ; but it is but reasonable I should have my share. Your worship looks like a good man, and, I hope, will consider my honesty ; for I might have kept every farthing, and nobody ever the wiser." " I promise thee, upon my honour," cries Jones, " that I know the right owner, and will restore it her." " Nay, your worship," answered the fellow, " may do as you please as to that ; if you will but give me my share, that is, one-half of the money, your honour may keep the rest yourself if you please ; " and concluded with swearing, by a very vehement oath, " that he would never mention a syllable of it to any man living."

" Lookee, friend," cries Jones, " the right owner shall certainly have again all that she lost ; and as for any farther gratuity, I really cannot give it you at present ; but let me know your name, and where you live, and it is more than possible you may hereafter have further reason to rejoice at this morning's adventure."

"I don't know what you mean by venture," cries the fellow; "it seems I must venture whether you will return the lady her money or no; but I hope your worship will consider—" "Come, come," said Partridge, "tell his honour your name, and where you may be found; I warrant you will never repent having put the money into his hands." The fellow, seeing no hopes of recovering the possession of the pocket-book, at last complied in giving in his name and place of abode, which Jones writ upon a piece of paper with the pencil of Sophia; and then, placing the paper in the same page where she had writ her name, he cried out, "There, friend, you are the happiest man alive; I have joined your name to that of an angel." "I don't know anything about angels," answered the fellow; "but I wish you would give me a little more money, or else return me the pocket-book." Partridge now waxed wrath: he called the poor cripple by several vile and opprobrious names, and was absolutely proceeding to beat him, but Jones would not suffer any such thing: and now, telling the fellow he would certainly find some opportunity of serving him, Mr Jones departed as fast as his heels would carry him; and Partridge, into whom the thoughts of the hundred pound had infused new spirits, followed his leader; while the man, who was obliged to stay behind, fell to cursing them both, as well as his parents; "for had they," says he, "sent me to charity-school to learn to write and read and cast accounts, I should have known the value of these matters as well as other people."

Chapter v.

Containing more adventures which Mr Jones and his companion met on the road.

OUR travellers now walked so fast, that they had very little time or breath for conversation; Jones meditating all the way on Sophia, and Partridge on the bank-bill, which, though it gave him some pleasure, caused him at the same time to repine at fortune, which, in all his walks, had never given him such an opportunity of showing his honesty. They had proceeded above three miles, when Partridge, being unable any longer to keep up with Jones, called to him, and begged him a little to slacken his pace: with this he was the more ready to comply, as he had for some time lost the footsteps of the horses, which the thaw had enabled him to trace for several miles, and he was now upon a wide common, where were several roads.

He here therefore stopt to consider which of these roads he should pursue; when on a sudden they heard the noise of a drum, that seemed at no great distance. This sound presently alarmed the fears of Partridge, and he cried out, "Lord have mercy upon us all; they are certainly a coming!" "Who is coming?" cries Jones; for fear had long since given place to softer ideas in his mind; and since his adventure with the lame man, he had been totally intent on pursuing Sophia, without entertaining one thought of an enemy. "Who?" cries Partridge, "why, the rebels: but why should I call them rebels? they may be very honest gentlemen, for anything I know to the contrary. The devil take him that affronts them, I say; I am sure, if they have nothing to say to me, I will have nothing to say to them, but in a civil way. For Heaven's sake, sir, don't affront them if they should come, and perhaps they may do us no harm ; but would it not be the wiser way to creep into some of yonder bushes, till they are gone by ? What can two unarmed men do perhaps against fifty thousand ? Certainly nobody but a madman ; I hope your honour is not offended ; but certainly no man who hath *mens sana in corpore sano*——" Here Jones interrupted this torrent of eloquence, which fear had inspired, saying, "That by the drum he perceived they were near some town." He then made directly towards the place whence the noise proceeded, bidding Partridge "take courage, for that he would lead him into no danger ; " and adding, " it was impossible the rebels should be so near."

Partridge was a little comforted with this last assurance ; and though he would more gladly have gone the contrary way, he followed his leader, his heart beating time, but not after the manner of heroes, to the music of the drum, which ceased not till they had traversed the common, and were come into a narrow lane.

And now Partridge, who kept even pace with Jones, discovered something painted flying in the air, a very few yards before him, which fancying to be the colours of the enemy, he fell a bellowing, "Oh Lord, sir, here they are ; there is the crown and coffin. Oh Lord ! I never saw anything so terrible ; and we are within gun-shot of them already."

Jones no sooner looked up, than he plainly perceived what it was which Partridge had thus mistaken.   " Partridge," says he, " I fancy you will be able to engage this whole army yourself ; for by the colours I guess what the drum was which we heard before, and which beats up for recruits to a puppet-show."

" A puppet-show ! " answered Partridge, with most eager transport.   " And is it really no more than that ? I love a puppet-show of all the pastimes upon earth.

Do, good sir, let us tarry and see it. Besides, I am quite famished to death; for it is now almost dark, and I have not eat a morsel since three o'clock in the morning."

They now arrived at an inn, or indeed an ale-house, where Jones was prevailed upon to stop, the rather as he had no longer any assurance of being in the road he desired. They walked both directly into the kitchen, where Jones began to enquire if no ladies had passed that way in the morning, and Partridge as eagerly examined into the state of their provisions; and indeed his enquiry met with the better success; for Jones could not hear news of Sophia; but Partridge, to his great satisfaction, found good reason to expect very shortly the agreeable sight of an excellent smoaking dish of eggs and bacon.

In strong and healthy constitutions love hath a very different effect from what it causes in the puny part of the species. In the latter it generally destroys all that appetite which tends towards the conservation of the individual; but in the former, though it often induces forgetfulness, and a neglect of food, as well as of everything else; yet place a good piece of well-powdered buttock before a hungry lover, and he seldom fails very handsomely to play his part. Thus it happened in the present case; for though Jones perhaps wanted a prompter, and might have travelled much farther, had he been alone, with an empty stomach; yet no sooner did he sit down to the bacon and eggs, than he fell to as heartily and voraciously as Partridge himself.

Before our travellers had finished their dinner, night came on, and as the moon was now past the full, it was extremely dark. Partridge therefore prevailed on Jones to stay and see the puppet-show, which was just going to begin, and to which they were very eagerly invited by the master of the said show, who declared that his figures were the finest which the world had ever produced, and that they had given great satisfaction to all the quality in every town in England.

The puppet-show was performed with great regularity and decency. It was called the fine and serious part of the Provoked Husband; and it was indeed a very grave and solemn entertainment, without any low wit or humour, or jests; or, to do it no more than justice, without anything which could provoke a laugh. The audience were all highly pleased. A grave matron told the master she would bring her two daughters the next night, as he did not show any stuff; and an attorney's clerk and an exciseman both declared, that the characters of Lord and Lady Townley were well preserved, and highly in nature. Partridge likewise concurred with this opinion.

The master was so highly elated with these encomiums, that he could not refrain from adding some more of his own. He said, "The present age was not improved in anything so much as in their puppet-shows; which, by throwing out Punch and his wife Joan, and such idle trumpery, were at last brought to be a rational entertainment. I remember," said he, "when I first took to the business, there was a great deal of low stuff that did very well to make folks laugh; but was never calculated to improve the morals of young people, which certainly ought to be principally aimed at in every puppet-show: for why may not good and instructive lessons be conveyed this way, as well as any other? My figures are as big as the life, and they represent the life in every particular; and I question not but people rise from my little drama as much improved as they do from the great." "I would by no means degrade the ingenuity of your profession," answered Jones, "but I should have been glad to have seen my old acquaintance master Punch, for all that; and so far from improving, I think, by leaving out him and his merry wife Joan, you have spoiled your puppet-show."

The dancer of wires conceived an immediate and high contempt for Jones, from these words. And with much disdain in his countenance, he replied, "Very probably, sir, that may be your opinion; but I have the satisfaction to know the best judges differ from you, and it is impossible to please every taste. I confess, indeed, some of the quality at Bath, two or three years ago, wanted mightily to bring Punch again upon the stage. I believe I lost some money for not agreeing to it; but let others do as they will; a little matter shall never bribe me to degrade my own profession, nor will I ever willingly consent to the spoiling the decency and regularity of my stage, by introducing any such low stuff upon it."

"Right, friend," cries the clerk, "you are very right. Always avoid what is low. There are several of my acquaintance in London, who are resolved to drive everything which is low from the stage." "Nothing can be more proper," cries the exciseman, pulling his pipe from his mouth. "I remember," added he, "(for I then lived with my lord) I was in the footman's gallery, the night when this play of the Provoked Husband was acted first. There was a great deal of low stuff in it about a country gentleman come up to town to stand for parliament-man; and there they brought a parcel of his servants upon the stage, his coachman I remember particularly; but the gentlemen in our gallery could not bear anything so low, and they damned it. I observe, friend, you have left all that matter out, and you are to be commended for it."

"Nay, gentlemen," cries Jones, "I can never maintain my opinion against so many; indeed, if the generality of his audience dislike him, the learned gentleman who conducts the show might have done very right in dismissing Punch from his service."

The master of the show then began a second harangue, and said much of the great force of example, and how much the inferior part of mankind would be deterred from vice, by observing how odious it was in their superiors; when he was unluckily interrupted by an incident, which, though perhaps we might have omitted it at another time, we cannot help relating at present, but not in this chapter.

Chapter vi.

From which it may be inferred that the best things are liable to be misunderstood and misinterpreted.

A VIOLENT uproar now arose in the entry, where my landlady was well cuffing her maid both with her fist and tongue. She had indeed missed the wench from her employment, and, after a little search, had found her on the puppet-show stage in company with the Merry Andrew, and in a situation not very proper to be described.

Though Grace (for that was her name) had forfeited all title to modesty; yet had she not impudence enough to deny a fact in which she was actually surprized; she, therefore, took another turn, and attempted to mitigate the offence. "Why do you beat me in this manner, mistress?" cries the wench. "If you don't like my doings, you may turn me away. If I am a w——e" (for the other had liberally bestowed that appellation on her), "my betters are so as well as I. What was the fine lady in the puppet-show just now? I suppose she did not lie all night out from her husband for nothing."

The landlady now burst into the kitchen, and fell foul on both her husband and the poor puppet-mover. "Here, husband," says she, "you see the consequence of harbouring these people in your house. If one doth draw a little drink the more for them, one is hardly made amends for the litter they make; and then to have one's house made a bawdy-house of by such lousy vermin. In short, I desire you would be gone to-morrow morning; for I will tolerate no more such doings. It is only the way to teach our servants idleness and nonsense; for to be sure nothing better can be learned by such idle shows as these. I remember when puppet-shows were made of good scripture stories, as Jephthah's Rash Vow, and such good things, and when wicked people were carried away by the devil. There was some sense in those matters; but as the parson told us last Sunday, nobody believes in the devil now-a-days; and here you bring about a parcel of puppets drest up like lords and ladies, only to turn the heads of poor country wenches; and when their heads are once turned topsy-turvy, no wonder everything else is so."

Virgil, I think, tells us, that when the mob are assembled in a riotous and tumultuous manner, and all sorts of missile weapons fly about, if a man of gravity and authority appears amongst them, the tumult is presently appeased, and the mob, which when collected into one body, may be well compared to an ass, erect their long ears at the grave man's discourse.

On the contrary, when a set of grave men and philosophers are disputing; when wisdom herself may in a manner be considered as present, and administering arguments to the disputants; should a tumult arise among the mob, or should one scold, who is herself equal in noise to a mighty mob, appear among the said philosophers; their disputes cease in a moment, wisdom no longer performs her ministerial office, and the attention of every one is immediately attracted by the scold alone.

Thus the uproar aforesaid, and the arrival of the landlady, silenced the master of the puppet-show, and put a speedy and final end to that grave and solemn harangue, of which we have given the reader a sufficient taste already. Nothing indeed could have happened so very inopportune as this accident; the most wanton malice of fortune could not have contrived such another stratagem to confound the poor fellow, while he was so triumphantly descanting on the good morals inculcated by his exhibitions. His mouth was now as effectually stopt, as that of quack must be, if, in the midst of a declamation on the great virtues of his pills and powders, the corpse of one of his martyrs should be brought forth, and deposited before the stage, as a testimony of his skill.

Instead, therefore, of answering my landlady, the puppet-show man ran out to punish his Merry Andrew; and now the moon beginning to put forth her silver light, as the poets call it (though she looked at that time more like a piece of copper), Jones called for his reckoning, and ordered Partridge, whom my landlady had just awaked from a profound nap, to prepare for his journey; but Partridge, having lately carried two points, as my reader hath seen before, was emboldened to attempt a third, which was to prevail with Jones to take up a lodging that evening in the house where he then was. He introduced this with an affected surprize at the intention which Mr Jones declared of removing; and, after urging many excellent arguments against it, he at last insisted strongly that it could be to no manner of purpose whatever; for that, unless Jones knew which way the lady was gone, every step he took might very possibly lead him the farther from her;

"for you find, sir," said he, "by all the people in the house, that she is not gone this way. How much better, therefore, would it be to stay till the morning, when we may expect to meet with somebody to enquire of?"

This last argument had indeed some effect on Jones, and while he was weighing it the landlord threw all the rhetoric of which he was master into the same scale. "Sure, sir," said he, "your servant gives you most excellent advice; for who would travel by night at this time of the year?" He then began in the usual stile to trumpet forth the excellent accommodation which his house afforded; and my landlady likewise opened on the occasion——But, not to detain the reader with what is common to every host and hostess, it is sufficient to tell him Jones was at last prevailed on to stay and refresh himself with a few hours' rest, which indeed he very much wanted; for he had hardly shut his eyes since he had left the inn where the accident of the broken head had happened.

As soon as Jones had taken a resolution to proceed no farther that night, he presently retired to rest, with his two bedfellows, the pocket-book and the muff; but Partridge, who at several times had refreshed himself with several naps, was more inclined to eating than to sleeping, and more to drinking than to either.

And now the storm which Grace had raised being at an end, and my landlady being again reconciled to the puppet-man, who on his side forgave the indecent reflections which the good woman in her passion had cast on his performances, a face of perfect peace and tranquillity reigned in the kitchen; where sat assembled round the fire the landlord and landlady of the house, the master of the puppet-show, the attorney's clerk, the exciseman, and the ingenious Mr Partridge; in which company past the agreeable conversation which will be found in the next chapter.

Chapter vij.

Containing a remark or two of our own, and many more of the good company assembled in the kitchen.

THOUGH the pride of Partridge did not submit to acknowledge himself a servant, yet he condescended in most particulars to imitate the manners of that rank. One instance of this was, his greatly magnifying the fortune of his companion, as he called Jones: such is a general custom with all servants among strangers, as none of them would willingly be thought the attendant on a beggar: for, the higher the situation of the master is, the higher consequently is that of the man in his own opinion; the truth of which observation appears from the behaviour of all the footmen of the nobility.

But, though title and fortune communicate a splendor all around them, and the footmen of men of quality and of estate think themselves entitled to a part of that respect which is paid to the quality and estate of their masters, it is clearly otherwise with regard to virtue and understanding. These advantages are strictly personal, and swallow themselves all the respect which is paid to them. To say the truth, this is so very little, that they cannot well afford to let any others partake with them. As these therefore reflect no honour on the domestic, so neither is he at all dishonoured by the most deplorable want of both in his master. Indeed it is otherwise in the want of what is called virtue in a mistress, the consequence of which we have before seen: for in this dishonour there is a kind of contagion, which, like that of poverty, communicates itself to all who approach it.

Now for these reasons we are not to wonder that servants (I mean among the men only) should have so great regard for the reputation of the wealth of their masters, and little or none at all for their character in other points, and that, though they would be ashamed to be the footman of a beggar, they are not so to attend upon a rogue or a blockhead; and do consequently make no scruple to spread the fame of the iniquities and follies of their said masters as far as possible, and this often with great humour and merriment. In reality, a footman is often a wit as well as a beau, at the expence of the gentleman whose livery he wears.

After Partridge, therefore, had enlarged greatly on the vast fortune to which Mr Jones was heir, he very freely communicated an apprehension, which he had begun to conceive the day before, and for which, as we hinted at that very time, the behaviour of Jones seemed to have furnished a sufficient foundation. In short, he was now pretty well confirmed in an opinion that his master was out of his wits, with which opinion he very bluntly acquainted the good company round the fire.

With this sentiment the puppet-show man immediately coincided. "I own," said he, "the gentleman surprized me very much, when he talked so absurdly about puppet-shows. It is indeed hardly to be conceived that any man in his senses should be so much mistaken; what you say now accounts very well for all his monstrous notions. Poor gentleman! I am heartily concerned for him; indeed he hath a strange wildness about his eyes, which I took notice of before, though I did not mention it."

The landlord agreed with this last assertion, and likewise claimed the sagacity of having observed it. "And certainly," added he, "it must be so; for no one but a madman would have thought of leaving so good a house to ramble about the country at that time of night."

The exciseman, pulling his pipe from his mouth, said, " He thought the gentleman looked and talked a little wildly ; " and then turning to Partridge, "if he be a madman," says he, " he should not be suffered to travel thus about the country ; for possibly he may do some mischief. It is a pity he was not secured and sent home to his relations."

Now some conceits of this kind were likewise lurking in the mind of Partridge ; for, as he was now persuaded that Jones had run away from Mr Allworthy, he promised himself the highest rewards if he could by any means convey him back. But fear of Jones, of whose fierceness and strength he had seen, and indeed felt, some instances, had however represented any such scheme as impossible to be executed, and had discouraged him from applying himself to form any regular plan for the purpose. But no sooner did he hear the sentiments of the exciseman than he embraced that opportunity of declaring his own, and expressed a hearty wish that such a matter could be brought about.

"Could be brought about ! " says the exciseman : " why, there is nothing easier."

"Ah ! sir," answered Partridge, "you don't know what a devil of a fellow he is. He can take me up with one hand, and throw me out at window ; and he would, too, if he did but imagine——"

"Pogh ! " says the exciseman, " I believe I am as good a man as he. Besides, here are five of us."

"I don't know what five," cries the landlady, "my husband shall have nothing to do in it. Nor shall any violent hands be laid upon anybody in my house. The young gentleman is as pretty a young gentleman as ever I saw in my life, and I believe he is no more mad than any of us. What do you tell of his having a wild look with his eyes ? they are the prettiest eyes I ever saw, and he hath the prettiest look with them ; and a very

modest civil young man he is. I am sure I have bepitied him heartily ever since the gentleman there in
the corner told us he was crost in love. Certainly that
is enough to make any man, especially such a sweet
young gentleman as he is, to look a little otherwise
than he did before. Lady, indeed! what the devil
would the lady have better than such a handsome man
with a great estate? I suppose she is one of your
quality folks, one of your Townly ladies that we saw
last night in the puppet-show, who don't know what
they would be at."

The attorney's clerk likewise declared he would
have no concern in the business without the advice of
counsel. "Suppose," says he, "an action of false
imprisonment should be brought against us, what defence could we make? Who knows what may be
sufficient evidence of madness to a jury? But I only
speak upon my own account; for it don't look well
for a lawyer to be concerned in these matters, unless it
be as a lawyer. Juries are always less favourable to us
than to other people. I don't therefore dissuade you,
Mr Thomson (to the exciseman), nor the gentleman,
nor anybody else."

The exciseman shook his head at this speech, and
the puppet-show man said, "Madness was sometimes a
difficult matter for a jury to decide: for I remember,"
says he, "I was once present at a tryal of madness,
where twenty witnesses swore that the person was as
mad as a March hare; and twenty others, that he was
as much in his senses as any man in England.—And
indeed it was the opinion of most people, that it was
only a trick of his relations to rob the poor man of
his right."

"Very likely!" cries the landlady. "I myself
knew a poor gentleman who was kept in a mad-house
all his life by his family, and they enjoyed his estate,

but it did them no good; for though the law gave it them, it was the right of another."

"Pogh!" cries the clerk, with great contempt, "who hath any right but what the law gives them? If the law gave me the best estate in the country, I should never trouble myself much who had the right."

"If it be so," says Partridge, "*Felix quem faciunt aliena pericula cautum.*"

My landlord, who had been called out by the arrival of a horseman at the gate, now returned into the kitchen, and with an affrighted countenance cried out, "What do you think, gentlemen? The rebels have given the duke the slip, and are got almost to London. It is certainly true, for a man on horseback just now told me so."

"I am glad of it with all my heart," cries Partridge; "then there will be no fighting in these parts."

"I am glad," cries the clerk, "for a better reason; "for I would always have right take place."

"Ay, but," answered the landlord, "I have heard some people say this man hath no right."

"I will prove the contrary in a moment," cries the clerk: "if my father dies seized of a right; do you mind me, seized of a right, I say; doth not that right descend to his son; and doth not one right descend as well as another?"

"But how can he have any right to make us papishes?" says the landlord.

"Never fear that," cries Partridge. "As to the matter of right, the gentleman there hath proved it as clear as the sun; and as to the matter of religion, it is quite out of the case. The papists themselves don't expect any such thing. A popish priest, whom I know very well, and who is a very honest man, told me upon his word and honour they had no such design."

"And another priest, of my acquaintance," said the

landlady, "hath told me the same thing; but my husband is always so afraid of papishes. I know a great many papishes that are very honest sort of people, and spend their money very freely; and it is always a maxim with me, that one man's money is as good as another's."

"Very true, mistress," said the puppet-show man, "I don't care what religion comes; provided the Presbyterians are not uppermost; for they are enemies to puppet-shows."

"And so you would sacrifice your religion to your interest," cries the exciseman; "and are desirous to see popery brought in, are you?"

"Not I, truly," answered the other; "I hate popery as much as any man; but yet it is a comfort to one, that one should be able to live under it, which I could not do among Presbyterians. To be sure, every man values his livelihood first; that must be granted; and I warrant, if you would confess the truth, you are more afraid of losing your place than anything else; but never fear, friend, there will be an excise under another government as well as under this."

"Why, certainly," replied the exciseman, "I should be a very ill man if I did not honour the king, whose bread I eat. That is no more than natural, as a man may say: for what signifies it to me that there would be an excise-office under another government, since my friends would be out, and I could expect no better than to follow them? No, no, friend, I shall never be bubbled out of my religion in hopes only of keeping my place under another government; for I should certainly be no better, and very probably might be worse."

"Why, that is what I say," cries the landlord, "whenever folks say who knows what may happen! Odsooks! should not I be a blockhead to lend my money to I know not who, because mayhap he may return it again? I am sure it is safe in my own bureau, and there I will keep it."

The attorney's clerk had taken a great fancy to the sagacity of Partridge. Whether this proceeded from the great discernment which the former had into men, as well as things, or whether it arose from the sympathy between their minds; for they were both truly Jacobites in principle; they now shook hands heartily, and drank bumpers of strong beer to healths which we think proper to bury in oblivion.

These healths were afterwards pledged by all present, and even by my landlord himself, though reluctantly; but he could not withstand the menaces of the clerk, who swore he would never set his foot within his house again, if he refused. The bumpers which were swallowed on this occasion soon put an end to the conversation. Here, therefore, we will put an end to the chapter.

Chapter viii.

In which fortune seems to have been in a better humour with Jones than we have hitherto seen her.

AS there is no wholesomer, so perhaps there are few stronger, sleeping potions than fatigue. Of this Jones might be said to have taken a very large dose, and it operated very forcibly upon him. He had already slept nine hours, and might perhaps have slept longer, had he not been awakened by a most violent noise at his chamber-door, where the sound of many heavy blows was accompanied with many exclamations of murder. Jones presently leapt from his bed, where he found the master of the puppet-show belabouring

again uneasy, as the people of the house could give him no fresh information concerning Sophia.

Their meal being over, Jones was again preparing to sally, notwithstanding the violence of the storm still continued; but Partridge begged heartily for another mug; and at last casting his eyes on a lad at the fire, who had entered into the kitchen, and who at that instant was looking as earnestly at him, he turned suddenly to Jones, and cried, "Master, give me your hand, a single mug shan't serve the turn this bout. Why, here's more news of Madam Sophia come to town. The boy there standing by the fire is the very lad that rode before her. I can swear to my own plaister on his face."—"Heavens bless you, sir," cries the boy, "it is your own plaister sure enough; I shall have always reason to remember your goodness; for it hath almost cured me."

At these words Jones started from his chair, and, bidding the boy follow him immediately, departed from the kitchen into a private apartment; for, so delicate was he with regard to Sophia, that he never willingly mentioned her name in the presence of many people; and, though he had, as it were, from the overflowings of his heart, given Sophia as a toast among the officers, where he thought it was impossible she should be known; yet, even there, the reader may remember how difficultly he was prevailed upon to mention her sirname.

Hard therefore was it, and perhaps, in the opinion of many sagacious readers, very absurd and monstrous, that he should principally owe his present misfortune to the supposed want of that delicacy with which he so abounded; for, in reality, Sophia was much more offended at the freedoms which she thought (and not without good reason) he had taken with her name and character, than at any freedoms, in which, under his present circumstances, he had indulged himself with the person of another woman; and to say truth, I believe Honour could never have prevailed on her to leave Upton without her seeing Jones, had it not been for those two strong instances of a levity in his behaviour, so void of respect, and indeed so highly inconsistent with any degree of love and tenderness in great and delicate minds.

But so matters fell out, and so I must relate them; and if any reader is shocked at their appearing unnatural, I cannot help it. I must remind such persons that I am not writing a system, but a history, and I am not obliged to reconcile every matter to the received notions concerning truth and nature. But if this was never so easy to do, perhaps it might be more prudent in me to avoid it. For instance, as the fact at present before us now stands, without any comment of mine upon it, though it may at first sight offend some readers, yet, upon more mature consideration, it must please all; for wise and good men may consider what happened to Jones at Upton as a just punishment for his wickedness with regard to women, of which it was indeed the immediate consequence; and silly and bad persons may comfort themselves in their vices by flattering their own hearts that the characters of men are rather owing to accident than to virtue. Now, perhaps the reflections which we should be here inclined to draw would alike contradict both these conclusions, and would show that these incidents contribute only to confirm the great, useful, and uncommon doctrine, which it is the purpose of this whole work to inculcate, and which we must not fill up our pages by frequently repeating, as an ordinary parson fills his sermon by repeating his text at the end of every paragraph.

We are contented that it must appear, however unhappily Sophia had erred in her opinion of Jones, she had sufficient reason for her opinion; since, I believe, every other young lady would, in her situation, have erred in the same manner. Nay, had she followed her lover at this very time, and had entered this very alehouse the moment he was departed from it, she would have found the landlord as well acquainted with her name and person as the wench at Upton had appeared to be. For while Jones was examining his boy in whispers in an inner room, Partridge, who had no such delicacy in his disposition, was in the kitchen very openly catechising the other guide who had attended Mrs Fitzpatrick; by which means the landlord, whose ears were open on all such occasions, became perfectly well acquainted with the tumble of Sophia from her horse, &c., with the mistake concerning Jenny Cameron, with the many consequences of the punch, and, in short, with almost everything which had happened at the inn whence we despatched our ladies in a coach-and-six when we last took our leaves of them.

<hr />

Chapter ix.

Containing little more than a few odd observations.

JONES had been absent a full half-hour, when he returned into the kitchen in a hurry, desiring the landlord to let him know that instant what was to pay. And now the concern which Partridge felt at being obliged to quit the warm chimney-corner, and a cup of excellent liquor, was somewhat compensated by hearing that he was to proceed no farther on foot, for Jones, by golden arguments, had prevailed with the boy to attend him back to the inn whither he had before conducted Sophia; but to this however the lad consented, upon condition that the other guide would wait for him at the alehouse; because, as the landlord at Upton was an intimate acquaintance of the landlord at Gloucester, it might some time or other come to the ears of the latter that his horses had been let to more than one person; and so the boy might be brought to account for money which he wisely intended to put in his own pocket.

We were obliged to mention this circumstance, trifling as it may seem, since it retarded Mr Jones a considerable time in his setting out; for the honesty of this latter boy was somewhat high—that is, somewhat high-priced, and would indeed have cost Jones very dear, had not Partridge, who, as we have said, was a very cunning fellow, artfully thrown in half-a-crown to be spent at that very alehouse, while the boy was waiting for his companion. This half-crown the landlord no sooner got scent of, than he opened after it with such vehement and persuasive outcry, that the boy was soon overcome, and consented to take half-a-crown more for his stay. Here we cannot help observing, that as there is so much of policy in the lowest life, great men often overvalue themselves on those refinements in imposture, in which they are frequently excelled by some of the lowest of the human species.

The horses being now produced, Jones directly leapt into the side-saddle, on which his dear Sophia had rid. The lad, indeed, very civilly offered him the use of his; but he chose the side-saddle, probably because it was softer. Partridge, however, though full as effeminate as Jones, could not bear the thoughts of degrading his manhood; he therefore accepted the boy's offer: and now, Jones being mounted on the side-saddle of his Sophia, the boy on that of Mrs Honour, and Partridge bestriding the third horse, they set forwards on their journey, and within four hours arrived at the inn where the reader hath already spent so much time. Partridge was in very high spirits during the whole way, and often mentioned to Jones the many good omens of his future success which had lately befriended him; and which the reader, without being the least superstitious, must allow to have been particularly fortunate. Partridge was moreover better pleased with the present pursuit of his companion than he had been with his pursuit of glory; and from these very omens, which assured the pedagogue of success, he likewise first acquired a clear idea of the amour between Jones and Sophia; to which he had before given very little attention, as he had originally taken a wrong scent concerning the reasons of Jones's departure; and as to what happened at Upton, he was too much frightened just before and after his leaving that place to draw any other conclusions from thence than that poor Jones was a downright madman: a conceit which was not at all disagreeable to the opinion he before had of his extraordinary wildness, of which, he thought, his behaviour on their quitting Gloucester so well justified all the accounts he had formerly received. He was now, however, pretty well satisfied with his present expedition, and henceforth began to conceive much worthier sentiments of his friend's understanding.

The clock had just struck three when they arrived, and Jones immediately bespoke post-horses; but unluckily there was not a horse to be procured in the whole place; which the reader will not wonder at when he considers the hurry in which the whole nation, and especially this part of it, was at this time engaged, when expresses were passing and repassing every hour of the day and night.

Jones endeavoured all he could to prevail with his former guide to escorte him to Coventry; but he was inexorable. While he was arguing with the boy in the inn-yard, a person came up to him, and saluting him by his name, enquired how all the good family did in Somersetshire; and now Jones casting his eyes upon this person, presently discovered him to be Mr Dowling, the lawyer, with whom he had dined at Gloucester, and with much courtesy returned the salutation.

Dowling very earnestly pressed Mr Jones to go no further that night; and backed his solicitations with many unanswerable arguments, such as, that it was almost dark, that the roads were very dirty, and that he would be able to travel much better by day-light, with many others equally good, some of which Jones had probably suggested to himself before; but as they were then ineffectual, so they were still: and he continued resolute in his design, even though he should be obliged to set out on foot.

When the good attorney found he could not prevail on Jones to stay, he as strenuously applied himself to persuade the guide to accompany him. He urged many motives to induce him to undertake this short journey, and at last concluded with saying, "Do you think the gentleman won't very well reward you for your trouble?"

Two to one are odds at every other thing as well as at foot-ball. But the advantage which this united force hath in persuasion or entreaty must have been visible to a curious observer; for he must have often seen, that when a father, a master, a wife, or any other person in authority, have stoutly adhered to a denial against all the reasons which a single man could produce, they have afterwards yielded to the repetition of the same sentiments by a second or third person, who hath undertaken the cause, without attempting to advance anything new in its behalf. And hence, perhaps, proceeds the phrase of seconding an argument or a motion, and the great consequence this is of in all assemblies of public debate. Hence, likewise, probably it is, that in our courts of law we often hear a learned gentleman (generally a serjeant) repeating for an hour together what another learned gentleman, who spoke just before him, had been saying.

Instead of accounting for this, we shall proceed in our usual manner to exemplify it in the conduct of the lad above mentioned, who submitted to the persuasions of Mr Dowling, and promised once more to admit Jones into his side-saddle; but insisted on first giving the poor creatures a good bait, saying, they had travelled a great way, and been rid very hard. Indeed this caution of the boy was needless; for Jones, notwithstanding his hurry and impatience, would have ordered this of himself; for he by no means agreed with the opinion of those who consider animals as mere machines, and when they bury their spurs in the belly of their horse, imagine the spur and the horse to have an equal capacity of feeling pain.

While the beasts were eating their corn, or rather were supposed to eat it (for, as the boy was taking care of himself in the kitchen, the ostler took great care that his corn should not be consumed in the stable), Mr Jones, at the earnest desire of Mr Dowling, accompanied that gentleman into his room, where they sat down together over a bottle of wine.

Chapter x.

In which Mr Jones and Mr Dowling drink a bottle together.

MR DOWLING, pouring out a glass of wine, named the health of the good Squire Allworthy; adding, "If you please, sir, we will likewise remember his nephew and heir, the young squire: Come, sir, here's Mr Blifil to you, a very pretty young gentleman; and who, I dare swear, will hereafter make a very considerable figure in his country. I have a borough for him myself in my eye."

"Sir," answered Jones, "I am convinced you don't intend to affront me, so I shall not resent it; but I promise you, you have joined two persons very improperly together; for one is the glory of the human species, and the other is a rascal who dishonours the name of man."

Dowling stared at this. He said, "He thought both the gentlemen had a very unexceptionable character. As for Squire Allworthy himself," says he, "I never had the happiness to see him; but all the world talks of his goodness. And, indeed, as to the young gentleman, I never saw him but once, when I carried him the news of the loss of his mother; and then I was so hurried, and drove, and tore with the multiplicity of business, that I had hardly time to converse with him; but he looked so like a very honest gentleman, and behaved himself so prettily, that I protest I never was more delighted with any gentleman since I was born."

"I don't wonder," answered Jones, "that he should impose upon you in so short an acquaintance; for he hath the cunning of the devil himself, and you may live with him many years, without discovering him. I was bred up with him from my infancy, and we were hardly ever asunder; but it is very lately only that I have discovered half the villany which is in him. I own I never greatly liked him. I thought he wanted that generosity of spirit, which is the sure foundation of all that is great and noble in human nature. I saw a selfishness in him long ago which I despised; but it is lately, very lately, that I have found him capable of the basest and blackest designs; for, indeed, I have at last found out, that he hath taken an advantage of the openness of my own temper, and hath concerted the deepest project, by a long train of wicked artifice, to work my ruin, which at last he hath effected."

"Ay! ay!" cries Dowling; "I protest, then, it is a pity such a person should inherit the great estate of your uncle Allworthy."

"Alas, sir," cries Jones, "you do me an honour to which I have no title. It is true, indeed, his goodness once allowed me the liberty of calling him by a much nearer name; but as this was only a voluntary act of goodness, I can complain of no injustice when he thinks proper to deprive me of this honour; since the loss cannot be more unmerited than the gift originally was. I assure you, sir, I am no relation of Mr Allworthy; and if the world, who are incapable of setting a true value on his virtue, should think, in his behaviour to me, he hath dealt hardly by a relation, they do an injustice to the best of men: for I—but I ask your pardon, I shall trouble you with no particulars relating to myself; only as you seemed to think me a relation of Mr Allworthy, I thought proper to set you right in a matter that might draw some censures upon him, which I promise you I would rather lose my life than give occasion to."

"I protest, sir," cried Dowling, "you talk very much like a man of honour; but instead of giving me any trouble, I protest it would give me great pleasure to know how you came to be thought a relation of Mr Allworthy's, if you are not. Your horses won't be ready this half-hour, and as you have sufficient opportunity, I wish you would tell me how all that happened; for I protest it seems very surprizing that you should pass for a relation of a gentleman, without being so."

Jones, who in the compliance of his disposition (though not in his prudence) a little resembled his lovely Sophia, was easily prevailed on to satisfy Mr Dowling's

curiosity, by relating the history of his birth and education, which he did, like Othello.

> ———Even from his boyish years,
> To th' very moment he was bad to tell:

the which to hear, Dowling, like Desdemona, did
seriously incline;

> He swore 'twas strange, 'twas passing strange;
> 'Twas pitiful, 'twas wonderous pitiful.

Mr Dowling was indeed very greatly affected with
this relation; for he had not divested himself of
humanity by being an attorney. Indeed, nothing is
more unjust than to carry our prejudices against a
profession into private life, and to borrow our idea of
a man from our opinion of his calling. Habit, it is
true, lessens the horror of those actions which the
profession makes necessary, and consequently habitual;
but in all other instances, Nature works in men of all
professions alike; nay, perhaps, even more strongly
with those who give her, as it were, a holiday, when
they are following their ordinary business. A butcher,
I make no doubt, would feel compunction at the
slaughter of a fine horse; and though a surgeon can
feel no pain in cutting off a limb, I have known him
compassionate a man in a fit of the gout. The common
hangman, who hath stretched the necks of hundreds,
is known to have trembled at his first operation on a
head: and the very professors of human blood-shedding,
who, in their trade of war, butcher thousands, not only
of their fellow-professors, but often of women and
children, without remorse; even these, I say, in times
of peace, when drums and trumpets are laid aside, often
lay aside all their ferocity, and become very gentle
members of civil society. In the same manner an
attorney may feel all the miseries and distresses of his

fellow-creatures, provided he happens not to be concerned against them.

Jones, as the reader knows, was yet unacquainted with the very black colours in which he had been represented to Mr Allworthy; and as to other matters, he did not shew them in the most disadvantageous light; for though he was unwilling to cast any blame on his former friend and patron; yet he was not very desirous of heaping too much upon himself. Dowling therefore observed, and not without reason, that very ill offices must have been done him by somebody: "For certainly," cries he, "the squire would never have disinherited you only for a few faults, which any young gentleman might have committed. Indeed, I cannot properly say disinherited: for to be sure by law you cannot claim as heir. That's certain; that nobody need go to counsel for. Yet when a gentleman had in a manner adopted you thus as his own son, you might reasonably have expected some very considerable part, if not the whole; nay, if you had expected the whole, I should not have blamed you: for certainly all men are for getting as much as they can, and they are not to be blamed on that account."

"Indeed you wrong me," said Jones; "I should have been contented with very little: I never had any view upon Mr Allworthy's fortune; nay, I believe I may truly say, I never once considered what he could or might give me. This I solemnly declare, if he had done a prejudice to his nephew in my favour, I would have undone it again. I had rather enjoy my own mind than the fortune of another man. What is the poor pride arising from a magnificent house, a numerous equipage, a splendid table, and from all the other advantages or appearances of fortune, compared to the warm, solid content, the swelling satisfaction, the thrilling transports, and the exulting triumphs, which a good mind enjoys, in the contemplation of a generous, virtuous, noble, benevolent action? I envy not Blifil in the prospect of his wealth; nor shall I envy him in the possession of it. I would not think myself a rascal half an hour, to exchange situations. I believe, indeed, Mr Blifil suspected me of the views you mention; and I suppose these suspicions, as they arose from the baseness of his own heart, so they occasioned his baseness to me. But, I thank Heaven, I know, I feel—I feel my innocence, my friend; and I would not part with that feeling for the world. For as long as I know I have never done, nor even designed, an injury to any being whatever,

> *Pone me pigris ubi nulla campis*
> *Arbor æstiva recreatur aura,*
> *Quod latus mundi nebulæ, malusque*
> *   Jupiter urget.*
>
> *Pone sub curru nimium propinqui*
> *Solis in terra dominibus negata;*
> *Dulce ridentem Lalagen amabo,*
> *   Dulce loquentem.**

He then filled a bumper of wine, and drunk it off to the health of his dear Lalage; and, filling Dowling's glass likewise up to the brim, insisted on his pledging him. "Why, then, here's Miss Lalage's health with all my heart," cries Dowling. "I have heard her toasted often, I protest, though I never saw her; but they say she's extremely handsome."

> * Place me where never summer breeze
>   Unbinds the glebe, or warms the trees:
>   Where ever-lowering clouds appear,
> And angry Jove deforms th' inclement year.
>
>   Place me beneath the burning ray,
>   Where rolls the rapid car of day;
>   Love and the nymph shall charm my toils,
> The nymph who sweetly speaks, and sweetly smiles.
>   MR FRANCIS.

Though the Latin was not the only part of this speech which Dowling did not perfectly understand; yet there was somewhat in it that made a very strong impression upon him.   And though he endeavoured by winking, nodding, sneering, and grinning, to hide the impression from Jones (for we are as often ashamed of thinking right as of thinking wrong), it is certain he secretly approved as much of his sentiments as he understood, and really felt a very strong impulse of compassion for him.   But we may possibly take some other opportunity of commenting upon this, especially if we should happen to meet Mr Dowling any more in the course of our history.   At present we are obliged to take our leave of that gentleman a little abruptly, in imitation of Mr Jones; who was no sooner informed, by Partridge, that his horses were ready, than he deposited his reckoning, wished his companion a good night, mounted, and set forward towards Coventry, though the night was dark, and it just then began to rain very hard.

Chapter xi.

The disasters which befel Jones on his departure for Coventry; with the sage remarks of Partridge.

NO road can be plainer than that from the place where they now were to Coventry; and though neither Jones, nor Partridge, nor the guide, had ever travelled it before, it would have been almost impossible to have missed their way, had it not been for the two reasons mentioned in the conclusion of the last chapter.

These two circumstances, however, happening both

unfortunately to intervene, our travellers deviated into a much less frequented track; and after riding full six miles, instead of arriving at the stately spires of Coventry, they found themselves still in a very dirty lane, where they saw no symptoms of approaching the suburbs of a large city.

Jones now declared that they must certainly have lost their way; but this the guide insisted upon was impossible; a word which, in common conversation, is often used to signify not only improbable, but often what is really very likely, and, sometimes, what hath certainly happened; an hyperbolical violence like that which is so frequently offered to the words infinite and eternal; by the former of which it is usual to express a distance of half a yard, and by the latter, a duration of five minutes. And thus it is as usual to assert the impossibility of losing what is already actually lost. This was, in fact, the case at present; for, notwithstanding all the confident assertions of the lad to the contrary, it is certain they were no more in the right road to Coventry, than the fraudulent, griping, cruel, canting miser is in the right road to heaven.

It is not, perhaps, easy for a reader, who hath never been in those circumstances, to imagine the horror with which darkness, rain, and wind, fill persons who have lost their way in the night; and who, consequently, have not the pleasant prospect of warm fires, dry cloaths, and other refreshments, to support their minds in struggling with the inclemencies of the weather. A very imperfect idea of this horror will, however, serve sufficiently to account for the conceits which now filled the head of Partridge, and which we shall presently be obliged to open.

Jones grew more and more positive that they were out of their road; and the boy himself at last acknowledged he believed they were not in the right road to

Coventry; though he affirmed, at the same time, it was impossible they should have mist the way. But Partridge was of a different opinion. He said, "When they first set out he imagined some mischief or other would happen.—Did not you observe, sir," said he to Jones, "that old woman who stood at the door just as you was taking horse? I wish you had given her a small matter, with all my heart; for she said then you might repent it; and at that very instant it began to rain, and the wind hath continued rising ever since. Whatever some people may think, I am very certain it is in the power of witches to raise the wind whenever they please. I have seen it happen very often in my time: and if ever I saw a witch in all my life, that old woman was certainly one. I thought so to myself at that very time; and if I had had any halfpence in my pocket, I would have given her some; for to be sure it is always good to be charitable to those sort of people, for fear what may happen; and many a person hath lost his cattle by saving a halfpenny."

Jones, though he was horridly vexed at the delay which this mistake was likely to occasion in his journey, could not help smiling at the superstition of his friend, whom an accident now greatly confirmed in his opinion. This was a tumble from his horse; by which, however, he received no other injury than what the dirt conferred on his cloaths.

Partridge had no sooner recovered his legs, than he appealed to his fall, as conclusive evidence of all he had asserted; but Jones finding he was unhurt, answered with a smile: "This witch of yours, Partridge, is a most ungrateful jade, and doth not, I find, distinguish her friends from others in her resentment. If the old lady had been angry with me for neglecting her, I don't see why she should tumble you from your horse, after all the respect you have expressed for her."

"It is ill jesting," cries Partridge, "with people who have power to do these things; for they are often very malicious. I remember a farrier, who provoked one of them, by asking her when the time she had bargained with the devil for would be out; and within three months from that very day one of his best cows was drowned. Nor was she satisfied with that; for a little time afterwards he lost a barrel of best-drink: for the old witch pulled out the spigot, and let it run all over the cellar, the very first evening he had tapped it to make merry with some of his neighbours. In short, nothing ever thrived with him afterwards; for she worried the poor man so, that he took to drinking; and in a year or two his stock was seized, and he and his family are now come to the parish."

The guide, and perhaps his horse too, were both so attentive to this discourse, that, either through want of care, or by the malice of the witch, they were now both sprawling in the dirt.

Partridge entirely imputed this fall, as he had done his own, to the same cause. He told Mr Jones, "I would certainly be his turn next; and earnestly entreated him to return back, and find out the old woman, and pacify her. We shall very soon," added he, "reach the inn; for though we have seemed to go forward, I am very certain we are in the identical place in which we were an hour ago; and I dare swear, if it was daylight, we might now see the inn we set out from."

Instead of returning any answer to this sage advice, Jones was entirely attentive to what had happened to the boy, who received no other hurt than what had before befallen Partridge, and which his cloaths very easily bore, as they had been for many years inured to

the like. He soon regained his side-saddle, and by
the hearty curses and blows which he bestowed on
his horse, quickly satisfied Mr Jones that no harm
was done.

Chapter rij.

*Relates that Mr Jones continued his journey, contrary to
the advice of Partridge, with what happened on
that occasion.*

THEY now discovered a light at some distance, to
the great pleasure of Jones, and to the no small
terror of Partridge, who firmly believed himself
to be bewitched, and that this light was a Jack-with-a-
lantern, or somewhat more mischievous.

But how were these fears increased, when, as they
approached nearer to this light (or lights as they now
appeared), they heard a confused sound of human
voices ; of singing, laughing, and hallowing, together
with a strange noise that seemed to proceed from some
instruments ; but could hardly be allowed the name of
music ! indeed, to favour a little the opinion of Partridge, it might very well be called music bewitched.

It is impossible to conceive a much greater degree of
horror than what now seized on Partridge ; the contagion of which had reached the post-boy, who had
been very attentive to many things that the other had
uttered. He now, therefore, joined in petitioning
Jones to return ; saying he firmly believed what Partridge had just before said, that though the horses
seemed to go on, they had not moved a step forwards
during at least the last half-hour.

Jones could not help smiling in the midst of his
vexation, at the fears of these poor fellows. " Either
we advance," says he, " towards the lights, or the

lights have advanced towards us; for we are now at a very little distance from them; but how can either of you be afraid of a set of people who appear only to be merry-making?"

"Merry-making, sir!" cries Partridge; "who could be merry-making at this time of night, and in such a place, and such weather? They can be nothing but ghosts or witches, or some evil spirits or other, that's certain."

"Let them be what they will," cries Jones, "I am resolved to go up to them, and enquire the way to Coventry. All witches, Partridge, are not such ill-natured hags as that we had the misfortune to meet with last."

"O Lord, sir," cries Partridge, "there is no know-ing what humour they will be in; to be sure it is always best to be civil to them; but what if we should meet with something worse than witches, with evil spirits themselves?——Pray, sir, be advised; pray, sir, do. If you had read so many terrible accounts as I have of these matters, you would not be so fool-hardy.—— The Lord knows whither we have got already, or whither we are going; for sure such darkness was never seen upon earth, and I question whether it can be darker in the other world."

Jones put forwards as fast as he could, notwithstand-ing all these hints and cautions, and poor Partridge was obliged to follow; for though he hardly dared to ad-vance, he dared still less to stay behind by himself.

At length they arrived at the place whence the lights and different noises had issued. This Jones perceived to be no other than a barn, where a great number of men and women were assembled, and diverting them-selves with much apparent jollity.

Jones no sooner appeared before the great doors of the barn, which were open, than a masculine and very

rough voice from within demanded, who was there?—
To which Jones gently answered, a friend; and immediately asked the road to Coventry.

"If you are a friend," cries another of the men in
the barn, "you had better alight till the storm is over"
(for indeed it was now more violent than ever;) "you
are very welcome to put up your horse; for there is
sufficient room for him at the end of the barn."

"You are very obliging," returned Jones; "and I
will accept your offer for a few minutes, whilst the rain
continues; and here are two more who will be glad of
the same favour." This was accorded with more
good-will than it was accepted: for Partridge would
rather have submitted to the utmost inclemency of the
weather than have trusted to the clemency of those
whom he took for hobgoblins; and the poor post-boy
was now infected with the same apprehensions; but
they were both obliged to follow the example of Jones;
the one because he durst not leave his horse, and the
other because he feared nothing so much as being left
by himself.

Had this history been writ in the days of superstition, I should have had too much compassion for the
reader to have left him so long in suspense, whether
Beelzebub or Satan was about actually to appear in
person, with all his hellish retinue; but as these doctrines are at present very unfortunate, and have but few,
if any believers, I have not been much aware of conveying any such terrors. To say truth, the whole furniture
of the infernal regions hath long been appropriated by
the managers of playhouses, who seem lately to have laid
them by as rubbish, capable only of affecting the upper
gallery; a place in which few of our readers ever sit.

However, though we do not suspect raising any
great terror on this occasion, we have reason to fear
some other apprehensions may here arise in our reader,

into which we would not willingly betray him; I mean that we are going to take a voyage into fairy-land, and introduce a set of beings into our history, which scarce any one was ever childish enough to believe, though many have been foolish enough to spend their time in writing and reading their adventures.

To prevent, therefore, any such suspicions, so prejudicial to the credit of an historian, who professes to draw his materials from nature only, we shall now proceed to acquaint the reader who these people were, whose sudden appearance had struck such terrors into Partridge, had more than half frightened the post-boy, and had a little surprized even Mr Jones himself.

The people then assembled in this barn were no other than a company of Egyptians, or, as they are vulgarly called, gypsies, and they were now celebrating the wedding of one of their society.

It is impossible to conceive a happier set of people than appeared here to be met together. The utmost mirth, indeed, shewed itself in every countenance; nor was their ball totally void of all order and decorum. Perhaps it had more than a country assembly is sometimes conducted with: for these people are subject to a formal government and laws of their own, and all pay obedience to one great magistrate, whom they call their king.

Greater plenty, likewise, was nowhere to be seen than what flourished in this barn. Here was indeed no nicety nor elegance, nor did the keen appetite of the guests require any. Here was good store of bacon, fowls, and mutton, to which every one present provided better sauce himself than the best and dearest French cook can prepare.

Æneas is not described under more consternation in the temple of Juno,

Dum stupet obtutuque hæret defixus in uno,

than was our heroe at what he saw in this barn. While
he was looking everywhere round him with astonishment, a venerable person approached him with many
friendly salutations, rather of too hearty a kind to be
called courtly. This was no other than the king of
the gypsies himself. He was very little distinguished
in dress from his subjects, nor had he any regalia of
majesty to support his dignity; and yet there seemed
(as Mr Jones said) to be somewhat in his air which
denoted authority, and inspired the beholders with an
idea of awe and respect; though all this was perhaps
imaginary in Jones; and the truth may be, that such
ideas are incident to power, and almost inseparable
from it.

There was somewhat in the open countenance and
courteous behaviour of Jones which, being accompanied
with much comeliness of person, greatly recommended
him at first sight to every beholder. These were, perhaps, a little heightened in the present instance, by
that profound respect which he paid to the king of the
gypsies, the moment he was acquainted with his dignity,
and which was the sweeter to his gypseian majesty, as
he was not used to receive such homage from any but
his own subjects.

The king ordered a table to be spread with the
choicest of their provisions for his accommodation;
and, having placed himself at his right hand, his majesty
began to discourse with our heroe in the following
manner :—

"Me doubt not, sir, but you have often seen some
of my people, who are what you call de parties detache:
for dey go about everywhere; but me fancy you imagine not we be so considrable body as we be; and
may be you will be surprize more when you hear de
gypsy be as orderly and well govern people as any
upon face of de earth.

"Me have honour, as me say, to be deir king, and no monarch can do boast of more dutiful subject, ne no more affectionate. How far me deserve deir good-will, me no say; but dis me can say, dat me never design anyting but to do dem good. Me sall no do boast of dat neider: for what can me do oderwise dan consider of de good of dose poor people who go about all day to give me always the best of what dey get. Dey love and honour me darefore, because me do love and take care of dem; dat is all, me know no oder reason.

"About a tousand or two tousand year ago, me cannot tell to a year or two, as can neider write nor read, dere was a great what you call—a volution among de gypsy; for dere was de lord gypsy in dose days; and dese lord did quarrel vid one anoder about de place; but de king of de gypsy did demolish dem all, and made all his subject equal vid each oder; and since dat time dey have agree very well; for dey no tink of being king, and may be it be better for dem as dey be; for me assure you it be ver troublesome ting to be king, and always to do justice; me have often wish to be de private gypsy when me have been forced to punish my dear friend and relation; for dough we never put to death, our punishments be ver severe. Dey make de gypsy ashamed of demselves, and dat be ver terrible punishment; me ave scarce ever known de gypsy so punish do harm any more."

The king then proceeded to express some wonder that there was no such punishment as shame in other governments. Upon which Jones assured him to the contrary; for that there were many crimes for which shame was inflicted by the English laws, and that it was indeed one consequence of all punishment. "Dat be ver strange," said the king; "for me know and hears good deal of your people, dough me no live among dem; and me have often hear dat sham is de consequence and de cause too of many of your rewards. Are your rewards and punishments den de same ting?"

While his majesty was thus discoursing with Jones, a sudden uproar arose in the barn, and as it seems upon this occasion :—the courtesy of these people had by degrees removed all the apprehensions of Partridge, and he was prevailed upon not only to stuff himself with their food, but to taste some of their liquors, which by degrees entirely expelled all fear from his composition, and in its stead introduced much more agreeable sensations.

A young female gypsy, more remarkable for her wit than her beauty, had decoyed the honest fellow aside, pretending to tell his fortune. Now, when they were alone together in a remote part of the barn, whether it proceeded from the strong liquor, which is never so apt to inflame inordinate desire as after moderate fatigue ; or whether the fair gypsy herself threw aside the delicacy and decency of her sex, and tempted the youth Partridge with express solicitations ; but they were discovered in a very improper manner by the husband of the gypsy, who, from jealousy it seems, had kept a watchful eye over his wife, and had dogged her to the place, where he found her in the arms of her gallant.

To the great confusion of Jones, Partridge was now hurried before the king ; who heard the accusation, and likewise the culprit's defence, which was indeed very trifling ; for the poor fellow was confounded by the plain evidence which appeared against him, and had very little to say for himself. His majesty, then turning towards Jones, said, "Sir, you have hear what dey say ; what punishment do you tink your man deserve?"

Jones answered, "He was sorry for what had happened, and that Partridge should make the husband all the amends in his power : he said, he had very little money about him at that time;" and, putting his hand into his pocket, offered the fellow a guinea. To which he immediately answered, "He hoped his honour would not think of giving him less than five."

This sum, after some altercation, was reduced to two; and Jones, having stipulated for the full forgiveness of both Partridge and the wife, was going to pay the money; when his majesty, restraining his hand, turned to the witness and asked him, "At what time he had discovered the criminals?" To which he answered, "That he had been desired by the husband to watch the motions of his wife from her first speaking to the stranger, and that he had never lost sight of her afterwards till the crime had been committed." The king then asked, "if the husband was with him all that time in his lurking-place?" To which he answered in the affirmative. His Egyptian majesty then addressed himself to the husband as follows: "Me be sorry to see any gypsy dat have no more honour dan to sell de honour of his wife for money. If you had de love for your wife, you would have prevented dis matter, and not endeavour to make her de whore dat you might discover her. Me do order dat you have no money given you, for you deserve punishment, not reward; me do order derefore, dat you be de infamous gypsy, and do wear pair of horns upon your forehead for one month, and dat your wife be called de whore, and pointed at all dat time; for you be de infamous gypsy, but she be no less de infamous whore."

The gypsies immediately proceeded to execute the sentence, and left Jones and Partridge alone with his majesty.

Jones greatly applauded the justice of the sentence: upon which the king, turning to him, said, "Me believe you be surprize: for me suppose you have ver bad opinion of my people; me suppose you tink us all de tieves."

"I must confess, sir," said Jones, "I have not heard so favourable an account of them as they seem to deserve."

"Me vil tell you," said the king, "how the difference is between you and us. My people rob your people, and your people rob one anoder."

Jones afterwards proceeded very gravely to sing forth the happiness of those subjects who live under such a magistrate.

Indeed their happiness appears to have been so compleat, that we are aware lest some advocate for arbitrary power should hereafter quote the case of those people, as an instance of the great advantages which attend that government above all others.

And here we will make a concession, which would not perhaps have been expected from us, that no limited form of government is capable of rising to the same degree of perfection, or of producing the same benefits to society, with this. Mankind have never been so happy, as when the greatest part of the then known world was under the dominion of a single master; and this state of their felicity continued during the reigns of five successive princes.* This was the true æra of the golden age, and the only golden age which ever had any existence, unless in the warm imaginations of the poets, from the expulsion from Eden down to this day.

In reality, I know but of one solid objection to absolute monarchy. The only defect in which excellent constitution seems to be, the difficulty of finding any man adequate to the office of an absolute monarch: for this indispensably requires three qualities very difficult, as it appears from history, to be found in princely natures: first, a sufficient quantity of moderation in the prince, to be contented with all the power

* Nerva, Trajan, Adrian, and the two Antonini.

which is possible for him to have. 2ndly, Enough of wisdom to know his own happiness. And, 3rdly, Goodness sufficient to support the happiness of others, when not only compatible with, but instrumental to his own.

Now if an absolute monarch, with all these great and rare qualifications, should be allowed capable of conferring the greatest good on society; it must be surely granted, on the contrary, that absolute power, vested in the hands of one who is deficient in them all, is likely to be attended with no less a degree of evil.

In short, our own religion furnishes us with adequate ideas of the blessing, as well as curse, which may attend absolute power. The pictures of heaven and of hell will place a very lively image of both before our eyes; for though the prince of the latter can have no power but what he originally derives from the omnipotent Sovereign in the former, yet it plainly appears from Scripture that absolute power in his infernal dominions is granted to their diabolical ruler. This is indeed the only absolute power which can by Scripture be derived from heaven. If, therefore, the several tyrannies upon earth can prove any title to a Divine authority, it must be derived from this original grant to the prince of darkness; and these subordinate deputations must consequently come immediately from him whose stamp they so expressly bear.

To conclude, as the examples of all ages shew us that mankind in general desire power only to do harm, and, when they obtain it, use it for no other purpose; it is not consonant with even the least degree of prudence to hazard an alteration, where our hopes are poorly kept in countenance by only two or three exceptions out of a thousand instances to alarm our fears. In this case it will be much wiser to submit to a few inconveniencies arising from the dispassionate deafness of laws, than to remedy them by applying to the passionate open ears of a tyrant.

Nor can the example of the gypsies, though possibly they may have long been happy under this form of government, be here urged; since we must remember the very material respect in which they differ from all other people, and to which perhaps this their happiness is entirely owing, namely, that they have no false honours among them, and that they look on shame as the most grievous punishment in the world.

Chapter xiii.

A dialogue between Jones and Partridge.

THE honest lovers of liberty will, we doubt not, pardon that long digression into which we were led at the close of the last chapter, to prevent our history from being applied to the use of the most pernicious doctrine which priestcraft had ever the wickedness or the impudence to preach.

We will now proceed with Mr Jones, who, when the storm was over, took leave of his Egyptian majesty, after many thanks for his courteous behaviour and kind entertainment, and set out for Coventry; to which place (for it was still dark) a gypsy was ordered to conduct him.

Jones having, by reason of his deviation, travelled eleven miles instead of six, and most of those through very execrable roads, where no expedition could have been made in quest of a midwife, did not arrive at Coventry till near twelve. Nor could he possibly get again into the saddle till past two; for post-horses were now not easy to get; nor were the hostler or post-boy in half so great a hurry as himself, but chose rather to imitate the tranquil disposition of Partridge; who, being denied the nourishment of sleep, took all opportunities to supply its place with every other kind of nourishment, and was never better pleased than when he arrived at an inn, nor ever more dissatisfied than when he was again forced to leave it.

Jones now travelled post; we will follow him, therefore, according to our custom, and to the rules of Longinus, in the same manner. From Coventry he arrived at Daventry, from Daventry at Stratford, and from Stratford at Dunstable, whither he came the next day a little after noon, and within a few hours after Sophia had left it; and though he was obliged to stay here longer than he wished, while a smith, with great deliberation, shoed the post-horse he was to ride, he doubted not but to overtake his Sophia before she should set out from St Albans; at which place he concluded, and very reasonably, that his lordship would stop and dine.

And had he been right in this conjecture, he most probably would have overtaken his angel at the aforesaid place; but unluckily my lord had appointed a dinner to be prepared for him at his own house in London, and, in order to enable him to reach that place in proper time, he had ordered a relay of horses to meet him at St Albans. When Jones therefore arrived there, he was informed that the coach-and-six had set out two hours before.

If fresh post-horses had been now ready, as they were not, it seemed so apparently impossible to overtake the coach before it reached London, that Partridge thought he had now a proper opportunity to remind his friend of a matter which he seemed entirely to have forgotten; what this was the reader will guess, when we inform him that Jones had eat nothing more than one poached egg since he had left the alehouse where he had first met the guide returning from Sophia; for with the gypsies he had feasted only his understanding.

The landlord so entirely agreed with the opinion of Mr Partridge, that he no sooner heard the latter desire his friend to stay and dine, than he very readily put in his word, and retracting his promise before given of furnishing the horses immediately, he assured Mr Jones he would lose no time in bespeaking a dinner, which, he said, could be got ready sooner than it was possible to get the horses up from grass, and to prepare them for their journey by a feed of corn.

Jones was at length prevailed on, chiefly by the latter argument of the landlord; and now a joint of mutton was put down to the fire. While this was preparing, Partridge, being admitted into the same apartment with his friend or master, began to harangue in the following manner.

"Certainly, sir, if ever man deserved a young lady, you deserve young Madam Western; for what a vast quantity of love must a man have, to be able to live upon it without any other food, as you do? I am positive I have eat thirty times as much within these last twenty-four hours as your honour, and yet I am almost famished; for nothing makes a man so hungry as travelling, especially in this cold raw weather. And yet I can't tell how it is, but your honour is seemingly in perfect good health, and you never looked better nor fresher in your life. It must be certainly love that you live upon."

"And a very rich diet too, Partridge," answered Jones. "But did not fortune send me an excellent dainty yesterday? Dost thou imagine I cannot live more than twenty-four hours on this dear pocket-book?"

"Undoubtedly," cries Partridge, "there is enough in that pocket-book to purchase many a good meal.

Fortune sent it to your honour very opportunely for present use, as your honour's money must be almost out by this time."

"What do you mean?" answered Jones; "I hope you don't imagine that I should be dishonest enough, even if it belonged to any other person, besides Miss Western——"

"Dishonest!" replied Partridge, "heaven forbid I should wrong your honour so much! but where's the dishonesty in borrowing a little for present spending, since you will be so well able to pay the lady hereafter? No, indeed, I would have your honour pay it again, as soon as it is convenient, by all means; but where can be the harm in making use of it now you want it? Indeed, if it belonged to a poor body, it would be another thing; but so great a lady, to be sure, can never want it, especially now as she is along with a lord, who, it can't be doubted, will let her have whatever she hath need of. Besides, if she should want a little, she can't want the whole, therefore I would give her a little; but I would be hanged before I mentioned the having found it at first, and before I got some money of my own; for London, I have heard, is the very worst of places to be in without money. Indeed, if I had not known to whom it belonged, I might have thought it was the devil's money, and have been afraid to use it; but as you know otherwise, and came honestly by it, it would be an affront to fortune to part with it all again, at the very time when you want it most; you can hardly expect she should ever do you such another good turn; for *fortuna nunquam perpetuo est bona.* You will do as you please, notwithstanding all I say; but for my part, I would be hanged before I mentioned a word of the matter."

"By what I can see, Partridge," cries Jones, "hanging is a matter *non longe alienum à Scævolæ studiis.*"

"You should say *alienus*," says Partridge.—"I remember the passage; it is an example under *communis, alienus, immunis, variis casibus serviunt.*" "If you do remember it," cries Jones, "I find you don't understand it; but I tell thee, friend, in plain English, that he who finds another's property, and wilfully detains it from the known owner, deserves, *in foro conscientiæ,* to be hanged, no less than if he had stolen it. And as for this very identical bill, which is the property of my angel, and was once in her dear possession, I will not deliver it into any hands but her own, upon any consideration whatever, no, though I was as hungry as thou art, and had no other means to satisfy my craving appetite; this I hope to do before I sleep; but if it should happen otherwise, I charge thee, if thou would'st not incur my displeasure for ever, not to shock me any more by the bare mention of such detestable baseness."

"I should not have mentioned it now," cries Partridge, "if it had appeared so to me; for I'm sure I scorn any wickedness as much as another; but perhaps you know better; and yet I might have imagined that I should not have lived so many years, and have taught school so long, without being able to distinguish between *fas et nefas ;* but it seems we are all to live and learn. I remember my old schoolmaster, who was a prodigious great scholar, used often to say, *Polly matete cry town is my daskalon.* The English of which, he told us, was, That a child may sometimes teach his grandmother to suck eggs. I have lived to a fine purpose, truly, if I am to be taught my grammar at this time of day. Perhaps, young gentleman, you may change your opinion, if you live to my years: for I remember I thought myself as wise when I was a stripling of one or two and twenty as I am now. I am sure I always taught *alienus,* and my master read it so before me."

There were not many instances in which Partridge could provoke Jones, nor were there many in which Partridge himself could have been hurried out of his respect. Unluckily, however, they had both hit on one of these. We have already seen Partridge could not bear to have his learning attacked, nor could Jones bear some passage or other in the foregoing speech. And now, looking upon his companion with a contemptuous and disdainful air (a thing not usual with him), he cried, "Partridge, I see thou art a conceited old fool, and I wish thou art not likewise an old rogue. Indeed, if I was as well convinced of the latter as I am of the former, thou should'st travel no farther in my company."

The sage pedagogue was contented with the vent which he had already given to his indignation; and, as the vulgar phrase is, immediately drew in his horns. He said, he was sorry he had uttered anything which might give offence, for that he had never intended it; but *Nemo omnibus horis sapit.*

As Jones had the vices of a warm disposition, he was entirely free from those of a cold one; and if his friends must have confest his temper to have been a little too easily ruffled, his enemies must at the same time have confest, that it as soon subsided; nor did it at all resemble the sea, whose swelling is more violent and dangerous after a storm is over than while the storm itself subsists. He instantly accepted the submission of Partridge, shook him by the hand, and with the most benign aspect imaginable, said twenty kind things, and at the same time very severely condemned himself, though not half so severely as he will most probably be condemned by many of our good readers.

Partridge was now highly comforted, as his fears of having offended were at once abolished, and his pride completely satisfied by Jones having owned himself in the wrong, which submission he instantly applied to what had principally nettled him, and repeated in a muttering voice, "To be sure, sir, your knowledge may be superior to mine in some things; but as to the grammar, I think I may challenge any man living. I think, at least, I have that at my finger's end."

If anything could add to the satisfaction which the poor man now enjoyed, he received this addition by the arrival of an excellent shoulder of mutton, that at this instant came smoking to the table. On which, having both plentifully feasted, they again mounted their horses, and set forward for London.

Chapter xiv.

What happened to Mr Jones in his journey from St Albans.

THEY were got about two miles beyond Barnet, and it was now the dusk of the evening, when a genteel-looking man, but upon a very shabby horse, rode up to Jones, and asked him whether he was going to London; to which Jones answered in the affirmative. The gentleman replied, "I should be obliged to you, sir, if you will accept of my company; for it is very late, and I am a stranger to the road." Jones readily complied with the request; and on they travelled together, holding that sort of discourse which is usual on such occasions.

Of this, indeed, robbery was the principal topic: upon which subject the stranger expressed great apprehensions; but Jones declared he had very little to lose, and consequently as little to fear. Here Partridge could not forbear putting in his word. "Your honour," said he, "may think it a little, but I am sure, if I had a hundred-pound bank-note in my pocket, as you have, I should be very sorry to lose it; but, for my part, I never was less afraid in my life; for we are four of us, and if we all stand by one another, the best man in England can't rob us.   Suppose he should have a pistol, he can kill but one of us, and a man can die but once.—That's my comfort, a man can die but once."

Besides the reliance on superior numbers, a kind of valour which hath raised a certain nation among the moderns to a high pitch of glory, there was another reason for the extraordinary courage which Partridge now discovered; for he had at present as much of that quality as was in the power of liquor to bestow.

Our company were now arrived within a mile of Highgate, when the stranger turned short upon Jones, and pulling out a pistol, demanded that little bank-note which Partridge had mentioned.

Jones was at first somewhat shocked at this unexpected demand; however, he presently recollected himself, and told the highwayman, all the money he had in his pocket was entirely at his service; and so saying, he pulled out upwards of three guineas, and offered to deliver it; but the other answered with an oath, That would not do.   Jones answered coolly, he was very sorry for it, and returned the money into his pocket.

The highwayman then threatened, if he did not deliver the bank-note that moment, he must shoot him; holding his pistol at the same time very near to his breast.   Jones instantly caught hold of the fellow's hand, which trembled so that he could scarce hold the pistol in it, and turned the muzzle from him.   A struggle then ensued, in which the former wrested the pistol from the hand of his antagonist, and both came from their horses on the ground together, the highwayman upon his back, and the victorious Jones upon him.

The poor fellow now began to implore mercy of the conqueror : for, to say the truth, he was in strength by no means a match for Jones. "Indeed, sir," says he, "I could have had no intention to shoot you; for you will find the pistol was not loaded. This is the first robbery I ever attempted, and I have been driven by distress to this."

At this instant, at about a hundred and fifty yards' distance, lay another person on the ground, roaring for mercy in a much louder voice than the highwayman. This was no other than Partridge himself, who, endeavouring to make his escape from the engagement, had been thrown from his horse, and lay flat on his face, not daring to look up, and expecting every minute to be shot.

In this posture he lay, till the guide, who was no otherwise concerned than for his horses, having secured the stumbling beast, came up to him, and told him his master had got the better of the highwayman.

Partridge leapt up at this news, and ran back to the place where Jones stood with his sword drawn in his hand to guard the poor fellow; which Partridge no sooner saw than he cried out, "Kill the villain, sir, run him through the body, kill him this instant!"

Luckily, however, for the poor wretch, he had fallen into more merciful hands; for Jones having examined the pistol, and found it to be really unloaded, began to believe all the man had told him, before Partridge came up : namely, that he was a novice in the trade, and that he had been driven to it by the distress he mentioned, the greatest indeed imaginable, that of five hungry children, and a wife lying in of the sixth, in the utmost want and misery. The truth of all which the highwayman most vehemently asserted, and offered to convince Mr Jones of it, if he would take the trouble to go to his house, which was not above two miles off; saying,

"That he desired no favour, but upon condition of proving all he had alledged."

Jones at first pretended that he would take the fellow at his word, and go with him, declaring that his fate should depend entirely on the truth of his story. Upon this the poor fellow immediately expressed so much alacrity, that Jones was perfectly satisfied with his veracity, and began now to entertain sentiments of compassion for him. He returned the fellow his empty pistol, advised him to think of honester means of relieving his distress, and gave him a couple of guineas for the immediate support of his wife and his family; adding, "he wished he had more for his sake, for the hundred pound that had been mentioned was not his own."

Our readers will probably be divided in their opinions concerning this action; some may applaud it perhaps as an act of extraordinary humanity, while those of a more saturnine temper will consider it as a want of regard to that justice which every man owes his country. Partridge certainly saw it in that light; for he testified much dissatisfaction on the occasion, quoted an old proverb, and said, he should not wonder if the rogue attacked them again before they reached London.

The highwayman was full of expressions of thankfulness and gratitude. He actually dropt tears, or pretended so to do. He vowed he would immediately return home, and would never afterwards commit such a transgression: whether he kept his word or no, perhaps may appear hereafter.

Our travellers having remounted their horses, arrived in town without encountering any new mishap. On the road much pleasant discourse passed between Jones and Partridge, on the subject of their last adventure: in which Jones exprest a great compassion for those highwaymen who are, by unavoidable distress, driven, as it were, to such illegal courses, as generally bring them to a shameful death : "I mean," said he, "those only whose highest guilt extends no farther than to robbery, and who are never guilty of cruelty nor insult to any person, which is a circumstance that, I must say, to the honour of our country, distinguishes the robbers of England from those of all other nations; for murder is, amongst those, almost inseparably incident to robbery."

"No doubt," answered Partridge, "it is better to take away one's money than one's life; and yet it is very hard upon honest men, that they can't travel about their business without being in danger of these villains. And to be sure it would be better that all rogues were hanged out of the way, than that one honest man should suffer. For my own part, indeed, I should not care to have the blood of any of them on my own hands; but it is very proper for the law to hang them all. What right hath any man to take sixpence from me, unless I give it him? Is there any honesty in such a man?"

"No, surely," cries Jones, "no more than there is in him who takes the horses out of another man's stable, or who applies to his own use the money which he finds, when he knows the right owner."

These hints stopt the mouth of Partridge; nor did he open it again till Jones, having thrown some sarcastical jokes on his cowardice, he offered to excuse himself on the inequality of fire-arms, saying, "A thousand naked men are nothing to one pistol; for though it is true it will kill but one at a single discharge, yet who can tell but that one may be himself?"

BOOK XIII.

CONTAINING THE SPACE OF TWELVE DAYS.

Chapter i.

An Invocation.

COME, bright love of fame, inspire my glowing breast: not thee I call, who, over swelling tides of blood and tears, dost bear the heroe on to glory, while sighs of millions waft his spreading sails; but thee, fair, gentle maid, whom Mnesis, happy nymph, first on the banks of Hebrus did produce. Thee, whom Mæonia educated, whom Mantua charmed, and who, on that fair hill which overlooks the proud metropolis of Britain, sat'st, with thy Milton, sweetly tuning the heroic lyre; fill my ravished fancy with the hopes of charming ages yet to come. Foretel me that some tender maid, whose grandmother is yet unborn, hereafter, when, under the fictitious name of Sophia, she reads the real worth which once existed in my Charlotte, shall from her sympathetic breast send forth the heaving sigh. Do thou teach me not only to foresee, but to enjoy, nay, even to feed on future praise. Comfort me by a solemn assurance, that when the little parlour in which I sit at this instant shall be reduced to a worse furnished box, I shall be read with honour by those who never knew nor saw me, and whom I shall neither know nor see.

And thou, much plumper dame, whom no airy forms nor phantoms of imagination cloathe; whom the well-seasoned beef, and pudding richly stained with plumes, delight: thee I call: of whom in a treck-schuyte, in some Dutch canal, the fat ufrow gelt, impregnated by a jolly merchant of Amsterdam, was delivered: in Grub-street school didst thou suck in the elements of thy erudition. Here hast thou, in thy maturer age, taught poetry to tickle not the fancy, but the pride of the patron. Comedy from thee learns a grave and solemn air; while tragedy storms aloud, and rends th' affrighted theatres with its thunders. To soothe thy wearied limbs in slumber, Alderman History tells his tedious tale; and, again, to awaken thee, Monsieur Romance performs his surprizing tricks of dexterity. Nor less thy well-fed bookseller obeys thy influence. By thy advice the heavy, unread, folio lump, which long had dozed on the dusty shelf, piece-mealed into numbers, runs nimbly through the nation. Instructed by thee, some books, like quacks, impose on the world by promising wonders; while others turn beaus, and trust all their merits to a gilded out-side. Come, thou jolly substance, with thy shining face, keep back thy inspiration, but hold forth thy tempting rewards; thy shining, chinking heap; thy quickly convertible bank-bill, big with unseen riches; thy often-varying stock; the warm, the comfortable house; and, lastly, a fair portion of that bounteous mother, whose flowing breasts yield redundant sus-tenance for all her numerous offspring, did not some too greedily and wantonly drive their brethren from the teat. Come thou, and if I am too tasteless of thy valuable treasures, warm my heart with the transporting thought of conveying them to others. Tell me, that through thy bounty, the pratling babes, whose innocent play hath often been interrupted by my labours, may one time be amply rewarded for them.

And now, this ill-yoked pair, this lean shadow and this fat substance, have prompted me to write, whose assistance shall I invoke to direct my pen?

First, Genius; thou gift of Heaven; without whose aid in vain we struggle against the stream of nature. Thou who dost sow the generous seeds which art nourishes, and brings to perfection. Do thou kindly take me by the hand, and lead me through all the mazes, the winding labyrinths of nature. Initiate me into all those mysteries which profane eyes never beheld. Teach me, which to thee is no difficult task, to know mankind better than they know themselves. Remove that mist which dims the intellects of mortals, and causes them to adore men for their art, or to detest them for their cunning, in deceiving others, when they are, in reality, the objects only of ridicule, for deceiving themselves. Strip off the thin disguise of wisdom from self-conceit, of plenty from avarice, and of glory from ambition. Come, thou that hast inspired thy Aristophanes, thy Lucian, thy Cervantes, thy Rabelais, thy Molière, thy Shakespear, thy Swift, thy Marivaux, fill my pages with humour; till mankind learn the good-nature to laugh only at the follies of others, and the humility to grieve at their own.

And thou, almost the constant attendant on true genius, Humanity, bring all thy tender sensations. If thou hast already disposed of them all between thy Allen and thy Lyttleton, steal them a little while from their bosoms. Not without these the tender scene is painted. From these alone proceed the noble, dis-interested friendship, the melting love, the generous sentiment, the ardent gratitude, the soft compassion, the candid opinion; and all those strong energies of a good mind, which fill the moistened eyes with tears, the glowing cheeks with blood, and swell the heart with tides of grief, joy, and benevolence.

And thou, O Learning! (for without thy assistance nothing pure, nothing correct, can genius produce) do thou guide my pen. Thee in thy favourite fields, where the limpid, gently-rolling Thames washes thy Etonian banks, in early youth I have worshipped. To thee, at thy birchen altar, with true Spartan devotion, I have sacrificed my blood. Come then, and from thy vast, luxuriant stores, in long antiquity piled up, pour forth the rich profusion. Open thy Mæonian and thy Mantuan coffers, with whatever else includes thy philosophic, thy poetic, and thy historical treasures, whether with Greek or Roman characters thou hast chosen to inscribe the ponderous chests: give me a while that key to all thy treasures, which to thy Warburton thou hast entrusted.

Lastly, come Experience, long conversant with the wise, the good, the learned, and the polite. Nor with them only, but with every kind of character, from the minister at his levee, to the bailiff in his spunging-house; from the dutchess at her drum, to the landlady behind her bar. From thee only can the manners of mankind be known; to which the recluse pedant, however great his parts or extensive his learning may be, hath ever been a stranger.

Come all these, and more, if possible; for arduous is the task I have undertaken; and, without all your assistance, will, I find, be too heavy for me to support. But if you all smile on my labours I hope still to bring them to a happy conclusion.

Chapter ij.

What befel Mr Jones on his arrival in London.

THE learned Dr Misaubin used to say, that the
proper direction to him was *To Dr* Misaubin,
in the World ; intimating that there were few
people in it to whom his great reputation was not known.
And, perhaps, upon a very nice examination into the
matter, we shall find that this circumstance bears no
inconsiderable part among the many blessings of
grandeur.

The great happiness of being known to posterity,
with the hopes of which we so delighted ourselves in
the preceding chapter, is the portion of few. To have
the several elements which compose our names, as
Sydenham expresses it, repeated a thousand years
hence, is a gift beyond the power of title and wealth ;
and is scarce to be purchased, unless by the sword and
the pen. But to avoid the scandalous imputation,
while we yet live, of being *one whom nobody knows*
(a scandal, by the bye, as old as the days of Homer*),
will always be the envied portion of those, who have a
legal title either to honour or estate.

From that figure, therefore, which the Irish peer,
who brought Sophia to town, hath already made in
this history, the reader will conclude, doubtless, it
must have been an easy matter to have discovered his
house in London without knowing the particular street
or square which he inhabited, since he must have been
one *whom everybody knows.* To say the truth, so it
would have been to any of those tradesmen who are
accustomed to attend the regions of the great ; for the
doors of the great are generally no less easy to find
than it is difficult to get entrance into them. But

* See the 2d Odyssey, ver. 175.

Jones, as well as Partridge, was an entire stranger in London; and as he happened to arrive first in a quarter of the town, the inhabitants of which have very little intercourse with the householders of Hanover or Grosvenor-square (for he entered through Gray's-inn-lane), so he rambled about some time before he could even find his way to those happy mansions where fortune segregates from the vulgar those magnanimous heroes, the descendants of antient Britons, Saxons, or Danes, whose ancestors, being born in better days, by sundry kinds of merit, have entailed riches and honour on their posterity.

Jones, being at length arrived at those terrestrial Elysian fields, would now soon have discovered his lordship's mansion; but the peer, unluckily quitted his former house when he went for Ireland; and as he was just entered into a new one, the fame of his equipage had not yet sufficiently blazed in the neighbourhood; so that, after a successless enquiry till the clock had struck eleven, Jones at last yielded to the advice of Partridge, and retreated to the Bull and Gate in Holborn, that being the inn where he had first alighted, and where he retired to enjoy that kind of repose which usually attends persons in his circumstances.

Early in the morning he again set forth in pursuit of Sophia; and many a weary step he took to no better purpose than before. At last, whether it was that Fortune relented, or whether it was no longer in her power to disappoint him, he came into the very street which was honoured by his lordship's residence; and, being directed to the house, he gave one gentle rap at the door.

The porter, who, from the modesty of the knock, had conceived no high idea of the person approaching, conceived but little better from the appearance of Mr

Jones, who was drest in a suit of fustian, and had by his side the weapon formerly purchased of the serjeant; of which, though the blade might be composed of well-tempered steel, the handle was composed only of brass, and that none of the brightest. When Jones, therefore, enquired after the young lady who had come to town with his lordship, this fellow answered surlily, "That there were no ladies there." Jones then desired to see the master of the house; but was informed that his lordship would see nobody that morning. And upon growing more pressing the porter said, " he had positive orders to let no person in; but if you think proper," said he, "to leave your name, I will acquaint his lordship; and if you call another time you shall know when he will see you."

Jones now declared, "that he had very particular business with the young lady, and could not depart without seeing her." Upon which the porter, with no very agreeable voice or aspect, affirmed, "that there was no young lady in that house, and consequently none could he see;" adding, "sure you are the strangest man I ever met with, for you will not take an answer."

I have often thought that, by the particular description of Cerberus, the porter of hell, in the 6th Æneid, Virgil might possibly intend to satirize the porters of the great men in his time; the picture, at least, resembles those who have the honour to attend at the doors of our great men. The porter in his lodge answers exactly to Cerberus in his den, and, like him, must be appeased by a sop before access can be gained to his master. Perhaps Jones might have seen him in that light, and have recollected the passage where the Sibyl, in order to procure an entrance for Æneas, presents the keeper of the Stygian avenue with such a sop. Jones, in like manner, now began to offer a bribe to the human

Cerberus, which a footman, overhearing, instantly advanced, and declared, "if Mr Jones would give him the sum proposed, he would conduct him to the lady." Jones instantly agreed, and was forthwith conducted to the lodging of Mrs Fitzpatrick by the very fellow who had attended the ladies thither the day before.

Nothing more aggravates ill success than the near approach to good. The gamester, who loses his party at piquet by a single point, laments his bad luck ten times as much as he who never came within a prospect of the game. So in a lottery, the proprietors of the next numbers to that which wins the great prize are apt to account themselves much more unfortunate than their fellow-sufferers. In short, these kind of hairbreadth missings of happiness look like the insults of Fortune, who may be considered as thus playing tricks with us, and wantonly diverting herself at our expense.

Jones, who more than once already had experienced this frolicsome disposition of the heathen goddess, was now again doomed to be tantalized in the like manner; for he arrived at the door of Mrs Fitzpatrick about ten minutes after the departure of Sophia. He now addressed himself to the waiting-woman belonging to Mrs Fitzpatrick; who told him the disagreeable news that the lady was gone, but could not tell him whither; and the same answer he afterwards received from Mrs Fitzpatrick herself. For as that lady made no doubt but that Mr Jones was a person detached from her uncle Western, in pursuit of his daughter, so she was too generous to betray her.

Though Jones had never seen Mrs Fitzpatrick, yet he had heard that a cousin of Sophia was married to a gentleman of that name. This, however, in the present tumult of his mind, never once recurred to his memory; but when the footman, who had conducted him from his lordship's, acquainted him with the great intimacy between the ladies, and with their calling each other cousin, he then recollected the story of the marriage which he had formerly heard; and as he was presently convinced that this was the same woman, he became more surprized at the answer which he had received, and very earnestly desired leave to wait on the lady herself; but she as positively refused him that honour.

Jones, who, though he had never seen a court, was better bred than most who frequent it, was incapable of any rude or abrupt behaviour to a lady. When he had received, therefore, a peremptory denial, he retired for the present, saying to the waiting-woman, "That if this was an improper hour to wait on her lady, he would return in the afternoon; and that he then hoped to have the honour of seeing her." The civility with which he uttered this, added to the great comeliness of his person, made an impression on the waiting-woman, and she could not help answering; "Perhaps, sir, you may;" and, indeed, she afterwards said everything to her mistress, which she thought most likely to prevail on her to admit a visit from the handsome young gentleman; for so she called him.

Jones very shrewdly suspected that Sophia herself was now with her cousin, and was denied to him; which he imputed to her resentment of what had happened at Upton. Having, therefore, dispatched Partridge to procure him lodgings, he remained all day in the street, watching the door where he thought his angel lay concealed; but no person did he see issue forth, except a servant of the house, and in the evening he returned to pay his visit to Mrs Fitzpatrick, which that good lady at last condescended to admit.

There is a certain air of natural gentility, which it is neither in the power of dress to give, nor to conceal. Mr Jones, as hath been before hinted, was possessed of this in a very eminent degree. He met, therefore, with a reception from the lady somewhat different from what his apparel seemed to demand; and after he had paid her his proper respects, was desired to sit down.

The reader will not, I believe, be desirous of knowing all the particulars of this conversation, which ended very little to the satisfaction of poor Jones. For though Mrs Fitzpatrick soon discovered the lover (as all women have the eyes of hawks in those matters), yet she still thought it was such a lover, as a generous friend of the lady should not betray her to. In short, she suspected this was the very Mr Blifil, from whom Sophia had flown; and all the answers which she artfully drew from Jones, concerning Mr Allworthy's family, confirmed her in this opinion. She therefore strictly denied any knowledge concerning the place whither Sophia was gone; nor could Jones obtain more than a permission to wait on her again the next evening.

When Jones was departed Mrs Fitzpatrick communicated her suspicion concerning Mr Blifil to her maid; who answered, "Sure, madam, he is too pretty a man, in my opinion, for any woman in the world to run away from. I had rather fancy it is Mr Jones." —"Mr Jones!" said the lady, "what Jones?" For Sophia had not given the least hint of any such person in all their conversation; but Mrs Honour had been much more communicative, and had acquainted her sister Abigail with the whole history of Jones, which this now again related to her mistress.

Mrs Fitzpatrick no sooner received this information, than she immediately agreed with the opinion of her maid; and, what is very unaccountable, saw charms in the gallant, happy lover, which she had overlooked in the slighted squire. "Betty," says she, "you are certainly in the right: he is a very pretty fellow, and

I don't wonder that my cousin's maid should tell you so many women are fond of him. I am sorry now I did not inform him where my cousin was; and yet, if he be so terrible a rake as you tell me, it is a pity she should ever see him any more; for what but her ruin can happen from marrying a rake and a beggar against her father's consent? I protest, if he be such a man as the wench described him to you, it is but an office of charity to keep her from him; and I am sure it would be unpardonable in me to do otherwise, who have tasted so bitterly of the misfortunes attending such marriages."

Here she was interrupted by the arrival of a visitor, which was no other than his lordship; and as nothing passed at this visit either new or extraordinary, or any ways material to this history, we shall here put an end to this chapter.

Chapter iii.

A project of Mrs Fitzpatrick, and her visit to Lady Bellaston.

WHEN Mrs Fitzpatrick retired to rest, her thoughts were entirely taken up by her cousin Sophia and Mr Jones. She was, indeed, a little offended with the former, for the disingenuity which she now discovered. In which meditation she had not long exercised her imagination before the following conceit suggested itself; that could she possibly become the means of preserving Sophia from this man, and of restoring her to her father, she should, in all human probability, by so great a service to the family, reconcile to herself both her uncle and her aunt Western.

As this was one of her most favourite wishes, so the hope of success seemed so reasonable, that nothing remained but to consider of proper methods to accomplish her scheme. To attempt to reason the case with Sophia did not appear to her one of those methods: for as Betty had reported from Mrs Honour, that Sophia had a violent inclination to Jones, she conceived that to dissuade her from the match was an endeavour of the same kind, as it would be very heartily and earnestly to entreat a moth not to fly into a candle.

If the reader will please to remember that the acquaintance which Sophia had with Lady Bellaston was contracted at the house of Mrs Western, and must have grown at the very time when Mrs Fitzpatrick lived with this latter lady, he will want no information, that Mrs Fitzpatrick must have been acquainted with her likewise.   They were, besides, both equally her distant relations.

After much consideration, therefore, she resolved to go early in the morning to that lady, and endeavour to see her, unknown to Sophia, and to acquaint her with the whole affair.   For she did not in the least doubt, but that the prudent lady, who had often ridiculed romantic love, and indiscreet marriages, in her conversation, would very readily concur in her sentiments concerning this match, and would lend her utmost assistance to prevent it.

This resolution she accordingly executed; and the next morning before the sun, she huddled on her cloaths, and at a very unfashionable, unseasonable, unvisitable hour, went to Lady Bellaston, to whom she got access, without the least knowledge or suspicion of Sophia, who, though not asleep, lay at that time awake in her bed, with Honour snoring by her side.

Mrs Fitzpatrick made many apologies for an early, abrupt visit, at an hour when, she said, "she should not have thought of disturbing her ladyship, but upon business of the utmost consequence." She then opened the whole affair, told all she had heard from Betty; and did not forget the visit which Jones had paid to herself the preceding evening.

Lady Bellaston answered with a smile, "Then you have seen this terrible man, madam; pray, is he so very fine a figure as he is represented? for Etoff entertained me last night almost two hours with him. The wench I believe is in love with him by reputation." Here the reader will be apt to wonder; but the truth is, that Mrs Etoff, who had the honour to pin and unpin the Lady Bellaston, had received compleat information concerning the said Mr Jones, and had faithfully conveyed the same to her lady last night (or rather that morning) while she was undressing; on which accounts she had been detained in her office above the space of an hour and a half.

The lady indeed, though generally well enough pleased with the narratives of Mrs Etoff at those seasons, gave an extraordinary attention to her account of Jones; for Honour had described him as a very handsome fellow, and Mrs Etoff, in her hurry, added so much to the beauty of his person to her report, that Lady Bellaston began to conceive him to be a kind of miracle in nature.

The curiosity which her woman had inspired was now greatly increased by Mrs Fitzpatrick, who spoke as much in favour of the person of Jones as she had before spoken in dispraise of his birth, character, and fortune.

When Lady Bellaston had heard the whole, she answered gravely, "Indeed, madam, this is a matter of great consequence. Nothing can certainly be more commendable than the part you act; and I shall be very glad to have my share in the preservation of a young lady of so much merit, and for whom I have so much esteem."

"Doth not your ladyship think," says Mrs Fitzpatrick eagerly, "that it would be the best way to write immediately to my uncle, and acquaint him where my cousin is?"

The lady pondered a little upon this, and thus answered—"Why, no, madam, I think not. Di Western hath described her brother to me to be such a brute, that I cannot consent to put any woman under his power who hath escaped from it. I have heard he behaved like a monster to his own wife, for he is one of those wretches who think they have a right to tyrannise over us, and from such I shall ever esteem it the cause of my sex to rescue any woman who is so unfortunate to be under their power.—The business, dear cousin, will be only to keep Miss Western from seeing this young fellow, till the good company, which she will have an opportunity of meeting here, give her a properer turn."

"If he should find her out, madam," answered the other, "your ladyship may be assured he will leave nothing unattempted to come at her."

"But, madam," replied the lady, "it is impossible he should come here—though indeed it is possible he may get some intelligence where she is, and then may lurk about the house—I wish therefore I knew his person.

"Is there no way, madam, by which I could have a sight of him? for, otherwise, you know, cousin, she may contrive to see him here without my knowledge." Mrs Fitzpatrick answered, "That he had threatened her with another visit that afternoon, and that, if her ladyship pleased to do her the honour of calling upon her then, she would hardly fail of seeing him between six and seven : and if he came earlier she would, by some means or other, detain him till her ladyship's arrival."—Lady Bellaston replied, " She would come the moment she could get from dinner, which she supposed would be by seven at farthest; for that it was absolutely necessary she should be acquainted with his person.   Upon my word, madam," says she, " it was very good to take this care of Miss Western; but common humanity, as well as regard to our family, requires it of us both; for it would be a dreadful match indeed."

Mrs Fitzpatrick failed not to make a proper return to the compliment which Lady Bellaston had bestowed on her cousin, and, after some little immaterial conversation, withdrew; and, getting as fast as she could into her chair, unseen by Sophia or Honour, returned home.

Chapter iv.

Which consists of visiting.

MR Jones had walked within sight of a certain door during the whole day, which, though one of the shortest, appeared to him to be one of the longest in the whole year.   At length, the clock having struck five, he returned to Mrs Fitzpatrick, who, though it was a full hour earlier than the decent time of visiting, received him very civilly; but still persisted in her ignorance concerning Sophia.

Jones, in asking for his angel, had dropped the word cousin, upon which Mrs Fitzpatrick said, " Then, sir, you know we are related : and, as we are, you will permit me the right of enquiring into the particulars of your business with my cousin."   Here Jones hesitated a good while, and at last answered, " He had a considerable sum of money of hers in his hands, which he desired to deliver to her." He then produced the pocket-book, and acquainted Mrs Fitzpatrick with the contents, and with the method in which they came into his hands. He had scarce finished his story, when a most violent noise shook the whole house. To attempt to describe this noise to those who have heard it would be in vain; and to aim at giving any idea of it to those who have never heard the like, would be still more vain: for it may be truly said—

———————*Non acuta*
Sic geminant Corybantes æra.

The priests of Cybele do not so rattle their sounding brass.

In short, a footman knocked, or rather thundered, at the door. Jones was a little surprized at the sound, having never heard it before; but Mrs Fitzpatrick very calmly said, that, as some company were coming, she could not make him any answer now; but if he pleased to stay till they were gone, she intimated she had something to say to him.

The door of the room now flew open, and, after pushing in her hoop sideways before her, entered Lady Bellaston, who having first made a very low courtesy to Mrs Fitzpatrick, and as low a one to Mr Jones, was ushered to the upper end of the room.

We mention these minute matters for the sake of some country ladies of our acquaintance, who think it contrary to the rules of modesty to bend their knees to a man.

The company were hardly well settled, before the arrival of the peer lately mentioned, caused a fresh disturbance, and a repetition of ceremonials.

These being over, the conversation began to be (as the phrase is) extremely brilliant. However, as nothing past in it which can be thought material to this history, or, indeed, very material in itself, I shall omit the relation; the rather, as I have known some very fine polite conversation grow extremely dull, when transcribed into books, or repeated on the stage. Indeed, this mental repast is a dainty, of which those who are excluded from polite assemblies must be contented to remain as ignorant as they must of the several dainties of French cookery, which are served only at the tables of the great. To say the truth, as neither of these are adapted to every taste, they might both be often thrown away on the vulgar.

Poor Jones was rather a spectator of this elegant scene, than an actor in it; for though, in the short interval before the peer's arrival, Lady Bellaston first, and afterwards Mrs Fitzpatrick, had addressed some of their discourse to him; yet no sooner was the noble lord entered, than he engrossed the whole attention of the two ladies to himself; and as he took no more notice of Jones than if no such person had been present, unless by now and then staring at him, the ladies followed his example.

The company had now staid so long, that Mrs Fitzpatrick plainly perceived they all designed to stay out each other. She therefore resolved to rid herself of Jones, he being the visitant to whom she thought the least ceremony was due. Taking therefore an opportunity of a cessation of chat, she addressed herself gravely to him, and said, " Sir, I shall not possibly be able to give you an answer to-night as to that business; but if you please to leave word where I may send to you to-morrow——"

Jones had natural, but not artificial good-breeding. Instead therefore of communicating the secret of his lodgings to a servant, he acquainted the lady herself with it particularly, and soon after very ceremoniously withdrew.

He was no sooner gone than the great personages, who had taken no notice of him present, began to take much notice of him in his absence; but if the reader hath already excused us from relating the more brilliant part of this conversation, he will surely be very ready to excuse the repetition of what may be called vulgar abuse; though, perhaps, it may be material to our history to mention an observation of Lady Bellaston, who took her leave in a few minutes after him, and then said to Mrs Fitzpatrick, at her departure, "I am satisfied on the account of my cousin; she can be in no danger from this fellow."

Our history shall follow the example of Lady Bellaston, and take leave of the present company, which was now reduced to two persons; between whom, as nothing passed, which in the least concerns us or our reader, we shall not suffer ourselves to be diverted by it from matters which must seem of more consequence to all those who are at all interested in the affairs of our heroe.

Chapter v.

An adventure which happened to Mr Jones at his lodgings, with some account of a young gentleman who lodged there, and of the mistress of the house, and her two daughters.

THE next morning, as early as it was decent, Jones attended at Mrs Fitzpatrick's door, where he was answered that the lady was not at home; an answer which surprized him the more, as he had walked backwards and forwards in the street from break of day; and if she had gone out, he must have seen her. This answer, however, he was obliged to receive, and not only now, but to five several visits which he made her that day.

To be plain with the reader, the noble peer had from some reason or other, perhaps from a regard for the lady's honour, insisted that she should not see Mr Jones, whom he looked on as a scrub, any more; and the lady had complied in making that promise to which we now see her so strictly adhere.

But as our gentle reader may possibly have a better opinion of the young gentleman than her ladyship, and may even have some concern, should it be apprehended that, during this unhappy separation from Sophia, he took up his residence either at an inn, or in the street; we shall now give an account of his lodging, which was indeed in a very reputable house, and in a very good part of the town.

Mr Jones, then, had often heard Mr Allworthy mention the gentlewoman at whose house he used to lodge when he was in town. This person, who, as Jones likewise knew, lived in Bond-street, was the widow of a clergyman, and was left by him, at his decease, in possession of two daughters, and of a compleat set of manuscript sermons.

Of these two daughters, Nancy, the elder, was now arrived at the age of seventeen, and Betty, the younger, at that of ten.

Hither Jones had despatched Partridge, and in this house he was provided with a room for himself in the second floor, and with one for Partridge in the fourth.

The first floor was inhabited by one of those young gentlemen, who, in the last age, were called men of wit and pleasure about town, and properly enough; for as men are usually denominated from their business or profession, so pleasure may be said to have been the only business or profession of those gentlemen to

whom fortune had made all useful occupations un-
necessary. Playhouses, coffeehouses, and taverns were
the scenes of their rendezvous. Wit and humour were
the entertainment of their looser hours, and love was
the business of their more serious moments. Wine and
the muses conspired to kindle the brightest flames in
their breasts; nor did they only admire, but some
were able to celebrate the beauty they admired, and
all to judge of the merit of such compositions.

Such, therefore, were properly called the men of
wit and pleasure; but I question whether the same
appellation may, with the same propriety, be given to
those young gentlemen of our times, who have the
same ambition to be distinguished for parts. Wit
certainly they have nothing to do with. To give
them their due, they soar a step higher than their
predecessors, and may be called men of wisdom and
vertù (take heed you do not read virtue). Thus at an
age when the gentlemen above mentioned employ their
time in toasting the charms of a woman, or in making
sonnets in her praise; in giving their opinion of a play
at the theatre, or of a poem at Will's or Button's;
these gentlemen are considering the methods to bribe a
corporation, or meditating speeches for the House of
Commons, or rather for the magazines. But the
science of gaming is that which above all others
employs their thoughts. These are the studies of
their graver hours, while for their amusements they
have the vast circle of connoisseurship, painting, music,
statuary, and natural philosophy, or rather *unnatural*,
which deals in the wonderful, and knows nothing of
Nature, except her monsters and imperfections.

When Jones had spent the whole day in vain en-
quiries after Mrs Fitzpatrick, he returned at last disconsolate to his apartment. Here, while he was
venting his grief in private, he heard a violent uproar

below-stairs; and soon after a female voice begged him
for heaven's sake to come and prevent murder. Jones,
who was never backward on any occasion to help the
distressed, immediately ran down-stairs; when stepping
into the dining-room, whence all the noise issued, he
beheld the young gentleman of wisdom and vertù just
before mentioned, pinned close to the wall by his
footman, and a young woman standing by, wringing
her hands, and crying out, "He will be murdered!
he will be murdered!" and, indeed, the poor gentleman seemed in some danger of being choaked, when
Jones flew hastily to his assistance, and rescued him,
just as he was breathing his last, from the unmerciful
clutches of the enemy.

Though the fellow had received several kicks and
cuffs from the little gentleman, who had more spirit
than strength, he had made it a kind of scruple of
conscience to strike his master, and would have contented himself with only choaking him; but towards
Jones he bore no such respect: he no sooner therefore
found himself a little roughly handled by his new
antagonist, than he gave him one of those punches in
the guts which, though the spectators at Broughton's
amphitheatre have such exquisite delight in seeing
them, convey but very little pleasure in the feeling.

The lusty youth had no sooner received this blow,
than he meditated a most grateful return; and now
ensued a combat between Jones and the footman,
which was very fierce, but short; for this fellow was
no more able to contend with Jones than his master
had before been to contend with him.

And now, Fortune, according to her usual custom,
reversed the face of affairs. The former victor lay
breathless on the ground, and the vanquished gentleman had recovered breath enough to thank Mr
Jones for his seasonable assistance; he received like-

wise the hearty thanks of the young woman present, who was indeed no other than Miss Nancy, the eldest daughter of the house.

The footman, having now recovered his legs, shook his head at Jones, and, with a sagacious look, cried— "O d—n me, I'll have nothing more to do with you; you have been upon the stage, or I'm d—nably mistaken." And indeed we may forgive this his suspicion; for such was the agility and strength of our heroe, that he was, perhaps, a match for one of the first-rate boxers, and could, with great ease, have beaten all the muffled * graduates of Mr Broughton's school.

The master, foaming with wrath, ordered his man immediately to strip, to which the latter very readily agreed, on condition of receiving his wages. This condition was presently complied with, and the fellow was discharged.

And now the young gentleman, whose name was Nightingale, very strenuously insisted that his deliverer should take part of a bottle of wine with him; to which Jones, after much entreaty, consented, though more out of complacence than inclination; for the uneasiness of his mind fitted him very little for conversation at this time. Miss Nancy likewise, who was

---

* Lest posterity should be puzzled by this epithet, I think proper to explain it by an advertisement which was published Feb. 1, 1747.

N.B.—Mr Broughton proposes, with proper assistance, to open an academy at his house in the Haymarket, for the instruction of those who are willing to be initiated in the mystery of boxing: where the whole theory and practice of that truly British art, with all the various stops, blows, cross-buttocks, &c., incident to combatants, will be fully taught and explained; and that persons of quality and distinction may not be deterred from entering into *A course of those lectures*, they will be given with the utmost tenderness and regard to the delicacy of the frame and constitution of the pupil, for which reason muffles are provided, that will effectually secure them from the inconveniency of black eyes, broken jaws, and bloody noses.

the only female then in the house, her mamma and sister being both gone to the play, condescended to favour them with her company.

When the bottle and glasses were on the table the gentleman began to relate the occasion of the preceding disturbance.

" I hope, sir," said he to Jones, " you will not from this accident conclude, that I make a custom of striking my servants, for I assure you this is the first time I have been guilty of it in my remembrance, and I have passed by many provoking faults in this very fellow, before he could provoke me to it; but when you hear what hath happened this evening, you will, I believe, think me excusable. I happened to come home several hours before my usual time, when I found four gentlemen of the cloth at whist by my fire ;—and my Hoyle, sir—my best Hoyle, which cost me a guinea, lying open on the table, with a quantity of porter spilt on one of the most material leaves of the whole book. This, you will allow, was provoking; but I said nothing till the rest of the honest company were gone, and then gave the fellow a gentle rebuke, who, instead of expressing any concern, made me a pert answer, " That servants must have their diversions as well as other people ; that he was sorry for the accident which had happened to the book, but that several of his acquaintance had bought the same for a shilling, and that I might stop as much in his wages, if I pleased." I now gave him a severer reprimand than before, when the rascal had the insolence to——In short, he imputed my early coming home to——In short, he cast a reflection——He mentioned the name of a young lady, in a manner—in such a manner that incensed me beyond all patience, and, in my passion, I struck him.

Jones answered, " That he believed no person living

would blame him; for my part," said he, "I confess I should, on the last-mentioned provocation, have done the same thing."

Our company had not sat long before they were joined by the mother and daughter, at their return from the play. And now they all spent a very chearful evening together; for all but Jones were heartily merry, and even he put on as much constrained mirth as possible. Indeed, half his natural flow of animal spirits, joined to the sweetness of his temper, was sufficient to make a most amiable companion; and notwithstanding the heaviness of his heart, so agreeable did he make himself on the present occasion, that, at their breaking up, the young gentleman earnestly desired his further acquaintance. Miss Nancy was well pleased with him; and the widow, quite charmed with her new lodger, invited him, with the other, next morning to breakfast.

Jones on his part was no less satisfied. As for Miss Nancy, though a very little creature, she was extremely pretty, and the widow had all the charms which can adorn a woman near fifty. As she was one of the most innocent creatures in the world, so she was one of the most chearful. She never thought, nor spoke, nor wished any ill, and had constantly that desire of pleasing, which may be called the happiest of all desires in this, that it scarce ever fails of attaining its ends, when not disgraced by affectation. In short, though her power was very small, she was in her heart one of the warmest friends. She had been a most affectionate wife, and was a most fond and tender mother. As our history doth not, like a newspaper, give great characters to people who never were heard of before, nor will ever be heard of again, the reader may hence conclude, that this excellent woman will hereafter appear to be of some importance in our history.

Nor was Jones a little pleased with the young gentleman himself, whose wine he had been drinking. He thought he discerned in him much good sense, though a little too much tainted with town-foppery; but what recommended him most to Jones were some sentiments of great generosity and humanity, which occasionally dropt from him; and particularly many expressions of the highest disinterestedness in the affair of love. On which subject the young gentleman delivered himself in a language which might have very well become an Arcadian shepherd of old, and which appeared very extraordinary when proceeding from the lips of a modern fine gentleman; but he was only one by imitation, and meant by nature for a much better character.

Chapter vi.

What arrived while the company were at breakfast, with some hints concerning the government of daughters.

OUR company brought together in the morning the same good inclinations towards each other, with which they had separated the evening before; but poor Jones was extremely disconsolate; for he had just received information from Partridge, that Mrs Fitzpatrick had left her lodging, and that he could not learn whither she was gone. This news highly afflicted him, and his countenance, as well as his behaviour, in defiance of all his endeavours to the contrary, betrayed manifest indications of a disordered mind.

The discourse turned at present, as before, on love; and Mr Nightingale again expressed many of those warm, generous, and disinterested sentiments upon this subject, which wise and sober men call romantic, but which wise and sober women generally regard in a better light. Mrs Miller (for so the mistress of the house was called) greatly approved these sentiments; but when the young gentleman appealed to Miss Nancy, she answered only, "That she believed the gentleman who had spoke the least was capable of feeling most."

This compliment was so apparently directed to Jones, that we should have been sorry had he passed it by unregarded. He made her indeed a very polite answer, and concluded with an oblique hint, that her own silence subjected her to a suspicion of the same kind: for indeed she had scarce opened her lips either now or the last evening.

"I am glad, Nanny," says Mrs Miller, "the gentleman hath made the observation; I protest I am almost of his opinion. What can be the matter with you, child? I never saw such an alteration. What is become of all your gaiety? Would you think, sir, I used to call her my little prattler? She hath not spoke twenty words this week."

Here their conversation was interrupted by the entrance of a maid-servant, who brought a bundle in her hand, which, she said, "was delivered by a porter for Mr Jones." She added, "That the man immediately went away, saying, it required no answer."

Jones expressed some surprize on this occasion, and declared it must be some mistake; but the maid persisting that she was certain of the name, all the women were desirous of having the bundle immediately opened; which operation was at length performed by little Betsy, with the consent of Mr Jones: and the contents were found to be a domino, a mask, and a masquerade ticket.

Jones was now more positive than ever in asserting, that these things must have been delivered by mistake; and Mrs Miller herself expressed some doubt, and said,

"She knew not what to think." But when Mr Nightingale was asked, he delivered a very different opinion. "All I can conclude from it, sir," said he, "is, that you are a very happy man; for I make no doubt but these were sent you by some lady whom you will have the happiness of meeting at the masquerade."

Jones had not a sufficient degree of vanity to entertain any such flattering imagination; nor did Mrs Miller herself give much assent to what Mr Nightingale had said, till Miss Nancy having lifted up the domino, a card dropt from the sleeve, in which was written as follows :—

To Mr Jones.

The queen of the fairies sends you this;
Use her favours not amiss.

Mrs Miller and Miss Nancy now both agreed with Mr Nightingale; nay, Jones himself was almost persuaded to be of the same opinion. And as no other lady but Mrs Fitzpatrick, he thought, knew his lodging, he began to flatter himself with some hopes, that it came from her, and that he might possibly see his Sophia. These hopes had surely very little foundation; but as the conduct of Mrs Fitzpatrick, in not seeing him according to her promise, and in quitting her lodgings, had been very odd and unaccountable, he conceived some faint hopes, that she (of whom he had formerly heard a very whimsical character) might possibly intend to do him that service in a strange manner, which she declined doing by more ordinary methods. To say the truth, as nothing certain could be concluded from so odd and uncommon an incident, he had the greater latitude to draw what imaginary conclusions from it he pleased. As his temper therefore was naturally sanguine, he indulged it on this occasion, and his imagination worked up a thousand

To confess the truth, Mr Jones was now in a situation, which sometimes happens to be the case of young gentlemen of much better figure than himself. In short, he had not one penny in his pocket; a situation in much greater credit among the antient philosophers than among the modern wise men who live in Lombard-street, or those who frequent White's chocolate-house. And, perhaps, the great honours which those philosophers have ascribed to an empty pocket may be one of the reasons of that high contempt in which they are held in the aforesaid street and chocolate-house.

Now if the antient opinion, that men might live very comfortably on virtue only, be, as the modern wise men just above-mentioned pretend to have discovered, a notorious error; no less false is, I apprehend, that position of some writers of romance, that a man can live altogether on love: for however delicious repasts this may afford to some of our senses or appetites, it is most certain it can afford none to others. Those, therefore, who have placed too great a confidence in such writers, have experienced their error when it was too late; and have found that love was no more capable of allaying hunger, than a rose is capable of delighting the ear, or a violin of gratifying the smell.

Notwithstanding, therefore, all the delicacies which love had set before him, namely, the hopes of seeing Sophia at the masquerade; on which, however ill-founded his imagination might be, he had voluptuously feasted during the whole day, the evening no sooner came than Mr Jones began to languish for some food of a grosser kind. Partridge discovered this by intuition, and took the occasion to give some oblique hints concerning the bank-bill; and, when these were rejected with disdain, he collected courage enough once more to mention a return to Mr Allworthy.

"Partridge," cries Jones, "you cannot see my fortune in a more desperate light than I see it myself; and I begin heartily to repent that I suffered you to leave a place where you was settled, and to follow me. However, I insist now on your returning home; and for the expense and trouble which you have so kindly put yourself to on my account, all the cloaths I left behind in your care I desire you would take as your own. I am sorry I can make you no other acknowledgment."

He spoke these words with so pathetic an accent, that Partridge, among whose vices ill-nature or hardness of heart were not numbered, burst into tears; and after swearing he would not quit him in his distress, he began with the most earnest entreaties to urge his return home. "For heaven's sake, sir," says he, "do but consider; what can your honour do?—how is it possible you can live in this town without money? Do what you will, sir, or go wherever you please, I am resolved not to desert you. But pray, sir, consider— do pray, sir, for your own sake, take it into your consideration; and I'm sure," says he, "that your own good sense will bid you return home."

"How often shall I tell thee," answered Jones, "that I have no home to return to? Had I any hopes that Mr Allworthy's doors would be open to receive me, I want no distress to urge me—nay, there is no other cause upon earth, which could detain me a moment from flying to his presence; but, alas! that I am for ever banished from. His last words were—O, Partridge, they still ring in my ears—his last words were, when he gave me a sum of money—what it was I know not, but considerable I'm sure it was—his last words were—'I am resolved from this day forward, on no account to converse with you any more.'"

Here passion stopt the mouth of Jones, as surprize for a moment did that of Partridge; but he soon recovered the use of speech, and after a short preface, in which he declared he had no inquisitiveness in his temper, enquired what Jones meant by a considerable sum—he knew not how much—and what was become of the money.

In both these points he now received full satisfaction; on which he was proceeding to comment, when he was interrupted by a message from Mr Nightingale, who desired his master's company in his apartment.

When the two gentlemen were both attired for the masquerade, and Mr Nightingale had given orders for chairs to be sent for, a circumstance of distress occurred to Jones, which will appear very ridiculous to many of my readers. This was how to procure a shilling; but if such readers will reflect a little on what they have themselves felt from the want of a thousand pounds, or, perhaps, of ten or twenty, to execute a favourite scheme, they will have a perfect idea of what Mr Jones felt on this occasion. For this sum, therefore, he applied to Partridge, which was the first he had permitted him to advance, and was the last he intended that poor fellow should advance in his service. To say the truth, Partridge had lately made no offer of this kind. Whether it was that he desired to see the bank-bill broke in upon, or that distress should prevail on Jones to return home, or from what other motive it proceeded, I will not determine.

<hr />

Chapter vij.

Containing the whole humours of a masquerade.

OUR cavaliers now arrived at that temple, where Heydegger, the great Arbiter Deliciarum, the great high-priest of pleasure, presides; and, like other heathen priests, imposes on his votaries by the pretended presence of the deity, when in reality no such deity is there.

Mr Nightingale, having taken a turn or two with his companion, soon left him, and walked off with a female, saying, "Now you are here, sir, you must beat about for your own game."

Jones began to entertain strong hopes that his Sophia was present; and these hopes gave him more spirits than the lights, the music, and the company; though these are pretty strong antidotes against the spleen. He now accosted every woman he saw, whose stature, shape, or air, bore any resemblance to his angel. To all of whom he endeavoured to say something smart, in order to engage an answer, by which he might discover that voice which he thought it impossible he should mistake. Some of these answered by a question, in a squeaking voice, Do you know me? Much the greater number said, I don't know you, sir, and nothing more. Some called him an impertinent fellow; some made him no answer at all; some said, Indeed I don't know your voice, and I shall have nothing to say to you; and many gave him as kind answers as he could wish, but not in the voice he desired to hear.

Whilst he was talking with one of these last (who was in the habit of a shepherdess) a lady in a domino came up to him, and slapping him on the shoulder, whispered him, at the same time, in the ear, "If you talk any longer with that trollop, I will acquaint Miss Western."

Jones no sooner heard that name, than, immediately quitting his former companion, he applied to the domino, begging and entreating her to show him the lady she had mentioned, if she was then in the room.

The mask walked hastily to the upper end of the innermost apartment before she spoke; and then, instead of answering him, sat down, and declared she was tired.

Jones sat down by her, and still persisted in his entreaties : at last the lady coldly answered, " I imagined Mr Jones had been a more discerning lover, than to suffer any disguise to conceal his mistress from him." " Is she here, then, madam?" replied Jones, with some vehemence. Upon which the lady cried—"Hush, sir, you will be observed. I promise you, upon my honour, Miss Western is not here."

Jones, now taking the mask by the hand, fell to entreating her in the most earnest manner, to acquaint him where he might find Sophia : and when he could obtain no direct answer, he began to upbraid her gently for having disappointed him the day before ; and concluded, saying, " Indeed, my good fairy queen, I know your majesty very well, notwithstanding the affected disguise of your voice. Indeed, Mrs Fitzpatrick, it is a little cruel to divert yourself at the expense of my torments."

The mask answered, " Though you have so ingeniously discovered me, I must still speak in the same voice, lest I should be known by others. And do you think, good sir, that I have no greater regard for my cousin, than to assist in carrying on an affair between you two, which must end in her ruin, as well as your own? Besides, I promise you, my cousin is not mad enough to consent to her own destruction, if you are so much her enemy as to tempt her to it."

" Alas, madam!" said Jones, " you little know my heart, when you call me an enemy of Sophia."

" And yet to ruin any one," cries the other, " you will allow, is the act of an enemy ; and when by the same act you must knowingly and certainly bring ruin on yourself, is it not folly or madness, as well as guilt? Now, sir, my cousin hath very little more than her father will please to give her ; very little for one of her fashion —you know him, and you know your own situation."

Jones vowed he had no such design on Sophia, "That he would rather suffer the most violent of deaths than sacrifice her interest to his desires." He said, "he knew how unworthy he was of her, every way, that he had long ago resolved to quit all such aspiring thoughts, but that some strange accidents had made him desirous to see her once more, when he promised he would take leave of her for ever. No, madam," concluded he, "my love is not of that base kind which seeks its own satisfaction at the expense of what is most dear to its object. I would sacrifice everything to the possession of my Sophia, but Sophia herself."

Though the reader may have already conceived no very sublime idea of the virtue of the lady in the mask; and though possibly she may hereafter appear not to deserve one of the first characters of her sex; yet, it is certain, these generous sentiments made a strong impression upon her, and greatly added to the affection she had before conceived for our young heroe.

The lady now, after silence of a few moments, said, "She did not see his pretensions to Sophia so much in the light of presumption, as of imprudence. Young fellows," says she, "can never have too aspiring thoughts. I love ambition in a young man, and I would have you cultivate it as much as possible. Perhaps you may succeed with those who are infinitely superior in fortune; nay, I am convinced there are women——but don't you think me a strange creature, Mr Jones, to be thus giving advice to a man with whom I am so little acquainted, and one with whose behaviour to me I have so little reason to be pleased?"

Here Jones began to apologize, and to hope he had not offended in anything he had said of her cousin.— To which the mask answered, "And are you so little

versed in the sex, to imagine you can well affront a
lady more than by entertaining her with your passion
for another woman? If the fairy queen had conceived
no better opinion of your gallantry, she would scarce
have appointed you to meet her at the masquerade."

Jones had never less inclination to an amour than
at present; but gallantry to the ladies was among his
principles of honour; and he held it as much incumbent
on him to accept a challenge to love, as if it had been
a challenge to fight. Nay, his very love to Sophia
made it necessary for him to keep well with the lady,
as he made no doubt but she was capable of bringing
him into the presence of the other.

He began therefore to make a very warm answer to
her last speech, when a mask, in the character of an
old woman, joined them. This mask was one of those
ladies who go to a masquerade only to vent ill-nature,
by telling people rude truths, and by endeavouring, as
the phrase is, to spoil as much sport as they are able.
This good lady, therefore, having observed Jones, and
his friend, whom she well knew, in close consultation
together in a corner of the room, concluded she could
nowhere satisfy her spleen better than by interrupting
them. She attacked them, therefore, and soon drove
them from their retirement; nor was she contented with
this, but pursued them to every place which they shifted
to avoid her; till Mr Nightingale, seeing the distress
of his friend, at last relieved him, and engaged the old
woman in another pursuit.

While Jones and his mask were walking together
about the room, to rid themselves of the teazer, he observed his lady speak to several masks, with the same
freedom of acquaintance as if they had been barefaced.
He could not help expressing his surprize at this; saying, " Sure, madam, you must have infinite discernment,
to know people in all disguises." To which the lady

answered, " You cannot conceive anything more insipid and childish than a masquerade to the people of fashion, who in general know one another as well here as when they meet in an assembly or a drawing-room ; nor will any woman of condition converse with a person with whom she is not acquainted. In short, the generality of persons whom you see here may more properly be said to kill time in this place than in any other ; and generally retire from hence more tired than from the longest sermon. To say the truth, I begin to be in that situation myself; and if I have any faculty at guessing, you are not much better pleased. I protest it would be almost charity in me to go home for your sake." " I know but one charity equal to it," cries Jones, " and that is to suffer me to wait on you home." " Sure," answered the lady, " you have a strange opinion of me, to imagine, that upon such an acquaintance, I would let you into my doors at this time of night. I fancy you impute the friendship I have shown my cousin to some other motive. Confess honestly ; don't you consider this contrived interview as little better than a downright assignation ? Are you used, Mr Jones, to make these sudden conquests ? " " I am not used, madam," said Jones, " to submit to such sudden conquests ; but as you have taken my heart by surprize, the rest of my body hath a right to follow ; so you must pardon me if I resolve to attend you wherever you go." He accompanied these words with some proper actions ; upon which the lady, after a gentle rebuke, and saying their familiarity would be observed, told him, " She was going to sup with an acquaintance, whither she hoped he would not follow her ; for if you should," said she, " I shall be thought an unaccountable creature, though my friend indeed is not censorious : yet I hope you won't follow me ; I protest I shall not know what to say if you do."

The lady presently after quitted the masquerade, and Jones, notwithstanding the severe prohibition he had received, presumed to attend her. He was now reduced to the same dilemma we have mentioned before, namely, the want of a shilling, and could not relieve it by borrowing as before. He therefore walked boldly on after the chair in which his lady rode, pursued by a grand huzza, from all the chairmen present, who wisely take the best care they can to discountenance all walking afoot by their betters. Luckily, however, the gentry who attend at the Opera-house were too busy to quit their stations, and as the lateness of the hour prevented him from meeting many of their brethren in the street, he proceeded without molestation, in a dress, which, at another season, would have certainly raised a mob at his heels.

The lady was set down in a street not far from Hanover-square, where the door being presently opened, she was carried in, and the gentleman, without any ceremony, walked in after her.

Jones and his companion were now together in a very well-furnished and well-warmed room ; when the female, still speaking in her masquerade voice, said she was surprized at her friend, who must absolutely have forgot her appointment ; at which, after venting much resentment, she suddenly exprest some apprehension from Jones, and asked him what the world would think of their having been alone together in a house at that time of night ? But instead of a direct answer to so important a question, Jones began to be very importunate with the lady to unmask ; and at length having prevailed, there appeared not Mrs Fitzpatrick, but the Lady Bellaston herself.

It would be tedious to give the particular conversation, which consisted of very common and ordinary occurrences, and which lasted from two till six o'clock in the morning. It is sufficient to mention all of it that is anywise material to this history. And this was a promise that the lady would endeavour to find out Sophia, and in a few days bring him to an interview with her, on condition that he would then take his leave of her. When this was thoroughly settled, and a second meeting in the evening appointed at the same place, they separated; the lady returned to her house, and Jones to his lodgings.

Chapter viij.

Containing a scene of distress, which will appear very extraordinary to most of our readers.

JONES having refreshed himself with a few hours' sleep, summoned Partridge to his presence; and delivering him a bank-note of fifty pounds, ordered him to go and change it. Partridge received this with sparkling eyes, though, when he came to reflect farther, it raised in him some suspicions not very advantageous to the honour of his master: to these the dreadful idea he had of the masquerade, the disguise in which his master had gone out and returned, and his having been abroad all night, contributed. In plain language, the only way he could possibly find to account for the possession of this note, was by robbery: and, to confess the truth, the reader, unless he should suspect it was owing to the generosity of Lady Bellaston, can hardly imagine any other.

To clear, therefore, the honour of Mr Jones, and to do justice to the liberality of the lady, he had really received this present from her, who, though she did not give much into the hackney charities of the age, such as building hospitals, &c., was not, however,

entirely void of that Christian virtue; and conceived
(very rightly I think) that a young fellow of merit,
without a shilling in the world, was no improper object
of this virtue.

Mr Jones and Mr Nightingale had been invited to
dine this day with Mrs Miller.   At the appointed
hour, therefore, the two young gentlemen, with the
two girls, attended in the parlour, where they waited
from three till almost five before the good woman
appeared.   She had been out of town to visit a relation, of whom, at her return, she gave the following
account.

" I hope, gentlemen, you will pardon my making
you wait; I am sure if you knew the occasion—I have
been to see a cousin of mine, about six miles off, who
now lies in.—It should be a warning to all persons
(says she, looking at her daughters) how they marry
indiscreetly.   There is no happiness in this world
without a competency.   O Nancy! how shall I describe the wretched condition in which I found your
poor cousin? she hath scarce lain in a week, and there
was she, this dreadful weather, in a cold room, without any curtains to her bed, and not a bushel of coals
in her house to supply her with fire: her second son,
that sweet little fellow, lies ill of a quinzy in the same
bed with his mother; for there is no other bed in the
house.   Poor little Tommy! I believe, Nancy, you
will never see your favourite any more; for he is really
very ill.   The rest of the children are in pretty good
health: but Molly, I am afraid, will do herself an
injury: she is but thirteen years old, Mr Nightingale,
and yet, in my life, I never saw a better nurse: she
tends both her mother and her brother; and, what is
wonderful in a creature so young, she shows all the
chearfulness in the world to her mother; and yet I
saw her—I saw the poor child, Mr Nightingale, turn

about, and privately wipe the tears from her eyes."
Here Mrs Miller was prevented, by her own tears,
from going on, and there was not, I believe, a person
present who did not accompany her in them ; at length
she a little recovered herself, and proceeded thus : "In
all this distress the mother supports her spirits in a
surprizing manner. The danger of her son sits heaviest
upon her, and yet she endeavours as much as possible
to conceal even this concern, on her husband's account.
Her grief, however, sometimes gets the better of all
her endeavours ; for she was always extravagantly fond
of this boy, and a most sensible, sweet-tempered creature it is. I protest I was never more affected in my
life than when I heard the little wretch, who is hardly
yet seven years old, while his mother was wetting him
with her tears, beg her to be comforted. 'Indeed,
mamma,' cried the child, 'I shan't die ; God Al-
mighty, I'm sure, won't take Tommy away ; let
heaven be ever so fine a place, I had rather stay here
and starve with you and my papa than go to it.'
Pardon me, gentlemen, I can't help it" (says she,
wiping her eyes), "such sensibility and affection in a
child.——And yet, perhaps, he is least the object of
pity ; for a day or two will, most probably, place him
beyond the reach of all human evils. The father is,
indeed, most worthy of compassion. Poor man, his
countenance is the very picture of horror, and he looks
like one rather dead than alive. Oh heavens ! what a
scene did I behold at my first coming into the room !
The good creature was lying behind the bolster, supporting at once both his child and his wife. He had
nothing on but a thin waistcoat ; for his coat was
spread over the bed, to supply the want of blankets.——
When he rose up at my entrance, I scarce knew him.
As comely a man, Mr Jones, within this fortnight, as
you ever beheld ; Mr Nightingale hath seen him.

His eyes sunk, his face pale, with a long beard. His body shivering with cold, and worn with hunger too; for my cousin says she can hardly prevail upon him to eat.—He told me himself in a whisper—he told me— I can't repeat it—he said he could not bear to eat the bread his children wanted. And yet, can you believe it, gentlemen? in all this misery his wife has as good caudle as if she lay in the midst of the greatest affluence; I tasted it, and I scarce ever tasted better.—The means of procuring her this, he said, he believed was sent him by an angel from heaven. I know not what he meant; for I had not spirits enough to ask a single question.

"This was a love-match, as they call it, on both sides; that is, a match between two beggars. I must, indeed, say, I never saw a fonder couple; but what is their fondness good for, but to torment each other?" "Indeed, mamma," cries Nancy, "I have always looked on my cousin Anderson" (for that was her name) "as one of the happiest of women." "I am sure," says Mrs Miller, "the case at present is much otherwise; for any one might have discerned that the tender consideration of each other's sufferings makes the most intolerable part of their calamity, both to the husband and wife. Compared to which, hunger and cold, as they affect their own persons only, are scarce evils. Nay, the very children, the youngest, which is not two years old, excepted, feel in the same manner; for they are a most loving family, and, if they had but a bare competency, would be the happiest people in the world." "I never saw the least sign of misery at her house," replied Nancy; "I am sure my heart bleeds for what you now tell me."—"O child," answered the mother, "she hath always endeavoured to make the best of everything. They have always been in great distress; but, indeed, this absolute ruin hath been brought upon them by others. The poor man was bail for the villain his brother; and about a week ago, the very day before her lying-in, their goods were all carried away, and sold by an execution. He sent a letter to me of it by one of the bailiffs, which the villain never delivered.——What must he think of my suffering a week to pass before he heard of me?"

It was not with dry eyes that Jones heard this narrative; when it was ended he took Mrs Miller apart with him into another room, and, delivering her his purse, in which was the sum of £50, desired her to send as much of it as she thought proper to these poor people. The look which Mrs Miller gave Jones, on this occasion, is not easy to be described. She burst into a kind of agony of transport, and cryed out ——" Good heavens! is there such a man in the world?" ——But recollecting herself, she said, " Indeed I know one such; but can there be another?" " I hope, madam," cries Jones, "there are many who have common humanity; for to relieve such distresses in our fellow-creatures, can hardly be called more." Mrs Miller then took ten guineas, which were the utmost he could prevail with her to accept, and said, " She would find some means of conveying them early the next morning;" adding, "that she had herself done some little matter for the poor people, and had not left them in quite so much misery as she found them."

They then returned to the parlour, where Nightingale expressed much concern at the dreadful situation of these wretches, whom indeed he knew; for he had seen them more than once at Mrs Miller's. He inveighed against the folly of making oneself liable for the debts of others; vented many bitter execrations against the brother; and concluded with wishing something could be done for the unfortunate family

"Suppose, madam," said he, "you should recommend them to Mr Allworthy? Or what think you of a collection? I will give them a guinea with all my heart."

Mrs Miller made no answer; and Nancy, to whom her mother had whispered the generosity of Jones, turned pale upon the occasion; though, if either of them was angry with Nightingale, it was surely without reason. For the liberality of Jones, if he had known it, was not an example which he had any obligation to follow; and there are thousands who would not have contributed a single halfpenny, as indeed he did not in effect, for he made no tender of anything; and therefore, as the others thought proper to make no demand, he kept his money in his pocket.

I have, in truth, observed, and shall never have a better opportunity than at present to communicate my observation, that the world are in general divided into two opinions concerning charity, which are the very reverse of each other. One party seems to hold, that all acts of this kind are to be esteemed as voluntary gifts, and, however little you give (if indeed no more than your good wishes), you acquire a great degree of merit in so doing. Others, on the contrary, appear to be as firmly persuaded, that beneficence is a positive duty, and that whenever the rich fall greatly short of their ability in relieving the distresses of the poor, their pitiful largesses are so far from being meritorious, that they have only performed their duty by halves, and are in some sense more contemptible than those who have entirely neglected it.

To reconcile these different opinions is not in my power. I shall only add, that the givers are generally of the former sentiment, and the receivers are almost universally inclined to the latter.

Chapter ix.

*Which treats of matters of a very different kind from those
in the preceding chapter.*

IN the evening Jones met his lady again, and a long
conversation again ensued between them : but as it
consisted only of the same ordinary occurrences as
before, we shall avoid mentioning particulars, which we
despair of rendering agreeable to the reader ; unless he
is one whose devotion to the fair sex, like that of the
papists to their saints, wants to be raised by the help
of pictures. But I am so far from desiring to exhibit
such pictures to the public, that I would wish to draw
a curtain over those that have been lately set forth in
certain French novels ; very bungling copies of which
have been presented us here under the name of trans-
lations.

Jones grew still more and more impatient to see
Sophia ; and finding, after repeated interviews with
Lady Bellaston, no likelihood of obtaining this by her
means (for, on the contrary, the lady began to treat
even the mention of the name of Sophia with resentment), he resolved to try some other method. He
made no doubt but that Lady Bellaston knew where
his angel was, so he thought it most likely that some
of her servants should be acquainted with the same
secret. Partridge therefore was employed to get acquainted with those servants, in order to fish this secret
out of them.

Few situations can be imagined more uneasy than that
to which his poor master was at present reduced ; for
besides the difficulties he met with in discovering Sophia,
besides the fears he had of having disobliged her, and
the assurances he had received from Lady Bellaston of
the resolution which Sophia had taken against him, and

of her having purposely concealed herself from him, which he had sufficient reason to believe might be true ; he had still a difficulty to combat which it was not in the power of his mistress to remove, however kind her inclination might have been.   This was the exposing of her to be disinherited of all her father's estate, the almost inevitable consequence of their coming together without a consent, which he had no hopes of ever obtaining.

Add to all these the many obligations which Lady Bellaston, whose violent fondness we can no longer conceal, had heaped upon him ; so that by her means he was now become one of the best-dressed men about town ; and was not only relieved from those ridiculous distresses we have before mentioned, but was actually raised to a state of affluence beyond what he had ever known.

Now, though there are many gentlemen who very well reconcile it to their consciences to possess themselves of the whole fortune of a woman, without making her any kind of return ; yet to a mind, the proprietor of which doth not deserved to be hanged, nothing is, I believe, more irksome than to support love with gratitude only ; especially where inclination pulls the heart a contrary way.   Such was the unhappy case of Jones ; for though the virtuous love he bore to Sophia, and which left very little affection for any other woman, had been entirely out of the question, he could never have been able to have made any adequate return to the generous passion of this lady, who had indeed been once an object of desire, but was now entered at least into the autumn of life, though she wore all the gaiety of youth, both in her dress and manner ; nay, she contrived still to maintain the roses in her cheeks ; but these, like flowers forced out of season by art, had none of that lively blooming freshness with which Nature, at the proper time, bedecks her own productions. She had, besides, a certain imperfection, which renders some flowers, though very beautiful to the eye, very improper to be placed in a wilderness of sweets, and what above all others is most disagreeable to the breath of love.

Though Jones saw all these discouragements on the one side, he felt his obligations full as strongly on the other; nor did he less plainly discern the ardent passion whence those obligations proceeded, the extreme violence of which if he failed to equal, he well knew the lady would think him ungrateful; and, what is worse, he would have thought himself so. He knew the tacit consideration upon which all her favours were conferred; and as his necessity obliged him to accept them, so his honour, he concluded, forced him to pay the price. This therefore he resolved to do, whatever misery it cost him, and to devote himself to her, from that great principle of justice, by which the laws of some countries oblige a debtor, who is no otherwise capable of discharging his debt, to become the slave of his creditor.

While he was meditating on these matters, he received the following note from the lady :—

" A very foolish, but a very perverse accident hath happened since our last meeting, which makes it improper I should see you any more at the usual place. I will, if possible, contrive some other place by tomorrow. In the meantime, adieu."

This disappointment, perhaps, the reader may conclude was not very great; but if it was, he was quickly relieved; for in less than an hour afterwards another note was brought him from the same hand, which contained as follows :—

" I have altered my mind since I wrote; a change

which, if you are no stranger to the tenderest of all passions, you will not wonder at. I am now resolved to see you this evening at my own house, whatever may be the consequence. Come to me exactly at seven; I dine abroad, but will be at home by that time. A day, I find, to those that sincerely love, seems longer than I imagined.

"If you should accidentally be a few moments before me, bid them show you into the drawing-room."

To confess the truth, Jones was less pleased with this last epistle than he had been with the former, as he was prevented by it from complying with the earnest entreaties of Mr Nightingale, with whom he had now contracted much intimacy and friendship. These entreaties were to go with that young gentleman and his company to a new play, which was to be acted that evening, and which a very large party had agreed to damn, from some dislike they had taken to the author, who was a friend to one of Mr Nightingale's acquaintance. And this sort of fun, our heroe, we are ashamed to confess, would willingly have preferred to the above kind appointment; but his honour got the better of his inclination.

Before we attend him to this intended interview with the lady, we think proper to account for both the preceding notes, as the reader may possibly be not a little surprized at the imprudence of Lady Bellaston, in bringing her lover to the very house where her rival was lodged.

First, then, the mistress of the house where these lovers had hitherto met, and who had been for some years a pensioner to that lady, was now become a methodist, and had that very morning waited upon her ladyship, and after rebuking her very severely for her past life, had positively declared that she would, on no account, be instrumental in carrying on any of her affairs for the future.

The hurry of spirits into which this accident threw the lady made her despair of possibly finding any other convenience to meet Jones that evening; but as she began a little to recover from her uneasiness at the disappointment, she set her thoughts to work, when luckily it came into her head to propose to Sophia to go to the play, which was immediately consented to, and a proper lady provided for her companion. Mrs Honour was likewise despatched with Mrs Etoff on the same errand of pleasure; and thus her own house was left free for the safe reception of Mr Jones, with whom she promised herself two or three hours of uninterrupted conversation after her return from the place where she dined, which was at a friend's house in a pretty distant part of the town, near her old place of assignation, where she had engaged herself before she was well apprized of the revolution that had happened in the mind and morals of her late confidante.

Chapter x.

A chapter which, though short, may draw tears from some eyes.

MR JONES was just dressed to wait on Lady Bellaston, when Mrs Miller rapped at his door; and, being admitted, very earnestly desired his company below-stairs, to drink tea in the parlour.

Upon his entrance into the room, she presently introduced a person to him, saying, "This, sir, is my cousin, who hath been so greatly beholden to your goodness, for which he begs to return you his sincerest thanks."

The man had scarce entered upon that speech which Mrs Miller had so kindly prefaced, when both Jones and he, looking stedfastly at each other, showed at once the utmost tokens of surprize. The voice of the latter began instantly to faulter; and, instead of finishing his speech, he sunk down into a chair, crying, "It is so, I am convinced it is so!"

"Bless me! what's the meaning of this?" cries Mrs Miller; "you are not ill, I hope, cousin? Some water, a dram this instant."

"Be not frighted, madam," cries Jones, "I have almost as much need of a dram as your cousin. We are equally surprized at this unexpected meeting. Your cousin is an acquaintance of mine, Mrs Miller."

"An acquaintance!" cries the man.——"Oh, heaven!"

"Ay, an acquaintance," repeated Jones, "and an honoured acquaintance too. When I do not love and honour the man who dares venture everything to preserve his wife and children from instant destruction, may I have a friend capable of disowning me in adversity!"

"Oh, you are an excellent young man," cries Mrs Miller:——"Yes, indeed, poor creature! he hath ventured everything.——If he had not had one of the best of constitutions, it must have killed him."

"Cousin," cries the man, who had now pretty well recovered himself, "this is the angel from heaven whom I meant. This is he to whom, before I saw you, I owed the preservation of my Peggy. He it was to whose generosity every comfort, every support which I have procured for her, was owing. He is, indeed, the worthiest, bravest, noblest, of all human beings. O cousin, I have obligations to this gentleman of such a nature!"

"Mention nothing of obligations," cries Jones

eagerly; "not a word, I insist upon it, not a word" (meaning, I suppose, that he would not have him betray the affair of the robbery to any person). "If, by the trifle you have received from me, I have preserved a whole family, sure pleasure was never bought so cheap."

"Oh, sir!" cries the man, "I wish you could this instant see my house. If any person had ever a right to the pleasure you mention, I am convinced it is yourself. My cousin tells me she acquainted you with the distress in which she found us. That, sir, is all greatly removed, and chiefly by your goodness.——— My children have now a bed to lie on———and they have———they have———eternal blessings reward you for it!———they have bread to eat. My little boy is recovered; my wife is out of danger, and I am happy. All, all owing to you, sir, and to my cousin here, one of the best of women. Indeed, sir, I must see you at my house.—Indeed my wife must see you, and thank you.—My children too must express their gratitude.———Indeed, sir, they are not without a sense of their obligation; but what is my feeling when I reflect to whom I owe that they are now capable of expressing their gratitude.———Oh, sir, the little hearts which you have warmed had now been cold as ice without your assistance."

Here Jones attempted to prevent the poor man from proceeding; but indeed the overflowing of his own heart would of itself have stopped his words. And now Mrs Miller likewise began to pour forth thanksgivings, as well in her own name, as in that of her cousin, and concluded with saying, "She doubted not but such goodness would meet a glorious reward."

Jones answered, "He had been sufficiently rewarded already. Your cousin's account, madam," said he, "hath given me a sensation more pleasing than I have ever known. He must be a wretch who is unmoved at hearing such a story; how transporting then must be the thought of having happily acted a part in this scene! If there are men who cannot feel the delight of giving happiness to others, I sincerely pity them, as they are incapable of tasting what is, in my opinion, a greater honour, a higher interest, and a sweeter pleasure than the ambitious, the avaricious, or the voluptuous man can ever obtain."

The hour of appointment being now come, Jones was forced to take a hasty leave, but not before he had heartily shaken his friend by the hand, and desired to see him again as soon as possible; promising that he would himself take the first opportunity of visiting him at his own house. He then stept into his chair, and proceeded to Lady Bellaston's, greatly exulting in the happiness which he had procured to this poor family; nor could he forbear reflecting, without horror, on the dreadful consequences which must have attended them, had he listened rather to the voice of strict justice than to that of mercy, when he was attacked on the high road.

Mrs Miller sung forth the praises of Jones during the whole evening, in which Mr Anderson, while he stayed, so passionately accompanied her, that he was often on the very point of mentioning the circumstance of the robbery. However, he luckily recollected himself, and avoided an indiscretion which would have been so much the greater, as he knew Mrs Miller to be extremely strict and nice in her principles. He was likewise well apprized of the loquacity of this lady; and yet such was his gratitude, that it had almost got the better both of discretion and shame, and made him publish that which would have defamed his own character, rather than omit any circumstances which might do the fullest honour to his benefactor.

Chapter ꜰɪ.

In which the reader will be surprized.

MR JONES was rather earlier than the time appointed, and earlier than the lady; whose arrival was hindered, not only by the distance of the place where she dined, but by some other cross accidents very vexatious to one in her situation of mind. He was accordingly shown into the drawing-room, where he had not been many minutes before the door opened, and in came——no other than Sophia herself, who had left the play before the end of the first act; for this, as we have already said, being a new play, at which two large parties met, the one to damn, and the other to applaud, a violent uproar, and an engagement between the two parties, had so terrified our heroine, that she was glad to put herself under the protection of a young gentleman who safely conveyed her to her chair.

As Lady Bellaston had acquainted her that she should not be at home till late, Sophia, expecting to find no one in the room, came hastily in, and went directly to a glass which almost fronted her, without once looking towards the upper end of the room, where the statue of Jones now stood motionless.——In this glass it was, after contemplating her own lovely face, that she first discovered the said statue; when, instantly turning about, she perceived the reality of the vision: upon which she gave a violent scream, and scarce preserved herself from fainting, till Jones was able to move to her, and support her in his arms.

To paint the looks or thoughts of either of these lovers, is beyond my power. As their sensations, from their mutual silence, may be judged to have been too big for their own utterance, it cannot be supposed that

I should be able to express them : and the misfortune is, that few of my readers have been enough in love to feel by their own hearts what past at this time in theirs.

After a short pause, Jones, with faultering accents, said—"I see, madam, you are surprised."—"Surprized!" answered she; "Oh heavens! Indeed, I am surprized. I almost doubt whether you are the person you seem."—"Indeed," cries he, "my Sophia, pardon me, madam, for this once calling you so, I am that very wretched Jones, whom fortune, after so many disappointments, hath, at last, kindly conducted to you. Oh! my Sophia, did you know the thousand torments I have suffered in this long, fruitless pursuit."—"Pursuit of whom?" said Sophia, a little recollecting herself, and assuming a reserved air.—"Can you be so cruel to ask that question?" cries Jones; "Need I say, of you?" "Of me!" answered Sophia: "Hath Mr Jones, then, any such important business with me?" —"To some, madam," cries Jones, "this might seem an important business" (giving her the pocket-book). "I hope, madam, you will find it of the same value as when it was lost." Sophia took the pocket-book, and was going to speak, when he interrupted her thus :— "Let us not, I beseech you, lose one of these precious moments which fortune hath so kindly sent us. O, my Sophia! I have business of a much superior kind. Thus, on my knees, let me ask your pardon."—"My pardon!" cries she; "Sure, sir, after what is past, you cannot expect, after what I have heard."—"I scarce know what I say," answered Jones. "By heavens! I scarce wish you should pardon me. O my Sophia! henceforth never cast away a thought on such a wretch as I am. If any remembrance of me should ever intrude to give a moment's uneasiness to that tender bosom, think of my unworthiness; and let the remembrance of what passed at Upton blot me for ever from your mind."

Sophia stood trembling all this while. Her face was whiter than snow, and her heart was throbbing through her stays. But, at the mention of Upton, a blush arose in her cheeks, and her eyes, which before she had scarce lifted up, were turned upon Jones with a glance of disdain. He understood this silent reproach, and replied to it thus: "O my Sophia! my only love! you cannot hate or despise me more for what happened there than I do myself; but yet do me the justice to think that my heart was never unfaithful to you. That had no share in the folly I was guilty of; it was even then unalterably yours. Though I despaired of possessing you, nay, almost of ever seeing you more, I doated still on your charming idea, and could seriously love no other woman. But if my heart had not been engaged, she, into whose company I accidently fell at that cursed place, was not an object of serious love. Believe me, my angel, I never have seen her from that day to this; and never intend or desire to see her again." Sophia, in her heart, was very glad to hear this; but forcing into her face an air of more coldness than she had yet assumed, "Why," said she, "Mr Jones, do you take the trouble to make a defence where you are not accused? If I thought it worth while to accuse you, I have a charge of unpardonable nature indeed."—"What is it, for heaven's sake?" answered Jones, trembling and pale, expecting to hear of his amour with Lady Bellaston. "Oh," said she, "how is it possible! can everything noble and everything base be lodged together in the same bosom?" Lady Bellaston, and the ignominious circumstance of having been kept, rose again in his mind, and stopt his mouth from any reply. "Could I have expected," proceeded Sophia, "such treatment from you? Nay, from any gentleman, from any man of honour? To have my name traduced in public; in inns, among the meanest vulgar! to have any little favours that my unguarded heart may have too lightly betrayed me to grant, boasted of there! nay, even to hear that you had been forced to fly from my love!"

Nothing could equal Jones's surprize at these words of Sophia; but yet, not being guilty, he was much less embarrassed how to defend himself than if she had touched that tender string at which his conscience had been alarmed. By some examination he presently found, that her supposing him guilty of so shocking an outrage against his love, and her reputation, was entirely owing to Partridge's talk at the inns before landlords and servants; for Sophia confessed to him it was from them that she received her intelligence. He had no very great difficulty to make her believe that he was entirely innocent of an offence so foreign to his character; but she had a great deal to hinder him from going instantly home, and putting Partridge to death, which he more than once swore he would do. This point being cleared up, they soon found themselves so well pleased with each other, that Jones quite forgot he had begun the conversation with conjuring her to give up all thoughts of him; and she was in a temper to have given ear to a petition of a very different nature; for before they were aware they had both gone so far, that he let fall some words that sounded like a proposal of marriage. To which she replied, "That, did not her duty to her father forbid her to follow her own inclinations, ruin with him would be more welcome to her than the most affluent fortune with another man." At the mention of the word ruin, he started, let drop her hand, which he had held for some time, and striking his breast with his own, cried out, "Oh, Sophia! can I then ruin thee? No; by heavens, no! I never will act so base a part. Dearest Sophia, whatever it costs me, I will renounce you; I will give you up; I will tear all such hopes from my heart as are inconsistent with your real good. My love I will ever retain, but it shall be in silence; it shall be at a distance from you; it shall be in some foreign land; from whence no voice, no sigh of my despair, shall ever reach and disturb your ears. And when I am dead" —He would have gone on, but was stopt by a flood of tears which Sophia let fall in his bosom, upon which she leaned, without being able to speak one word. He kissed them off, which, for some moments, she allowed him to do without any resistance; but then recollecting herself, gently withdrew out of his arms; and, to turn the discourse from a subject too tender, and which she found she could not support, bethought herself to ask him a question she never had time to put to him before, "How he came into that room?" He began to stammer, and would, in all probability, have raised her suspicions by the answer he was going to give, when, at once, the door opened, and in came Lady Bellaston.

Having advanced a few steps, and seeing Jones and Sophia together, she suddenly stopt; when, after a pause of a few moments, recollecting herself with admirable presence of mind, she said—though with sufficient indications of surprize both in voice and countenance—"I thought, Miss Western, you had been at the play?"

Though Sophia had no opportunity of learning of Jones by what means he had discovered her, yet, as she had not the least suspicion of the real truth, or that Jones and Lady Bellaston were acquainted, so she was very little confounded; and the less, as the lady had, in all their conversations on the subject, entirely taken her side against her father. With very little hesitation, therefore, she went through the whole story of what had happened at the play-house, and the cause of her hasty return.

The length of this narrative gave Lady Bellaston an opportunity of rallying her spirits, and of considering in what manner to act. And as the behaviour of Sophia gave her hopes that Jones had not betrayed her, she put on an air of good humour, and said, "I should not have broke in so abruptly upon you, Miss Western, if I had known you had company."

Lady Bellaston fixed her eyes on Sophia whilst she spoke these words. To which that poor young lady, having her face overspread with blushes and confusion, answered, in a stammering voice, "I am sure, madam, I shall always think the honour of your ladyship's company——" "I hope, at least," cries Lady Bellaston, "I interrupt no business."—"No, madam," answered Sophia, "our business was at an end. Your ladyship may be pleased to remember I have often mentioned the loss of my pocket-book, which this gentleman, having very luckily found, was so kind to return it to me with the bill in it."

Jones, ever since the arrival of Lady Bellaston, had been ready to sink with fear. He sat kicking his heels, playing with his fingers, and looking more like a fool, if it be possible, than a young booby squire, when he is first introduced into a polite assembly. He began, however, now to recover himself; and taking a hint from the behaviour of Lady Bellaston, who he saw did not intend to claim any acquaintance with him, he resolved as entirely to affect the stranger on his part. He said, "Ever since he had the pocket-book in his possession, he had used great diligence in enquiring out the lady whose name was writ in it; but never till that day could be so fortunate to discover her."

Sophia had indeed mentioned the loss of her pocket-book to Lady Bellaston; but as Jones, for some reason or other, had never once hinted to her that it was in his possession, she believed not one syllable of what Sophia now said, and wonderfully admired the extreme quickness of the young lady in inventing such an excuse. The reason of Sophia's leaving the playhouse met with no better credit; and though she could not account for the meeting between these two lovers, she was firmly persuaded it was not accidental.

With an affected smile, therefore, she said, " Indeed, Miss Western, you have had very good luck in re-covering your money. Not only as it fell into the hands of a gentleman of honour, but as he happened to discover to whom it belonged. I think you would not consent to have it advertised.——It was great good fortune, sir, that you found out to whom the note belonged."

" Oh, madam," cries Jones, "it was enclosed in a pocket-book, in which the young lady's name was written."

" That was very fortunate, indeed," cries the lady :—— " And it was no less so, that you heard Miss Western was at my house; for she is very little known."

Jones had at length perfectly recovered his spirits; and as he conceived he had now an opportunity of satisfying Sophia as to the question she had asked him just before Lady Bellaston came in, he proceeded thus : " Why, madam," answered he, " it was by the luckiest chance imaginable I made this discovery. I was men-tioning what I had found, and the name of the owner, the other night to a lady at the masquerade, who told me she believed she knew where I might see Miss Western ; and if I would come to her house the next morning she would inform me. I went according to her appointment, but she was not at home ; nor could

I ever meet with her till this morning, when she directed me to your ladyship's house. I came accordingly, and did myself the honour to ask for your ladyship; and upon my saying that I had very particular business, a servant showed me into this room; where I had not been long before the young lady returned from the play."

Upon his mentioning the masquerade, he looked very slily at Lady Bellaston, without any fear of being remarked by Sophia; for she was visibly too much confounded to make any observations. This hint a little alarmed the lady, and she was silent; when Jones, who saw the agitation of Sophia's mind, resolved to take the only method of relieving her, which was by retiring; but, before he did this, he said, "I believe, madam, it is customary to give some reward on these occasions;—I must insist on a very high one for my honesty;—it is, madam, no less than the honour of being permitted to pay another visit here."

"Sir," replied the lady, "I make no doubt that you are a gentleman, and my doors are never shut to people of fashion."

Jones then, after proper ceremonials, departed, highly to his own satisfaction, and no less to that of Sophia; who was terribly alarmed lest Lady Bellaston should discover what she knew already but too well.

Upon the stairs Jones met his old acquaintance, Mrs Honour, who, notwithstanding all she had said against him, was now so well bred to behave with great civility. This meeting proved indeed a lucky circumstance, as he communicated to her the house where he lodged, with which Sophia was unacquainted.

Chapter xij.

In which the thirteenth book is concluded.

THE elegant Lord Shaftesbury somewhere objects to telling too much truth: by which it may be fairly inferred, that, in some cases, to lie is not only excusable but commendable.

And surely there are no persons who may so properly challenge a right to this commendable deviation from truth, as young women in the affair of love; for which they may plead precept, education, and above all, the sanction, nay, I may say the necessity of custom, by which they are restrained, not from submitting to the honest impulses of nature (for that would be a foolish prohibition), but from owning them.

We are not, therefore, ashamed to say, that our heroine now pursued the dictates of the above-mentioned right honourable philosopher. As she was perfectly satisfied then, that Lady Bellaston was ignorant of the person of Jones, so she determined to keep her in that ignorance, though at the expense of a little fibbing.

Jones had not been long gone, before Lady Bellaston cryed, "Upon my word, a good pretty young fellow; I wonder who he is; for I don't remember ever to have seen his face before."

"Nor I neither, madam," cries Sophia. "I must say he behaved very handsomely in relation to my note."

"Yes; and he is a very handsome fellow," said the lady: "don't you think so?"

"I did not take much notice of him," answered Sophia, "but I thought he seemed rather awkward, and ungenteel than otherwise."

"You are extremely right," cries Lady Bellaston:

"you may see, by his manner, that he hath not kept good company. Nay, notwithstanding his returning your note, and refusing the reward, I almost question whether he is a gentleman.———I have always observed there is a something in persons well born, which others can never acquire.———I think I will give orders not to be at home to him."

"Nay, sure, madam," answered Sophia, "one can't suspect after what he hath done;—besides, if your ladyship observed him, there was an elegance in his discourse, a delicacy, a prettiness of expression that, that———"

"I confess," said Lady Bellaston, "the fellow hath words———And indeed, Sophia, you must forgive me, indeed you must."

"I forgive your ladyship!" said Sophia.

"Yes, indeed you must," answered she, laughing; "for I had a horrible suspicion when I first came into the room———I vow you must forgive it; but I suspected it was Mr Jones himself."

"Did your ladyship, indeed?" cries Sophia, blushing, and affecting a laugh.

"Yes, I vow I did," answered she. "I can't imagine what put it into my head: for, give the fellow his due, he was genteely drest; which, I think, dear Sophy, is not commonly the case with your friend."

"This raillery," cries Sophia, "is a little cruel, Lady Bellaston, after my promise to your ladyship."

"Not at all, child," said the lady;———"It would have been cruel before; but after you have promised me never to marry without your father's consent, in which you know is implied your giving up Jones, sure you can bear a little raillery on a passion which was pardonable enough in a young girl in the country, and of which you tell me you have so entirely got the better. What must I think, my dear Sophy, if you cannot bear a little ridicule even on his dress? I shall begin to fear you are very far gone indeed; and almost question whether you have dealt ingenuously with me."

"Indeed, madam," cries Sophia, "your ladyship mistakes me, if you imagine I had any concern on his account."

"On his account!" answered the lady: "You must have mistaken me; I went no farther than his dress; ——for I would not injure your taste by any other comparison——I don't imagine, my dear Sophy, if your Mr Jones had been such a fellow as this——"

"I thought," says Sophia, "your ladyship had allowed him to be handsome"——

"Whom, pray?" cried the lady hastily.

"Mr Jones," answered Sophia;—and immediately recollecting herself, "Mr Jones!—no, no; I ask your pardon;—I mean the gentleman who was just now here."

"O Sophy! Sophy!" cries the lady; "this Mr Jones, I am afraid, still runs in your head."

"Then, upon my honour, madam," said Sophia, "Mr Jones is as entirely indifferent to me, as the gentleman who just now left us."

"Upon my honour," said Lady Bellaston, "I believe it. Forgive me, therefore, a little innocent raillery; but I promise you I will never mention his name any more."

And now the two ladies separated, infinitely more to the delight of Sophia than of Lady Bellaston, who would willingly have tormented her rival a little longer, had not business of more importance called her away. As for Sophia, her mind was not perfectly easy under this first practice of deceit; upon which, when she retired to her chamber, she reflected with the highest uneasiness and conscious shame. Nor could the peculiar hardship of her situation, and the necessity of the case, at all reconcile her mind to her conduct; for the frame of her mind was too delicate to bear the thought of having been guilty of a falsehood, however qualified by circumstances.   Nor did this thought once suffer her to close her eyes during the whole succeeding night.

BOOK XIV

CONTAINING TWO DAYS.

Chapter i.

An essay to prove that an author will write the better for having some knowledge of the subject on which he writes.

AS several gentlemen in these times, by the wonderful force of genius only, without the least assistance of learning, perhaps, without being well able to read, have made a considerable figure in the republic of letters; the modern critics, I am told, have lately begun to assert, that all kind of learning is entirely useless to a writer; and, indeed, no other than a kind of fetters on the natural sprightliness and activity of the imagination, which is thus weighed down, and prevented from soaring to those high flights which otherwise it would be able to reach.

This doctrine, I am afraid, is at present carried much too far: for why should writing differ so much from all other arts? The nimbleness of a dancing-master is not at all prejudiced by being taught to move; nor doth any mechanic, I believe, exercise his tools the worse by having learnt to use them. For my own part, I cannot conceive that Homer or Virgil would

have writ with more fire, if instead of being masters of
all the learning of their times, they had been as ignorant
as most of the authors of the present age.   Nor do I
believe that all the imagination, fire, and judgment of
Pitt, could have produced those orations that have
made the senate of England, in these our times, a rival
in eloquence to Greece and Rome, if he had not been
so well read in the writings of Demosthenes and Cicero,
as to have transferred their whole spirit into his speeches,
and, with their spirit, their knowledge too.

I would not here be understood to insist on the same
fund of learning in any of my brethren, as Cicero persuades us is necessary to the composition of an orator.
On the contrary, very little reading is, I conceive,
necessary to the poet, less to the critic, and the least
of all to the politician.   For the first, perhaps, Byshe's
Art of Poetry, and a few of our modern poets, may
suffice; for the second, a moderate heap of plays;
and, for the last, an indifferent collection of political
journals.

To say the truth, I require no more than that a man
should have some little knowledge of the subject on
which he treats, according to the old maxim of law,
Quam quisque nôrit artem in eâ se exerceat.   With this
alone a writer may sometimes do tolerably well; and,
indeed, without this, all the other learning in the world
will stand him in little stead.

For instance, let us suppose that Homer and Virgil,
Aristotle and Cicero, Thucydides and Livy, could have
met all together, and have clubbed their several talents
to have composed a treatise on the art of dancing: I
believe it will be readily agreed they could not have
equalled the excellent treatise which Mr Essex hath
given us on that subject, entitled, The Rudiments of
Genteel Education.   And, indeed, should the excellent
Mr Broughton be prevailed on to set fist to paper, and

to complete the above-said rudiments, by delivering down the true principles of athletics, I question whether the world will have any cause to lament, that none of the great writers, either antient or modern, have ever treated about that noble and useful art.

To avoid a multiplicity of examples in so plain a case, and to come at once to my point, I am apt to conceive, that one reason why many English writers have totally failed in describing the manners of upper life, may possibly be, that in reality they know nothing of it.

This is a knowledge unhappily not in the power of many authors to arrive at. Books will give us a very imperfect idea of it; nor will the stage a much better: the fine gentleman formed upon reading the former will almost always turn out a pedant, and he who forms himself upon the latter, a coxcomb.

Nor are the characters drawn from these models better supported. Vanbrugh and Congreve copied nature; but they who copy them draw as unlike the present age as Hogarth would do if he was to paint a rout or a drum in the dresses of Titian and of Vandyke. In short, imitation here will not do the business. The picture must be after Nature herself. A true knowledge of the world is gained only by conversation, and the manners of every rank must be seen in order to be known.

Now it happens that this higher order of mortals is not to be seen, like all the rest of the human species, for nothing, in the streets, shops, and coffee-houses: nor are they shown, like the upper rank of animals, for so much a-piece. In short, this is a sight to which no persons are admitted without one or other of these qualifications, viz., either birth or fortune, or, what is equivalent to both, the honourable profession of a gamester. And, very unluckily for the world, persons so qualified very seldom care to take upon themselves the bad trade of writing; which is generally entered upon by the lower and poorer sort, as it is a trade which many think requires no kind of stock to set up with.

Hence those strange monsters in lace and embroidery, in silks and brocades, with vast wigs and hoops; which, under the name of lords and ladies, strut the stage, to the great delight of attorneys and their clerks in the pit, and of the citizens and their apprentices in the galleries; and which are no more to be found in real life than the centaur, the chimera, or any other creature of mere fiction. But to let my reader into a secret, this knowledge of upper life, though very necessary for preventing mistakes, is no very great resource to a writer whose province is comedy, or that kind of novels which, like this I am writing, is of the comic class.

What Mr Pope says of women is very applicable to most in this station, who are, indeed, so entirely made up of form and affectation, that they have no character at all, at least none which appears. I will venture to say the highest life is much the dullest, and affords very little humour or entertainment. The various callings in lower spheres produce the great variety of humorous characters; whereas here, except among the few who are engaged in the pursuit of ambition, and the fewer still who have a relish for pleasure, all is vanity and servile imitation. Dressing and cards, eating and drinking, bowing and courtesying, make up the business of their lives.

Some there are, however, of this rank upon whom passion exercises its tyranny, and hurries them far beyond the bounds which decorum prescribes; of these the ladies are as much distinguished by their noble intrepidity, and a certain superior contempt of reputation, from the frail ones of meaner degree, as a virtuous woman of quality is by the elegance and delicacy of her sentiments from the honest wife of a yeoman and shopkeeper. Lady Bellaston was of this intrepid character; but let not my country readers conclude from her, that this is the general conduct of women of fashion, or that we mean to represent them as such. They might as well suppose that every clergyman was represented by Thwackum, or every soldier by ensign Northerton.

There is not, indeed, a greater error than that which universally prevails among the vulgar, who, borrowing their opinion from some ignorant satirists, have affixed the character of lewdness to these times. On the contrary, I am convinced there never was less of love intrigue carried on among persons of condition than now. Our present women have been taught by their mothers to fix their thoughts only on ambition and vanity, and to despise the pleasures of love as unworthy their regard; and being afterwards, by the care of such mothers, married without having husbands, they seem pretty well confirmed in the justness of those sentiments; whence they content themselves, for the dull remainder of life, with the pursuit of more innocent, but I am afraid more childish amusements, the bare mention of which would ill suit with the dignity of this history. In my humble opinion, the true characteristic of the present beau monde is rather folly than vice, and the only epithet which it deserves is that of frivolous.

Chapter ij.

Containing letters and other matters which attend amours.

JONES had not been long at home before he received the following letter :—

"I was never more surprized than when I found you was gone. When you left the room I little imagined you intended to have left the house without seeing me again. Your behaviour is all of a piece, and convinces me how much I ought to despise a heart which can doat upon an idiot; though I know not whether I should not admire her cunning more than her simplicity : wonderful both ! For though she understood not a word of what passed between us, yet she had the skill, the assurance, the——what shall I call it ? to deny to my face that she knows you, or ever saw you before.——Was this a scheme laid between you, and have you been base enough to betray me ?——O how I despise her, you, and all the world, but chiefly myself ! for——I dare not write what I should afterwards run mad to read ; but remember, I can detest as violently as I have loved."

Jones had but little time given him to reflect on this letter, before a second was brought him from the same hand ; and this, likewise, we shall set down in the precise words.

"When you consider the hurry of spirits in which I must have writ, you cannot be surprized at any expressions in my former note.——Yet, perhaps, on reflection, they were rather too warm. At least I would, if possible, think all owing to the odious playhouse, and to the impertinence of a fool, which detained me beyond my appointment.——How easy is it to think well of

those we love !——Perhaps you desire I should think
so. I have resolved to see you to-night ; so come to
me immediately.

"*P.S.*—I have ordered to be at home to none but
yourself.

"*P.S.*—Mr Jones will imagine I shall assist him in
his defence ; for I believe he cannot desire to impose
on me more than I desire to impose on myself.

"*P.S.*—Come immediately."

To the men of intrigue I refer the determination,
whether the angry or the tender letter gave the greatest
uneasiness to Jones. Certain it is, he had no violent
inclination to pay any more visits that evening, unless
to one single person. However, he thought his honour
engaged, and had not this been motive sufficient, he
would not have ventured to blow the temper of Lady
Bellaston into that flame of which he had reason to
think it susceptible, and of which he feared the consequence might be a discovery to Sophia, which he
dreaded. After some discontented walks therefore
about the room, he was preparing to depart, when the
lady kindly prevented him, not by another letter, but
by her own presence. She entered the room very
disordered in her dress, and very discomposed in her
looks, and threw herself into a chair, where, having
recovered her breath, she said—"You see, sir, when
women have gone one length too far, they will stop at
none. If any person would have sworn this to me a
week ago, I would not have believed it of myself."
"I hope, madam," said Jones, "my charming Lady
Bellaston will be as difficult to believe anything against
one who is so sensible of the many obligations she hath
conferred upon him." "Indeed !" says she, "sensible
of obligations ! Did I expect to hear such cold lan-

guage from Mr Jones?"   "Pardon me, my dear
angel," said he, "if, after the letters I have received,
the terrors of your anger, though I know not how I
have deserved it"——"And have I then," says she,
with a smile, "so angry a countenance?—Have I
really brought a chiding face with me?"——"If there
be honour in man," said he, "I have done nothing to
merit your anger. — You remember the appointment
you sent me; I went in pursuance."—"I beseech
you," cried she, "do not run through the odious
recital.—Answer me but one question, and I shall
be easy. Have you not betrayed my honour to her?"
—Jones fell upon his knees, and began to utter the
most violent protestations, when Partridge came dancing
and capering into the room, like one drunk with joy,
crying out, "She's found! she's found!—Here, sir,
here, she's here—Mrs Honour is upon the stairs."
"Stop her a moment," cries Jones—"Here, madam,
step behind the bed, I have no other room nor closet,
nor place on earth to hide you in; sure never was so
damned an accident."—"D—n'd indeed!" said the
lady, as she went to her place of concealment; and
presently afterwards in came Mrs Honour. "Hey-
day!" says she, "Mr Jones, what's the matter?—
That impudent rascal your servant would scarce let me
come upstairs. I hope he hath not the same reason
to keep me from you as he had at Upton.—I suppose
you hardly expected to see me; but you have certainly
bewitched my lady. Poor dear young lady! To be
sure, I loves her as tenderly as if she was my own
sister. Lord have mercy upon you, if you don't make
her a good husband! and to be sure, if you do not,
nothing can be bad enough for you." Jones begged
her only to whisper, for that there was a lady dying in
the next room. "A lady!" cries she; "ay, I suppose one of your ladies.—O Mr Jones, there are too

many of them in the world; I believe we are got into the house of one, for my Lady Bellaston I darst to say is no better than she should be."—"Hush! hush!" cries Jones, "every word is overheard in the next room." "I don't care a farthing," cries Honour, "I speaks no scandal of any one; but to be sure the servants make no scruple of saying as how her ladyship meets men at another place—where the house goes under the name of a poor gentlewoman; but her ladyship pays the rent, and many's the good thing besides, they say, she hath of her."—Here Jones, after expressing the utmost uneasiness, offered to stop her mouth:—"Hey-day! why sure, Mr Jones, you will let me speak; I speaks no scandal, for I only says what I heard from others—and thinks I to myself, much good may it do the gentlewoman with her riches, if she comes by it in such a wicked manner. To be sure it is better to be poor and honest." "The servants are villains," cries Jones, "and abuse their lady unjustly." — "Ay, to be sure, servants are always villains, and so my lady says, and won't hear a word of it."—"No, I am convinced," says Jones, "my Sophia is above listening to such base scandal." "Nay, I believe it is no scandal, neither," cries Honour, "for why should she meet men at another house?—It can never be for any good: for if she had a lawful design of being courted, as to be sure any lady may lawfully give her company to men upon that account: why, where can be the sense?"—"I protest," cries Jones, "I can't hear all this of a lady of such honour, and a relation of Sophia; besides, you will distract the poor lady in the next room.—Let me entreat you to walk with me down stairs."—"Nay, sir, if you won't let me speak, I have done.—Here, sir, is a letter from my young lady—what would some men give to have this? But, Mr Jones, I think you are not over and above generous, and yet I have heard some servants say——but I am sure you will do me the justice to own I never saw the colour of your money." Here Jones hastily took the letter, and presently after slipped five pieces into her hand. He then returned a thousand thanks to his dear Sophia in a whisper, and begged her to leave him to read her letter : she presently departed, not without expressing much grateful sense of his generosity.

Lady Bellaston now came from behind the curtain. How shall I describe her rage? Her tongue was at first incapable of utterance ; but streams of fire darted from her eyes, and well indeed they might, for her heart was all in a flame. And now as soon as her voice found way, instead of expressing any indignation against Honour or her own servants, she began to attack poor Jones. "You see," said she, "what I have sacrificed to you ; my reputation, my honour— gone for ever! And what return have I found? Neglected, slighted for a country girl, for an idiot." —"What neglect, madam, or what slight," cries Jones, "have I been guilty of?"—"Mr Jones," said she, "it is in vain to dissemble ; if you will make me easy, you must entirely give her up ; and as a proof of your intention, show me the letter."——"What letter, madam?" said Jones. "Nay, surely," said she, "you cannot have the confidence to deny your having received a letter by the hands of that trollop."——"And can your ladyship," cries he, "ask of me what I must part with my honour before I grant? Have I acted in such a manner by your ladyship? Could I be guilty of betraying this poor innocent girl to you, what security could you have that I should not act the same part by yourself? A moment's reflection will, I am sure, convince you that a man with whom the secrets of a lady are not safe must be the most contemptible of wretches."—"Very well," said she—"I need not insist on your becoming this contemptible wretch in your own opinion; for the inside of the letter could inform me of nothing more than I know already. I see the footing you are upon."—Here ensued a long conversation, which the reader, who is not too curious, will thank me for not inserting at length. It shall suffice, therefore, to inform him, that Lady Bellaston grew more and more pacified, and at length believed, or affected to believe, his protestations, that his meeting with Sophia that evening was merely accidental, and every other matter which the reader already knows, and which, as Jones set before her in the strongest light, it is plain that she had in reality no reason to be angry with him.

She was not, however, in her heart perfectly satisfied with his refusal to show her the letter; so deaf are we to the clearest reason, when it argues against our prevailing passions. She was, indeed, well convinced that Sophia possessed the first place in Jones's affections; and yet, haughty and amorous as this lady was, she submitted at last to bear the second place; or, to express it more properly in a legal phrase, was contented with the possession of that of which another woman had the reversion.

It was at length agreed that Jones should for the future visit at the house: for that Sophia, her maid, and all the servants, would place these visits to the account of Sophia; and that she herself would be considered as the person imposed upon.

This scheme was contrived by the lady, and highly relished by Jones, who was indeed glad to have a prospect of seeing his Sophia at any rate; and the lady herself was not a little pleased with the imposition on Sophia, which Jones, she thought, could not possibly discover to her for his own sake.

The next day was appointed for the first visit, and then, after proper ceremonials, the Lady Bellaston returned home.

Chapter iii.

Containing various matters.

JONES was no sooner alone than he eagerly broke open his letter, and read as follows :—

"Sir, it is impossible to express what I have suffered since you left this house; and as I have reason to think you intend coming here again, I have sent Honour, though so late at night, as she tells me she knows your lodgings, to prevent you. I charge you, by all the regard you have for me, not to think of visiting here; for it will certainly be discovered; nay, I almost doubt, from some things which have dropt from her ladyship, that she is not already without some suspicion. Something favourable perhaps may happen; we must wait with patience; but I once more entreat you, if you have any concern for my ease, do not think of returning hither."

This letter administered the same kind of consolation to poor Jones, which Job formerly received from his friends. Besides disappointing all the hopes which he promised to himself from seeing Sophia, he was reduced to an unhappy dilemma, with regard to Lady Bellaston; for there are some certain engagements, which, as he well knew, do very difficultly admit of any excuse for the failure; and to go, after the strict prohibition from Sophia, he was not to be forced by any human power. At length, after much deliberation, which during that night supplied the place of sleep, he determined to feign himself sick : for this suggested itself as the only means of failing the appointed visit, without incensing Lady Bellaston, which he had more than one reason of desiring to avoid.

The first thing, however, which he did in the morning, was, to write an answer to Sophia, which he inclosed in one to Honour. He then despatched another to Lady Bellaston, containing the abovementioned excuse ; and to this he soon received the following answer :—

"I am vexed that I cannot see you here this afternoon, but more concerned for the occasion ; take great care of yourself, and have the best advice, and I hope there will be no danger.—I am so tormented all this morning with fools, that I have scarce a moment's time to write to you. Adieu.

"*P.S.*—I will endeavour to call on you this evening, at nine.—Be sure to be alone."

Mr Jones now received a visit from Mrs Miller, who, after some formal introduction, began the following speech :—"I am very sorry, sir, to wait upon you on such an occasion ; but I hope you will consider the ill consequence which it must be to the reputation of my poor girls, if my house should once be talked of as a house of ill-fame. I hope you won't think me, therefore, guilty of impertinence, if I beg you not to bring any more ladies in at that time of night. The clock had struck two before one of them went away."—"I do assure you, madam," said Jones, "the lady who was here last night, and who staid the latest (for the other only brought me a letter), is a woman of very great fashion, and my near relation."—"I don't know what fashion she is of," answered Mrs Miller ; "but I am sure no woman of virtue, unless a very near relation indeed, would visit a young gentleman at ten at night, and stay four hours in his room with him alone ; besides, sir, the behaviour of her chairmen shows what she was ; for they did nothing but make jests all the evening in the entry, and asked Mr Partridge, in the hearing of my own maid, if madam intended to stay with his master all night ; with a great deal of stuff not proper to be repeated.   I have really a great respect for you, Mr Jones, upon your own account ; nay, I have a very high obligation to you for your generosity to my cousin.   Indeed, I did not know how very good you had been till lately.   Little did I imagine to what dreadful courses the poor man's distress had driven him.   Little did I think, when you gave me the ten guineas, that you had given them to a highwayman ! O heavens ! what goodness have you shown !   How have you preserved this family !—The character which Mr Allworthy hath formerly given me of you was, I find, strictly true.—And indeed, if I had no obligation to you, my obligations to him are such, that, on his account, I should shew you the utmost respect in my power. — Nay, believe me, dear Mr Jones, if my daughters' and my own reputation were out of the case, I should, for your own sake, be sorry that so pretty a young gentleman should converse with these women ; but if you are resolved to do it, I must beg you to take another lodging ; for I do not myself like to have such things carried on under my roof ; but more especially upon the account of my girls, who have little, heaven knows, besides their characters, to recommend them." Jones started and changed colour at the name of Allworthy.   "Indeed, Mrs Miller," answered he, a little warmly, "I do not take this at all kind.   I will never bring any slander on your house ; but I must insist on seeing what company I please in my own room ; and if that gives you any offence, I shall, as soon as I am able, look for another lodging."—"I am sorry we must part then, sir," said she ; "but I am convinced

Mr Allworthy himself would never come within my doors, if he had the least suspicion of my keeping an ill house."—"Very well, madam," said Jones.—"I hope, sir," said she, "you are not angry; for I would not for the world offend any of Mr Allworthy's family. I have not slept a wink all night about this matter."— "I am sorry I have disturbed your rest, madam," said Jones, "but I beg you will send Partridge up to me immediately;" which she promised to do, and then with a very low courtesy retired.

As soon as Partridge arrived, Jones fell upon him in the most outrageous manner. "How often," said he, "am I to suffer for your folly, or rather for my own in keeping you? is that tongue of yours resolved upon my destruction?" "What have I done, sir?" answered affrighted Partridge. "Who was it gave you authority to mention the story of the robbery, or that the man you saw here was the person?" "I, sir?" cries Partridge. "Now don't be guilty of a falsehood in denying it," said Jones. "If I did mention such a matter," answers Partridge, "I am sure I thought no harm; for I should not have opened my lips, if it had not been to his own friends and relations, who, I imagined, would have let it go no farther." "But I have a much heavier charge against you," cries Jones, "than this. How durst you, after all the precautions I gave you, mention the name of Mr Allworthy in this house?" Partridge denied that he ever had, with many oaths. "How else," said Jones, "should Mrs Millar be acquainted that there was any connexion between him and me? And it is but this moment she told me she respected me on his account." "O Lord, sir," said Partridge, "I desire only to be heard out; and to be sure, never was anything so unfortunate: hear me but out, and you will own how wrongfully you have accused me. When Mrs Honour

came downstairs last night she met me in the entry,
and asked me when my master had heard from Mr
Allworthy; and to be sure Mrs Miller heard the very
words; and the moment Madam Honour was gone, she
called me into the parlour to her. 'Mr Partridge,'
says she, 'what Mr Allworthy is it that the gentlewoman mentioned? is it the great Mr Allworthy of
Somersetshire?' 'Upon my word, madam,' says I,
'I know nothing of the matter.' 'Sure,' says she,
'your master is not the Mr Jones I have heard Mr
Allworthy talk of?' 'Upon my word, madam,' says
I, 'I know nothing of the matter.' 'Then,' says she,
turning to her daughter Nancy, says she, 'as sure as
tenpence this is the very young gentleman, and he agrees
exactly with the squire's description.' The Lord above
knows who it was told her: for I am the arrantest
villain that ever walked upon two legs if ever it came
out of my mouth. I promise you, sir, I can keep a
secret when I am desired. Nay, sir, so far was I from
telling her anything about Mr Allworthy, that I told
her the very direct contrary; for, though I did not
contradict it at that moment, yet, as second thoughts,
they say, are best, so when I came to consider that
somebody must have informed her, thinks I to myself,
I will put an end to the story; and so I went back
again into the parlour some time afterwards, and says
I, upon my word, says I, whoever, says I, told you
that this gentleman was Mr Jones; that is, says I, that
this Mr Jones was that Mr Jones, told you a confounded
lie: and I beg, says I, you will never mention any such
matter, says I; for my master, says I, will think I
must have told you so; and I defy anybody in the
house ever to say I mentioned any such word. To be
certain, sir, it is a wonderful thing, and I have been
thinking with myself ever since, how it was she came
to know it; not but I saw an old woman here t'other

day a begging at the door, who looked as like her we saw in Warwickshire, that caused all that mischief to us. To be sure it is never good to pass by an old woman without giving her something, especially if she looks at you; for all the world shall never persuade me but that they have a great power to do mischief, and to be sure I shall never see an old woman again, but I shall think to myself, *Infandum, regina, jubes renovare dolorem.*"

The simplicity of Partridge set Jones a laughing, and put a final end to his anger, which had indeed seldom any long duration in his mind; and, instead of commenting on his defence, he told him he intended presently to leave those lodgings, and ordered him to go and endeavour to get him others.

Chapter ix.

Which we hope will be very attentively perused by young people of both sexes.

PARTRIDGE had no sooner left Mr Jones than Mr Nightingale, with whom he had now contracted a great intimacy, came to him, and, after a short salutation, said, "So, Tom, I hear you had company very late last night. Upon my soul you are a happy fellow, who have not been in town above a fortnight, and can keep chairs waiting at your door till two in the morning." He then ran on with much commonplace raillery of the same kind, till Jones at last interrupted him, saying, "I suppose you have received all this information from Mrs Miller, who hath been up here a little while ago to give me warning. The good woman is afraid, it seems, of the reputation of her daughters." "Oh! she is wonderfully nice," says Nightingale, "upon that account; if you remember, she would not let Nancy go with us to the masquerade." "Nay, upon my honour, I think she's in the right of it," says Jones: "however, I have taken her at her word, and have sent Partridge to look for another lodging." "If you will," says Nightingale, "we may, I believe, be again together; for, to tell you a secret, which I desire you won't mention in the family, I intend to quit the house to-day." "What, hath Mrs Miller given you warning too, my friend?" cries Jones. "No," answered the other; "but the rooms are not convenient enough. Besides, I am grown weary of this part of the town. I want to be nearer the places of diversion; so I am going to Pall-mall." "And do you intend to make a secret of your going away?" said Jones. "I promise you," answered Nightingale, "I don't intend to bilk my lodgings; but I have a private reason for not taking a formal leave." "Not so private," answered Jones; "I promise you, I have seen it ever since the second day of my coming to the house. Here will be some wet eyes on your departure. Poor Nancy, I pity her, faith! Indeed, Jack, you have played the fool with that girl. You have given her a longing, which I am afraid nothing will ever cure her of." Nightingale answered, "What the devil would you have me do? would you have me marry her to cure her?" "No," answered Jones, "I would not have had you make love to her, as you have often done in my presence. I have been astonished at the blindness of her mother in never seeing it." "Pugh, see it!" cries Nightingale. "What the devil should she see?" "Why, see," said Jones, "that you have made her daughter distractedly in love with you. The poor girl cannot conceal it a moment; her eyes are never off from you, and she always colours every time you come into the room. Indeed, I pity her heartily; for she seems to be one of the best-natured and honestest of human creatures." "And so," answered Nightingale, "according to your doctrine, one must not amuse oneself by any common gallantries with women, for fear they should fall in love with us." "Indeed, Jack," said Jones, "you wilfully misunderstand me; I do not fancy women are so apt to fall in love; but you have gone far beyond common gallantries." "What, do you suppose," says Nightingale, "that we have been a-bed together?" "No, upon my honour," answered Jones, very seriously, "I do not suppose so ill of you; nay, I will go farther, I do not imagine you have laid a regular premeditated scheme for the destruction of the quiet of a poor little creature, or have even foreseen the consequence: for I am sure thou art a very good-natured fellow, and such a one can never be guilty of a cruelty of that kind; but at the same time you have pleased your own vanity, without considering that this poor girl was made a sacrifice to it; and while you have had no design but of amusing an idle hour, you have actually given her reason to flatter herself that you had the most serious designs in her favour. Prithee, Jack, answer me honestly; to what have tended all those elegant and luscious descriptions of happiness arising from violent and mutual fondness? all those warm professions of tenderness, and generous disinterested love? Did you imagine she would not apply them? or, speak ingenuously, did not you intend she should?" "Upon my soul, Tom," cries Nightingale, "I did not think this was in thee. Thou wilt make an admirable parson. So I suppose you would not go to bed to Nancy now, if she would let you?" "No," cries Jones, "may I be d—n'd if I would." "Tom, Tom," answered Nightingale, "last night; remember last night——

> When every eye was closed, and the pale moon,
> And silent stars, shone conscious of the theft."

"Lookee, Mr Nightingale," said Jones, "I am no canting hypocrite, nor do I pretend to the gift of chastity, more than my neighbours. I have been guilty with women, I own it; but am not conscious that I have ever injured any.—Nor would I, to procure pleasure to myself, be knowingly the cause of misery to any human being."

"Well, well," said Nightingale, "I believe you, and I am convinced you acquit me of any such thing."

"I do, from my heart," answered Jones, " of having debauched the girl, but not from having gained her affections."

"If I have," said Nightingale, "I am sorry for it; but time and absence will soon wear off such impressions. It is a receipt I must take myself; for, to confess the truth to you—I never liked any girl half so much in my whole life; but I must let you into the whole secret, Tom. My father hath provided a match for me with a woman I never saw; and she is now coming to town, in order for me to make my addresses to her."

At these words Jones burst into a loud fit of laughter; when Nightingale cried—"Nay, prithee, don't turn me into ridicule. The devil take me if I am not half mad about this matter! my poor Nancy! Oh! Jones, Jones, I wish I had a fortune in my own possession."

"I heartily wish you had," cries Jones; "for, if this be the case, I sincerely pity you both; but surely you don't intend to go away without taking your leave of her?"

"I would not," answered Nightingale, "undergo the pain of taking leave, for ten thousand pounds; besides, I am convinced, instead of answering any good purpose, it would only serve to inflame my poor Nancy the more. I beg, therefore, you would not mention a word of it to-day, and in the evening, or to-morrow morning, I intend to depart."

II.   K

Jones promised he would not ; and said, upon reflection, he thought, as he had determined and was obliged to leave her, he took the most prudent method. He then told Nightingale he should be very glad to lodge in the same house with him ; and it was accordingly agreed between them, that Nightingale should procure him either the ground floor, or the two pair of stairs ; for the young gentleman himself was to occupy that which was between them.

This Nightingale, of whom we shall be presently obliged to say a little more, was in the ordinary transactions of life a man of strict honour, and, what is more rare among young gentlemen of the town, one of strict honesty too ; yet in affairs of love he was somewhat loose in his morals ; not that he was even here as void of principle as gentlemen sometimes are, and oftener affect to be ; but it is certain he had been guilty of some indefensible treachery to women, and had, in a certain mystery, called making love, practised many deceits, which, if he had used in trade, he would have been counted the greatest villain upon earth.

But as the world, I know not well for what reason, agree to see this treachery in a better light, he was so far from being ashamed of his iniquities of this kind, that he gloried in them, and would often boast of his skill in gaining of women, and his triumphs over their hearts, for which he had before this time received some rebukes from Jones, who always exprest great bitterness against any misbehaviour to the fair part of the species, who, if considered, he said, as they ought to be, in the light of the dearest friends, were to be cultivated, honoured, and caressed with the utmost love and tenderness ; but, if regarded as enemies, were a conquest of which a man ought rather to be ashamed than to value himself upon it.

Chapter v.

A short account of the history of Mrs Miller.

JONES this day eat a pretty good dinner for a sick man, that is to say, the larger half of a shoulder of mutton.   In the afternoon he received an invitation from Mrs Miller to drink tea; for that good woman, having learnt, either by means of Partridge, or by some other means natural or supernatural, that he had a connexion with Mr Allworthy, could not endure the thoughts of parting with him in an angry manner.

Jones accepted the invitation; and no sooner was the tea-kettle removed, and the girls sent out of the room, than the widow, without much preface, began as follows : " Well, there are very surprizing things happen in this world; but certainly it is a wonderful business that I should have a relation of Mr Allworthy in my house, and never know anything of the matter.   Alas! sir, you little imagine what a friend that best of gentlemen hath been to me and mine.   Yes, sir, I am not ashamed to own it; it is owing to his goodness that I did not long since perish for want, and leave my poor little wretches, two destitute, helpless, friendless orphans, to the care, or rather to the cruelty, of the world.

" You must know, sir, though I am now reduced to get my living by letting lodgings, I was born and bred a gentlewoman.   My father was an officer of the army, and died in a considerable rank : but he lived up to his pay; and, as that expired with him, his family, at his death, became beggars.   We were three sisters. One of us had the good luck to die soon after of the small-pox; a lady was so kind as to take the second out of charity, as she said, to wait upon her.   The mother of this lady had been a servant to my grandmother; and, having inherited a vast fortune from her father, which he had got by pawnbroking, was married to a gentleman of great estate and fashion. She used my sister so barbarously, often upbraiding her with her birth and poverty, calling her in derision a gentlewoman, that I believe she at length broke the heart of the poor girl. In short, she likewise died within a twelvemonth after my father. Fortune thought proper to provide better for me, and within a month from his decease I was married to a clergyman, who had been my lover a long time before, and who had been very ill used by my father on that account: for though my poor father could not give any of us a shilling, yet he bred us up as delicately, considered us, and would have had us consider ourselves, as highly as if we had been the richest heiresses. But my dear husband forgot all this usage, and the moment we were become fatherless he immediately renewed his addresses to me so warmly, that I, who always liked, and now more than ever esteemed him, soon complied. Five years did I live in a state of perfect happiness with that best of men, till at last—Oh! cruel! cruel fortune, that ever separated us, that deprived me of the kindest of husbands and my poor girls of the tenderest parent.—O my poor girls! you never knew the blessing which ye lost.—I am ashamed, Mr Jones, of this womanish weakness; but I shall never mention him without tears." "I ought rather, madam," said Jones, "to be ashamed that I do not accompany you." "Well, sir," continued she, "I was now left a second time in a much worse condition than before; besides the terrible affliction I was to encounter, I had now two children to provide for; and was, if possible, more pennyless than ever; when that great, that good, that glorious man, Mr Allworthy, who had some little acquaintance with my husband, accidentally heard of my distress, and im-

mediately writ this letter to me.   Here, sir, here it is ;
I put it into my pocket to shew it you.   This is the
letter, sir ; I must and will read it to you.

" ' MADAM,

" ' I heartily condole with you on your late grievous loss, which your own good sense, and the excellent
lessons you must have learnt from the worthiest of men,
will better enable you to bear than any advice which I
am capable of giving.   Nor have I any doubt that you,
whom I have heard to be the tenderest of mothers, will
suffer any immoderate indulgence of grief to prevent
you from discharging your duty to those poor infants,
who now alone stand in need of your tenderness.

" ' However, as you must be supposed at present to
be incapable of much worldly consideration, you will
pardon my having ordered a person to wait on you,
and to pay you twenty guineas, which I beg you will
accept till I have the pleasure of seeing you, and believe
me to be, madam, &c.'

" This letter, sir, I received within a fortnight after
the irreparable loss I have mentioned ; and within a
fortnight afterwards, Mr Allworthy—the blessed Mr
Allworthy, came to pay me a visit, when he placed
me in the house where you now see me, gave me a
large sum of money to furnish it, and settled an annuity
of £50 a-year upon me, which I have constantly
received ever since.   Judge, then, Mr Jones, in what
regard I must hold a benefactor, to whom I owe the
preservation of my life, and of those dear children, for
whose sake alone my life is valuable.   Do not, therefore, think me impertinent, Mr Jones (since I must
esteem one for whom I know Mr Allworthy hath so
much value), if I beg you not to converse with these
wicked women.   You are a young gentleman, and do

not know half their artful wiles. Do not be angry with me, sir, for what I said upon account of my house; you must be sensible it would be the ruin of my poor dear girls. Besides, sir, you cannot but be acquainted that Mr Allworthy himself would never forgive my conniving at such matters, and particularly with you."

"Upon my word, madam," said Jones, "you need make no farther apology; nor do I in the least take anything ill you have said; but give me leave, as no one can have more value than myself for Mr Allworthy, to deliver you from one mistake, which, perhaps, would not be altogether for his honour; I do assure you, I am no relation of his."

"Alas! sir," answered she, "I know you are not, I know very well who you are; for Mr Allworthy hath told me all; but I do assure you, had you been twenty times his son, he could not have expressed more regard for you than he hath often expressed in my presence. You need not be ashamed, sir, of what you are; I promise you no good person will esteem you the less on that account. No, Mr Jones, the words 'dishonourable birth' are nonsense, as my dear, dear husband used to say, unless the word 'dishonourable' be applied to the parents; for the children can derive no real dishonour from an act of which they are intirely innocent."

Here Jones heaved a deep sigh, and then said, "Since I perceive, madam, you really do know me, and Mr Allworthy hath thought proper to mention my name to you; and since you have been so explicit with me as to your own affairs, I will acquaint you with some more circumstances concerning myself." And these Mrs Miller having expressed great desire and curiosity to hear, he began and related to her his whole history, without once mentioning the name of Sophia.

There is a kind of sympathy in honest minds, by means of which they give an easy credit to each other. Mrs Miller believed all which Jones told her to be true, and exprest much pity and concern for him. She was beginning to comment on the story, but Jones interrupted her; for, as the hour of assignation now drew nigh, he began to stipulate for a second interview with the lady that evening, which he promised should be the last at her house; swearing, at the same time, that she was one of great distinction, and that nothing but what was intirely innocent was to pass between them; and I do firmly believe he intended to keep his word.

Mrs Miller was at length prevailed on, and Jones departed to his chamber, where he sat alone till twelve o'clock, but no Lady Bellaston appeared.

As we have said that this lady had a great affection for Jones, and as it must have appeared that she really had so, the reader may perhaps wonder at the first failure of her appointment, as she apprehended him to be confined by sickness, a season when friendship seems most to require such visits. This behaviour, therefore, in the lady, may, by some, be condemned as unnatural; but that is not our fault; for our business is only to record truth.

Chapter vi.

Containing a scene which we doubt not will affect all our readers.

MR JONES closed not his eyes during all the former part of the night; not owing to any uneasiness which he conceived at being disappointed by Lady Bellaston; nor was Sophia herself, though most of his waking hours were justly to be charged to her account, the present cause of dispelling his slumbers. In fact, poor Jones was one of the best-natured fellows alive, and had all that weakness which is called compassion, and which distinguishes this imperfect character from that noble firmness of mind, which rolls a man, as it were, within himself, and like a polished bowl, enables him to run through the world without being once stopped by the calamities which happen to others. He could not help, therefore, compassionating the situation of poor Nancy, whose love for Mr Nightingale seemed to him so apparent, that he was astonished at the blindness of her mother, who had more than once, the preceding evening, remarked to him the great change in the temper of her daughter, " who from being," she said, " one of the liveliest, merriest girls in the world, was, on a sudden, become all gloom and melancholy."

Sleep, however, at length got the better of all resistance ; and now, as if he had already been a deity, as the antients imagined, and an offended one too, he seemed to enjoy his dear-bought conquest.—To speak simply, and without any metaphor, Mr Jones slept till eleven the next morning, and would, perhaps, have continued in the same quiet situation much longer, had not a violent uproar awakened him.

Partridge was now summoned, who, being asked what was the matter, answered, " That there was a dreadful hurricane below-stairs ; that Miss Nancy was in fits ; and that the other sister, and the mother, were both crying and lamenting over her." Jones expressed much concern at this news ; which Partridge endeavoured to relieve, by saying, with a smile, " he fancied the young lady was in no danger of death ; for that Susan " (which was the name of the maid) " had given him to understand, it was nothing more than a common affair. In short," said he, " Miss Nancy hath had a mind to be as wise as her mother ; that's all ; she was a little hungry, it seems, and so sat down to dinner before grace was said ; and so there is a child coming for the Foundling Hospital."—— " Prithee, leave thy stupid jesting," cries Jones. " Is the misery of these poor wretches a subject of mirth ? Go immediately to Mrs Miller, and tell her I beg leave—Stay, you will make some blunder ; I will go myself ; for she desired me to breakfast with her." He then rose and dressed himself as fast as he could ; and while he was dressing, Partridge, notwithstanding many severe rebukes, could not avoid throwing forth certain pieces of brutality, commonly called jests, on this occasion. Jones was no sooner dressed than he walked downstairs, and knocking at the door, was presently admitted by the maid, into the outward parlour, which was as empty of company as it was of any apparatus for eating. Mrs Miller was in the inner room with her daughter, whence the maid presently brought a message to Mr Jones, " That her mistress hoped he would excuse the disappointment, but an accident had happened, which made it impossible for her to have the pleasure of his company at breakfast that day ; and begged his pardon for not sending him up notice sooner." Jones desired, " She would give herself no trouble about anything so trifling as his disappointment ; that he was heartily sorry for the occasion ; and that if he could be of any service to her, she might command him."

He had scarce spoke these words, when Mrs Miller, who heard them all, suddenly threw open the door, and coming out to him, in a flood of tears, said, " O Mr Jones ! you are certainly one of the best young men alive. I give you a thousand thanks for your kind offer of your service ; but, alas ! sir, it is out of your power to preserve my poor girl.—O my child! my child! she is undone, she is ruined for ever!" "I hope, madam," said Jones, "no villain"——"O Mr Jones!" said she, "that villain who yesterday left my lodgings, hath betrayed my poor girl; hath destroyed her.—I know you are a man of honour. You have a good—a noble heart, Mr Jones. The actions to which I have been myself a witness, could proceed from no other. I will tell you all: nay, indeed, it is impossible, after what hath happened, to keep it a secret. That Nightingale, that barbarous villain, hath undone my daughter. She is—she is—oh! Mr Jones, my girl is with child by him; and in that condition he hath deserted her. Here! here, sir, is his cruel letter: read it, Mr Jones, and tell me if such another monster lives."

The letter was as follows:

"DEAR NANCY,

"As I found it impossible to mention to you what, I am afraid, will be no less shocking to you, than it is to me, I have taken this method to inform you, that my father insists upon my immediately paying my addresses to a young lady of fortune, whom he hath provided for my—I need not write the detested word. Your own good understanding will make you sensible, how entirely I am obliged to an obedience, by which I shall be for ever excluded from your dear arms. The fondness of your mother may encourage you to trust her with the unhappy consequence of our love, which may be easily kept a secret from the world, and for which I will take care to provide, as I will for you. I wish you may feel less on this account than I have suffered; but summon all your fortitude to your assistance, and forgive and forget the man, whom nothing but the prospect of certain ruin could have forced to write this letter. I bid you forget me, I mean only as a lover; but the best of friends you shall ever find in your faithful, though unhappy,

"J. N."

When Jones had read this letter, they both stood silent during a minute, looking at each other; at last he began thus: "I cannot express, madam, how much I am shocked at what I have read; yet let me beg you, in one particular, to take the writer's advice. Consider the reputation of your daughter."——"It is gone, it is lost, Mr Jones," cryed she, "as well as her innocence. She received the letter in a room full of company, and immediately swooning away upon opening it, the contents were known to every one present. But the loss of her reputation, bad as it is, is not the worst; I shall lose my child; she hath attempted twice to destroy herself already; and though she hath been hitherto prevented, vows she will not outlive it; nor could I myself outlive any accident of that nature.—— What then will become of my little Betsy, a helpless infant orphan? and the poor little wretch will, I believe, break her heart at the miseries with which she sees her sister and myself distracted, while she is ignorant of the cause. O 'tis the most sensible, and best-natured little thing! The barbarous, cruel—— hath destroyed us all. O my poor children! Is this the reward of all my cares? Is this the fruit of all my prospects? Have I so chearfully undergone all the labours and duties of a mother? Have I been so tender of their infancy, so careful of their education? Have I been toiling so many years, denying myself even the conveniences of life, to provide some little sustenance for them, to lose one or both in such a manner?" "Indeed, madam," said Jones, with tears in his eyes, "I pity you from my soul."——"O! Mr

Jones," answered she, "even you, though I know the goodness of your heart, can have no idea of what I feel. The best, the kindest, the most dutiful of children! O my poor Nancy, the darling of my soul! the delight of my eyes! the pride of my heart! too much, indeed, my pride; for to those foolish, ambitious hopes, arising from her beauty, I owe her ruin. Alas! I saw with pleasure the liking which this young man had for her. I thought it an honourable affection; and flattered my foolish vanity with the thoughts of seeing her married to one so much her superior. And a thousand times in my presence, nay, often in yours, he hath endeavoured to soothe and encourage these hopes by the most generous expressions of disinterested love, which he hath always directed to my poor girl, and which I, as well as she, believed to be real. Could I have believed that these were only snares laid to betray the innocence of my child, and for the ruin of us all?"—At these words little Betsy came running into the room, crying, "Dear mamma, for heaven's sake come to my sister; for she is in another fit, and my cousin can't hold her." Mrs Miller immediately obeyed the summons; but first ordered Betsy to stay with Mr Jones, and begged him to entertain her a few minutes, saying, in the most pathetic voice, "Good heaven! let me preserve one of my children at least."

Jones, in compliance with this request, did all he could to comfort the little girl, though he was, in reality, himself very highly affected with Mrs Miller's story. He told her "Her sister would be soon very well again; that by taking on in that manner she would not only make her sister worse, but make her mother ill too." "Indeed, sir," says she, "I would not do anything to hurt them for the world. I would burst my heart rather than they should see me cry.—But

.my poor sister can't see me cry.——I am afraid she will
never be able to see me cry any more. Indeed, I
can't part with her; indeed, I can't.——And then poor
mamma too, what will become of her?——She says she
will die too, and leave me: but I am resolved I won't
be left behind." "And are you not afraid to die,
my little Betsy?" said Jones. "Yes," answered she,
"I was always afraid to die; because I must have left
my mamma, and my sister; but I am not afraid of
going anywhere with those I love."

Jones was so pleased with this answer, that he
eagerly kissed the child; and soon after Mrs Miller
returned, saying, "She thanked heaven Nancy was now
come to herself. And now, Betsy," says she, "you
may go in, for your sister is better, and longs to see
you." She then turned to Jones, and began to
renew her apologies for having disappointed him of his
breakfast.

"I hope, madam," said Jones, "I shall have a
more exquisite repast than any you could have provided for me. This, I assure you, will be the case,
if I can do any service to this little family of love.
But whatever success may attend my endeavours, I
am resolved to attempt it. I am very much deceived
in Mr Nightingale, if, notwithstanding what hath happened, he hath not much goodness of heart at the
bottom, as well as a very violent affection for your
daughter. If this be the case, I think the picture
which I shall lay before him will affect him. Endeavour, madam, to comfort yourself, and Miss Nancy,
as well as you can. I will go instantly in quest of
Mr Nightingale; and I hope to bring you good
news."

Mrs Miller fell upon her knees and invoked all the
blessings of heaven upon Mr Jones; to which she
afterwards added the most passionate expressions of

gratitude. He then departed to find Mr Nightingale, and the good woman returned to comfort her daughter, who was somewhat cheared at what her mother told her; and both joined in resounding the praises of Mr Jones.

Chapter vij.

The interview between Mr Jones and Mr Nightingale.

THE good or evil we confer on others very often, I believe, recoils on ourselves. For as men of a benign disposition enjoy their own acts of beneficence equally with those to whom they are done, so there are scarce any natures so entirely diabolical, as to be capable of doing injuries, without paying themselves some pangs for the ruin which they bring on their fellow-creatures.

Mr Nightingale, at least, was not such a person. On the contrary, Jones found him in his new lodgings, sitting melancholy by the fire, and silently lamenting the unhappy situation in which he had placed poor Nancy. He no sooner saw his friend appear than he arose hastily to meet him; and after much congratulation said, "Nothing could be more opportune than this kind visit; for I was never more in the spleen in my life."

"I am sorry," answered Jones, "that I bring news very unlikely to relieve you: nay, what I am convinced must, of all other, shock you the most. However, it is necessary you should know it. Without further preface, then, I come to you, Mr Nightingale, from a worthy family, which you have involved in misery and ruin." Mr Nightingale changed colour at these words; but Jones, without regarding it, proceeded, in the liveliest manner, to paint the tragical story with which the reader was acquainted in the last chapter.

Nightingale never once interrupted the narration, though he discovered violent emotions at many parts of it. But when it was concluded, after fetching a deep sigh, he said, " What you tell me, my friend, affects me in the tenderest manner. Sure there never was so cursed an accident as the poor girl's betraying my letter. Her reputation might otherwise have been safe, and the affair might have remained a profound secret; and then the girl might have gone off never the worse; for many such things happen in this town: and if the husband should suspect a little, when it is too late, it will be his wiser conduct to conceal his suspicion both from his wife and the world."

" Indeed, my friend," answered Jones, " this could not have been the case with your poor Nancy. You have so entirely gained her affections, that it is the loss of you, and not of her reputation, which afflicts her, and will end in the destruction of her and her family." " Nay, for that matter, I promise you," cries Nightingale, " she hath my affections so absolutely, that my wife, whoever she is to be, will have very little share in them." " And is it possible then," said Jones, " you can think of deserting her?" " Why, what can I do?" answered the other. " Ask Miss Nancy," replied Jones warmly. " In the condition to which you have reduced her, I sincerely think she ought to determine what reparation you shall make her. Her interest alone, and not yours, ought to be your sole consideration. But if you ask me what you shall do, what can you do less," cries Jones, " than fulfil the expectations of her family, and her own? Nay, I sincerely tell you, they were mine too, ever since I first saw you together. You will pardon me if I presume on the friendship you have favoured me with, moved as I am with compassion for those poor creatures. But your own heart will best suggest to you, whether you have never intended, by your conduct, to persuade the mother, as well as the daughter, into an opinion, that you designed honourably : and if so, though there may have been no direct promise of marriage in the case, I will leave to your own good understanding, how far you are bound to proceed."

"Nay, I must not only confess what you have hinted," said Nightingale ; "but I am afraid even that very promise you mention I have given." "And can you, after owning that," said Jones, "hesitate a moment ?" "Consider, my friend," answered the other ; "I know you are a man of honour, and would advise no one to act contrary to its rules ; if there were no other objection, can I, after this publication of her disgrace, think of such an alliance with honour?" "Undoubtedly," replied Jones, "and the very best and truest honour, which is goodness, requires it of you. As you mention a scruple of this kind, you will give me leave to examine it. Can you with honour be guilty of having under false pretences deceived a young woman and her family, and of having by these means treacherously robbed her of her innocence ? Can you, with honour, be the knowing, the wilful occasion, nay, the artful contriver of the ruin of a human being ? Can you, with honour, destroy the fame, the peace, nay, probably, both the life and soul too, of this creature ? Can honour bear the thought, that this creature is a tender, helpless, defenceless, young woman ? A young woman, who loves, who doats on you, who dies for you ; who hath placed the utmost confidence in your promises ; and to that confidence hath sacrificed everything which is dear to her ? Can honour support such contemplations as these a moment ? "

"Common sense, indeed," said Nightingale, "warrants all you say; but yet you well know the opinion of the world is so contrary to it, that, was I to marry a whore, though my own, I should be ashamed of ever showing my face again."

"Fie upon it, Mr Nightingale!" said Jones, "do not call her by so ungenerous a name: when you promised to marry her she became your wife; and she hath sinned more against prudence than virtue. And what is this world which you would be ashamed to face but the vile, the foolish, and the profligate? Forgive me if I say such a shame must proceed from false modesty, which always attends false honour as its shadow.——But I am well assured there is not a man of real sense and goodness in the world who would not honour and applaud the action. But, admit no other would, would not your own heart, my friend, applaud it? And do not the warm, rapturous sensations, which we feel from the consciousness of an honest, noble, generous, benevolent action, convey more delight to the mind than the undeserved praise of millions? Set the alternative fairly before your eyes. On the one side, see this poor, unhappy, tender, believing girl, in the arms of her wretched mother, breathing her last. Hear her breaking heart in agonies, sighing out your name; and lamenting, rather than accusing, the cruelty which weighs her down to destruction. Paint to your imagination the circumstances of her fond despairing parent, driven to madness, or, perhaps, to death, by the loss of her lovely daughter. View the poor, helpless, orphan infant; and when your mind hath dwelt a moment only on such ideas, consider yourself as the cause of all the ruin of this poor, little, worthy, defenceless family. On the other side, consider yourself as relieving them from their temporary sufferings. Think with what joy, with what transports that lovely creature will fly to your arms. See her blood returning to her pale cheeks, her fire to her languid eyes, and raptures to her tortured breast. Consider the exultations of her mother, the happiness of all. Think of this little family made by one act of yours completely happy. Think of this alternative, and sure I am mistaken in my friend if it requires any long deliberation whether he will sink these wretches down for ever, or, by one generous, noble resolution, raise them all from the brink of misery and despair to the highest pitch of human happiness. Add to this but one consideration more; the consideration that it is your duty so to do—That the misery from which you will relieve these poor people is the misery which you yourself have wilfully brought upon them."

"O, my dear friend!" cries Nightingale, "I wanted not your eloquence to rouse me. I pity poor Nancy from my soul, and would willingly give anything in my power that no familiarities had ever passed between us. Nay, believe me, I had many struggles with my passion before I could prevail with myself to write that cruel letter, which hath caused all the misery in that unhappy family. If I had no inclinations to consult but my own, I would marry her to-morrow morning: I would, by heaven! but you will easily imagine how impossible it would be to prevail on my father to consent to such a match; besides, he hath provided another for me; and to-morrow, by his express command, I am to wait on the lady."

"I have not the honour to know your father," said Jones; "but, suppose he could be persuaded, would you yourself consent to the only means of preserving these poor people?" "As eagerly as I would pursue my happiness," answered Nightingale: "for I never shall find it in any other woman.—O, my dear friend! could you imagine what I have felt within these twelve hours for my poor girl, I am convinced she would not engross all your pity. Passion leads me only to her; and, if I had any foolish scruples of honour, you have fully satisfied them: could my father be induced to comply with my desires, nothing would be wanting to compleat my own happiness or that of my Nancy."

"Then I am resolved to undertake it," said Jones. "You must not be angry with me, in whatever light it may be necessary to set this affair, which, you may depend on it, could not otherwise be long hid from him: for things of this nature make a quick progress when once they get abroad, as this unhappily hath already. Besides, should any fatal accident follow, as upon my soul I am afraid will, unless immediately prevented, the public would ring of your name in a manner which, if your father hath common humanity, must offend him. If you will therefore tell me where I may find the old gentleman, I will not lose a moment in the business; which, while I pursue, you cannot do a more generous action than by paying a visit to the poor girl. You will find I have not exaggerated in the account I have given of the wretchedness of the family."

Nightingale immediately consented to the proposal; and now, having acquainted Jones with his father's lodging, and the coffee-house where he would most probably find him, he hesitated a moment, and then said, "My dear Tom, you are going to undertake an impossibility. If you knew my father you would never think of obtaining his consent.——Stay, there is one way——suppose you told him I was already married, it might be easier to reconcile him to the fact after it was done; and, upon my honour, I am so affected with what you have said, and I love my Nancy so passionately, I almost wish it was done, whatever might be the consequence."

Jones greatly approved the hint, and promised to pursue it. They then separated, Nightingale to visit his Nancy, and Jones in quest of the old gentleman.

<hr />

Chapter viii.

What passed between Jones and old Mr Nightingale ; with the arrival of a person not yet mentioned in this history.

NOTWITHSTANDING the sentiment of the Roman satirist, which denies the divinity of fortune, and the opinion of Seneca to the same purpose ; Cicero, who was, I believe, a wiser man than either of them, expressly holds the contrary ; and certain it is, there are some incidents in life so very strange and unaccountable, that it seems to require more than human skill and foresight in producing them.

Of this kind was what now happened to Jones, who found Mr Nightingale the elder in so critical a minute, that Fortune, if she was really worthy all the worship she received at Rome, could not have contrived such another. In short, the old gentleman, and the father of the young lady whom he intended for his son, had been hard at it for many hours ; and the latter was just now gone, and had left the former delighted with the thoughts that he had succeeded in a long contention, which had been between the two fathers of the future bride and bridegroom ; in which both endeavoured to overreach the other, and, as it not rarely happens in such cases, both had retreated fully satisfied of having obtained the victory.

This gentleman, whom Mr Jones now visited, was what they call a man of the world ; that is to say, a man who directs his conduct in this world as one who, being fully persuaded there is no other, is resolved to make the most of this. In his early years he had been bred to trade ; but, having acquired a very good fortune, he had lately declined his business ; or, to speak more properly, had changed it from dealing in goods, to dealing only in money, of which he had always a plentiful fund at command, and of which he knew very well how to make a very plentiful advantage, sometimes of the necessities of private men, and sometimes of those of the public. He had indeed conversed so entirely with money, that it may be almost doubted whether he imagined there was any other thing really existing in the world ; this at least may be certainly averred, that he firmly believed nothing else to have any real value.

The reader will, I fancy, allow that Fortune could not have culled out a more improper person for Mr Jones to attack with any probability of success ; nor could the whimsical lady have directed this attack at a more unseasonable time.

As money then was always uppermost in this gentleman's thoughts, so the moment he saw a stranger within his doors it immediately occurred to his imagination, that such stranger was either come to bring him money, or to fetch it from him. And according as one or other of these thoughts prevailed, he conceived a favourable or unfavourable idea of the person who approached him.

Unluckily for Jones, the latter of these was the ascendant at present ; for as a young gentleman had visited him the day before, with a bill from his son for a play debt, he apprehended, at the first sight of Jones, that he was come on such another errand. Jones therefore had no sooner told him that he was come on his son's account than the old gentleman, being confirmed in his suspicion, burst forth into an exclamation,

"That he would lose his labour." "Is it then possible, sir," answered Jones, "that you can guess my business?" "If I do guess it," replied the other, "I repeat again to you, you will lose your labour. What, I suppose you are one of those sparks who lead my son into all those scenes of riot and debauchery, which will be his destruction? but I shall pay no more of his bills, I promise you. I expect he will quit all such company for the future. If I had imagined otherwise, I should not have provided a wife for him; for I would be instrumental in the ruin of nobody." "How, sir," said Jones, "and was this lady of your providing?" "Pray, sir," answered the old gentleman, "how comes it to be any concern of yours?"—"Nay, dear sir," replied Jones, "be not offended that I interest myself in what regards your son's happiness, for whom I have so great an honour and value. It was upon that very account I came to wait upon you. I can't express the satisfaction you have given me by what you say; for I do assure you your son is a person for whom I have the highest honour.—Nay, sir, it is not easy to express the esteem I have for you; who could be so generous, so good, so kind, so indulgent to provide such a match for your son; a woman, who, I dare swear, will make him one of the happiest men upon earth."

There is scarce anything which so happily introduces men to our good liking, as having conceived some alarm at their first appearance; when once those apprehensions begin to vanish we soon forget the fears which they occasioned, and look on ourselves as indebted for our present ease to those very persons who at first raised our fears.

Thus it happened to Nightingale, who no sooner found that Jones had no demand on him, as he suspected, than he began to be pleased with his presence.

"Pray, good sir," said he, "be pleased to sit down.
I do not remember to have ever had the pleasure of
seeing you before; but if you are a friend of my son,
and have anything to say concerning this young lady, I
shall be glad to hear you. As to her making him
happy, it will be his own fault if she doth not. I have
discharged my duty, in taking care of the main article.
She will bring him a fortune capable of making any
reasonable, prudent, sober man, happy." "Undoubtedly," cries Jones, "for she is in herself a
fortune; so beautiful, so genteel, so sweet-tempered,
and so well-educated; she is indeed a most accom-
plished young lady; sings admirably well, and hath
a most delicate hand at the harpsichord." "I did
not know any of these matters," answered the old
gentleman, "for I never saw the lady: but I do not
like her the worse for what you tell me; and I am the
better pleased with her father for not laying any stress
on these qualifications in our bargain. I shall always
think it a proof of his understanding. A silly fellow
would have brought in these articles as an addition to
her fortune; but, to give him his due, he never mentioned any such matter; though to be sure they are
no disparagements to a woman." "I do assure you,
sir," cries Jones, "she hath them all in the most
eminent degree: for my part, I own I was afraid you
might have been a little backward, a little less inclined to
the match; for your son told me you had never seen
the lady; therefore I came, sir, in that case, to entreat you, to conjure you, as you value the happiness of
your son, not to be averse to his match with a woman
who hath not only all the good qualities I have mentioned, but many more."——"If that was your business,
sir," said the old gentleman, "we are both obliged to
you; and you may be perfectly easy; for I give you
my word I was very well satisfied with her fortune."

"Sir," answered Jones, "I honour you every moment more and more. To be so easily satisfied, so very moderate on that account, is a proof of the soundness of your understanding, as well as the nobleness of your mind."——"Not so very moderate, young gentleman, not so very moderate," answered the father.——"Still more and more noble," replied Jones; "and give me leave to add, sensible: for sure it is little less than madness to consider money as the sole foundation of happiness. Such a woman as this with her little, her nothing of a fortune"——"I find," cries the old gentleman, "you have a pretty just opinion of money, my friend, or else you are better acquainted with the person of the lady than with her circumstances. Why, pray, what fortune do you imagine this lady to have?" "What fortune?" cries Jones, "why, too contemptible a one to be named for your son."——"Well, well, well," said the other, "perhaps he might have done better." ——"That I deny," said Jones, "for she is one of the best of women."——"Ay, ay, but in point of fortune I mean," answered the other. "And yet, as to that now, how much do you imagine your friend is to have?" ——"How much?" cries Jones, "how much? Why, at the utmost, perhaps £200." "Do you mean to banter me, young gentleman?" said the father, a little angry. "No, upon my soul," answered Jones, "I am in earnest: nay, I believe I have gone to the utmost farthing. If I do the lady an injury, I ask her pardon." "Indeed you do," cries the father; "I am certain she hath fifty times that sum, and she shall produce fifty to that before I consent that she shall marry my son." "Nay," said Jones, "it is too late to talk of consent now; if she had not fifty farthings your son is married." ——"My son married!" answered the old gentleman, with surprize. "Nay," said Jones, "I thought you was unacquainted with it." "My son married to Miss

Harris!" answered he again. "To Miss Harris!" said Jones; "no, sir; to Miss Nancy Miller, the daughter of Mrs Miller, at whose house he lodged; a young lady, who, though her mother is reduced to let lodgings—"—"Are you bantering, or are you in earnest?" cries the father, with a most solemn voice. "Indeed, sir," answered Jones, "I scorn the character of a banterer. I came to you in most serious earnest, imagining, as I find true, that your son had never dared acquaint you with a match so much inferior to him in point of fortune, though the reputation of the lady will suffer it no longer to remain a secret."

While the father stood like one struck suddenly dumb at this news, a gentleman came into the room, and saluted him by the name of brother.

But though these two were in consanguinity so nearly related, they were in their dispositions almost the opposites to each other. The brother who now arrived had likewise been bred to trade, in which he no sooner saw himself worth £6000 than he purchased a small estate with the greatest part of it, and retired into the country; where he married the daughter of an unbeneficed clergyman; a young lady, who, though she had neither beauty nor fortune, had recommended herself to his choice entirely by her good humour, of which she possessed a very large share.

With this woman he had, during twenty-five years, lived a life more resembling the model which certain poets ascribe to the golden age, than any of those patterns which are furnished by the present times. By her he had four children, but none of them arrived at maturity, except only one daughter, whom, in vulgar language, he and his wife had spoiled; that is, had educated with the utmost tenderness and fondness, which she returned to such a degree, that she had actually refused a very extraordinary match with a gentleman a little turned of forty, because she could not bring herself to part with her parents.

The young lady whom Mr Nightingale had intended for his son was a near neighbour of his brother, and an acquaintance of his niece; and in reality it was upon the account of his projected match that he was now come to town; not, indeed, to forward, but to dissuade his brother from a purpose which he conceived would inevitably ruin his nephew; for he foresaw no other event from a union with Miss Harris, notwithstanding the largeness of her fortune, as neither her person nor mind seemed to him to promise any kind of matrimonial felicity: for she was very tall, very thin, very ugly, very affected, very silly, and very ill-natured.

His brother, therefore, no sooner mentioned the marriage of his nephew with Miss Miller, than he exprest the utmost satisfaction; and when the father had very bitterly reviled his son, and pronounced sentence of beggary upon him, the uncle began in the following manner:

"If you was a little cooler, brother, I would ask you whether you love your son for his sake or for your own. You would answer, I suppose, and so I suppose you think, for his sake; and doubtless it is his happiness which you intended in the marriage you proposed for him.

"Now, brother, to prescribe rules of happiness to others hath always appeared to me very absurd, and to insist on doing this, very tyrannical. It is a vulgar error, I know; but it is, nevertheless, an error. And if this be absurd in other things, it is mostly so in the affair of marriage, the happiness of which depends entirely on the affection which subsists between the parties.

"I have therefore always thought it unreasonable in parents to desire to chuse for their children on this occasion; since to force affection is an impossible attempt; nay, so much doth love abhor force, that I know not whether, through an unfortunate but uncurable perverseness in our natures, it may not be even impatient of persuasion.

"It is, however, true that, though a parent will not, I think, wisely prescribe, he ought to be consulted on this occasion; and, in strictness, perhaps, should at least have a negative voice. My nephew, therefore, I own, in marrying, without asking your advice, hath been guilty of a fault. But, honestly speaking, brother, have you not a little promoted this fault? Have not your frequent declarations on this subject given him a moral certainty of your refusal, where there was any deficiency in point of fortune? Nay, doth not your present anger arise solely from that deficiency? And if he hath failed in his duty here, did you not as much exceed that authority when you absolutely bargained with him for a woman, without his knowledge, whom you yourself never saw, and whom, if you had seen and known as well as I, it must have been madness in you to have ever thought of bringing her into your family?

"Still I own my nephew in a fault; but surely it is not an unpardonable fault. He hath acted indeed without your consent, in a matter in which he ought to have asked it, but it is in a matter in which his interest is principally concerned; you yourself must and will acknowledge that you consulted his interest only, and if he unfortunately differed from you, and hath been mistaken in his notion of happiness, will you, brother, if you love your son, carry him still wider from the point? Will you increase the ill consequences of his simple choice? Will you endeavour to make an event certain misery to him, which may accidentally prove so? In a word, brother, because he hath put it out of your power to make his circumstances as affluent as you would, will you distress them as much as you can?"

By the force of the true Catholic faith St Anthony won upon the fishes. Orpheus and Amphion went a little farther, and by the charms of music enchanted things merely inanimate. Wonderful, both! but neither history nor fable have ever yet ventured to record an instance of any one, who, by force of argument and reason, hath triumphed over habitual avarice.

Mr Nightingale, the father, instead of attempting to answer his brother, contented himself with only observing, that they had always differed in their sentiments concerning the education of their children. "I wish," said he, "brother, you would have confined your care to your own daughter, and never have troubled yourself with my son, who hath, I believe, as little profited by your precepts, as by your example." For young Nightingale was his uncle's godson, and had lived more with him than with his father. So that the uncle had often declared he loved his nephew almost equally with his own child.

Jones fell into raptures with this good gentleman; and when, after much persuasion, they found the father grew still more and more irritated, instead of appeased, Jones conducted the uncle to his nephew at the house of Mrs Miller.

Chapter ix.

Containing strange matters.

AT his return to his lodgings, Jones found the situation of affairs greatly altered from what they had been in at his departure. The mother, the two daughters, and young Mr Nightingale, were now sat down to supper together, when the uncle was, at his own desire, introduced without any ceremony into the company, to all of whom he was well known; for he had several times visited his nephew at that house.

The old gentleman immediately walked up to Miss Nancy, saluted and wished her joy, as he did afterwards the mother and the other sister; and lastly, he paid the proper compliments to his nephew, with the same good humour and courtesy, as if his nephew had married his equal or superior in fortune, with all the previous requisites first performed.

Miss Nancy and her supposed husband both turned pale, and looked rather foolish than otherwise upon the occasion; but Mrs Miller took the first opportunity of withdrawing; and, having sent for Jones into the dining-room, she threw herself at his feet, and in a most passionate flood of tears, called him her good angel, the preserver of her poor little family, with many other respectful and endearing appellations, and made him every acknowledgment which the highest benefit can extract from the most grateful heart.

After the first gust of her passion was a little over, which she declared, if she had not vented, would have burst her, she proceeded to inform Mr Jones that all matters were settled between Mr Nightingale and her daughter, and that they were to be married the next morning; at which Mr Jones having expressed much pleasure, the poor woman fell again into a fit of joy and thanksgiving, which he at length with difficulty silenced, and prevailed on her to return with him back to the company, whom they found in the same good humour in which they had left them.

This little society now past two or three very agreeable hours together, in which the uncle, who was a very great lover of his bottle, had so well plyed his nephew, that this latter, though not drunk, began to be somewhat flustered; and now Mr Nightingale, taking the old gentleman with him upstairs into the apartment he had lately occupied, unbosomed himself as follows :—

"As you have been always the best and kindest of uncles to me, and as you have shown such unparalleled goodness in forgiving this match, which to be sure may be thought a little improvident, I should never forgive myself if I attempted to deceive you in anything." He then confessed the truth, and opened the whole affair.

"How, Jack?" said the old gentleman, "and are you really then not married to this young woman?" "No, upon my honour," answered Nightingale, "I have told you the simple truth." "My dear boy," cries the uncle, kissing him, "I am heartily glad to hear it. I never was better pleased in my life. If you had been married I should have assisted you as much as was in my power to have made the best of a bad matter; but there is a great difference between considering a thing which is already done and irrecoverable, and that which is yet to do. Let your reason have fair play, Jack, and you will see this match in so foolish and preposterous a light, that there will be no need of any dissuasive arguments." "How, sir?" replies young Nightingale, "is there this difference between having already done an act, and being in honour engaged to do it?" "Pugh!" said the uncle, "honour is a creature of the world's making, and the world hath the power of a creator over it, and may govern and direct it as they please. Now you well know how trivial these breaches of contract are thought; even the grossest make but the wonder and conversation of a day. Is there a man who afterwards will be more backward in giving you his sister, or daughter? or is there any sister or daughter who would be more backward to receive you? Honour is not concerned in these engagements." "Pardon me, dear sir," cries Nightingale, "I can never think so; and not only honour, but conscience and humanity, are concerned. I am well satisfied, that, was I now to disappoint the young creature, her death would be the consequence, and I should look upon myself as her murderer; nay, as her murderer by the cruellest of all methods, by breaking her heart." "Break her heart, indeed! no, no, Jack," cries the uncle, "the hearts of women are not so soon broke; they are tough, boy, they are tough." "But, sir," answered Nightingale, "my own affections are engaged, and I never could be happy with any other woman. How often have I heard you say, that children should be always suffered to chuse for themselves, and that you would let my cousin Harriet do so?" "Why, ay," replied the old gentleman, "so I would have them; but then I would have them chuse wisely.—Indeed, Jack, you must and shall leave the girl."——"Indeed, uncle," cries the other, "I must and will have her." "You will, young gentleman;" said the uncle; "I did not expect such a word from you. I should not wonder if you had used such language to your father, who hath always treated you like a dog, and kept you at the distance which a tyrant preserves over his subjects; but I, who have lived with you upon an equal footing, might surely expect better usage: but I know how to account for it all: it is all owing to your preposterous education, in which I have had too little share. There is my daughter, now, whom I have brought up as my friend, never doth anything without my advice, nor ever refuses to take it when I give it her." "You have never yet given her advice in an affair of this kind," said Nightingale; "for I am greatly mistaken in my cousin, if she would be very ready to obey even your

most positive commands in abandoning her inclinations."
"Don't abuse my girl," answered the old gentleman
with some emotion; "don't abuse my Harriet. I
have brought her up to have no inclinations contrary to
my own. By suffering her to do whatever she pleases,
I have enured her to a habit of being pleased to do
whatever I like." "Pardon, me, sir," said Nightingale, "I have not the least design to reflect on my
cousin, for whom I have the greatest esteem; and
indeed I am convinced you will never put her to so
severe a tryal, or lay such hard commands on her as
you would do on me.—But, dear sir, let us return to
the company; for they will begin to be uneasy at our
long absence. I must beg one favour of my dear uncle,
which is that he would not say anything to shock the
poor girl or her mother." "Oh! you need not fear
me," answered he, "I understand myself too well to
affront women; so I will readily grant you that favour;
and in return I must expect another of you." "There
are but few of your commands, sir," said Nightingale,
"which I shall not very chearfully obey." "Nay,
sir, I ask nothing," said the uncle, "but the honour of
your company home to my lodging, that I may reason
the case a little more fully with you; for I would, if
possible, have the satisfaction of preserving my family,
notwithstanding the headstrong folly of my brother,
who, in his own opinion, is the wisest man in the
world."

Nightingale, who well knew his uncle to be as headstrong as his father, submitted to attend him home, and
then they both returned back into the room, where the
old gentleman promised to carry himself with the same
decorum which he had before maintained.

Chapter x.

A short chapter, which concludes the book.

THE long absence of the uncle and nephew had
occasioned some disquiet in the minds of all
whom they had left behind them; and the
more, as, during the preceding dialogue, the uncle had
more than once elevated his voice, so as to be heard
downstairs; which, though they could not distinguish
what he said, had caused some evil foreboding in Nancy
and her mother, and, indeed, even in Jones himself.

When the good company, therefore, again assembled,
there was a visible alteration in all their faces; and the
good-humour which, at their last meeting, universally
shone forth in every countenance, was now changed
into a much less agreeable aspect. It was a change,
indeed, common enough to the weather in this climate,
from sunshine to clouds, from June to December.

This alteration was not, however, greatly remarked
by any present; for as they were all now endeavouring
to conceal their own thoughts, and to act a part, they
became all too busily engaged in the scene to be spectators of it. Thus neither the uncle nor nephew saw
any symptoms of suspicion in the mother or daughter;
nor did the mother or daughter remark the overacted
complacence of the old man, nor the counterfeit satisfaction which grinned in the features of the young one.

Something like this, I believe, frequently happens,
where the whole attention of two friends being engaged
in the part which each is to act, in order to impose on
the other, neither sees nor suspects the arts practised
against himself; and thus the thrust of both (to borrow
no improper metaphor on the occasion) alike takes
place.

From the same reason it is no unusual thing for both

II.   L

parties to be overreached in a bargain, though the one must be always the greater loser; as was he who sold a blind horse, and received a bad note in payment.

Our company in about half an hour broke up, and the uncle carried off his nephew; but not before the latter had assured Miss Nancy, in a whisper, that he would attend her early in the morning, and fulfil all his engagements.

Jones, who was the least concerned in this scene, saw the most. He did indeed suspect the very fact; for, besides observing the great alteration in the behaviour of the uncle, the distance he assumed, and his overstrained civility to Miss Nancy; the carrying off a bridegroom from his bride at that time of night was so extraordinary a proceeding that it could be accounted for only by imagining that young Nightingale had revealed the whole truth, which the apparent openness of his temper, and his being flustered with liquor, made too probable.

While he was reasoning with himself, whether he should acquaint these poor people with his suspicion, the maid of the house informed him that a gentlewoman desired to speak with him.——He went immediately out, and, taking the candle from the maid, ushered his visitant upstairs, who, in the person of Mrs Honour, acquainted him with such dreadful news concerning his Sophia, that he immediately lost all consideration for every other person; and his whole stock of compassion was entirely swallowed up in reflections on his own misery, and on that of his unfortunate angel.

What this dreadful matter was, the reader will be informed, after we have first related the many preceding steps which produced it, and those will be the subject of the following book.

BOOK XV.

IN WHICH THE HISTORY ADVANCES ABOUT TWO DAYS.

Chapter i.

Too short to need a preface.

THERE are a set of religious, or rather moral writers, who teach that virtue is the certain road to happiness, and vice to misery, in this world. A very wholesome and comfortable doctrine, and to which we have but one objection, namely, that it is not true.

Indeed, if by virtue these writers mean the exercise of those cardinal virtues, which like good housewives stay at home, and mind only the business of their own family, I shall very readily concede the point; for so surely do all these contribute and lead to happiness, that I could almost wish, in violation of all the antient and modern sages, to call them rather by the name of wisdom, than by that of virtue; for, with regard to this life, no system, I conceive, was ever wiser than that of the antient Epicureans, who held this wisdom to constitute the chief good; nor foolisher than that of their opposites, those modern epicures, who place all felicity in the abundant gratification of every sensual appetite.

But if by virtue is meant (as I almost think it ought) a certain relative quality, which is always busying itself without-doors, and seems as much interested in pursuing the good of others as its own; I cannot so easily agree that this is the surest way to human happiness; because I am afraid we must then include poverty and contempt, with all the mischiefs which backbiting, envy, and ingratitude, can bring on mankind, in our idea of happiness; nay, sometimes perhaps we shall be obliged to wait upon the said happiness to a jail; since many by the above virtue have brought themselves thither.

I have not now leisure to enter upon so large a field of speculation, as here seems opening upon me; my design was to wipe off a doctrine that lay in my way; since, while Mr Jones was acting the most virtuous part imaginable in labouring to preserve his fellow-creatures from destruction, the devil, or some other evil spirit, one perhaps cloathed in human flesh, was hard at work to make him completely miserable in the ruin of his Sophia.

This therefore would seem an exception to the above rule, if indeed it was a rule; but as we have in our voyage through life seen so many other exceptions to it, we chuse to dispute the doctrine on which it is founded, which we don't apprehend to be Christian, which we are convinced is not true, and which is indeed destructive of one of the noblest arguments that reason alone can furnish for the belief of immortality.

But as the reader's curiosity (if he hath any) must be now awake, and hungry, we shall provide to feed it as fast as we can.

Chapter ij.

In which is opened a very black design against Sophia.

I REMEMBER a wise old gentleman who used to say, "When children are doing nothing, they are doing mischief." I will not enlarge this quaint saying to the most beautiful part of the creation in general; but so far I may be allowed, that when the effects of female jealousy do not appear openly in their proper colours of rage and fury, we may suspect that mischievous passion to be at work privately, and attempting to undermine, what it doth not attack above-ground.

This was exemplified in the conduct of Lady Bellaston, who, under all the smiles which she wore in her countenance, concealed much indignation against Sophia; and as she plainly saw that this young lady stood between her and the full indulgence of her desires, she resolved to get rid of her by some means or other; nor was it long before a very favourable opportunity of accomplishing this presented itself to her.

The reader may be pleased to remember, that when Sophia was thrown into that consternation at the playhouse, by the wit and humour of a set of young gentlemen who call themselves the town, we informed him, that she had put herself under the protection of a young nobleman, who had very safely conducted her to her chair.

This nobleman, who frequently visited Lady Bellaston, had more than once seen Sophia there, since her arrival in town, and had conceived a very great liking to her; which liking, as beauty never looks more amiable than in distress, Sophia had in this fright so encreased, that he might now, without any great impropriety, be said to be actually in love with her.

It may easily be believed, that he would not suffer so handsome an occasion of improving his acquaintance with the beloved object as now offered itself to elapse, when even good breeding alone might have prompted him to pay her a visit.

The next morning therefore, after this accident, he waited on Sophia, with the usual compliments, and hopes that she had received no harm from her last night's adventure.

As love, like fire, when once thoroughly kindled, is soon blown into a flame, Sophia in a very short time compleated her conquest. Time now flew away unperceived, and the noble lord had been two hours in company with the lady, before it entered into his head that he had made too long a visit. Though this circumstance alone would have alarmed Sophia, who was somewhat more a mistress of computation at present; she had indeed much more pregnant evidence from the eyes of her lover of what past within his bosom; nay, though he did not make any open declaration of his passion, yet many of his expressions were rather too warm, and too tender, to have been imputed to complacence, even in the age when such complacence was in fashion; the very reverse of which is well known to be the reigning mode at present.

Lady Bellaston had been apprized of his lordship's visit at his first arrival; and the length of it very well satisfied her, that things went as she wished, and as indeed she had suspected the second time she saw this young couple together. This business, she rightly I think concluded, that she should by no means forward by mixing in the company while they were together; she therefore ordered her servants, that when my lord was going, they should tell him she desired to speak with him; and employed the intermediate time in meditating how best to accomplish a scheme, which she made no doubt but his lordship would very readily embrace the execution of.

Lord Fellamar (for that was the title of this young nobleman) was no sooner introduced to her ladyship, than she attacked him in the following strain : " Bless me, my lord, are you here yet ? I thought my servants had made a mistake, and let you go away ; and I wanted to see you about an affair of some importance."———" Indeed, Lady Bellaston," said he, " I don't wonder you are astonished at the length of my visit; for I have staid above two hours, and I did not think I had staid above half-a-one."———" What am I to conclude from thence, my lord ? " said she. " The company must be very agreeable which can make time slide away so very deceitfully."———" Upon my honour," said he, " the most agreeable I ever saw. Pray tell me, Lady Bellaston, who is this blazing star which you have produced among us all of a sudden ? "———" What blazing star, my lord ? " said she, affecting a surprize. " I mean," said he, " the lady I saw here the other day, whom I had last night in my arms at the play-house, and to whom I have been making that un-reasonable visit."———" O, my cousin Western ! " said she ; " why, that blazing star, my lord, is the daughter of a country booby squire, and hath been in town about a fortnight, for the first time."——— " Upon my soul," said he, " I should swear she had been bred up in a court; for besides her beauty, I never saw anything so genteel, so sensible, so polite." ———" O brave ! " cries the lady, " my cousin hath you, I find."———" Upon my honour," answered he, " I wish she had ; for I am in love with her to distraction."———" Nay, my lord," said she, " it is not wishing yourself very ill neither, for she is a very great fortune : I assure you she is an only child, and her father's estate is a good £3000 a-year." " Then

I can assure you, madam," answered the lord, "I think her the best match in England." "Indeed, my lord," replied she, "if you like her, I heartily wish you had her." "If you think so kindly of me, madam," said he, "as she is a relation of yours, will you do me the honour to propose it to her father?" "And are you really then in earnest?" cries the lady, with an affected gravity. "I hope, madam," answered he, "you have a better opinion of me, than to imagine I would jest with your ladyship in an affair of this kind." "Indeed, then," said the lady, "I will most readily propose your lordship to her father; and I can, I believe, assure you of his joyful acceptance of the proposal; but there is a bar, which I am almost ashamed to mention; and yet it is one you will never be able to conquer. You have a rival, my lord, and a rival who, though I blush to name him, neither you, nor all the world, will ever be able to conquer." "Upon my word, Lady Bellaston," cries he, "you have struck a damp to my heart, which hath almost deprived me of being." "Fie, my lord," said she, "I should rather hope I had struck fire into you. A lover, and talk of damps in your heart! I rather imagined you would have asked your rival's name, that you might have immediately entered the lists with him." "I promise you, madam," answered he, "there are very few things I would not undertake for your charming cousin; but pray, who is this happy man?"—"Why, he is," said she, "what I am sorry to say most happy men with us are, one of the lowest fellows in the world. He is a beggar, a bastard, a foundling, a fellow in meaner circumstances than one of your lordship's footmen." "And is it possible," cried he, "that a young creature with such perfections should think of bestowing herself so unworthily?" "Alas! my lord," answered she, "consider the country—the bane of all young women is the country. There they learn a set of romantic notions of love, and I know not what folly, which this town and good company can scarce eradicate in a whole winter." "Indeed, madam," replied my lord, "your cousin is of too immense a value to be thrown away; such ruin as this must be prevented." "Alas!" cries she, "my lord, how can it be prevented? The family have already done all in their power; but the girl is, I think, intoxicated, and nothing less than ruin will content her. And to deal more openly with you, I expect every day to hear she is run away with him." "What you tell me, Lady Bellaston," answered his lordship, "affects me most tenderly, and only raises my compassion, instead of lessening my adoration of your cousin. Some means must be found to preserve so inestimable a jewel. Hath your ladyship endeavoured to reason with her?" Here the lady affected a laugh, and cried, "My dear lord, sure you know us better than to talk of reasoning a young woman out of her inclinations? These inestimable jewels are as deaf as the jewels they wear: time, my lord, time is the only medicine to cure their folly; but this is a medicine which I am certain she will not take; nay, I live in hourly horrors on her account. In short, nothing but violent methods will do." "What is to be done?" cries my lord; "what methods are to be taken?—Is there any method upon earth?—Oh! Lady Bellaston! there is nothing which I would not undertake for such a reward."——"I really know not," answered the lady, after a pause; and then pausing again, she cried out—"Upon my soul, I am at my wit's end on this girl's account.—If she can be preserved, something must be done immediately; and, as I say, nothing but violent methods will do. ——If your lordship hath really this attachment to my cousin (and to do her justice, except in this silly inclination, of which she will soon see her folly, she is every way deserving), I think there may be one way, indeed, it is a very disagreeable one, and what I am almost afraid to think of.——It requires a great spirit, I promise you." "I am not conscious, madam," said he, "of any defect there; nor am I, I hope, suspected of any such. It must be an egregious defect indeed, which could make me backward on this occasion." "Nay, my lord," answered she, "I am so far from doubting you, I am much more inclined to doubt my own courage; for I must run a monstrous risque. In short, I must place such a confidence in your honour as a wise woman will scarce ever place in a man on any consideration." In this point likewise my lord very well satisfied her; for his reputation was extremely clear, and common fame did him no more than justice, in speaking well of him. "Well, then," said she, "my lord,——I——I vow, I can't bear the apprehension of it.——No, it must not be.——At least every other method shall be tried. Can you get rid of your engagements, and dine here to-day? Your lordship will have an opportunity of seeing a little more of Miss Western.——I promise you we have no time to lose. Here will be nobody but Lady Betty, and Miss Eagle, and Colonel Hampsted, and Tom Edwards; they will all go soon——and I shall be at home to nobody. Then your lordship may be a little more explicit. Nay, I will contrive some method to convince you of her attachment to this fellow." My lord made proper compliments, accepted the invitation, and then they parted to dress, it being now past three in the morning, or to reckon by the old style, in the afternoon.

Chapter iii.

A further explanation of the foregoing design.

THOUGH the reader may have long since concluded Lady Bellaston to be a member (and no inconsiderable one) of the great world; she was in reality a very considerable member of the little world; by which appellation was distinguished a very worthy and honourable society which not long since flourished in this kingdom.

Among other good principles upon which this society was founded, there was one very remarkable; for, as it was a rule of an honourable club of heroes, who assembled at the close of the late war, that all the members should every day fight once at least; so 'twas in this, that every member should, within the twenty-four hours, tell at least one merry fib, which was to be propagated by all the brethren and sisterhood.

Many idle stories were told about this society, which from a certain quality may be, perhaps not unjustly, supposed to have come from the society themselves. As, that the devil was the president; and that he sat in person in an elbow-chair at the upper end of the table; but, upon very strict enquiry, I find there is not the least truth in any of those tales, and that the assembly consisted in reality of a set of very good sort of people, and the fibs which they propagated were of a harmless kind, and tended only to produce mirth and good humour.

Edwards was likewise a member of this comical society. To him therefore Lady Bellaston applied as a proper instrument for her purpose, and furnished him with a fib, which he was to vent whenever the lady gave him her cue; and this was not to be till the evening, when all the company but Lord Fellamar and himself were gone, and while they were engaged in a rubber at whist.

To this time then, which was between seven and eight in the evening, we will convey our reader; when Lady Bellaston, Lord Fellamar, Miss Western, and Tom, being engaged at whist, and in the last game of their rubbers, Tom received his cue from Lady Bellaston, which was, " I protest, Tom, you are grown intolerable lately ; you used to tell us all the news of the town, and now you know no more of the world than if you lived out of it."

Mr Edwards then began as follows : " The fault is not mine, madam : it lies in the dulness of the age, that doth nothing worth talking of.——O la ! though now I think on't there hath a terrible accident befallen poor Colonel Wilcox.——Poor Ned.——You know him, my lord, everybody knows him ; faith ! I am very much concerned for him."

" What is it, pray ? " says Lady Bellaston.

" Why, he hath killed a man this morning in a duel, that's all."

His lordship, who was not in the secret, asked gravely, whom he had killed ? To which Edwards answered, " A young fellow we none of us know ; a Somersetshire lad just came to town, one Jones his name is ; a near relation of one Mr Allworthy, of whom your lordship I believe hath heard. I saw the lad lie dead in a coffee-house.——Upon my soul, he is one of the finest corpses I ever saw in my life ! "

Sophia, who had just began to deal as Tom had mentioned that a man was killed, stopt her hand, and listened with attention (for all stories of that kind affected her), but no sooner had he arrived at the latter part of the story than she began to deal again ; and having dealt three cards to one, and seven to another, and ten to a third, at last dropt the rest from her hand, and fell back in her chair.

The company behaved as usually on these occasions. The usual disturbance ensued, the usual assistance was summoned, and Sophia at last, as it is usual, returned again to life, and was soon after, at her earnest desire, led to her own apartment; where, at my lord's request, Lady Bellaston acquainted her with the truth, attempted to carry it off as a jest of her own, and comforted her with repeated assurances, that neither his lordship nor Tom, though she had taught him the story, were in the true secret of the affair.

There was no farther evidence necessary to convince Lord Fellamar how justly the case had been represented to him by Lady Bellaston; and now, at her return into the room, a scheme was laid between these two noble persons, which, though it appeared in no very heinous light to his lordship (as he faithfully promised, and faithfully resolved too, to make the lady all the subsequent amends in his power by marriage), yet many of our readers, we doubt not, will see with just detestation.

The next evening at seven was appointed for the fatal purpose, when Lady Bellaston undertook that Sophia should be alone, and his lordship should be introduced to her. The whole family were to be regulated for the purpose, most of the servants despatched out of the house; and for Mrs Honour, who, to prevent suspicion, was to be left with her mistress till his lordship's arrival, Lady Bellaston herself was to engage her in an apartment as distant as possible from the scene of the intended mischief, and out of the hearing of Sophia.

Matters being thus agreed on, his lordship took his leave, and her ladyship retired to rest, highly pleased with a project, of which she had no reason to doubt the success, and which promised so effectually to remove

Sophia from being any further obstruction to her amour
with Jones, by a means of which she should never appear to be guilty, even if the fact appeared to the world ;
but this she made no doubt of preventing by huddling
up a marriage, to which she thought the ravished
Sophia would easily be brought to consent, and at
which all the rest of her family would rejoice.

But affairs were not in so quiet a situation in the
bosom of the other conspirator ; his mind was tost in
all the distracting anxiety so nobly described by
Shakespear—

> " Between the acting of a dreadful thing,
> And the first motion, all the interim is
> Like a phantasma, or a hideous dream ;
> The genius and the mortal instruments
> Are then in council ; and the state of man,
> Like to a little kingdom, suffers then
> The nature of an insurrection."——

Though the violence of his passion had made him
eagerly embrace the first hint of this design, especially
as it came from a relation of the lady, yet when that
friend to reflection, a pillow, had placed the action itself in all its natural black colours before his eyes, with
all the consequences which must, and those which
might probably attend it, his resolution began to abate,
or rather indeed to go over to the other side ; and after
a long conflict, which lasted a whole night, between
honour and appetite, the former at length prevailed, and
he determined to wait on Lady Bellaston, and to relinquish the design.

Lady Bellaston was in bed, though very late in the
morning, and Sophia sitting by her bed-side, when the
servant acquainted her that Lord Fellamar was below
in the parlour ; upon which her ladyship desired him
to stay, and that she would see him presently ; but the
servant was no sooner departed than poor Sophia began

to intreat her cousin not to encourage the visits of that odious lord (so she called him, though a little unjustly) upon her account. "I see his design," said she; "for he made downright love to me yesterday morning; but as I am resolved never to admit it, I beg your ladyship not to leave us alone together any more, and to order the servants that, if he enquires for me, I may be always denied to him."

"La! child," says Lady Bellaston, "you country girls have nothing but sweethearts in your head; you fancy every man who is civil to you is making love. He is one of the most gallant young fellows about town, and I am convinced means no more than a little gallantry. Make love to you indeed! I wish with all my heart he would, and you must be an arrant mad woman to refuse him."

"But as I shall certainly be that mad woman," cries Sophia, "I hope his visits shall not be intruded upon me."

"O child!" said Lady Bellaston, "you need not be so fearful; if you resolve to run away with that Jones, I know no person who can hinder you."

"Upon my honour, madam," cries Sophia, "your ladyship injures me. I will never run away with any man; nor will I ever marry contrary to my father's inclinations."

"Well, Miss Western," said the lady, "if you are not in a humour to see company this morning, you may retire to your own apartment; for I am not frightened at his lordship, and must send for him up into my dressing-room."

Sophia thanked her ladyship, and withdrew; and presently afterwards Fellamar was admitted upstairs.

Chapter iv.

*By which it will appear how dangerous an advocate a lady
is when she applies her eloquence to an ill purpose.*

WHEN Lady Bellaston heard the young lord's
scruples, she treated them with the same
disdain with which one of those sages of
the law, called Newgate solicitors, treats the qualms of
conscience in a young witness. "My dear lord," said
she, "you certainly want a cordial. I must send to
Lady Edgely for one of her best drams. Fie upon it!
have more resolution. Are you frightened by the word
rape? Or are you apprehensive——? Well! if the
story of Helen was modern, I should think it unnatural.
I mean the behaviour of Paris, not the fondness of the
lady; for all women love a man of spirit. There is
another story of the Sabine ladies—and that too, I
thank heaven, is very antient. Your lordship, perhaps,
will admire my reading; but I think Mr Hook tells us,
they made tolerable good wives afterwards. I fancy
few of my married acquaintance were ravished by their
husbands." "Nay, dear Lady Bellaston," cried he,
"don't ridicule me in this manner." "Why, my good
lord," answered she, "do you think any woman in
England would not laugh at you in her heart, whatever
prudery she might wear in her countenance?——You
force me to use a strange kind of language, and to
betray my sex most abominably; but I am contented
with knowing my intentions are good, and that I am
endeavouring to serve my cousin; for I think you will
make her a husband notwithstanding this; or, upon my
soul, I would not even persuade her to fling herself
away upon an empty title. She should not upbraid me
hereafter with having lost a man of spirit; for that his
enemies allow this poor young fellow to be."

Let those who have had the satisfaction of hearing reflections of this kind from a wife or a mistress, declare whether they are at all sweetened by coming from a female tongue. Certain it is, they sunk deeper into his lordship than anything which Demosthenes or Cicero could have said on the occasion.

Lady Bellaston, perceiving she had fired the young lord's pride, began now, like a true orator, to rouse other passions to its assistance. "My lord," says she, in a graver voice, "you will be pleased to remember, you mentioned this matter to me first; for I would not appear to you in the light of one who is endeavouring to put off my cousin upon you. Fourscore thousand pounds do not stand in need of an advocate to recommend them." "Nor doth Miss Western," said he, "require any recommendation from her fortune; for, in my opinion, no woman ever had half her charms." "Yes, yes, my lord," replied the lady, looking in the glass, "there have been women with more than half her charms, I assure you; not that I need lessen her on that account: she is a most delicious girl, that's certain; and within these few hours she will be in the arms of one, who surely doth not deserve her, though I will give him his due, I believe he is truly a man of spirit."

"I hope so, madam," said my lord; "though I must own he doth not deserve her; for, unless heaven or your ladyship disappoint me, she shall within that time be in mine."

"Well spoken, my lord," answered the lady; "I promise you no disappointment shall happen from my side; and within this week I am convinced I shall call your lordship my cousin in public."

The remainder of this scene consisted entirely of raptures, excuses, and compliments, very pleasant to have heard from the parties; but rather dull when related at second hand. Here, therefore, we shall put an end to this dialogue, and hasten to the fatal hour when everything was prepared for the destruction of poor Sophia.

But this being the most tragical matter in our whole history, we shall treat it in a chapter by itself.

Chapter v.

Containing some matters which may affect, and others which may surprize, the reader.

THE clock had now struck seven, and poor Sophia, alone and melancholy, sat reading a tragedy. It was the Fatal Marriage; and she was now come to that part where the poor distrest Isabella disposes of her wedding-ring.

Here the book dropt from her hand, and a shower of tears ran down into her bosom. In this situation she had continued a minute, when the door opened, and in came Lord Fellamar. Sophia started from her chair at his entrance; and his lordship advancing forwards, and making a low bow, said, "I am afraid, Miss Western, I break in upon you abruptly." "Indeed, my lord," says she, "I must own myself a little surprized at this unexpected visit." "If this visit be unexpected, madam," answered Lord Fellamar, "my eyes must have been very faithless interpreters of my heart, when last I had the honour of seeing you; for surely you could not otherwise have hoped to detain my heart in your possession, without receiving a visit from its owner." Sophia, confused as she was, answered this bombast (and very properly I think) with a look of inconceivable disdain. My lord then made another and a longer speech of the same sort. Upon which

Sophia, trembling, said, "Am I really to conceive your lordship to be out of your senses? Sure, my lord, there is no other excuse for such behaviour." "I am, indeed, madam, in the situation you suppose," cries his lordship; "and sure you will pardon the effects of a frenzy which you yourself have occasioned; for love hath so totally deprived me of reason, that I am scarce accountable for any of my actions." "Upon my word, my lord," said Sophia, "I neither understand your words nor your behaviour." "Suffer me then, madam," cries he, "at your feet to explain both, by laying open my soul to you, and declaring that I doat on you to the highest degree of distraction. O most adorable, most divine creature! what language can express the sentiments of my heart?" "I do assure you, my lord," said Sophia, "I shall not stay to hear any more of this." "Do not," cries he, "think of leaving me thus cruelly; could you know half the torments which I feel, that tender bosom must pity what those eyes have caused." Then fetching a deep sigh, and laying hold of her hand, he ran on for some minutes in a strain which would be little more pleasing to the reader than it was to the lady; and at last concluded with a declaration, "That if he was master of the world, he would lay it at her feet." Sophia then, forcibly pulling away her hand from his, answered with much spirit, "I promise you, sir, your world and its master I should spurn from me with equal contempt." She then offered to go; and Lord Fellamar, again laying hold of her hand, said, "Pardon me, my beloved angel, freedoms which nothing but despair could have tempted me to take.——Believe me, could I have had any hope that my title and fortune, neither of them inconsiderable, unless when compared with your worth, would have been accepted, I had, in the humblest manner, presented them to your acceptance.——But

I cannot lose you.—By heaven, I will sooner part with my soul!—You are, you must, you shall be only mine." "My lord," says she, "I intreat you to desist from a vain pursuit; for, upon my honour, I will never hear you on this subject. Let go my hand, my lord; for I am resolved to go from you this moment; nor will I ever see you more." "Then, madam," cries his lordship, "I must make the best use of this moment; for I cannot live, nor will I live without you."——"What do you mean, my lord?" said Sophia; "I will raise the family." "I have no fear, madam," answered he, "but of losing you, and that I am resolved to prevent, the only way which despair points to me."—He then caught her in his arms: upon which she screamed so loud, that she must have alarmed some one to her assistance, had not Lady Bellaston taken care to remove all ears.

But a more lucky circumstance happened for poor Sophia; another noise now broke forth, which almost drowned her cries; for now the whole house rang with, "Where is she? D—n me, I'll unkennel her this instant. Show me her chamber, I say. Where is my daughter? I know she's in the house, and I'll see her if she's above-ground. Show me where she is."—At which last words the door flew open, and in came Squire Western, with his parson and a set of myrmidons at his heels.

How miserable must have been the condition of poor Sophia, when the enraged voice of her father was welcome to her ears! Welcome indeed it was, and luckily did he come; for it was the only accident upon earth which could have preserved the peace of her mind from being for ever destroyed.

Sophia, notwithstanding her fright, presently knew her father's voice; and his lordship, notwithstanding his passion, knew the voice of reason, which peremp-

torily assured him, it was not now a time for the per-
petration of his villany. Hearing, therefore, the voice
approach, and hearing likewise whose it was (for as
the squire more than once roared forth the word
daughter, so Sophia, in the midst of her struggling,
cried out upon her father), he thought proper to relinquish his prey, having only disordered her handkerchief, and with his rude lips committed violence on her
lovely neck.

If the reader's imagination doth not assist me, I
shall never be able to describe the situation of these
two persons when Western came into the room.
Sophia tottered into a chair, where she sat disordered,
pale, breathless, bursting with indignation at Lord
Fellamar; affrighted, and yet more rejoiced, at the
arrival of her father.

His lordship sat down near her, with the bag of his
wig hanging over one of his shoulders, the rest of his
dress being somewhat disordered, and rather a greater
proportion of linen than is usual appearing at his bosom.
As to the rest, he was amazed, affrighted, vexed, and
ashamed.

As to Squire Western, he happened at this time to
be overtaken by an enemy, which very frequently pur-
sues, and seldom fails to overtake, most of the country
gentlemen in this kingdom. He was, literally speaking, drunk; which circumstance, together with his
natural impetuosity, could produce no other effect
than his running immediately up to his daughter,
upon whom he fell foul with his tongue in the most
inveterate manner; nay, he had probably committed
violence with his hands, had not the parson interposed, saying, "For heaven's sake, sir, animadvert
that you are in the house of a great lady. Let me
beg you to mitigate your wrath; it should minister a
fulness of satisfaction that you have found your daughter;

for as to revenge, it belongeth not unto us. I discern great contrition in the countenance of the young lady. I stand assured, if you will forgive her, she will repent her of all past offences, and return unto her duty."

The strength of the parson's arms had at first been of more service than the strength of his rhetoric. However, his last words wrought some effect, and the squire answered, "I'll forgee her if she wull ha un. If wot ha un, Sophy, I'll forgee thee all. Why dost unt speak? Shat ha un! d——n me, shat ha un! Why dost unt answer? Was ever such a stubborn tuoad?"

"Let me intreat you, sir, to be a little more moderate," said the parson; "you frighten the young lady so, that you deprive her of all power of utterance."

"Power of mine a——," answered the squire. "You take her part then, you do? A pretty parson, truly, to side with an undutiful child! Yes, yes, I will gee you a living with a pox. I'll gee un to the devil sooner."

"I humbly crave your pardon," said the parson; "I assure your worship I meant no such matter."

My Lady Bellaston now entered the room, and came up to the squire, who no sooner saw her, than, resolving to follow the instructions of his sister, he made her a very civil bow, in the rural manner, and paid her some of his best compliments. He then immediately proceeded to his complaints, and said, "There, my lady cousin; there stands the most undutiful child in the world; she hankers after a beggarly rascal, and won't marry one of the greatest matches in all England, that we have provided for her."

"Indeed, cousin Western," answered the lady, "I am persuaded you wrong my cousin. I am sure she hath a better understanding. I am convinced she will not refuse what she must be sensible is so much to her advantage."

This was a wilful mistake in Lady Bellaston, for she well knew whom Mr Western meant; though perhaps she thought he would easily be reconciled to his lordship's proposals.

"Do you hear there," quoth the squire, "what her ladyship says? All your family are for the match. Come, Sophy, be a good girl, and be dutiful, and make your father happy."

"If my death will make you happy, sir," answered Sophia, "you will shortly be so."

"It's a lye, Sophy; it's a d—n'd lye, and you know it," said the squire.

"Indeed, Miss Western," said Lady Bellaston, "you injure your father; he hath nothing in view but your interest in this match; and I and all your friends must acknowledge the highest honour done to your family in the proposal."

"Ay, all of us," quoth the squire; "nay, it was no proposal of mine. She knows it was her aunt proposed it to me first.——Come, Sophy, once more let me beg you to be a good girl, and gee me your consent before your cousin."

"Let me give him your hand, cousin," said the lady. "It is the fashion now-a-days to dispense with time and long courtships."

"Pugh!" said the squire, "what signifies time; won't they have time enough to court afterwards? People may court very well after they have been a-bed together."

As Lord Fellamar was very well assured that he was meant by Lady Bellaston, so, never having heard nor suspected a word of Blifil, he made no doubt of his being meant by the father. Coming up, therefore, to the squire, he said, "Though I have not the honour,

sir, of being personally known to you, yet, as I find I
have the happiness to have my proposals accepted, let
me intercede, sir, in behalf of the young lady, that she
may not be more solicited at this time."

"You intercede, sir!" said the squire; "why, who
the devil are you?"

"Sir, I am Lord Fellamar," answered he, "and am
the happy man whom I hope you have done the honour
of accepting for a son-in-law."

"You are a son of a b——," replied the squire,
"for all your laced coat.   You my son-in-law, and be
d——n'd to you!"

"I shall take more from you, sir, than from any
man," answered the lord; "but I must inform you
that I am not used to hear such language without
resentment."

"Resent my a——," quoth the squire.   "Don't think
I am afraid of such a fellow as thee art! because hast
got a spit there dangling at thy side.   Lay by your
spit, and I'll give thee enough of meddling with what
doth not belong to thee.   I'll teach you to father-in-
law me.   I'll lick thy jacket."

"It's very well, sir," said my lord, "I shall make
no disturbance before the ladies.   I am very well
satisfied.   Your humble servant, sir; Lady Bellaston,
your most obedient."

His lordship was no sooner gone, than Lady Bellaston, coming up to Mr Western, said, "Bless me, sir,
what have you done?   You know not whom you have
affronted; he is a nobleman of the first rank and fortune, and yesterday made proposals to your daughter;
and such as I am sure you must accept with the highest
pleasure."

"Answer for yourself, lady cousin," said the squire,
"I will have nothing to do with any of your lords.   My
daughter shall have an honest country gentleman; I

have pitched upon one for her—and she shall ha' un.
—I am sorry for the trouble she hath given your ladyship with all my heart." Lady Bellaston made a civil
speech upon the word trouble; to which the squire
answered—"Why, that's kind—and I would do as
much for your ladyship. To be sure relations should
do for one another. So I wish your ladyship a good
night.—Come, madam, you must go along with me
by fair means, or I'll have you carried down to the
coach."

Sophia said she would attend him without force;
but begged to go in a chair, for she said she should not
be able to ride any other way.

"Prithee," cries the squire, "wout unt persuade me
canst not ride in a coach, wouldst? That's a pretty
thing surely! No, no, I'll never let thee out of my
sight any more till art married, that I promise thee."
Sophia told him, she saw he was resolved to break her
heart. "O break thy heart and be d—n'd," quoth
he, "if a good husband will break it. I don't value
a brass varden, not a halfpenny, of any undutiful b—
upon earth." He then took violent hold of her hand;
upon which the parson once more interfered, begging
him to use gentle methods. At that the squire thundered
out a curse, and bid the parson hold his tongue, saying,
"At'nt in pulpit now? when art a got up there I never
mind what dost say; but I won't be priest-ridden, nor
taught how to behave myself by thee. I wish your
ladyship a good-night. Come along, Sophy; be a
good girl, and all shall be well. Shat ha' un, d—n
me, shat ha' un!"

Mrs Honour appeared below-stairs, and with a low
curtesy to the squire offered to attend her mistress; but
he pushed her away, saying, "Hold, madam, hold, you
come no more near my house." "And will you take
my maid away from me?" said Sophia. "Yes, in-

deed, madam, will I," cries the squire : "you need not fear being without a servant; I will get you another maid, and a better maid than this, who, I'd lay five pounds to a crown, is no more a maid than my grannum. No, no, Sophy, she shall contrive no more escapes, I promise you." He then packed up his daughter and the parson into the hackney coach, after which he mounted himself, and ordered it to drive to his lodgings. In the way thither he suffered Sophia to be quiet, and entertained himself with reading a lecture to the parson on good manners, and a proper behaviour to his betters.

It is possible he might not so easily have carried off his daughter from Lady Bellaston, had that good lady desired to have detained her ; but, in reality, she was not a little pleased with the confinement into which Sophia was going; and as her project with Lord Fellamar had failed of success, she was well contented that other violent methods were now going to be used in favour of another man.

Chapter vi.

By what means the squire came to discover his daughter.

THOUGH the reader, in many histories, is obliged to digest much more unaccountable appearances than this of Mr Western, without any satisfaction at all; yet, as we dearly love to oblige him whenever it is in our power, we shall now proceed to shew by what method the squire discovered where his daughter was.

In the third chapter, then, of the preceding book, we gave a hint (for it is not our custom to unfold at any time more than is necessary for the occasion) that Mrs Fitzpatrick, who was very desirous of reconciling her uncle and aunt Western, thought she had a probable opportunity, by the service of preserving Sophia from committing the same crime which had drawn on herself the anger of her family. After much deliberation, therefore, she resolved to inform her aunt Western where her cousin was, and accordingly she writ the following letter, which we shall give the reader at length, for more reasons than one.

" HONOURED MADAM,

"The occasion of my writing this will perhaps make a letter of mine agreeable to my dear aunt, for the sake of one of her nieces, though I have little reason to hope it will be so on the account of another.

"Without more apology, as I was coming to throw my unhappy self at your feet, I met, by the strangest accident in the world, my cousin Sophy, whose history you are better acquainted with than myself, though, alas! I know infinitely too much; enough indeed to satisfy me, that unless she is immediately prevented, she is in danger of running into the same fatal mischief, which, by foolishly and ignorantly refusing your most wise and prudent advice, I have unfortunately brought on myself.

"In short, I have seen the man, nay, I was most part of yesterday in his company, and a charming young fellow I promise you he is. By what accident he came acquainted with me is too tedious to tell you now; but I have this morning changed my lodgings to avoid him, lest he should by my means discover my cousin; for he doth not yet know where she is, and it is adviseable he should not, till my uncle hath secured her.——No time therefore is to be lost; and I need only inform you, that she is now with Lady Bellaston, whom I have seen, and who hath, I find, a design of concealing her from her family. You know, madam, she is a strange woman; but nothing could misbecome me more than to presume to give any hint to one of your great understanding and great knowledge of the world, besides barely informing you of the matter of fact.

"I hope, madam, the care which I have shewn on this occasion for the good of my family will recommend me again to the favour of a lady who hath always exerted so much zeal for the honour and true interest of us all; and that it may be a means of restoring me to your friendship, which hath made so great a part of my former, and is so necessary to my future happiness.

"I am,

    with the utmost respect,

       honoured madam,

          your most dutiful obliged niece,

            and most obedient humble servant,

               HARRIET FITZPATRICK."

Mrs Western was now at her brother's house, where she had resided ever since the flight of Sophia, in order to administer comfort to the poor squire in his affliction. Of this comfort, which she doled out to him in daily portions, we have formerly given a specimen.

She was now standing with her back to the fire, and, with a pinch of snuff in her hand, was dealing forth this daily allowance of comfort to the squire, while he smoaked his afternoon pipe, when she received the above letter; which she had no sooner read than she delivered it to him, saying, "There, sir, there is an account of your lost sheep. Fortune hath again restored her to you, and if you will be governed by my advice, it is possible you may yet preserve her."

The squire had no sooner read the letter than he

leaped from his chair, threw his pipe into the fire, and gave a loud huzza for joy. He then summoned his servants, called for his boots, and ordered the Chevalier and several other horses to be saddled, and that parson Supple should be immediately sent for. Having done this, he turned to his sister, caught her in his arms, and gave her a close embrace, saying, "Zounds! you don't seem pleased; one would imagine you was sorry I have found the girl."

"Brother," answered she, "the deepest politicians, who see to the bottom, discover often a very different aspect of affairs, from what swims on the surface. It is true, indeed, things do look rather less desperate than they did formerly in Holland, when Lewis the Fourteenth was at the gates of Amsterdam; but there is a delicacy required in this matter, which you will pardon me, brother, if I suspect you want. There is a decorum to be used with a woman of figure, such as Lady Bellaston, brother, which requires a knowledge of the world, superior, I am afraid, to yours."

"Sister," cries the squire, "I know you have no opinion of my parts; but I'll shew you on this occasion who is a fool. Knowledge, quotha! I have not been in the country so long without having some knowledge of warrants and the law of the land. I know I may take my own wherever I can find it. Shew me my own daughter, and if I don't know how to come at her, I'll suffer you to call me a fool as long as I live. There be justices of peace in London, as well as in other places."

"I protest," cries she, "you make me tremble for the event of this matter, which, if you will proceed by my advice, you may bring to so good an issue. Do you really imagine, brother, that the house of a woman of figure is to be attacked by warrants and brutal justices of the peace? I will inform you how to proceed. As soon as you arrive in town, and have got yourself into a decent dress (for indeed, brother, you have none at present fit to appear in), you must send your compliments to Lady Bellaston, and desire leave to wait on her. When you are admitted to her presence, as you certainly will be, and have told her your story, and have made proper use of my name (for I think you just know one another only by sight, though you are relations), I am confident she will withdraw her protection from my niece, who hath certainly imposed upon her. This is the only method. — Justices of peace, indeed! do you imagine any such event can arrive to a woman of figure in a civilised nation?"

"D—n their figures," cries the squire; "a pretty civilised nation, truly, where women are above the law. And what must I stand sending a parcel of compliments to a confounded whore, that keeps away a daughter from her own natural father? I tell you, sister, I am not so ignorant as you think me——I know you would have women above the law, but it is all a lye; I heard his lordship say at size, that no one is above the law. But this of yours is Hanover law, I suppose."

"Mr Western," said she, "I think you daily improve in ignorance.——I protest you are grown an arrant bear."

"No more a bear than yourself, sister Western," said the squire.——"Pox! you may talk of your civility an you will, I am sure you never shew any to me. I am no bear, no, nor no dog neither, though I know somebody, that is something that begins with a b; but pox! I will show you I have got more good manners than some folks."

"Mr Western," answered the lady, "you may say what you please, *je vous mesprise de tout mon cœur*. I shall not therefore be angry.——Besides, as my cousin,

with that odious Irish name, justly says, I have that
regard for the honour and true interest of my family,
and that concern for my niece, who is a part of it,
that I have resolved to go to town myself upon this
occasion; for indeed, indeed, brother, you are not a fit
minister to be employed at a polite court.—Greenland
—Greenland should always be the scene of the tra-
montane negociation."

"I thank Heaven," cries the squire, "I don't
understand you now. You are got to your Hanoverian
linguo. However, I'll shew you I scorn to be behind-
hand in civility with you; and as you are not angry
for what I have said, so I am not angry for what you
have said. Indeed I have always thought it a folly
for relations to quarrel; and if they do now and then
give a hasty word, why, people should give and take;
for my part, I never bear malice; and I take it very
kind of you to go up to London; for I never was
there but twice in my life, and then I did not stay
above a fortnight at a time, and to be sure I can't be
expected to know much of the streets and the folks in
that time. I never denied that you know'd all these
matters better than I. For me to dispute that would
be all as one as for you to dispute the management of a
pack of dogs, or the finding a hare sitting, with me."
—"Which I promise you," says she, "I never will."
—"Well, and I promise you," returned he, "that I
never will dispute the t'other."

Here then a league was struck (to borrow a phrase
from the lady) between the contending parties; and
now the parson arriving, and the horses being ready,
the squire departed, having promised his sister to
follow her advice, and she prepared to follow him
the next day.

But having communicated these matters to the parson
on the road, they both agreed that the prescribed

formalities might very well be dispensed with; and the squire, having changed his mind, proceeded in the manner we have already seen.

Chapter vii.

In which various misfortunes befel poor Jones.

AFFAIRS were in the aforesaid situation when Mrs Honour arrived at Mrs Miller's, and called Jones out from the company, as we have before seen, with whom, when she found herself alone, she began as follows :—

"O, my dear sir! how shall I get spirits to tell you; you are undone, sir, and my poor lady's undone, and I am undone." "Hath anything happened to Sophia?" cries Jones, staring like a madman. "All that is bad," cries Honour: "Oh, I shall never get such another lady! Oh that I should ever live to see this day!" At these words Jones turned pale as ashes, trembled, and stammered; but Honour went on—"O! Mr Jones, I have lost my lady for ever." "How? what! for Heaven's sake, tell me. O, my dear Sophia!" "You may well call her so," said Honour; "she was the dearest lady to me. I shall never have such another place."——"D—n your place!" cries Jones; "where is—what—what is become of my Sophia?" "Ay, to be sure," cries she, "servants may be d—n'd. It signifies nothing what becomes of them, though they are turned away, and ruined ever so much. To be sure they are not flesh and blood like other people. No, to be sure, it signifies nothing what becomes of them." "If you have any pity, any compassion," cries Jones, "I beg you will instantly tell me what hath happened to Sophia?" "To be sure, I have more pity for you than you have for me," answered Honour; "I don't d—n you because you have lost the sweetest lady in the world. To be sure you are worthy to be pitied, and I am worthy to be pitied too: for, to be sure, if ever there was a good mistress——" "What hath happened?" cries Jones, in almost a raving fit. "What?—What?" said Honour: "Why, the worst that could have happened both for you and for me.—Her father is come to town, and hath carried her away from us both." Here Jones fell on his knees in thanksgiving that it was no worse. "No worse!" repeated Honour; "what could be worse for either of us? He carried her off, swearing she should marry Mr Blifil; that's for your comfort; and, for poor me, I am turned out of doors." "Indeed, Mrs Honour," answered Jones, "you frightened me out of my wits. I imagined some most dreadful sudden accident had happened to Sophia; something, compared to which, even seeing her married to Blifil would be a trifle; but while there is life there are hopes, my dear Honour. Women in this land of liberty, cannot be married by actual brutal force." "To be sure, sir," said she, "that's true. There may be some hopes for you; but alack-a-day! what hopes are there for poor me? And to be sure, sir, you must be sensible I suffer all this upon your account. All the quarrel the squire hath to me is for taking your part, as I have done, against Mr Blifil." "Indeed, Mrs Honour," answered he, "I am sensible of my obligations to you, and will leave nothing in my power undone to make you amends." "Alas! sir," said she, "what can make a servant amends for the loss of one place but the getting another altogether as good?" "Do not despair, Mrs Honour," said Jones, "I hope to reinstate you again in the same." "Alack-a-day, sir," said she, "how

can I flatter myself with such hopes when I know it is
a thing impossible? for the squire is so set against me:
and yet, if you should ever have my lady, as to be sure
I now hopes heartily you will; for you are a generous,
good-natured gentleman; and I am sure you loves her,
and to be sure she loves you as dearly as her own soul;
it is a matter in vain to deny it; because as why, everybody, that is in the least acquainted with my lady, must
see it; for, poor dear lady, she can't dissemble: and
if two people who loves one another a'n't happy, why
who should be so? Happiness don't always depend
upon what people has; besides, my lady has enough for
both. To be sure, therefore, as one may say, it would
be all the pity in the world to keep two such loviers
asunder; nay, I am convinced, for my part, you will
meet together at last; for, if it is to be, there is no
preventing it. If a marriage is made in heaven, all the
justices of peace upon earth can't break it off. To be
sure I wishes that parson Supple had but a little more
spirit, to tell the squire of his wickedness in endeavouring to force his daughter contrary to her liking; but
then his whole dependance is on the squire; and so the
poor gentleman, though he is a very religious good sort
of man, and talks of the badness of such doings behind
the squire's back, yet he dares not say his soul is his
own to his face. To be sure I never saw him make
so bold as just now; I was afeard the squire would
have struck him. I would not have your honour be
melancholy, sir, nor despair; things may go better, as
long as you are sure of my lady, and that I am certain
you may be; for she never will be brought to consent
to marry any other man. Indeed I am terribly afeared
the squire will do her a mischief in his passion, for he
is a prodigious passionate gentleman; and I am afeared
too the poor lady will be brought to break her heart,
for she is as tender-hearted as a chicken. It is pity,

methinks, she had not a little of my courage.   If I was
in love with a young man, and my father offered to
lock me up, I'd tear his eyes out but I'd come at him;
but then there's a great fortune in the case, which it is
in her father's power either to give her or not; that,
to be sure, may make some difference."

Whether Jones gave strict attention to all the foregoing harangue, or whether it was for want of any
vacancy in the discourse, I cannot determine; but he
never once attempted to answer, nor did she once stop
till Partridge came running into the room, and informed
him that the great lady was upon the stairs.

Nothing could equal the dilemma to which Jones
was now reduced.   Honour knew nothing of any acquaintance that subsisted between him and Lady
Bellaston, and she was almost the last person in the
world to whom he would have communicated it.   In
this hurry and distress, he took (as is common
enough) the worst course, and, instead of exposing
her to the lady, which would have been of little consequence, he chose to expose the lady to her; he therefore resolved to hide Honour, whom he had but just time
to convey behind the bed, and to draw the curtains.

The hurry in which Jones had been all day engaged
on account of his poor landlady and her family, the
terrors occasioned by Mrs Honour, and the confusion
into which he was thrown by the sudden arrival of
Lady Bellaston, had altogether driven former thoughts
out of his head; so that it never once occurred to his
memory to act the part of a sick man; which, indeed,
neither the gaiety of his dress, nor the freshness of his
countenance, would have at all supported.

He received her ladyship therefore rather agreeably
to her desires than to her expectations, with all the good
humour he could muster in his countenance, and without
any real or affected appearance of the least disorder.

Lady Bellaston no sooner entered the room, than she squatted herself down on the bed: "So, my dear Jones," said she, "you find nothing can detain me long from you. Perhaps I ought to be angry with you, that I have neither seen nor heard from you all day; for I perceive your distemper would have suffered you to come abroad: nay, I suppose you have not sat in your chamber all day drest up like a fine lady to see company after a lying-in; but, however, don't think I intend to scold you; for I never will give you an excuse for the cold behaviour of a husband, by putting on the ill-humour of a wife."

"Nay, Lady Bellaston," said Jones, "I am sure your ladyship will not upbraid me with neglect of duty, when I only waited for orders. Who, my dear creature, hath reason to complain? Who missed an appointment last night, and left an unhappy man to expect, and wish, and sigh, and languish?"

"Do not mention it, my dear Mr Jones," cried she. "If you knew the occasion, you would pity me. In short, it is impossible to conceive what women of condition are obliged to suffer from the impertinence of fools, in order to keep up the farce of the world. I am glad, however, all your languishing and wishing have done you no harm; for you never looked better in your life. Upon my faith! Jones, you might at this instant sit for the picture of Adonis."

There are certain words of provocation which men of honour hold can properly be answered only by a blow. Among lovers possibly there may be some expressions which can be answered only by a kiss. Now the compliment which Lady Bellaston now made Jones seems to be of this kind, especially as it was attended with a look, in which the lady conveyed more soft ideas than it was possible to express with her tongue.

Jones was certainly at this instant in one of the most disagreeable and distressed situations imaginable; for, to carry on the comparison we made use of before, though the provocation was given by the lady, Jones could not receive satisfaction, nor so much as offer to ask it, in the presence of a third person; seconds in this kind of duels not being according to the law of arms. As this objection did not occur to Lady Bellaston, who was ignorant of any other woman being there but herself, she waited some time in great astonishment for an answer from Jones, who, conscious of the ridiculous figure he made, stood at a distance, and, not daring to give the proper answer, gave none at all. Nothing can be imagined more comic, nor yet more tragical, than this scene would have been if it had lasted much longer. The lady had already changed colour two or three times; had got up from the bed and sat down again, while Jones was wishing the ground to sink under him, or the house to fall on his head, when an odd accident freed him from an embarrassment out of which neither the eloquence of a Cicero, nor the politics of a Machiavel, could have delivered him, without utter disgrace.

This was no other than the arrival of young Nightingale, dead drunk; or rather in that state of drunkenness which deprives men of the use of their reason without depriving them of the use of their limbs.

Mrs Miller and her daughters were in bed, and Partridge was smoaking his pipe by the kitchen fire; so that he arrived at Mr Jones's chamber-door without any interruption. This he burst open, and was entering without any ceremony, when Jones started from his seat and ran to oppose him, which he did so effectually, that Nightingale never came far enough within the door to see who was sitting on the bed.

Nightingale had in reality mistaken Jones's apart‹ ment for that in which himself had lodged; he therefore strongly insisted on coming in, often swearing that he would not be kept from his own bed. Jones, however, prevailed over him, and delivered him into the hands of Partridge, whom the noise on the stairs soon summoned to his master's assistance.

And now Jones was unwillingly obliged to return to his own apartment, where at the very instant of his entrance he heard Lady Bellaston venting an exclamation, though not a very loud one; and at the same time saw her flinging herself into a chair in a vast agitation, which in a lady of a tender constitution would have been an hysteric fit.

In reality the lady, frightened with the struggle between the two men, of which she did not know what would be the issue, as she heard Nightingale swear many oaths he would come to his own bed, attempted to retire to her known place of hiding, which to her great confusion she found already occupied by another.

"Is this usage to be borne, Mr Jones?" cries the lady.—"Basest of men?——What wretch is this to whom you have exposed me?" "Wretch!" cries Honour, bursting in a violent rage from her place of concealment——"Marry come up!——Wretch forsooth?——as poor a wretch as I am, I am honest; this is more than some folks who are richer can say."

Jones, instead of applying himself directly to take off the edge of Mrs Honour's resentment, as a more experienced gallant would have done, fell to cursing his stars, and lamenting himself as the most unfortunate man in the world; and presently after, addressing himself to Lady Bellaston, he fell to some very absurd protestations of innocence. By this time the lady, having recovered the use of her reason, which she had as ready as any woman in the world, especially on such occasions, calmly replied; "Sir, you need make no apologies, I see now who the person is; I did not at first know Mrs Honour: but now I do, I can suspect nothing wrong between her and you; and I am sure she is a woman of too good sense to put any wrong constructions upon my visit to you; I have been always her friend, and it may be in my power to be much more hereafter."

Mrs Honour was altogether as placable as she was passionate. Hearing, therefore, Lady Bellaston assume the soft tone, she likewise softened hers.——"I'm sure, madam," says she, "I have been always ready to acknowledge your ladyship's friendships to me; sure I never had so good a friend as your ladyship——and to be sure, now I see it is your ladyship that I spoke to, I could almost bite my tongue off for very mad.—— I constructions upon your ladyship—to be sure it doth not become a servant as I am to think about such a great lady—I mean I was a servant: for indeed I am nobody's servant now, the more miserable wretch is me.—I have lost the best mistress——" Here Honour thought fit to produce a shower of tears.—— "Don't cry, child," says the good lady; "ways perhaps may be found to make you amends. Come to me to-morrow morning." She then took up her fan which lay on the ground, and without even looking at Jones walked very majestically out of the room; there being a kind of dignity in the impudence of women of quality, which their inferiors vainly aspire to attain to in circumstances of this nature.

Jones followed her downstairs, often offering her his hand, which she absolutely refused him, and got into her chair without taking any notice of him as he stood bowing before her.

At his return upstairs, a long dialogue past between

him and Mrs Honour, while she was adjusting herself after the discomposure she had undergone. The subject of this was his infidelity to her young lady; on which she enlarged with great bitterness; but Jones at last found means to reconcile her, and not only so, but to obtain a promise of most inviolable secrecy, and that she would the next morning endeavour to find out Sophia, and bring him a further account of the proceedings of the squire.

Thus ended this unfortunate adventure to the satisfaction only of Mrs Honour; for a secret (as some of my readers will perhaps acknowledge from experience) is often a very valuable possession: and that not only to those who faithfully keep it, but sometimes to such as whisper it about till it come to the ears of every one except the ignorant person who pays for the supposed concealing of what is publickly known.

Chapter viij.

Short and sweet.

NOTWITHSTANDING all the obligations she had received from Jones, Mrs Miller could not forbear in the morning some gentle remonstrances for the hurricane which had happened the preceding night in his chamber. These were, however, so gentle and so friendly, professing, and indeed truly, to aim at nothing more than the real good of Mr Jones himself, that he, far from being offended, thankfully received the admonition of the good woman, expressed much concern for what had past, excused it as well as he could, and promised never more to bring the same disturbances into the house.

But though Mrs Miller did not refrain from a short

expostulation in private at their first meeting, yet the occasion of his being summoned downstairs that morning was of a much more agreeable kind, being indeed to perform the office of a father to Miss Nancy, and to give her in wedlock to Mr Nightingale, who was now ready drest, and full as sober as many of my readers will think a man ought to be who receives a wife in so imprudent a manner.

And here perhaps it may be proper to account for the escape which this young gentleman had made from his uncle, and for his appearance in the condition in which we have seen him the night before.

Now when the uncle had arrived at his lodgings with his nephew, partly to indulge his own inclinations (for he dearly loved his bottle), and partly to disqualify his nephew from the immediate execution of his purpose, he ordered wine to be set on the table; with which he so briskly plyed the young gentleman, that this latter, who, though not much used to drinking, did not detest it so as to be guilty of disobedience or want of complacence by refusing, was soon completely finished.

Just as the uncle had obtained this victory, and was preparing a bed for his nephew, a messenger arrived with a piece of news, which so entirely disconcerted and shocked him, that he in a moment lost all consideration for his nephew, and his whole mind became entirely taken up with his own concerns.

This sudden and afflicting news was no less than that his daughter had taken the opportunity of almost the first moment of his absence, and had gone off with a neighbouring young clergyman; against whom, though her father could have had but one objection, namely, that he was worth nothing, yet she had never thought proper to communicate her amour even to that father; and so artfully had she managed, that it had never been once suspected by any, till now that it was consummated.

Old Mr Nightingale no sooner received this account, than in the utmost confusion he ordered a post-chaise to be instantly got ready, and, having recommended his nephew to the care of a servant, he directly left the house, scarce knowing what he did, nor whither he went.

The uncle thus departed, when the servant came to attend the nephew to bed, had waked him for that purpose, and had at last made him sensible that his uncle was gone, he, instead of accepting the kind offices tendered him, insisted on a chair being called; with this the servant, who had received no strict orders to the contrary, readily complied; and, thus being conducted back to the house of Mrs Miller, he had staggered up to Mr Jones's chamber, as hath been before recounted.

This bar of the uncle being now removed (though young Nightingale knew not as yet in what manner), and all parties being quickly ready, the mother, Mr Jones, Mr Nightingale, and his love, stept into a hackney-coach, which conveyed them to Doctors' Commons; where Miss Nancy was, in vulgar language, soon made an honest woman, and the poor mother became, in the purest sense of the word, one of the happiest of all human beings.

And now Mr Jones, having seen his good offices to that poor woman and her family brought to a happy conclusion, began to apply himself to his own concerns; but here, lest many of my readers should censure his folly for thus troubling himself with the affairs of others, and lest some few should think he acted more disinterestedly than indeed he did, we think proper to assure our reader, that he was so far from being unconcerned in this matter, that he had indeed a very considerable interest in bringing it to that final consummation.

To explain this seeming paradox at once, he was one who could truly say with him in Terence, *Homo sum : humani nihil a me alienum puto.* He was never an indifferent spectator of the misery or happiness of any one ; and he felt either the one or the other in great proportion as he himself contributed to either. He could not, therefore, be the instrument of raising a whole family from the lowest state of wretchedness to the highest pitch of joy without conveying great felicity to himself ; more perhaps than worldly men often purchase to themselves by undergoing the most severe labour, and often by wading through the deepest iniquity.

Those readers who are of the same complexion with him will perhaps think this short chapter contains abundance of matter ; while others may probably wish, short as it is, that it had been totally spared as impertinent to the main design, which I suppose they conclude is to bring Mr Jones to the gallows, or, if possible, to a more deplorable catastrophe.

Chapter ix.

Containing love-letters of several sorts.

MR JONES, at his return home, found the following letters lying on his table, which he luckily opened in the order they were sent.

LETTER I.

"Surely I am under some strange infatuation ; I cannot keep my resolutions a moment, however strongly made or justly founded. Last night I resolved never to see you more ; this morning I am willing to hear if you can, as you say, clear up this affair. And yet I know that to be impossible. I have said everything to myself which you can invent.——Perhaps not. Perhaps your invention is stronger. Come to me, therefore, the moment you receive this. If you can forge an excuse I almost promise you to believe it. Betrayed too——I will think no more.——Come to me directly.——This is the third letter I have writ, the two former are burnt——I am almost inclined to burn this too ——I wish I may preserve my senses.——Come to me presently."

LETTER II.

"If you ever expect to be forgiven, or even suffered within my doors, come to me this instant."

LETTER III.

"I now find you was not at home when my notes came to your lodgings. The moment you receive this let me see you;——I shall not stir out; nor shall anybody be let in but yourself. Sure nothing can detain you long."

Jones had just read over these three billets when Mr Nightingale came into the room. "Well, Tom," said he, "any news from Lady Bellaston, after last night's adventure?" (for it was now no secret to any one in that house who the lady was). "The Lady Bellaston?" answered Jones very gravely.——"Nay, dear Tom," cries Nightingale, "don't be so reserved to your friends. Though I was too drunk to see her last night, I saw her at the masquerade. Do you think I am ignorant who the queen of the fairies is?" "And did you really then know the lady at the masquerade?" said Jones. "Yes, upon my soul, did I," said Nightingale, "and have given you twenty hints of it since, though you seemed always so tender on that point, that I would not speak plainly. I fancy, my friend, by your extreme nicety in this matter, you are not so well acquainted with the character of the lady as with her person. Don't be angry, Tom, but upon my honour, you are not the first young fellow she hath debauched. Her reputation is in no danger, believe me."

Though Jones had no reason to imagine the lady to have been of the vestal kind when his amour began; yet, as he was thoroughly ignorant of the town, and had very little acquaintance in it, he had no knowledge of that character which is vulgarly called a demirep; that is to say, a woman who intrigues with every man she likes, under the name and appearance of virtue; and who, though some over-nice ladies will not be seen with her, is visited (as they term it) by the whole town, in short, whom everybody knows to be what nobody calls her.

When he found, therefore, that Nightingale was perfectly acquainted with his intrigue, and began to suspect that so scrupulous a delicacy as he had hitherto observed was not quite necessary on the occasion, he gave a latitude to his friend's tongue, and desired him to speak plainly what he knew, or had ever heard of the lady.

Nightingale, who, in many other instances, was rather too effeminate in his disposition, had a pretty strong inclination to tittle-tattle. He had no sooner, therefore, received a full liberty of speaking from Jones, than he entered upon a long narrative concerning the lady; which, as it contained many particulars highly to her dishonour, we have too great a tenderness for all women of condition to repeat. We would cautiously avoid giving an opportunity to the future commentators on our works, of making any malicious application and of forcing us to be, against our will, the author of scandal, which never entered into our head.

Jones, having very attentively heard all that Nightingale had to say, fetched a deep sigh; which the other, observing, cried, "Heyday! why, thou art not in love, I hope! Had I imagined my stories would have affected you, I promise you should never have heard them." "O my dear friend!" cries Jones, "I am so entangled with this woman, that I know not how to extricate myself. In love, indeed! no, my friend, but I am under obligations to her, and very great ones. Since you know so much, I will be very explicit with you. It is owing, perhaps, solely to her, that I have not, before this, wanted a bit of bread. How can I possibly desert such a woman? and yet I must desert her, or be guilty of the blackest treachery to one who deserves infinitely better of me than she can; a woman, my Nightingale, for whom I have a passion which few can have an idea of. I am half distracted with doubts how to act." "And is this other, pray, an honourable mistress?" cries Nightingale. "Honourable!" answered Jones; "no breath ever yet durst sully her reputation. The sweetest air is not purer, the limpid stream not clearer, than her honour. She is all over, both in mind and body, consummate perfection. She is the most beautiful creature in the universe: and yet she is mistress of such noble elevated qualities, that, though she is never from my thoughts, I scarce ever think of her beauty but when I see it."—"And can you, my good friend," cries Nightingale, "with such an engagement as this upon your hands, hesitate a moment about quitting such a—" "Hold," said Jones, "no more abuse of her: I detest the thought of ingratitude." "Pooh!" answered the other, "you are not the first upon whom she hath conferred obligations of this kind. She is remarkably liberal where she likes; though, let me tell you, her favours are so prudently bestowed, that they should rather raise a man's vanity than his gratitude." In short, Nightingale proceeded so far on this head, and told his friend so many stories of the lady, which he swore to the truth of, that he entirely removed all esteem for her from the breast of Jones; and his gratitude was lessened in proportion. Indeed, he began to look on all the favours he had received rather as wages than benefits, which depreciated not only her, but himself too in his own conceit, and put him quite out of humour with both. From this disgust, his mind, by a natural transition, turned towards Sophia; her virtue, her purity, her love to him, her sufferings on his account, filled all his thoughts, and made his commerce with Lady Bellaston appear still more odious. The result of all was, that, though his turning himself out of her service, in which light he now saw his affair with her, would be the loss of his bread; yet he determined to quit her, if he could but find a handsome pretence: which being communicated to his friend, Nightingale considered a little, and then said, "I have it, my boy! I have found out a sure method; propose marriage to her, and I would venture hanging upon the success." "Marriage?" cries Jones. "Ay, propose marriage," answered Nightingale, "and she will declare off in a moment. I knew a young fellow whom she kept formerly, who made the offer to her in earnest, and was presently turned off for his pains."

Jones declared he could not venture the experiment. "Perhaps," said he, "she may be less shocked at this proposal from one man than from another. And if she should take me at my word, where am I then? caught in my own trap, and undone for ever." "No;" answered Nightingale, "not if I can give you an expedient by which you may at any time get out of the trap."——"What expedient can that be?" replied Jones. "This," answered

Nightingale. "The young fellow I mentioned, who is one of the most intimate acquaintances I have in the world, is so angry with her for some ill offices she hath since done him, that I am sure he would, without any difficulty, give you a sight of her letters; upon which you may decently break with her; and declare off before the knot is tyed, if she should really be willing to tie it, which I am convinced she will not."

After some hesitation, Jones, upon the strength of this assurance, consented; but, as he swore he wanted the confidence to propose the matter to her face, he wrote the following letter, which Nightingale dictated:—

" MADAM,

"I am extremely concerned, that, by an unfortunate engagement abroad, I should have missed receiving the honour of your ladyship's commands the moment they came; and the delay which I must now suffer of vindicating myself to your ladyship greatly adds to this misfortune. O, Lady Bellaston! what a terror have I been in for fear your reputation should be exposed by these perverse accidents! There is one only way to secure it. I need not name what that is. Only permit me to say, that as your honour is as dear to me as my own, so my sole ambition is to have the glory of laying my liberty at your feet; and believe me when I assure you, I can never be made completely happy without you generously bestow on me a legal right of calling you mine for ever.—I am,

madam,

with most profound respect,

your ladyship's most obliged,

obedient, humble servant,

THOMAS JONES."

To this she presently returned the following answer:

" Sir,

" When I read over your serious epistle, I could, from its coldness and formality, have sworn that you already had the legal right you mention ; nay, that we had for many years composed that monstrous animal a husband and wife. Do you really then imagine me a fool ? or do you fancy yourself capable of so entirely persuading me out of my senses, that I should deliver my whole fortune into your power, in order to enable you to support your pleasures at my expense ? Are these the proofs of love which I expected ? Is this the return for——? but I scorn to upbraid you, and am in great admiration of your profound respect.

" *P.S.* I am prevented from revising :——Perhaps I have said more than I meant.——Come to me at eight this evening."

Jones, by the advice of his privy-council, replied :

" Madam,

" It is impossible to express how much I am shocked at the suspicion you entertain of me. Can Lady Bellaston have conferred favours on a man whom she could believe capable of so base a design ? or can she treat the most solemn tie of love with contempt ? Can you imagine, madam, that if the violence of my passion, in an unguarded moment, overcame the tenderness which I have for your honour, I would think of indulging myself in the continuance of an intercourse which could not possibly escape long the notice of the world ; and which, when discovered, must prove so fatal to your reputation ? If such be your opinion of me, I must pray for a sudden opportunity of returning those pecuniary obligations, which I have been so unfortunate to receive at your hands ; and for those of a more tender kind, I shall ever remain, &c." And so concluded in the very words with which he had concluded the former letter.

The lady answered as follows:

"I see you are a villain! and I despise you from my soul. If you come here I shall not be at home."

Though Jones was well satisfied with his deliverance from a thraldom which those who have ever experienced it will, I apprehend, allow to be none of the lightest, he was not, however, perfectly easy in his mind. There was in this scheme too much of fallacy to satisfy one who utterly detested every species of falshood or dishonesty: nor would he, indeed, have submitted to put it in practice, had he not been involved in a distressful situation, where he was obliged to be guilty of some dishonour, either to the one lady or the other; and surely the reader will allow, that every good principle, as well as love, pleaded strongly in favour of Sophia.

Nightingale highly exulted in the success of his stratagem, upon which he received many thanks and much applause from his friend. He answered, "Dear Tom, we have conferred very different obligations on each other. To me you owe the regaining your liberty; to you I owe the loss of mine. But if you are as happy in the one instance as I am in the other, I promise you we are the two happiest fellows in England."

The two gentlemen were now summoned down to dinner, where Mrs Miller, who performed herself the office of cook, had exerted her best talents to celebrate the wedding of her daughter. This joyful circumstance she ascribed principally to the friendly behaviour of Jones, her whole soul was fired with gratitude towards him, and all her looks, words, and actions, were so busied in expressing it, that her daughter, and even

her new son-in-law, were very little objects of her
consideration.

Dinner was just ended when Mrs Miller received a
letter ; but as we have had letters enow in this chapter,
we shall communicate its contents in our next.

Chapter x.

*Consisting partly of facts, and partly of observations
upon them.*

THE letter then which arrived at the end of the
preceding chapter was from Mr Allworthy,
and the purport of it was, his intention to
come immediately to town, with his nephew Blifil, and
a desire to be accommodated with his usual lodgings,
which were the first floor for himself, and the second
for his nephew.

The chearfulness which had before displayed itself
in the countenance of the poor woman was a little
clouded on this occasion. This news did indeed a
good deal disconcert her. To requite so disinterested
a match with her daughter, by presently turning her
new son-in-law out of doors, appeared to her very
unjustifiable on the one hand ; and on the other, she
could scarce bear the thoughts of making any excuse
to Mr Allworthy, after all the obligations received
from him, for depriving him of lodgings which were
indeed strictly his due ; for that gentleman, in conferring all his numberless benefits on others, acted by
a rule diametrically opposite to what is practised by
most generous people. He contrived, on all occasions,
to hide his beneficence, not only from the world, but
even from the object of it. He constantly used the
words Lend and Pay, instead of Give ; and by every

other method he could invent, always lessened with his tongue the favours he conferred, while he was heaping them with both his hands. When he settled the annuity of £50 a year therefore on Mrs Miller, he told her, "it was in consideration of always having her first-floor when he was in town (which he scarce ever intended to be), but that she might let it at any other time, for that he would always send her a month's warning." He was now, however, hurried to town so suddenly, that he had no opportunity of giving such notice; and this hurry probably prevented him, when he wrote for his lodgings, adding, if they were then empty; for he would most certainly have been well satisfied to have relinquished them, on a less sufficient excuse than what Mrs Miller could now have made.

But there are a sort of persons, who, as Prior excellently well remarks, direct their conduct by something

> Beyond the fix'd and settled rules
> Of vice and virtue in the schools,
> Beyond the letter of the law.

To these it is so far from being sufficient that their defence would acquit them at the Old Bailey, that they are not even contented, though conscience, the severest of all judges, should discharge them. Nothing short of the fair and honourable will satisfy the delicacy of their minds; and if any of their actions fall short of this mark, they mope and pine, are as uneasy and restless as a murderer, who is afraid of a ghost, or of the hangman.

Mrs Miller was one of these. She could not conceal her uneasiness at this letter; with the contents of which she had no sooner acquainted the company, and given some hints of her distress, than Jones, her good angel, presently relieved her anxiety. "As for myself, madam," said he, "my lodging is at your service at a moment's warning; and Mr Nightingale, I am sure, as he cannot yet prepare a house fit to receive his lady, will consent to return to his new lodging, whither Mrs Nightingale will certainly consent to go." With which proposal both husband and wife instantly agreed.

The reader will easily believe, that the cheeks of Mrs Miller began again to glow with additional gratitude to Jones; but, perhaps, it may be more difficult to persuade him, that Mr Jones having in his last speech called her daughter Mrs Nightingale (it being the first time that agreeable sound had ever reached her ears), gave the fond mother more satisfaction, and warmed her heart more towards Jones, than his having dissipated her present anxiety.

The next day was then appointed for the removal of the new-married couple, and of Mr Jones, who was likewise to be provided for in the same house with his friend. And now the serenity of the company was again restored, and they past the day in the utmost chearfulness, all except Jones, who, though he outwardly accompanied the rest in their mirth, felt many a bitter pang on the account of his Sophia, which were not a little heightened by the news of Mr Blifil's coming to town (for he clearly saw the intention of his journey); and what greatly aggravated his concern was, that Mrs Honour, who had promised to inquire after Sophia, and to make her report to him early the next evening, had disappointed him.

In the situation that he and his mistress were in at this time, there were scarce any grounds for him to hope that he should hear any good news; yet he was as impatient to see Mrs Honour as if he had expected she would bring him a letter with an assignation in it from Sophia, and bore the disappointment as ill. Whether this impatience arose from that natural weakness of the human mind, which makes it desirous to know the worst, and renders uncertainty the most

intolerable of pains ; or whether he still flattered himself with some secret hopes, we will not determine.
But that it might be the last, whoever has loved cannot but know. For of all the powers exercised by
this passion over our minds, one of the most wonderful
is that of supporting hope in the midst of despair.
Difficulties, improbabilities, nay, impossibilities, are
quite overlooked by it ; so that to any man extremely
in love, may be applied what Addison says of Cæsar,

    " The Alps, and Pyrenæans, sink before him ! "

Yet it is equally true, that the same passion will sometimes make mountains of molehills, and produce despair
in the midst of hope ; but these cold fits last not long
in good constitutions. Which temper Jones was now
in, we leave the reader to guess, having no exact information about it ; but this is certain, that he had spent
two hours in expectation, when, being unable any
longer to conceal his uneasiness, he retired to his room ;
where his anxiety had almost made him frantick, when
the following letter was brought him from Mrs Honour,
with which we shall present the reader *verbatim et
literatim.*

    " Sir,

      " I shud sartenly haf kaled on you a cordin too
mi prommiss haddunt itt bin that hur lashipp prevent mee ;
for to bee sur, Sir, you nose very well that evere persun
must luk furst at ome, and sartenly such anuther offar
mite not have ever hapned, so as I shud ave bin justly
to blam, had I not excepted of it when her lashipp was
so veri kind as to offar to mak mee hur one uman
without mi ever askin any such thing, to be sur shee is
won of thee best ladis in thee wurld, and pepil who
sase to the kontrari must bee veri wiket pepil in thare
harts. To bee sur if ever I ave sad any thing of that

kine it as bin thru ignorens, and I am hartili sorri for it. I nose your onur to be a genteelman of more onur and onesty, if I ever said ani such thing, to repete it to hurt a pore servant that as alwais add thee gratest respect in thee wurld for ure onur. To be sur won shud kepe wons tung within wons teeth, for no boddi nose what may hapen ; and to bee sur if ani boddi ad tolde mee yesterday, that I shud haf bin in so gud a plase to day, I shud not haf beleeved it ; for to be sur I never was a dremd of any such thing, nor shud I ever have soft after ani other bodi's plase ; but as her laship wass so kine of her one a cord too give it mee without askin, to be sur Mrs Etoff herself, nor no other boddi can blam mee for exceptin such a thing when it fals in mi waye. I beg ure Onur not to menshion ani thing of what I haf sad, for I wish ure Onur all thee gud luk in the wurld ; and I don't cuestion butt thatt u will haf Madam Sofia in the end ; butt ass to miself ure onur nose I kant bee of ani farder sarvis to u in that matar, nou bein under thee cumand off anuther parson, and nott mi one mistress, I begg ure Onur to say nothing of what past, and belive me to be, sir, ure Onur's umble servant to cumand till deth,

" HONOUR BLACKMORE."

Various were the conjectures which Jones entertained on this step of Lady Bellaston ; who, in reality, had little farther design than to secure within her own house the repository of a secret, which she chose should make no farther progress than it had made already ; but mostly, she desired to keep it from the ears of Sophia ; for though that young lady was almost the only one who would never have repeated it again, her ladyship could not persuade herself of this ; since, as she now hated poor Sophia with most implacable hatred, she conceived a reciprocal hatred to herself to be lodged in the tender breast of our heroine, where no such passion had ever yet found an entrance.

While Jones was terrifying himself with the apprehension of a thousand dreadful machinations, and deep political designs, which he imagined to be at the bottom of the promotion of Honour, Fortune, who hitherto seems to have been an utter enemy to his match with Sophia, tried a new method to put a final end to it, by throwing a temptation in his way, which in his present desperate situation it seemed unlikely he should be able to resist.

Chapter ri.

Containing curious, but not unprecedented matter.

THERE was a lady, one Mrs Hunt, who had often seen Jones at the house where he lodged, being intimately acquainted with the women there, and indeed a very great friend to Mrs Miller. Her age was about thirty, for she owned six-and-twenty; her face and person very good, only inclining a little too much to be fat. She had been married young by her relations to an old Turkey merchant, who, having got a great fortune, had left off trade. With him she lived without reproach, but not without pain, in a state of great self-denial, for about twelve years; and her virtue was rewarded by his dying and leaving her very rich. The first year of her widowhood was just at an end, and she had past it in a good deal of retirement, seeing only a few particular friends, and dividing her time between her devotions and novels, of which she was always extremely fond. Very good health, a very warm constitution, and a good deal of religion, made it absolutely necessary for her to marry again; and she resolved to please herself in her second husband, as she had done her friends in the first. From her the following billet was brought to Jones:—

" SIR,

" From the first day I saw you, I doubt my eyes have told you too plainly that you were not indifferent to me; but neither my tongue nor my hand should have ever avowed it, had not the ladies of the family where you are lodged given me such a character of you, and told me such proofs of your virtue and goodness, as convince me you are not only the most agreeable, but the most worthy of men. I have also the satisfaction to hear from them, that neither my person, understanding, or character, are disagreeable to you. I have a fortune sufficient to make us both happy, but which cannot make me so without you. In thus disposing of myself, I know I shall incur the censure of the world; but if I did not love you more than I fear the world, I should not be worthy of you. One only difficulty stops me: I am informed you are engaged in a commerce of gallantry with a woman of fashion. If you think it worth while to sacrifice that to the possession of me, I am yours; if not, forget my weakness, and let this remain an eternal secret between you and

" ARABELLA HUNT."

At the reading of this, Jones was put into a violent flutter. His fortune was then at a very low ebb, the source being stopt from which hitherto he had been supplied. Of all he had received from Lady Bellaston, not above five guineas remained; and that very morning he had been dunned by a tradesman for twice that sum. His honourable mistress was in the hands of her father, and he had scarce any hopes ever to get her out of them again. To be subsisted at her expense, from that little fortune she had independent of her father, went much against the delicacy both of his pride and his love. This lady's fortune would have been exceeding convenient to him, and he could have no objection to her in any respect. On the contrary, he liked her as well as he did any woman except Sophia. But to abandon Sophia, and marry another, that was impossible; he could not think of it upon any account. Yet why should he not, since it was plain she could not be his? Would it not be kinder to her, than to continue her longer engaged in a hopeless passion for him? Ought he not to do so in friendship to her? This notion prevailed some moments, and he had almost determined to be false to her from a high point of honour: but that refinement was not able to stand very long against the voice of nature, which cried in his heart that such friendship was treason to love. At last he called for pen, ink, and paper, and writ as follows to Mrs Hunt :—

" MADAM,

"It would be but a poor return to the favour you have done me to sacrifice any gallantry to the possession of you, and I would certainly do it, though I were not disengaged, as at present I am, from any affair of that kind. But I should not be the honest man you think me, if I did not tell you that my affections are engaged to another, who is a woman of virtue, and one that I never can leave, though it is probable I shall never possess her. God forbid that, in return of your kindness to me, I should do you such an injury as to give you my hand when I cannot give my heart. No; I had much rather starve than be guilty of that. Even though my mistress were married to another, I would not marry you unless my heart had entirely effaced all impressions of her. Be assured that your secret was not more safe in your own breast, than in that of your most obliged, and grateful humble servant,

"T. Jones."

When our heroe had finished and sent this letter, he went to his scrutore, took out Miss Western's muff, kissed it several times, and then strutted some turns about his room, with more satisfaction of mind than ever any Irishman felt in carrying off a fortune of fifty thousand pounds.

Chapter xij.

A discovery made by Partridge.

WHILE Jones was exulting in the consciousness of his integrity, Partridge came capering into the room, as was his custom when he brought, or fancied he brought, any good tidings. He had been despatched that morning by his master, with orders to endeavour, by the servants of Lady Bellaston, or by any other means, to discover whither Sophia had been conveyed; and he now returned, and with a joyful countenance told our heroe that he had found the lost bird. "I have seen, sir," says he, "Black George, the gamekeeper, who is one of the servants whom the squire hath brought with him to town. I knew him presently, though I have not seen him these several years; but you know, sir, he is a very remarkable man, or, to use a purer phrase, he hath a most remarkable beard, the largest and blackest I ever saw. It was some time, however, before Black George could recollect me." "Well, but what is your good news?"

cries Jones; "what do you know of my Sophia?"
"You shall know presently, sir," answered Partridge,
"I am coming to it as fast as I can. You are so
impatient, sir, you would come at the infinitive mood
before you can get to the imperative. As I was saying, sir, it was some time before he recollected my
face."——"Confound your face!" cries Jones, "what
of my Sophia?" "Nay, sir," answered Partridge,
"I know nothing more of Madam Sophia than what I
am going to tell you; and I should have told you all
before this if you had not interrupted me; but if you
look so angry at me you will frighten all of it out of my
head, or, to use a purer phrase, out of my memory. I
never saw you look so angry since the day we left
Upton, which I shall remember if I was to live a
thousand years."——"Well, pray go on your own
way," said Jones: "you are resolved to make me mad
I find." "Not for the world," answered Partridge,
"I have suffered enough for that already; which, as I
said, I shall bear in my remembrance the longest day
I have to live." "Well, but Black George?" cries
Jones. "Well, sir, as I was saying, it was a long
time before he could recollect me; for, indeed, I am
very much altered since I saw him. *Non sum qualis
eram.* I have had troubles in the world, and nothing
alters a man so much as grief. I have heard it will
change the colour of a man's hair in a night. However, at last, know me he did, that's sure enough; for
we are both of an age, and were at the same charity
school. George was a great dunce, but no matter for
that; all men do not thrive in the world according to
their learning. I am sure I have reason to say so;
but it will be all one a thousand years hence. Well,
sir, where was I?——O—well, we no sooner knew
each other, than, after many hearty shakes by the hand,
we agreed to go to an alehouse and take a pot, and by

good luck the beer was some of the best I have met with since I have been in town. Now, sir, I am coming to the point; for no sooner did I name you, and told him that you and I came to town together, and had lived together ever since, than he called for another pot, and swore he would drink to your health; and indeed he drank your health so heartily that I was overjoyed to see there was so much gratitude left in the world; and after we had emptied that pot I said I would be my pot too, and so we drank another to your health; and then I made haste home to tell you the news.''

"What news?'' cries Jones, "you have not mentioned a word of my Sophia!'' "Bless me! I had like to have forgot that. Indeed, we mentioned a great deal about young Madam Western, and George told me all; that Mr Blifil is coming to town in order to be married to her. He had best make haste then, says I, or somebody will have her before he comes; and, indeed, says I, Mr Seagrim, it is a thousand pities somebody should not have her; for he certainly loves her above all the women in the world. I would have both you and she know, that it is not for her fortune he follows her; for I can assure you, as to matter of that, there is another lady, one of much greater quality and fortune than she can pretend to, who is so fond of somebody that she comes after him day and night.''

Here Jones fell into a passion with Partridge, for having, as he said, betrayed him; but the poor fellow answered, he had mentioned no name: "Besides, sir,'' said he, "I can assure you George is sincerely your friend, and wished Mr Blifil at the devil more than once; nay, he said he would do anything in his power upon earth to serve you; and so I am convinced he will. Betray you, indeed! why, I question whether you have a better friend than George upon earth, except myself, or one that would go farther to serve you."

"Well," says Jones, a little pacified, "you say this fellow, who, I believe, indeed, is enough inclined to be my friend, lives in the same house with Sophia?"

"In the same house!" answered Partridge; "why, sir, he is one of the servants of the family, and very well drest I promise you he is; if it was not for his black beard you would hardly know him."

"One service then at least he may do me," says Jones: "sure he can certainly convey a letter to my Sophia."

"You have hit the nail *ad unguem*," cries Partridge; "how came I not to think of it? I will engage he shall do it upon the very first mentioning."

"Well, then," said Jones, "do you leave me at present, and I will write a letter, which you shall deliver to him to-morrow morning; for I suppose you know where to find him."

"O yes, sir," answered Partridge, "I shall certainly find him again; there is no fear of that. The liquor is too good for him to stay away long. I make no doubt but he will be there every day he stays in town."

"So you don't know the street then where my Sophia is lodged?" cries Jones.

"Indeed, sir, I do," says Partridge.

"What is the name of the street?" cries Jones.

"The name, sir? why, here, sir, just by," answered Partridge, "not above a street or two off. I don't, indeed, know the very name; for, as he never told me, if I had asked, you know, it might have put some suspicion into his head. No, no, sir, let me alone for that. I am too cunning for that, I promise you."

"Thou art most wonderfully cunning, indeed," replied Jones; "however, I will write to my charmer, since I believe you will be cunning enough to find him to-morrow at the alehouse."

And now, having dismissed the sagacious Partridge, Mr Jones sat himself down to write, in which employment we shall leave him for a time. And here we put an end to the fifteenth book.

BOOK XVI.

Chapter i.

Of prologues.

I HAVE heard of a dramatic writer who used to say, he would rather write a play than a prologue; in like manner, I think, I can with less pains write one of the books of this history than the prefatory chapter to each of them.

To say the truth, I believe many a hearty curse hath been devoted on the head of that author who first instituted the method of prefixing to his play that portion of matter which is called the prologue; and which at first was part of the piece itself, but of latter years hath had usually so little connexion with the drama before which it stands, that the prologue to one play might as well serve for any other. Those indeed of more modern date, seem all to be written on the same three topics, viz., an abuse of the taste of the town, a condemnation of all contemporary authors, and an eulogium on the performance just about to be represented. The sentiments in all these are very little varied, nor is it possible they should; and indeed I have often wondered at the great invention of authors, who have been capable of finding such various phrases to express the same thing.

In like manner I apprehend, some future historian (if any one shall do me the honour of imitating my manner) will, after much scratching his pate, bestow some good wishes on my memory, for having first established these several initial chapters; most of which, like modern prologues, may as properly be prefixed to any other book in this history as to that which they introduce, or indeed to any other history as to this.

But however authors may suffer by either of these inventions, the reader will find sufficient emolument in the one as the spectator hath long found in the other.

First, it is well known that the prologue serves the critic for an opportunity to try his faculty of hissing, and to tune his cat-call to the best advantage; by which means, I have known those musical instruments so well prepared, that they have been able to play in full concert at the first rising of the curtain.

The same advantages may be drawn from these chapters, in which the critic will be always sure of meeting with something that may serve as a whetstone to his noble spirit; so that he may fall with a more hungry appetite for censure on the history itself. And here his sagacity must make it needless to observe how artfully these chapters are calculated for that excellent purpose; for in these we have always taken care to intersperse somewhat of the sour or acid kind, in order to sharpen and stimulate the said spirit of criticism.

Again, the indolent reader, as well as spectator, finds great advantage from both these; for, as they are not obliged either to see the one or read the others, and both the play and the book are thus protracted, by the former they have a quarter of an hour longer allowed them to sit at dinner, and by the latter they have the advantage of beginning to read at the fourth or fifth page instead of the first, a matter by no means of trivial consequence to persons who read books with no other

view than to say they have read them, a more general
motive to reading than is commonly imagined; and
from which not only law books, and good books, but
the pages of Homer and Virgil, of Swift and Cervantes,
have been often turned over.

Many other are the emoluments which arise from
both these, but they are for the most part so obvious,
that we shall not at present stay to enumerate them;
especially since it occurs to us that the principal merit
of both the prologue and the preface is that they be
short.

Chapter ij.

*A whimsical adventure which befel the squire, with the
distressed situation of Sophia.*

WE must now convey the reader to Mr Western's
lodgings, which were in Piccadilly, where
he was placed by the recommendation of the
landlord at the Hercules Pillars at Hyde Park Corner;
for at the inn, which was the first he saw on his arrival
in town, he placed his horses, and in those lodgings,
which were the first he heard of, he deposited himself.

Here, when Sophia alighted from the hackney-coach,
which brought her from the house of Lady Bellaston,
she desired to retire to the apartment provided for her;
to which her father very readily agreed, and whither he
attended her himself. A short dialogue, neither very
material nor pleasant to relate minutely, then passed
between them, in which he pressed her vehemently to
give her consent to the marriage with Blifil, who, as
he acquainted her, was to be in town in a few days;
but, instead of complying, she gave a more peremptory
and resolute refusal than she had ever done before

This so incensed her father, that after many bitter vows, that he would force her to have him whether she would or no, he departed from her with many hard words and curses, locked the door, and put the key into his pocket.

While Sophia was left with no other company than what attend the closest state prisoner, namely, fire and candle, the squire sat down to regale himself over a bottle of wine, with his parson and the landlord of the Hercules Pillars, who, as the squire said, would make an excellent third man, and could inform them of the news of the town, and how affairs went; for to be sure, says he, he knows a great deal, since the horses of many of the quality stand at his house.

In this agreeable society Mr Western past that evening and great part of the succeeding day, during which period nothing happened of sufficient consequence to find a place in this history. All this time Sophia past by herself; for her father swore she should never come out of her chamber alive, unless she first consented to marry Blifil; nor did he ever suffer the door to be unlocked, unless to convey her food, on which occasions he always attended himself.

The second morning after his arrival, while he and the parson were at breakfast together on a toast and tankard, he was informed that a gentleman was below to wait on him.

" A gentleman! " quoth the squire, "who the devil can he be? Do, doctor, go down and see who 'tis. Mr Blifil can hardly be come to town yet.—Go down, do, and know what his business is."

The doctor returned with an account that it was a very well-drest man, and by the ribbon in his hat he took him for an officer of the army; that he said he had some particular business, which he could deliver to none but Mr Western himself.

"An officer!" cries the squire; "what can any such fellow have to do with me? If he wants an order for baggage-waggons, I am no justice of peace here, nor can I grant a warrant.—Let un come up then, if he must speak to me."

A very genteel man now entered the room; who, having made his compliments to the squire, and desired the favour of being alone with him, delivered himself as follows:—

"Sir, I come to wait upon you by the command of my Lord Fellamar; but with a very different message from what I suppose you expect, after what past the other night."

"My lord who?" cries the squire; "I never heard the name o'un."

"His lordship," said the gentleman, "is willing to impute everything to the effect of liquor, and the most trifling acknowledgment of that kind will set everything right; for as he hath the most violent attachment to your daughter, you, sir, are the last person upon earth from whom he would resent an affront; and happy is it for you both that he hath given such public demonstrations of his courage as to be able to put up an affair of this kind without danger of any imputation on his honour. All he desires, therefore, is, that you will before me make some acknowledgment; the slightest in the world will be sufficient; and he intends this afternoon to pay his respects to you, in order to obtain your leave of visiting the young lady on the footing of a lover."

"I don't understand much of what you say, sir," said the squire; "but I suppose, by what you talk about my daughter, that this is the lord which my cousin, Lady Bellaston, mentioned to me, and said something about his courting my daughter. If so be that how that be the case—you may give my service to his lordship, and tell un the girl is disposed of already."

"Perhaps, sir," said the gentleman, "you are not sufficiently apprized of the greatness of this offer. I believe such a person, title, and fortune would be nowhere refused."

"Lookee, sir," answered the squire; "to be very plain, my daughter is bespoke already; but if she was not, I would not marry her to a lord upon any account; I hate all lords; they are a parcel of courtiers and Hanoverians, and I will have nothing to do with them."

"Well, sir," said the gentleman, "if that is your resolution, the message I am to deliver to you is that my lord desires the favour of your company this morning in Hyde Park."

"You may tell my lord," answered the squire, "that I am busy and cannot come. I have enough to look after at home, and can't stir abroad on any account."

"I am sure, sir," quoth the other, "you are too much a gentleman to send such a message; you will not, I am convinced, have it said of you, that, after having affronted a noble peer, you refuse him satisfaction. His lordship would have been willing, from his great regard to the young lady, to have made up matters in another way; but unless he is to look on you as a father, his honour will not suffer his putting up such an indignity as you must be sensible you offered him."

"I offered him!" cries the squire; "it is a d—n'd lie! I never offered him anything."

Upon these words the gentleman returned a very short verbal rebuke, and this he accompanied at the same time with some manual remonstrances, which no sooner reached the ears of Mr Western, than that worthy squire began to caper very briskly about the room, bellowing at the same time with all his might, as if desirous to summon a greater number of spectators to behold his agility.

The parson, who had left great part of the tankard unfinished, was not retired far ; he immediately attended therefore on the squire's vociferation, crying, " Bless me ! sir, what's the matter ? "—" Matter ! " quoth the squire, " here's a highwayman, I believe, who wants to rob and murder me—for he hath fallen upon me with that stick there in his hand, when I wish I may be d—n'd if I gid un the least provocation."

" How, sir," said the captain, " did you not tell me I lyed ? "

" No, as I hope to be saved," answered the squire, "—I believe I might say, 'Twas a lie that I had offered any affront to my lord—but I never said the word, ' you lie.'—I understand myself better, and you might have understood yourself better than to fall upon a naked man.   If I had a stick in my hand, you would not have dared strike me.   I'd have knocked thy lantern jaws about thy ears.   Come down into yard this minute, and I'll take a bout with thee at single stick for a broken head, that I will ; or I will go into naked room and box thee for a belly-full.   At unt half a man, at unt, I'm sure."

The captain, with some indignation, replied, " I see, sir, you are below my notice, and I shall inform his lordship you are below his.   I am sorry I have dirtied my fingers with you."   At which words he withdrew, the parson interposing to prevent the squire from stopping him, in which he easily prevailed, as the other, though he made some efforts for the purpose, did not seem very violently bent on success.   However, when the captain was departed, the squire sent many curses and some menaces after him; but as these did not set out from his lips till the officer was at the bottom of the stairs, and grew louder and louder as he was more and more remote, they did not reach his ears, or at least did not retard his departure.

Poor Sophia, however, who, in her prison, heard all her father's outcries from first to last, began now first to thunder with her foot, and afterwards to scream as loudly as the old gentleman himself had done before, though in a much sweeter voice. These screams soon silenced the squire, and turned all his consideration towards his daughter, whom he loved so tenderly, that the least apprehension of any harm happening to her, threw him presently into agonies; for, except in that single instance in which the whole future happiness of her life was concerned, she was sovereign mistress of his inclinations.

Having ended his rage against the captain, with swearing he would take the law of him, the squire now mounted upstairs to Sophia, whom, as soon as he had unlocked and opened the door, he found all pale and breathless. The moment, however, that she saw her father, she collected all her spirits, and, catching him hold by the hand, she cryed passionately, "O my dear sir, I am almost frightened to death! I hope to heaven no harm hath happened to you." "No, no," cries the squire, "no great harm. The rascal hath not hurt me much, but rat me if I don't ha the la o' un." "Pray, dear sir," says she, "tell me what's the matter; who is it that hath insulted you?" "I don't know the name o' un," answered Western; "some officer fellow, I suppose, that we are to pay for beating us; but I'll make him pay this bout, if the rascal hath got anything, which I suppose he hath not. For thof he was drest out so vine, I question whether he had got a voot of land in the world." "But, dear sir," cries she, "what was the occasion of your quarrel?"   "What should it be, Sophy," answered the squire, "but about you, Sophy?   All my misfortunes are about you; you will be the death of your poor father at last.   Here's a varlet of a lord, the Lord knows who, forsooth! who hath a taan a liking to you, and because I would not gi un my consent, he sent me a kallenge.   Come, do be a good girl, Sophy, and put an end to all your father's troubles; come, do consent to ha un; he will be in town within this day or two; do but promise me to marry un as soon as he comes, and you will make me the happiest man in the world, and I will make you the happiest woman; you shall have the finest cloaths in London, and the finest jewels, and a coach and six at your command.   I promised Allworthy already to give up half my estate—odrabbet it! I should hardly stick at giving up the whole."   "Will my papa be so kind," says she, "as to hear me speak?"—"Why wout ask, Sophy?" cries he, "when dost know I had rather hear thy voice than the musick of the best pack of dogs in England.—Hear thee, my dear little girl!   I hope I shall hear thee as long as I live; for if I was ever to lose that pleasure, I would not gee a brass varden to live a moment longer.   Indeed, Sophy, you do not know how I love you, indeed you don't, or you never could have run away and left your poor father, who hath no other joy, no other comfort upon earth, but his little Sophy."   At these words the tears stood in his eyes; and Sophia (with the tears streaming from hers) answered, "Indeed, my dear papa, I know you have loved me tenderly, and heaven is my witness how sincerely I have re-turned your affection; nor could anything but an apprehension of being forced into the arms of this man have driven me to run from a father whom I love so passionately, that I would, with pleasure.

sacrifice my life to his happiness; nay, I have endeavoured to reason myself into doing more, and had almost worked up a resolution to endure the most miserable of all lives, to comply with your inclination. It was that resolution alone to which I could not force my mind; nor can I ever." Here the squire began to look wild, and the foam appeared at his lips, which Sophia, observing, begged to be heard out, and then proceeded: "If my father's life, his health, or any real happiness of his was at stake, here stands your resolved daughter; may heaven blast me if there is a misery I would not suffer to preserve you!—No, that most detested, most loathsome of all lots would I embrace. I would give my hand to Blifil for your sake."—"I tell thee, it will preserve me," answers the father; "it will give me health, happiness, life, everything.—Upon my soul I shall die if dost refuse me; I shall break my heart, I shall, upon my soul." —"Is it possible," says she, "you can have such a desire to make me miserable?"—"I tell thee noa," answered he loudly, "d——n me if there is a thing upon earth I would not do to see thee happy."—"And will not my dear papa allow me to have the least knowledge of what will make me so? If it be true that happiness consists in opinion, what must be my condition, when I shall think myself the most miserable of all the wretches upon earth?" "Better think yourself so," said he, "than know it by being married to a poor bastardly vagabond." "If it will content you, sir," said Sophia, "I will give you the most solemn promise never to marry him, nor any other, while my papa lives, without his consent. Let me dedicate my whole life to your service; let me be again your poor Sophy, and my whole business and pleasure be, as it hath been, to please and divert you." "Lookee, Sophy," answered the squire, "I am not to be choused in this

manner. Your aunt Western would then have reason
to think me the fool she doth. No, no, Sophy, I'd
have you to know I have a got more wisdom, and
know more of the world, than to take the word of
a woman in a matter where a man is concerned."
"How, sir, have I deserved this want of confidence?"
said she; "have I ever broke a single promise to you?
or have I ever been found guilty of a falsehood from
my cradle?" "Lookee, Sophy," cries he; "that's
neither here nor there. I am determined upon this
match, and have him you shall, d—n me if shat unt.
D—n me if shat unt, though dost hang thyself the
next morning." At repeating which words he clinched
his fist, knit his brows, bit his lips, and thundered so
loud, that the poor afflicted, terrified Sophia sunk
trembling into her chair, and, had not a flood of
tears come immediately to her relief, perhaps worse
had followed.

Western beheld the deplorable condition of his
daughter with no more contrition or remorse than
the turnkey of Newgate feels at viewing the agonies
of a tender wife, when taking her last farewell of
her condemned husband; or rather he looked down
on her with the same emotions which arise in an
honest fair tradesman, who sees his debtor dragged to
prison for £10, which, though a just debt, the wretch
is wickedly unable to pay. Or, to hit the case still
more nearly, he felt the same compunction with a
bawd, when some poor innocent, whom she hath en-
snared into her hands, falls into fits at the first proposal
of what is called seeing company. Indeed this resemblance would be exact, was it not that the bawd
hath an interest in what she doth, and the father,
though perhaps he may blindly think otherwise, can,
in reality, have none in urging his daughter to almost
an equal prostitution.

In this condition he left his poor Sophia, and, departing with a very vulgar observation on the effect of tears, he locked the room, and returned to the parson, who said everything he durst in behalf of the young lady, which, though perhaps it was not quite so much as his duty required, yet was it sufficient to throw the squire into a violent rage, and into many indecent reflections on the whole body of the clergy, which we have too great an honour for that sacred function to commit to paper.

Chapter iij.

What happened to Sophia during her confinement.

THE landlady of the house where the squire lodged had begun very early to entertain a strange opinion of her guests. However, as she was informed that the squire was a man of vast fortune, and as she had taken care to exact a very extraordinary price for her rooms, she did not think proper to give any offence; for, though she was not without some concern for the confinement of poor Sophia, of whose great sweetness of temper and affability the maid of the house had made so favourable a report, which was confirmed by all the squire's servants, yet she had much more concern for her own interest than to provoke one, whom, as she said, she perceived to be a very hastish kind of a gentleman.

Though Sophia eat but little, yet she was regularly served with her meals; indeed, I believe, if she had liked any one rarity, that the squire, however angry, would have spared neither pains nor cost to have procured it for her; since, however strange it may appear to some of my readers, he really doated on his daughter, and to give her any kind of pleasure was the highest satisfaction of his life.

The dinner-hour being arrived, Black George carried her up a pullet, the squire himself (for he had sworn not to part with the key) attending the door. As George deposited the dish, some compliments passed between him and Sophia (for he had not seen her since she left the country, and she treated every servant with more respect than some persons shew to those who are in a very slight degree their inferiors). Sophia would have had him take the pullet back, saying, she could not eat; but George begged her to try, and particularly recommended to her the eggs, of which he said it was full.

All this time the squire was waiting at the door; but George was a great favourite with his master, as his employment was in concerns of the highest nature, namely, about the game, and was accustomed to take many liberties. He had officiously carried up the dinner, being, as he said, very desirous to see his young lady; he made therefore no scruple of keeping his master standing above ten minutes, while civilities were passing between him and Sophia, for which he received only a good-humoured rebuke at the door when he returned.

The eggs of pullets, partridges, pheasants, &c., were, as George well knew, the most favourite dainties of Sophia. It was therefore no wonder that he, who was a very good-natured fellow, should take care to supply her with this kind of delicacy, at a time when all the servants in the house were afraid she would be starved; for she had scarce swallowed a single morsel in the last forty hours.

Though vexation hath not the same effect on all persons as it usually hath on a widow, whose appetite it often renders sharper than it can be rendered by the air on Bansted Downs, or Salisbury Plain; yet the sublimest grief, notwithstanding what some people may say to the contrary, will eat at last. And Sophia, herself, after some little consideration, began to dissect the fowl, which she found to be as full of eggs as George had reported it.

But, if she was pleased with these, it contained something which would have delighted the Royal Society much more; for if a fowl with three legs be so invaluable a curiosity, when perhaps time hath produced a thousand such, at what price shall we esteem a bird which so totally contradicts all the laws of animal œconomy, as to contain a letter in its belly? Ovid tells us of a flower into which Hyacinthus was metamorphosed, that bears letters on its leaves, which Virgil recommended as a miracle to the Royal Society of his day; but no age nor nation hath ever recorded a bird with a letter in its maw.

But though a miracle of this kind might have engaged all the *Académies des Sciences* in Europe, and perhaps in a fruitless enquiry; yet the reader, by barely recollecting the last dialogue which passed between Messieurs Jones and Partridge, will be very easily satisfied from whence this letter came, and how it found its passage into the fowl.

Sophia, notwithstanding her long fast, and notwithstanding her favourite dish was there before her, no sooner saw the letter than she immediately snatched it up, tore it open, and read as follows :—

"Madam,

"Was I not sensible to whom I have the honour of writing, I should endeavour, however difficult, to paint the horrors of my mind at the account brought me by Mrs Honour; but as tenderness alone can have any true idea of the pangs which tenderness is capable of feeling, so can this most amiable quality, which my Sophia possesses in the most eminent degree, sufficiently inform her what her Jones must have suffered on this melancholy occasion. Is there a circumstance in the world which can heighten my agonies, when I hear of any misfortune which hath befallen you? Surely there is one only, and with that I am accursed. It is, my Sophia, the dreadful consideration that I am myself the wretched cause. Perhaps I here do myself too much honour, but none will envy me an honour which costs me so extremely dear. Pardon me this presumption, and pardon me a greater still, if I ask you, whether my advice, my assistance, my presence, my absence, my death, or my tortures can bring you any relief? Can the most perfect admiration, the most watchful observance, the most ardent love, the most melting tenderness, the most resigned submission to your will, make you amends for what you are to sacrifice to my happiness? If they can, fly, my lovely angel, to those arms which are ever open to receive and protect you; and to which, whether you bring yourself alone, or the riches of the world with you, is, in my opinion, an alternative not worth regarding. If, on the contrary, wisdom shall predominate, and, on the most mature reflection, inform you, that the sacrifice is too great; and if there be no way left to reconcile your father, and restore the peace of your dear mind, but by abandoning me, I conjure you drive me for ever from your thoughts, exert your resolution, and let no compassion for my sufferings bear the least weight in that tender bosom. Believe me, madam, I so sincerely love you better than myself, that my great and principal end is your happiness. My first wish (why would not fortune indulge me in it?) was, and pardon me if I say, still is, to see you every moment the happiest of women; my second wish is, to hear you are so; but no misery on earth can equal mine, while I think you owe an uneasy moment to him who is,

    Madam,
        in every sense, and to every purpose,
            your devoted,
                Thomas Jones."

What Sophia said, or did, or thought, upon this letter, how often she read it, or whether more than once, shall all be left to our reader's imagination. The answer to it he may perhaps see hereafter, but not at present: for this reason, among others, that she did not now write any, and that for several good causes, one of which was this, she had no paper, pen, nor ink.

In the evening, while Sophia was meditating on the letter she had received, or on something else, a violent noise from below disturbed her meditations. This noise was no other than a round bout at altercation between two persons. One of the combatants, by his voice, she immediately distinguished to be her father; but she did not so soon discover the shriller pipes to belong to the organ of her aunt Western, who was just arrived in town, where having, by means of one of her servants, who stopt at the Hercules Pillars, learned where her brother lodged, she drove directly to his lodgings.

We shall therefore take our leave at present of Sophia, and, with our usual good-breeding, attend her ladyship.

Chapter iv.

In which Sophia is delivered from her confinement.

THE squire and the parson (for the landlord was now otherwise engaged) were smoking their pipes together, when the arrival of the lady was first signified. The squire no sooner heard her name, than he immediately ran down to usher her upstairs; for he was a great observer of such ceremonials, especially to his sister, of whom he stood more in awe than of any other human creature, though he never would own this, nor did he perhaps know it himself.

Mrs Western, on her arrival in the dining-room, having flung herself into a chair, began thus to harangue: "Well, surely, no one ever had such an intolerable journey. I think the roads, since so many turnpike acts, are grown worse than ever. La, brother, how could you get into this odious place? no person of condition, I dare swear, ever set foot here before." "I don't know," cries the squire, "I think they do well enough; it was landlord recommended them. I thought, as he knew most of the quality, he could best shew me where to get among um." "Well, and where's my niece?" says the lady; "have you been to wait upon Lady Bellaston yet?" "Ay, ay," cries the squire, "your niece is safe enough; she is upstairs in chamber." "How!" answered the lady, "is my niece in this house, and does she not know of my being here?" "No, nobody can well get to her," says the squire, "for she is under lock and key. I have her safe; I vetched her from my lady cousin the first night I came to town, and I have taken care o' her ever since; she is as secure as a fox in a bag, I promise you." "Good heaven!" returned Mrs Western, "what do I hear? I thought what a fine piece of work would be the consequence of my consent to your coming to town yourself; nay, it was indeed your own headstrong will, nor can I charge myself with having ever consented to it. Did not you promise me, brother, that you would take none of these headstrong measures? Was it not by these headstrong measures that you forced my niece to run away from you in the country? Have you a mind to oblige her to take such another step?" "Z——ds and the devil!" cries the squire, dashing his pipe on the ground; "did ever mortal hear the like? when I expected you would have commended me for all I have done, to be fallen upon in this manner!" "How, brother!" said the lady, "have I ever given you the least reason to imagine I should commend you for locking up your daughter? Have I not often told you that women in a free country are not to be treated with such arbitrary power? We are as free as the men, and I heartily wish I could not say we deserve that freedom better. If you expect I should stay a moment longer in this wretched house, or that I should ever own you again as my relation, or that I should ever trouble myself again with the affairs of your family, I insist upon it that my niece be set at liberty this instant." This she spoke with so commanding an air, standing with her back to the fire, with one hand behind her, and a pinch of snuff in the other, that I question whether Thalestris, at the head of her Amazons, ever made a more tremendous figure. It is no wonder, therefore, that the poor squire was not proof against the awe which she inspired. "There," he cried, throwing down the key, "there it is, do whatever you please. I intended only to have kept her up till Blifil came to town, which can't be long; and now if any harm happens in the mean time, remember who is to be blamed for it."

"I will answer it with my life," cried Mrs Western, "but I shall not intermeddle at all, unless upon one condition, and that is, that you will commit the whole entirely to my care, without taking any one measure yourself, unless I shall eventually appoint you to act. If you ratify these preliminaries, brother, I yet will endeavour to preserve the honour of your family; if not, I shall continue in a neutral state."

"I pray you, good sir," said the parson, "permit yourself this once to be admonished by her ladyship: peradventure, by communing with young Madam Sophia, she will effect more than you have been able to perpetrate by more rigorous measures."

"What, dost thee open upon me?" cries the squire: "if thee dost begin to babble, I shall whip thee in presently."

"Fie, brother," answered the lady, "is this language to a clergyman? Mr Supple is a man of sense, and gives you the best advice; and the whole world, I believe, will concur in his opinion; but I must tell you I expect an immediate answer to my categorical proposals. Either cede your daughter to my disposal, or take her wholly to your own surprizing discretion, and then I here, before Mr Supple, evacuate the garrison, and renounce you and your family for ever."

"I pray you let me be a mediator," cries the parson, "let me supplicate you."

"Why, there lies the key on the table," cries the squire. "She may take un up, if she pleases: who hinders her?"

"No, brother," answered the lady, "I insist on the formality of its being delivered me, with a full ratification of all the concessions stipulated."

"Why then I will deliver it to you.—There 'tis," cries the squire. "I am sure, sister, you can't accuse me of ever denying to trust my daughter to you. She hath a-lived wi' you a whole year and muore to a time, without my ever zeeing her."

"And it would have been happy for her," answered the lady, "if she had always lived with me. Nothing of this kind would have happened under my eye."

"Ay, certainly," cries he, "I only am to blame."

"Why, you are to blame, brother," answered she. "I have been often obliged to tell you so, and shall always be obliged to tell you so. However, I hope you will now amend, and gather so much experience from past errors, as not to defeat my wisest machinations by your blunders. Indeed, brother, you are not qualified for these negociations. All your whole scheme of politics is wrong. I once more, therefore, insist, that you do not intermeddle. Remember only what is past."——

"Z——ds and bl——d, sister," cries the squire, "what would you have me say? You are enough to provoke the devil."

"There, now," said she, "just according to the old custom. I see, brother, there is no talking to you. I will appeal to Mr Supple, who is a man of sense, if I said anything which could put any human creature into a passion; but you are so wrongheaded every way."

"Let me beg you, madam," said the parson, "not to irritate his worship."

"Irritate him?" said the lady; "sure, you are as great a fool as himself. Well, brother, since you have promised not to interfere, I will once more undertake the management of my niece. Lord have mercy upon all affairs which are under the directions of men! The head of one woman is worth a thousand of yours." And now having summoned a servant to show her to Sophia, she departed, bearing the key with her.

She was no sooner gone, than the squire (having first shut the door) ejaculated twenty bitches, and as many hearty curses against her, not sparing himself for having ever thought of her estate; but added, " Now one hath been a slave so long, it would be pity to lose it at last, for want of holding out a little longer. The bitch can't live for ever, and I know I am down for it upon the will."

The parson greatly commended this resolution: and now the squire having ordered in another bottle, which was his usual method when anything either pleased or vexed him, did, by drinking plentifully of this medicinal julap, so totally wash away his choler, that his temper was become perfectly placid and serene, when Mrs Western returned with Sophia into the room. The young lady had on her hat and capuchin, and the aunt acquainted Mr Western, " that she intended to take her niece with her to her own lodgings; for, indeed, brother," says she, " these rooms are not fit to receive a Christian soul in."

" Very well, madam," quoth Western, " whatever you please. The girl can never be in better hands than yours; and the parson here can do me the justice to say, that I have said fifty times behind your back, that you was one of the most sensible women in the world."

" To this," cries the parson, " I am ready to bear testimony."

" Nay, brother," says Mrs Western, " I have always, I'm sure, given you as favourable a character. You must own you have a little too much hastiness in your temper; but when you will allow yourself time to reflect I never knew a man more reasonable."

" Why then, sister, if you think so," said the squire, " here's your good health with all my heart. I am a little passionate sometimes, but I scorn to bear any malice. Sophy, do you be a good girl, and do every-thing your aunt orders you."

"I have not the least doubt of her," answered Mrs Western. "She hath had already an example before her eyes in the behaviour of that wretch her cousin Harriet, who ruined herself by neglecting my advice. O brother, what think you? You was hardly gone out of hearing, when you set out for London, when who should arrive but that impudent fellow with the odious Irish name—that Fitzpatrick. He broke in abruptly upon me without notice, or I would not have seen him. He ran on a long, unintelligible story about his wife, to which he forced me to give him a hearing; but I made him very little answer, and delivered him the letter from his wife, which I bid him answer himself. I suppose the wretch will endeavour to find us out, but I beg you will not see her, for I am determined I will not."

"I zee her!" answered the squire; "you need not fear me. I'll ge no encouragemant to such undutiful wenches. It is well for the fellow, her husband, I was not at huome. Od rabbit it, he should have taken a dance thru the horse-pond, I promise un. You zee, Sophy, what undutifulness brings volks to. You have an example in your own family."

"Brother," cries the aunt, "you need not shock my niece by such odious repetitions. Why will you not leave everything entirely to me?" "Well, well, I wull, I wull," said the squire.

And now Mrs Western, luckily for Sophia, put an end to the conversation by ordering chairs to be called. I say luckily, for had it continued much longer, fresh matter of dissension would, most probably, have arisen between the brother and sister; between whom education and sex made the only difference; for both were equally violent and equally positive: they had both a vast affection for Sophia, and both a sovereign contempt for each other.

Chapter v.

In which Jones receives a letter from Sophia, and goes to a play with Mrs Miller and Partridge.

THE arrival of Black George in town, and the good offices which that grateful fellow had promised to do for his old benefactor, greatly comforted Jones in the midst of all the anxiety and uneasiness which he had suffered on the account of Sophia; from whom, by the means of the said George, he received the following answer to his letter, which Sophia, to whom the use of pen, ink, and paper was restored with her liberty, wrote the very evening when she departed from her confinement:

" SIR,

"As I do not doubt your sincerity in what you write, you will be pleased to hear that some of my afflictions are at an end, by the arrival of my aunt Western, with whom I am at present, and with whom I enjoy all the liberty I can desire. One promise my aunt hath insisted on my making, which is, that I will not see or converse with any person without her knowledge and consent. This promise I have most solemnly given, and shall most inviolably keep: and though she hath not expressly forbidden me writing, yet that must be an omission from forgetfulness; or this, perhaps, is included in the word conversing. However, as I cannot but consider this as a breach of her generous confidence in my honour, you cannot expect that I shall, after this, continue to write myself or to receive letters, without her knowledge. A promise is with me a very sacred thing, and to be extended to everything understood from it, as well as to what is expressed by it; and this consideration may, perhaps, on reflection, afford you some comfort.   But why should I mention a comfort to you of this kind ; for though there is one thing in which I can never comply with the best of fathers, yet am I firmly resolved never to act in defiance of him, or to take any step of consequence without his consent.   A firm persuasion of this must teach you to divert your thoughts from what fortune hath (perhaps) made impossible.   This your own interest persuades you.   This may reconcile, I hope, Mr Allworthy to you ; and if it will, you have my injunctions to pursue it.   Accidents have laid some obligations on me, and your good intentions probably more.   Fortune may, perhaps, be some time kinder to us both than at present. Believe this, that I shall always think of you as I think you deserve, and am,

Sir,
your obliged humble servant,
SOPHIA WESTERN.

" I charge you write to me no more—at present at least ; and accept this, which is now of no service to me, which I know you must want, and think you owe the trifle only to that fortune by which you found it." *

A child who hath just learnt his letters would have spelt this letter out in less time than Jones took in reading it.   The sensations it occasioned were a mixture of joy and grief ; somewhat like what divide the mind of a good man when he peruses the will of his deceased friend, in which a large legacy, which his distresses make the more welcome, is bequeathed to him.   Upon the whole, however, he was more pleased than displeased ; and, indeed, the reader may probably wonder that he was displeased at all ; but the reader is not quite so much in love as was poor Jones ; and love

* Meaning, perhaps, the bank-bill for £100.

is a disease which, though it may, in some instances, resemble a consumption (which it sometimes causes), in others proceeds in direct opposition to it, and particularly in this, that it never flatters itself, or sees any one symptom in a favourable light.

One thing gave him complete satisfaction, which was, that his mistress had regained her liberty, and was now with a lady where she might at least assure herself of a decent treatment. Another comfortable circumstance was the reference which she made to her promise of never marrying any other man; for however disinterested he might imagine his passion, and notwithstanding all the generous overtures made in his letter, I very much question whether he could have heard a more afflicting piece of news than that Sophia was married to another, though the match had been never so great, and never so likely to end in making her completely happy. That refined degree of Platonic affection which is absolutely detached from the flesh, and is, indeed, entirely and purely spiritual, is a gift confined to the female part of the creation; many of whom I have heard declare (and, doubtless, with great truth), that they would, with the utmost readiness, resign a lover to a rival, when such resignation was proved to be necessary for the temporal interest of such lover. Hence, therefore, I conclude that this affection is in nature, though I cannot pretend to say I have ever seen an instance of it.

Mr Jones having spent three hours in reading and kissing the aforesaid letter, and being, at last, in a state of good spirits, from the last-mentioned considerations, he agreed to carry an appointment, which he had before made, into execution. This was, to attend Mrs Miller, and her younger daughter, into the gallery at the play-house, and to admit Mr Partridge as one of the company. For as Jones had really that taste for humour which many affect, he expected to enjoy much entertainment in the criticisms of Partridge, from whom he expected the simple dictates of nature, unimproved, indeed, but likewise unadulterated, by art.

In the first row then of the first gallery did Mr Jones, Mrs Miller, her youngest daughter, and Partridge, take their places. Partridge immediately declared it was the finest place he had ever been in. When the first music was played, he said, " It was a wonder how so many fiddlers could play at one time, without putting one another out." While the fellow was lighting the upper candles, he cried out to Mrs Miller, " Look, look, madam, the very picture of the man in the end of the common-prayer book before the gunpowder-treason service." Nor could he help observing, with a sigh, when all the candles were lighted, " That here were candles enough burnt in one night, to keep an honest poor family for a whole twelvemonth."

As soon as the play, which was Hamlet, Prince of Denmark, began, Partridge was all attention, nor did he break silence till the entrance of the ghost; upon which he asked Jones, " What man that was in the strange dress; something," said he, " like what I have seen in a picture. Sure it is not armour, is it?" Jones answered, " That is the ghost." To which Partridge replied with a smile, " Persuade me to that, sir, if you can. Though I can't say I ever actually saw a ghost in my life, yet I am certain I should know one, if I saw him, better than that comes to. No, no, sir, ghosts don't appear in such dresses as that, neither." In this mistake, which caused much laughter in the neighbourhood of Partridge, he was suffered to continue, till the scene between the ghost and Hamlet, when Partridge gave that credit to Mr Garrick, which he had denied to Jones, and fell into so violent a trembling, that his knees knocked against each other. Jones asked him what was the matter, and whether he was afraid of the warrior upon the stage? "O la! sir," said he, "I perceive now it is what you told me. I am not afraid of anything; for I know it is but a play. And if it was really a ghost, it could do one no harm at such a distance, and in so much company; and yet if I was frightened, I am not the only person." "Why, who," cries Jones, "dost thou take to be such a coward here besides thyself?" "Nay, you may call me coward if you will; but if that little man there upon the stage is not frightened, I never saw any man frightened in my life. Ay, ay: go along with you: Ay, to be sure! Who's fool then? Will you? Lud have mercy upon such fool-hardiness!—Whatever happens, it is good enough for you.——Follow you? I'd follow the devil as soon. Nay, perhaps it is the devil——for they say he can put on what likeness he pleases.—Oh! here he is again.——No farther! No, you have gone far enough already; farther than I'd have gone for all the king's dominions." Jones offered to speak, but Partridge cried "Hush, hush! dear sir, don't you hear him?" And during the whole speech of the ghost, he sat with his eyes fixed partly on the ghost and partly on Hamlet, and with his mouth open; the same passions which succeeded each other in Hamlet, succeeding likewise in him.

When the scene was over Jones said, "Why, Partridge, you exceed my expectations. You enjoy the play more than I conceived possible." "Nay, sir," answered Partridge, "if you are not afraid of the devil, I can't help it; but to be sure, it is natural to be surprized at such things, though I know there is nothing in them: not that it was the ghost that surprized me, neither; for I should have known that to have been only a man in a strange dress; but when I saw the little man so frightened himself, it was that which took hold of me." "And dost thou imagine, then, Partridge," cries Jones, "that he was really frightened?" "Nay, sir," said Partridge, "did not you yourself observe afterwards, when he found it was his own father's spirit, and how he was murdered in the garden, how his fear forsook him by degrees, and he was struck dumb with sorrow, as it were, just as I should have been, had it been my own case?—But hush! O la! what noise is that? There he is again.——Well to be certain, though I know there is nothing at all in it, I am glad I am not down yonder, where those men are." Then turning his eyes again upon Hamlet, "Ay, you may draw your sword; what signifies a sword against the power of the devil?"

During the second act, Partridge made very few remarks. He greatly admired the fineness of the dresses; nor could he help observing upon the king's countenance. "Well," said he, "how people may be deceived by faces! *Nulla fides fronti* is, I find, a true saying. Who would think, by looking in the king's face, that he had ever committed a murder?" He then enquired after the ghost; but Jones, who intended he should be surprized, gave him no other satisfaction, than, "that he might possibly see him again soon, and in a flash of fire."

Partridge sat in a fearful expectation of this; and now, when the ghost made his next appearance, Partridge cried out, "There, sir, now; what say you now? is he frightened now or no? As much frightened as you think me, and, to be sure, nobody can help some fears. I would not be in so bad a condition as what's his name, squire Hamlet, is there, for all the world. Bless me! what's become of the spirit? As I am a living soul, I thought I saw him sink into the earth." "Indeed, you saw right," answered Jones. "Well,

well," cries Partridge, "I know it is only a play : and besides, if there was anything in all this, Madam Miller would not laugh so ; for as to you, sir, you would not be afraid, I believe, if the devil was here in person. ——There, there——Ay, no wonder you are in such a passion, shake the vile wicked wretch to pieces. If she was my own mother, I would serve her so. To be sure all duty to a mother is forfeited by such wicked doings.——Ay, go about your business, I hate the sight of you."

Our critic was now pretty silent till the play, which Hamlet introduces before the king. This he did not at first understand, till Jones explained it to him ; but he no sooner entered into the spirit of it, than he began to bless himself that he had never committed murder. Then turning to Mrs Miller, he asked her, "If she did not imagine the king looked as if he was touched ; though he is," said he, "a good actor, and doth all he can to hide it. Well, I would not have so much to answer for, as that wicked man there hath, to sit upon a much higher chair than he sits upon. No wonder he run away ; for your sake I'll never trust an innocent face again."

The grave-digging scene next engaged the attention of Partridge, who expressed much surprize at the number of skulls thrown upon the stage. To which Jones answered, "That it was one of the most famous burial-places about town." "No wonder then," cries Partridge, "that the place is haunted. But I never saw in my life a worse grave-digger. I had a sexton, when I was clerk, that should have dug three graves while he is digging one. The fellow handles a spade as if it was the first time he had ever had one in his hand. Ay, ay, you may sing. You had rather sing than work, I believe."——Upon Hamlet's taking up the skull, he cried out, "Well ! it is strange to see how fearless some men are : I never could bring myself to touch anything belonging to a dead man, on any account.—He seemed frightened enough too at the ghost, I thought. *Nemo omnibus horis sapit.*"

Little more worth remembering occurred during the play, at the end of which Jones asked him, "Which of the players he had liked best?" To this he answered, with some appearance of indignation at the question, "The king, without doubt." "Indeed, Mr Partridge," says Mrs Miller, "you are not of the same opinion with the town ; for they are all agreed, that Hamlet is acted by the best player who ever was on the stage." "He the best player ! " cries Partridge, with a contemptuous sneer, "why, I could act as well as he myself. I am sure, if I had seen a ghost, I should have looked in the very same manner, and done just as he did. And then, to be sure, in that scene, as you called it, between him and his mother, where you told me he acted so fine, why, Lord help me, any man, that is, any good man, that had such a mother, would have done exactly the same. I know you are only joking with me ; but indeed, madam, though I was never at a play in London, yet I have seen acting before in the country ; and the king for my money ; he speaks all his words distinctly, half as loud again as the other.—Anybody may see he is an actor."

While Mrs Miller was thus engaged in conversation with Partridge, a lady came up to Mr Jones, whom he immediately knew to be Mrs Fitzpatrick. She said, she had seen him from the other part of the gallery, and had taken that opportunity of speaking to him, as she had something to say, which might be of great service to himself. She then acquainted him with her lodgings, and made him an appointment the next day in the morning ; which, upon recollection, she presently changed to the afternoon; at which time Jones promised to attend her.

Thus ended the adventure at the playhouse; where Partridge had afforded great mirth, not only to Jones and Mrs Miller, but to all who sat within hearing, who were more attentive to what he said, than to anything that passed on the stage.

He durst not go to bed all that night, for fear of the ghost; and for many nights after sweated two or three hours before he went to sleep, with the same apprehensions, and waked several times in great horrors, crying out, " Lord have mercy upon us ! there it is."

Chapter vi.

In which the history is obliged to look back.

IT is almost impossible for the best parent to observe an exact impartiality to his children, even though no superior merit should bias his affection; but sure a parent can hardly be blamed, when that superiority determines his preference.

As I regard all the personages of this history in the light of my children; so I must confess the same inclination of partiality to Sophia; and for that I hope the reader will allow me the same excuse, from the superiority of her character.

This extraordinary tenderness which I have for my heroine never suffers me to quit her any long time without the utmost reluctance. I could now, therefore, return impatiently to enquire what hath happened to this lovely creature since her departure from her father's, but that I am obliged first to pay a short visit to Mr Blifil.

Mr Western, in the first confusion into which his

mind was cast upon the sudden news he received of his daughter, and in the first hurry to go after her, had not once thought of sending any account of the discovery to Blifil. He had not gone far, however, before he recollected himself, and accordingly stopt at the very first inn he came to, and dispatched away a messenger to acquaint Blifil with his having found Sophia, and with his firm resolution to marry her to him immediately, if he would come up after him to town.

As the love which Blifil had for Sophia was of that violent kind, which nothing but the loss of her fortune, or some such accident, could lessen, his inclination to the match was not at all altered by her having run away, though he was obliged to lay this to his own account. He very readily, therefore, embraced this offer. Indeed, he now proposed the gratification of a very strong passion besides avarice, by marrying this young lady, and this was hatred; for he concluded that matrimony afforded an equal opportunity of satisfying either hatred or love; and this opinion is very probably verified by much experience. To say the truth, if we are to judge by the ordinary behaviour of married persons to each other, we shall perhaps be apt to conclude that the generality seek the indulgence of the former passion only, in their union of everything but of hearts.

There was one difficulty, however, in his way, and this arose from Mr Allworthy. That good man, when he found by the departure of Sophia (for neither that, nor the cause of it, could be concealed from him), the great aversion which she had for his nephew, began to be seriously concerned that he had been deceived into carrying matters so far. He by no means concurred with the opinion of those parents, who think it as immaterial to consult the inclinations of their children in the affair of marriage, as to solicit the good pleasure of their servants when they intend to take a journey; and who are by law, or decency at least, withheld often from using absolute force. On the contrary, as he esteemed the institution to be of the most sacred kind, he thought every preparatory caution necessary to preserve it holy and inviolate; and very wisely concluded, that the surest way to effect this was by laying the foundation in previous affection.

Blifil indeed soon cured his uncle of all anger on the score of deceit, by many vows and protestations that he had been deceived himself, with which the many declarations of Western very well tallied; but now to persuade Allworthy to consent to the renewing his addresses was a matter of such apparent difficulty, that the very appearance was sufficient to have deterred a less enterprizing genius; but this young gentleman so well knew his own talents, that nothing within the province of cunning seemed to him hard to be atchieved.

Here then he represented the violence of his own affection, and the hopes of subduing aversion in the lady by perseverance. He begged that, in an affair on which depended all his future repose, he might at least be at liberty to try all fair means for success. Heaven forbid, he said, that he should ever think of prevailing by any other than the most gentle methods! "Besides, sir," said he, "if they fail, you may then (which will be surely time enough) deny your consent." He urged the great and eager desire which Mr Western had for the match; and lastly, he made great use of the name of Jones, to whom he imputed all that had happened; and from whom, he said, to preserve so valuable a young lady was even an act of charity.

All these arguments were well seconded by Thwackum, who dwelt a little stronger on the authority of parents than Mr Blifil himself had done.

He ascribed the measures which Mr Blifil was desirous to take to Christian motives; "and though," says he, "the good young gentleman hath mentioned charity last, I am almost convinced it is his first and principal consideration."

Square, possibly, had he been present, would have sung to the same tune, though in a different key, and would have discovered much moral fitness in the proceeding: but he was now gone to Bath for the recovery of his health.

Allworthy, though not without reluctance, at last yielded to the desires of his nephew. He said he would accompany him to London, where he might be at liberty to use every honest endeavour to gain the lady: "But I declare," said he, "I will never give my consent to any absolute force being put on her inclinations, nor shall you ever have her, unless she can be brought freely to compliance."

Thus did the affection of Allworthy for his nephew betray the superior understanding to be triumphed over by the inferior; and thus is the prudence of the best of heads often defeated by the tenderness of the best of hearts.

Blifil, having obtained this unhoped-for acquiescence in his uncle, rested not till he carried his purpose into execution. And as no immediate business required Mr Allworthy's presence in the country, and little preparation is necessary to men for a journey, they set out the very next day, and arrived in town that evening, when Mr Jones, as we have seen, was diverting himself with Partridge at the play.

The morning after his arrival Mr Blifil waited on Mr Western, by whom he was most kindly and graciously received, and from whom he had every possible assurance (perhaps more than was possible) that he should very shortly be as happy as Sophia could make him; nor would the squire suffer the young gentleman to return to his uncle till he had, almost against his will, carried him to his sister.

Chapter vij.

In which Mr Western pays a visit to his sister, in company with Mr Blifil.

MRS WESTERN was reading a lecture on prudence, and matrimonial politics, to her niece, when her brother and Blifil broke in with less ceremony than the laws of visiting require. Sophia no sooner saw Blifil than she turned pale, and almost lost the use of all her faculties; but her aunt, on the contrary, waxed red, and, having all her faculties at command, began to exert her tongue on the squire.

"Brother," said she, "I am astonished at your behaviour; will you never learn any regard to decorum? Will you still look upon every apartment as your own, or as belonging to one of your country tenants? Do you think yourself at liberty to invade the privacies of women of condition, without the least decency or notice?"——"Why, what a pox is the matter now?" quoth the squire; "one would think I had caught you at—"——"None of your brutality, sir, I beseech you," answered she.——"You have surprized my poor niece so, that she can hardly, I see, support herself.——Go, my dear, retire, and endeavour to recruit your spirits; for I see you have occasion." At which words Sophia, who never received a more welcome command, hastily withdrew.

"To be sure, sister," cries the squire, "you are mad, when I have brought Mr Blifil here to court her, to force her away."

"Sure, brother," says she, "you are worse than mad, when you know in what situation affairs are, to——I am sure I ask Mr Blifil's pardon, but he knows very well to whom to impute so disagreeable a reception. For my own part, I am sure I shall always be very glad to see Mr Blifil; but his own good sense would not have suffered him to proceed so abruptly, had you not compelled him to it."

Blifil bowed and stammered, and looked like a fool; but Western, without giving him time to form a speech for the purpose, answered, "Well, well, I am to blame, if you will, I always am, certainly; but come, let the girl be fetched back again, or let Mr Blifil go to her. ——He's come up on purpose, and there is no time to be lost."

"Brother," cries Mrs Western, "Mr Blifil, I am confident, understands himself better than to think of seeing my niece any more this morning, after what hath happened. Women are of a nice contexture; and our spirits, when disordered, are not to be recomposed in a moment. Had you suffered Mr Blifil to have sent his compliments to my niece, and to have desired the favour of waiting on her in the afternoon, I should possibly have prevailed on her to have seen him; but now I despair of bringing about any such matter."

"I am very sorry, madam," cried Blifil, "that Mr Western's extraordinary kindness to me, which I can never enough acknowledge, should have occasioned——"
"Indeed, sir," said she, interrupting him, "you need make no apologies, we all know my brother so well."

"I don't care what anybody knows of me," answered the squire;——"but when must he come to see her? for, consider, I tell you, he is come up on purpose, and so is Allworthy."——"Brother," said she, "whatever message Mr Blifil thinks proper to send to my niece shall be delivered to her; and I suppose she will want no instructions to make a proper answer. I am convinced she will not refuse to see Mr Blifil at a proper time."—"The devil she won't!" answered the squire.—"Odsbud!—Don't we know—I say nothing, but some volk are wiser than all the world.——If I might have had my will, she had not run away before: and now I expect to hear every moment she is guone again. For as great a fool as some volk think me, I know very well she hates——" "No matter, brother," replied Mrs Western, "I will not hear my niece abused. It is a reflection on my family. She is an honour to it; and she will be an honour to it, I promise you. I will pawn my whole reputation in the world on her conduct.——I shall be glad to see you, brother, in the afternoon; for I have somewhat of importance to mention to you.—At present, Mr Blifil, as well as you, must excuse me; for I am in haste to dress." "Well, but," said the squire, "do appoint a time." "Indeed," said she, "I can appoint no time. I tell you I will see you in the afternoon."—"What the devil would you have me do?" cries the squire, turning to Blifil; "I can no more turn her, than a beagle can turn an old hare. Perhaps she will be in a better humour in the afternoon."—"I am condemned, I see, sir, to misfortune," answered Blifil; "but I shall always own my obligations to you." He then took a ceremonious leave of Mrs Western, who was altogether as ceremonious on her part; and then they departed, the squire muttering to himself with an oath, that Blifil should see his daughter in the afternoon.

If Mr Western was little pleased with this interview, Blifil was less. As to the former, he imputed the whole behaviour of his sister to her humour only, and to her dissatisfaction at the omission of ceremony in the visit; but Blifil saw a little deeper into things.

He suspected somewhat of more consequence, from two or three words which dropt from the lady; and, to say the truth, he suspected right, as will appear when I have unfolded the several matters which will be contained in the following chapter.

Chapter viii.

Schemes of Lady Bellaston for the ruin of Jones.

LOVE had taken too deep a root in the mind of Lord Fellamar to be plucked up by the rude hands of Mr Western. In the heat of resentment he had, indeed, given a commission to Captain Egglane, which the captain had far exceeded in the execution; nor had it been executed at all, had his lordship been able to find the captain after he had seen Lady Bellaston, which was in the afternoon of the day after he had received the affront; but so industrious was the captain in the discharge of his duty, that, having after long enquiry found out the squire's lodgings very late in the evening, he sat up all night at a tavern, that he might not miss the squire in the morning, and by that means missed the revocation which my lord had sent to his lodgings.

In the afternoon then next after the intended rape of Sophia, his lordship, as we have said, made a visit to Lady Bellaston, who laid open so much of the character of the squire, that his lordship plainly saw the absurdity he had been guilty of in taking any offence at his words, especially as he had those honourable designs on his daughter. He then unbosomed the violence of his passion to Lady Bellaston, who readily undertook the cause, and encouraged him with certain assurance of a most favourable reception from all the elders of the family, and from the father himself when he should be sober, and should be made acquainted with the nature of the offer made to his daughter. The only danger, she said, lay in the fellow she had formerly mentioned, who, though a beggar and a vagabond, had, by some means or other, she knew not what, procured himself tolerable cloaths, and past for a gentleman. "Now," says she, "as I have, for the sake of my cousin, made it my business to enquire after this fellow, I have luckily found out his lodgings;" with which she then acquainted his lordship. "I am thinking, my lord," added she "(for this fellow is too mean for your personal resentment), whether it would not be possible for your lordship to contrive some method of having him pressed and sent on board a ship. Neither law nor conscience forbid this project: for the fellow, I promise you, however well drest, is but a vagabond, and as proper as any fellow in the streets to be pressed into the service; and as for the conscientious part, surely the preservation of a young lady from such ruin is a most meritorious act; nay, with regard to the fellow himself, unless he could succeed (which Heaven forbid) with my cousin, it may probably be the means of preserving him from the gallows, and perhaps may make his fortune in an honest way."

Lord Fellamar very heartily thanked her ladyship for the part which she was pleased to take in the affair, upon the success of which his whole future happiness entirely depended. He said, he saw at present no objection to the pressing scheme, and would consider of putting it in execution. He then most earnestly recommended to her ladyship to do him the honour of immediately mentioning his proposals to the family; to whom he said he offered a *carte blanche*, and would settle his fortune in almost any manner they should require.   And after uttering many ecstasies and raptures concerning Sophia, he took his leave and departed, but not before he had received the strongest charge to beware of Jones, and to lose no time in securing his person, where he should no longer be in a capacity of making any attempts to the ruin of the young lady.

The moment Mrs Western was arrived at her lodgings, a card was despatched with her compliments to Lady Bellaston; who no sooner received it than, with the impatience of a lover, she flew to her cousin, rejoiced at this fair opportunity, which beyond her hopes offered itself, for she was much better pleased with the prospect of making the proposals to a woman of sense, and who knew the world, than to a gentleman whom she honoured with the appellation of Hottentot; though, indeed, from him she apprehended no danger of a refusal.

The two ladies being met, after very short previous ceremonials, fell to business, which was indeed almost as soon concluded as begun; for Mrs Western no sooner heard the name of Lord Fellamar than her cheeks glowed with pleasure; but when she was acquainted with the eagerness of his passion, the earnestness of his proposals, and the generosity of his offer, she declared her full satisfaction in the most explicit terms.

In the progress of their conversation their discourse turned to Jones, and both cousins very pathetically lamented the unfortunate attachment which both agreed Sophia had to that young fellow; and Mrs Western entirely attributed it to the folly of her brother's management.   She concluded, however, at last, with declaring her confidence in the good understanding of her niece, who, though she would not give up her affection in favour of Blifil, will, I doubt not, says she, soon be prevailed upon to sacrifice a simple inclination to the addresses of a fine gentleman, who brings her both a title and a large estate: "For, indeed," added she, "I must do Sophy the justice to confess this Blifil is but a hideous kind of fellow, as you know, Bellaston, all country gentlemen are, and hath nothing but his fortune to recommend him."

"Nay," said Lady Bellaston, "I don't then so much wonder at my cousin; for I promise you this Jones is a very agreeable fellow, and hath one virtue, which the men say is a great recommendation to us. What do you think, Mrs Western—I shall certainly make you laugh; nay, I can hardly tell you myself for laughing—will you believe that the fellow hath had the assurance to make love to me? But if you should be inclined to disbelieve it, here is evidence enough, his own handwriting, I assure you." She then delivered her cousin the letter with the proposals of marriage, which, if the reader hath a desire to see, he will find already on record in the XVth book of this history.

"Upon my word I am astonished," said Mrs Western; "this is, indeed, a masterpiece of assurance. With your leave I may possibly make some use of this letter." "You have my full liberty," cries Lady Bellaston, "to apply it to what purpose you please. However, I would not have it shewn to any but Miss Western, nor to her unless you find occasion." "Well, and how did you use the fellow?" returned Mrs Western. "Not as a husband," said the lady; "I am not married, I promise you, my dear. You know, Bell, I have tried the comforts once already; and once, I think, is enough for any reasonable woman."

This letter Lady Bellaston thought would certainly turn the balance against Jones in the mind of Sophia, and she was emboldened to give it up, partly by her hopes of having him instantly dispatched out of the way, and partly by having secured the evidence of Honour, who, upon sounding her, she saw sufficient reason to imagine was prepared to testify whatever she pleased.

But perhaps the reader may wonder why Lady Bellaston, who in her heart hated Sophia, should be so desirous of promoting a match which was so much to the interest of the young lady. Now, I would desire such readers to look carefully into human nature, page almost the last, and there he will find, in scarce legible characters, that women, notwithstanding the preposterous behaviour of mothers, aunts, &c., in matrimonial matters, do in reality think it so great a misfortune to have their inclinations in love thwarted, that they imagine they ought never to carry enmity higher than upon these disappointments; again, he will find it written much about the same place, that a woman who hath once been pleased with the possession of a man, will go above halfway to the devil, to prevent any other woman from enjoying the same.

If he will not be contented with these reasons, I freely confess I see no other motive to the actions of that lady, unless we will conceive she was bribed by Lord Fellamar, which for my own part I see no cause to suspect.

Now this was the affair which Mrs Western was preparing to introduce to Sophia, by some prefatory discourse on the folly of love, and on the wisdom of legal prostitution for hire, when her brother and Blifil broke abruptly in upon her; and hence arose all that coldness in her behaviour to Blifil, which, though the squire, as was usual with him, imputed to a wrong cause, infused into Blifil himself (he being a much more cunning man) a suspicion of the real truth.

Chapter ix.

In which Jones pays a visit to Mrs Fitzpatrick.

THE reader may now, perhaps, be pleased to return with us to Mr Jones, who, at the appointed hour, attended on Mrs Fitzpatrick; but before we relate the conversation which now past it may be proper, according to our method, to return a little back, and to account for so great an alteration of behaviour in this lady, that from changing her lodging principally to avoid Mr Jones, she had now industriously, as hath been seen, sought this interview.

And here we shall need only to resort to what happened the preceding day, when, hearing from Lady Bellaston that Mr Western was arrived in town, she went to pay her duty to him, at his lodgings at Piccadilly, where she was received with many scurvy compellations too coarse to be repeated, and was even threatened to be kicked out of doors. From hence, an old servant of her aunt Western, with whom she was well acquainted, conducted her to the lodgings of that lady, who treated her not more kindly, but more politely; or, to say the truth, with rudeness in another way. In short, she returned from both, plainly convinced, not only that her scheme of reconciliation had proved abortive, but that she must for ever give over all thoughts of bringing it about by any means whatever. From this moment desire of revenge only filled her mind; and in this temper meeting Jones at the play, an opportunity seemed to her to occur of effecting this purpose.

The reader must remember that he was acquainted by Mrs Fitzpatrick, in the account she gave of her own story, with the fondness Mrs Western had formerly shewn for Mr Fitzpatrick at Bath, from the disappointment of which Mrs Fitzpatrick derived the great bitterness her aunt had expressed toward her. She had, therefore, no doubt but that the good lady would as easily listen to the addresses of Mr Jones as she had before done to the other; for the superiority of charms was clearly on the side of Mr Jones; and the advance which her aunt had since made in age, she concluded (how justly I will not say), was an argument rather in favour of her project than against it.

Therefore, when Jones attended, after a previous declaration of her desire of serving him, arising, as she said, from a firm assurance how much she should by so doing oblige Sophia; and after some excuses for her former disappointment, and after acquainting Mr Jones in whose custody his mistress was, of which she thought him ignorant; she very explicitly mentioned her scheme to him, and advised him to make sham addresses to the older lady, in order to procure an easy access to the younger, informing him at the same time of the success which Mr Fitzpatrick had formerly owed to the very same stratagem.

Mr Jones expressed great gratitude to the lady for the kind intentions towards him which she had expressed, and indeed testified, by this proposal; but, besides intimating some diffidence of success from the lady's knowledge of his love to her niece, which had not been her case in regard to Mr Fitzpatrick, he said, he was afraid Miss Western would never agree to an imposition of this kind, as well from her utter detestation of all fallacy as from her avowed duty to her aunt.

Mrs Fitzpatrick was a little nettled at this; and indeed, if it may not be called a lapse of the tongue, it was a small deviation from politeness in Jones, and into which he scarce would have fallen, had not the delight he felt in praising Sophia hurried him out of all reflection; for this commendation of one cousin was more than a tacit rebuke on the other.

"Indeed, sir," answered the lady, with some warmth, "I cannot think there is anything easier than to cheat an old woman with a profession of love, when her complexion is amorous; and, though she is my aunt, I must say there never was a more liquorish one than her ladyship. Can't you pretend that the despair of possessing her niece, from her being promised to Blifil, has made you turn your thoughts towards her? As to my cousin Sophia, I can't imagine her to be such a simpleton as to have the least scruple on such an account, or to conceive any harm in punishing one of these haggs for the many mischiefs they bring upon families by their tragi-comic passions; for which I think it is a pity they are not punishable by law. I had no such scruple myself; and yet I hope my cousin Sophia will not think it an affront when I say she cannot detest every real species of falsehood more than her cousin Fitzpatrick. To my aunt, indeed, I pretend no duty, nor doth she deserve any. However, sir, I have given you my advice; and if you decline pursuing it, I shall have the less opinion of your understanding —that's all."

Jones now clearly saw the error he had committed, and exerted his utmost power to rectify it; but he only faultered and stuttered into nonsense and contradiction. To say the truth, it is often safer to abide by the consequences of the first blunder than to endeavour to rectify it; for by such endeavours we generally plunge deeper instead of extricating ourselves; and few persons will on such occasions have the good-nature which Mrs Fitzpatrick displayed to Jones, by saying, with a smile, "You need attempt no more excuses; for I can easily forgive a real lover, whatever is the effect of fondness for his mistress."

She then renewed her proposal, and very fervently recommended it, omitting no argument which her invention could suggest on the subject; for she was so violently incensed against her aunt, that scarce anything was capable of affording her equal pleasure with exposing her; and, like a true woman, she would see no difficulties in the execution of a favourite scheme.

Jones, however, persisted in declining the undertaking, which had not, indeed, the least probability of success. He easily perceived the motives which induced Mrs Fitzpatrick to be so eager in pressing her advice. He said he would not deny the tender and passionate regard he had for Sophia; but was so conscious of the inequality of their situations, that he could never flatter himself so far as to hope that so divine a young lady would condescend to think on so unworthy a man; nay, he protested, he could scarce bring himself to wish she should. He concluded with a profession of generous sentiments, which we have not at present leisure to insert.

There are some fine women (for I dare not here speak in too general terms) with whom self is so predominant, that they never detach it from any subject; and, as vanity is with them a ruling principle, they are apt to lay hold of whatever praise they meet with; and, though the property of others, convey it to their own use. In the company of these ladies it is impossible to say anything handsome of another woman which they will not apply to themselves; nay, they often improve the praise they seize; as, for instance, if her beauty, her wit, her gentility, her good humour deserve so much commendation, what do I deserve, who possess those qualities in so much more eminent a degree?

To these ladies a man often recommends himself while he is commending another woman; and, while he is expressing ardour and generous sentiments for his mistress, they are considering what a charming lover this man would make to them, who can feel all this tenderness for an inferior degree of merit. Of this, strange as it may seem, I have seen many instances besides Mrs Fitzpatrick, to whom all this really happened, and who now began to feel a somewhat for Mr Jones, the symptoms of which she much sooner understood than poor Sophia had formerly done.

To say the truth, perfect beauty in both sexes is a more irresistible object than it is generally thought; for, notwithstanding some of us are contented with more homely lots, and learn by rote (as children to repeat what gives them no idea) to despise outside, and to value more solid charms; yet I have always observed, at the approach of consummate beauty, that these more solid charms only shine with that kind of lustre which the stars have after the rising of the sun.

When Jones had finished his exclamations, many of which would have become the mouth of Oroöndates himself, Mrs Fitzpatrick heaved a deep sigh, and, taking her eyes off from Jones, on whom they had been some time fixed, and dropping them on the ground, she cried, "Indeed, Mr Jones, I pity you; but it is the curse of such tenderness to be thrown away on those who are insensible of it. I know my cousin better than you, Mr Jones, and I must say, any woman who makes no return to such a passion, and such a person, is unworthy of both."

"Sure, madam," said Jones, "you can't mean——" "Mean!" cries Mrs Fitzpatrick, "I know not what I mean; there is something, I think, in true tenderness bewitching; few women ever meet with it in men, and fewer still know how to value it when they do. I never heard such truly noble sentiments, and I can't tell how it is, but you force one to believe you. Sure she must be the most contemptible of women who can overlook such merit."

The manner and look with which all this was spoke infused a suspicion into Jones which we don't care to convey in direct words to the reader. Instead of making any answer, he said, " I am afraid, madam, I have made too tiresome a visit ; " and offered to take his leave.

" Not at all, sir," answered Mrs Fitzpatrick.——— " Indeed I pity you, Mr Jones ; indeed I do : but if you are going, consider of the scheme I have mentioned——I am convinced you will approve it——and let me see you again as soon as you can.——To-morrow morning if you will, or at least some time to-morrow. I shall be at home all day."

Jones, then, after many expressions of thanks, very respectfully retired ; nor could Mrs Fitzpatrick forbear making him a present of a look at parting, by which if he had understood nothing, he must have had no understanding in the language of the eyes. In reality, it confirmed his resolution of returning to her no more ; for, faulty as he hath hitherto appeared in this history, his whole thoughts were now so confined to his Sophia, that I believe no woman upon earth could have now drawn him into an act of inconstancy.

Fortune, however, who was not his friend, resolved, as he intended to give her no second opportunity, to make the best of this ; and accordingly produced the tragical incident which we are now in sorrowful notes to record.

Chapter x.

The consequence of the preceding visit.

MR FITZPATRICK having received the letter before mentioned from Mrs Western, and being by that means acquainted with the place to which his wife was retired, returned directly to Bath, and thence the day after set forward to London.

The reader hath been already often informed of the jealous temper of this gentleman. He may likewise be pleased to remember the suspicion which he had conceived of Jones at Upton, upon his finding him in the room with Mrs Waters ; and, though sufficient reasons had afterwards appeared entirely to clear up that suspicion, yet now the reading so handsome a character of Mr Jones from his wife, caused him to reflect that she likewise was in the inn at the same time, and jumbled together such a confusion of circumstances in a head which was naturally none of the clearest, that the whole produced that green-eyed monster mentioned by Shakespear in his tragedy of Othello.

And now, as he was enquiring in the street after his wife, and had just received directions to the door, unfortunately Mr Jones was issuing from it.

Fitzpatrick did not yet recollect the face of Jones ; however, seeing a young well-dressed fellow coming from his wife, he made directly up to him, and asked him what he had been doing in that house ? " for I am sure," said he, " you must have been in it, as I saw you come out of it."

Jones answered very modestly, " That he had been visiting a lady there." To which Fitzpatrick replied, " What business have you with the lady ?" Upon which Jones, who now perfectly remembered the voice, features, and indeed coat, of the gentleman, cried out

————" Ha, my good friend! give me your hand; I hope there is no ill blood remaining between us, upon a small mistake which happened so long ago."

" Upon my soul, sir," said Fitzpatrick, " I don't know your name nor your face." " Indeed, sir," said Jones, " neither have I the pleasure of knowing your name, but your face I very well remember to have seen before at Upton, where a foolish quarrel happened between us, which, if it is not made up yet, we will now make up over a bottle."

" At Upton!" cried the other;————" Ha! upon my soul, I believe your name is Jones?" " Indeed," answered he, " it is."—" O! upon my soul," cries Fitzpatrick, " you are the very man I wanted to meet. —Upon my soul I will drink a bottle with you presently; but first I will give you a great knock over the pate. There is for you, you rascal. Upon my soul, if you do not give me satisfaction for that blow, I will give you another." And then, drawing his sword, put himself in a posture of defence, which was the only science he understood.

Jones was a little staggered by the blow, which came somewhat unexpectedly; but presently recovering himself he also drew, and though he understood nothing of fencing, prest on so boldly upon Fitzpatrick, that he beat down his guard, and sheathed one half of his sword in the body of the said gentleman, who had no sooner received it than he stept backwards, dropped the point of his sword, and leaning upon it, cried, " I have satisfaction enough: I am a dead man."

" I hope not," cries Jones, " but whatever be the consequence, you must be sensible you have drawn it upon yourself." At this instant a number of fellows rushed in and seized Jones, who told them he should make no resistance, and begged some of them at least would take care of the wounded gentleman.

"Ay," cries one of the fellows, "the wounded gentleman will be taken care enough of; for I suppose he hath not many hours to live. As for you, sir, you have a month at least good yet." "D——n me, Jack," said another, "he hath prevented his voyage; he's bound to another port now;" and many other such jests was our poor Jones made the subject of by these fellows, who were indeed the gang employed by Lord Fellamar, and had dogged him into the house of Mrs Fitzpatrick, waiting for him at the corner of the street when this unfortunate accident happened.

The officer who commanded this gang very wisely concluded that his business was now to deliver his prisoner into the hands of the civil magistrate. He ordered him, therefore, to be carried to a public-house, where, having sent for a constable, he delivered him to his custody.

The constable, seeing Mr Jones very well drest, and hearing that the accident had happened in a duel, treated his prisoner with great civility, and at his request dispatched a messenger to enquire after the wounded gentleman, who was now at a tavern under the surgeon's hands. The report brought back was, that the wound was certainly mortal, and there were no hopes of life. Upon which the constable informed Jones that he must go before a justice. He answered, "Wherever you please; I am indifferent as to what happens to me; for though I am convinced I am not guilty of murder in the eye of the law, yet the weight of blood I find intolerable upon my mind."

Jones was now conducted before the justice, where the surgeon who dressed Mr Fitzpatrick appeared, and deposed that he believed the wound to be mortal; upon which the prisoner was committed to the Gatehouse. It was very late at night, so that Jones would not send for Partridge till the next morning; and, as he never shut his eyes till seven, so it was near twelve before the poor fellow, who was greatly frightened at not hearing from his master so long, received a message which almost deprived him of his being when he heard it.

He went to the Gatehouse with trembling knees and a beating heart, and was no sooner arrived in the presence of Jones than he lamented the misfortune that had befallen him with many tears, looking all the while frequently about him in great terror; for as the news now arrived that Mr Fitzpatrick was dead, the poor fellow apprehended every minute that his ghost would enter the room. At last he delivered him a letter, which he had like to have forgot, and which came from Sophia by the hands of Black George.

Jones presently dispatched every one out of the room, and, having eagerly broke open the letter, read as follows:—

"You owe the hearing from me again to an accident which I own surprizes me. My aunt hath just now shown me a letter from you to Lady Bellaston, which contains a proposal of marriage. I am convinced it is your own hand; and what more surprizes me is, that it is dated at the very time when you would have me imagine you was under such concern on my account.—I leave you to comment on this fact. All I desire is, that your name may never more be mentioned to

"S. W."

Of the present situation of Mr Jones's mind, and of the pangs with which he was now tormented, we cannot give the reader a better idea than by saying, his misery was such that even Thwackum would almost have pitied him. But, bad as it is, we shall at present leave him in it, as his good genius (if he really had any) seems to have done. And here we put an end to the sixteenth book of our history.

BOOK XVII.

CONTAINING THREE DAYS.

Chapter i.

Containing a portion of introductory writing.

WHEN a comic writer hath made his principal characters as happy as he can, or when a tragic writer hath brought them to the highest pitch of human misery, they both conclude their business to be done, and that their work is come to a period.

Had we been of the tragic complexion, the reader must now allow we were very nearly arrived at this period, since it would be difficult for the devil, or any of his representatives on earth, to have contrived much greater torments for poor Jones than those in which we left him in the last chapter; and as for Sophia, a good-natured woman would hardly wish more uneasiness to a rival than what she must at present be supposed to feel. What then remains to complete the tragedy but a murder or two and a few moral sentences!

But to bring our favourites out of their present anguish and distress, and to land them at last on the shore of happiness, seems a much harder task;

a task indeed so hard that we do not undertake to execute it. In regard to Sophia, it is more than probable that we shall somewhere or other provide a good husband for her in the end—either Blifil, or my lord, or somebody else ; but as to poor Jones, such are the calamities in which he is at present involved, owing to his imprudence, by which if a man doth not become felon to the word, he is at least a *felo de se ;* so destitute is he now of friends, and so persecuted by enemies, that we almost despair of bringing him to any good ; and if our reader delights in seeing executions, I think he ought not to lose any time in taking a first row at Tyburn.

This I faithfully promise, that, notwithstanding any affection which we may be supposed to have for this rogue, whom we have unfortunately made our heroe, we will lend him none of that supernatural assistance with which we are entrusted, upon condition that we use it only on very important occasions. If he doth not therefore find some natural means of fairly extricating himself from all his distresses, we will do no violence to the truth and dignity of history for his sake ; for we had rather relate that he was hanged at Tyburn (which may very probably be the case) than forfeit our integrity, or shock the faith of our reader.

In this the antients had a great advantage over the moderns. Their mythology, which was at that time more firmly believed by the vulgar than any religion is at present, gave them always an opportunity of delivering a favourite heroe. Their deities were always ready at the writer's elbow, to execute any of his purposes ; and the more extraordinary the invention was, the greater was the surprize and delight of the credulous reader. Those writers could with greater ease have conveyed a heroe from one country to another, nay from one world to another, and have brought him back again, than a poor circumscribed modern can deliver him from a jail.

The Arabians and Persians had an equal advantage in writing their tales from the genii and fairies, which they believe in as an article of their faith, upon the authority of the Koran itself. But we have none of these helps. To natural means alone we are confined; let us try therefore what, by these means, may be done for poor Jones; though to confess the truth, something whispers me in the ear that he doth not yet know the worst of his fortune; and that a more shocking piece of news than any he hath yet heard remains for him in the unopened leaves of fate.

Chapter ij.

The generous and grateful behaviour of Mrs Miller.

MR ALLWORTHY and Mrs Miller were just sat down to breakfast, when Blifil, who had gone out very early that morning, returned to make one of the company.

He had not been long seated before he began as follows: "Good Lord! my dear uncle, what do you think hath happened? I vow I am afraid of telling it you, for fear of shocking you with the remembrance of ever having shewn any kindness to such a villain." "What is the matter, child?" said the uncle. "I fear I have shewn kindness in my life to the unworthy more than once. But charity doth not adopt the vices of its objects." "O, sir!" returned Blifil, "it is not without the secret direction of Providence that you mention the word adoption. Your adopted son, sir, that Jones, that wretch whom you nourished in your bosom, hath proved one of the greatest villains upon earth." "By all that's sacred 'tis false," cries Mrs Miller. "Mr Jones is no villain. He is one of the worthiest creatures breathing; and if any other person had called him villain, I would have thrown all this boiling water in his face." Mr Allworthy looked very much amazed at this behaviour. But she did not give him leave to speak, before, turning to him, she cried, "I hope you will not be angry with me; I would not offend you, sir, for the world; but, indeed, I could not bear to hear him called so." "I must own, madam," said Allworthy, very gravely, "I am a little surprized to hear you so warmly defend a fellow you do not know." "O! I do know him, Mr Allworthy," said she, "indeed I do; I should be the most ungrateful of all wretches if I denied it. O! he hath preserved me and my little family; we have all reason to bless him while we live.——And I pray Heaven to bless him, and turn the hearts of his malicious enemies. I know, I find, I see, he hath such." "You surprize me, madam, still more," said Allworthy; "sure you must mean some other. It is impossible you should have any such obligations to the man my nephew mentions." "Too surely," answered she, "I have obligations to him of the greatest and tenderest kind. He hath been the preserver of me and mine. Believe me, sir, he hath been abused, grossly abused to you; I know he hath, or you, whom I know to be all goodness and honour, would not, after the many kind and tender things I have heard you say of this poor helpless child, have so disdainfully called him fellow.——Indeed, my best of friends, he deserves a kinder appellation from you, had you heard the good, the kind, the grateful things which I have heard him utter of you. He never mentions your name but with a sort of adoration. In this very room I have seen him on his knees, imploring all the blessings of heaven upon your head. I do not love that child there better than he loves you."

"I see, sir, now," said Blifil, with one of those grinning sneers with which the devil marks his best beloved, "Mrs Miller really doth know him. I suppose you will find she is not the only one of your acquaintance to whom he hath exposed you. As for my character, I perceive, by some hints she hath thrown out, he hath been very free with it, but I forgive him." "And the Lord forgive you, sir!" said Mrs Miller; "we have all sins enough to stand in need of his forgiveness."

"Upon my word, Mrs Miller," said Allworthy, "I do not take this behaviour of yours to my nephew kindly; and I do assure you, as any reflections which you cast upon him must come only from that wickedest of men, they would only serve, if that were possible, to heighten my resentment against him: for I must tell you, Mrs Miller, the young man who now stands before you hath ever been the warmest advocate for the ungrateful wretch whose cause you espouse. This, I think, when you hear it from my own mouth, will make you wonder at so much baseness and ingratitude."

"You are deceived, sir," answered Mrs Miller; "if they were the last words which were to issue from my lips, I would say you were deceived; and I once more repeat it, the Lord forgive those who have deceived you! I do not pretend to say the young man is without faults; but they are all the faults of wildness and of youth; faults which he may, nay, which I am certain he will, relinquish, and, if he should not, they are vastly overbalanced by one of the most humane, tender, honest hearts that ever man was blest with."

"Indeed, Mrs Miller," said Allworthy, "had this

been related of you, I should not have believed it."
"Indeed, sir," answered she, "you will believe everything I have said, I am sure you will: and when you have heard the story which I shall tell you (for I will tell you all), you will be so far from being offended, that you will own (I know your justice so well), that I must have been the most despicable and most ungrateful of wretches if I had acted any other part than I have."

"Well, madam," said Allworthy, "I shall be very glad to hear any good excuse for a behaviour which, I must confess, I think wants an excuse. And now, madam, will you be pleased to let my nephew proceed in his story without interruption. He would not have introduced a matter of slight consequence with such a preface. Perhaps even this story will cure you of your mistake."

Mrs Miller gave tokens of submission, and then Mr Blifil began thus: "I am sure, sir, if you don't think proper to resent the ill-usage of Mrs Miller, I shall easily forgive what affects me only. I think your goodness hath not deserved this indignity at her hands." "Well, child," said Allworthy, "but what is this new instance? What hath he done of late?" "What," cries Blifil, "notwithstanding all Mrs Miller hath said, I am very sorry to relate, and what you should never have heard from me, had it not been a matter impossible to conceal from the whole world. In short he hath killed a man; I will not say murdered —for perhaps it may not be so construed in law, and I hope the best for his sake."

Allworthy looked shocked, and blessed himself; and then, turning to Mrs Miller, he cried, "Well, madam, what say you now?"

"Why, I say, sir," answered she, "that I never was more concerned at anything in my life; but, if the fact be true, I am convinced the man, whoever he is, was in fault. Heaven knows there are many villains in this town who make it their business to provoke young gentlemen. Nothing but the greatest provocation could have tempted him; for of all the gentlemen I ever had in my house, I never saw one so gentle or so sweet-tempered. He was beloved by every one in the house, and every one who came near it."

While she was thus running on, a violent knocking at the door interrupted their conversation, and prevented her from proceeding further, or from receiving any answer; for, as she concluded this was a visitor to Mr Allworthy, she hastily retired, taking with her her little girl, whose eyes were all over blubbered at the melancholy news she heard of Jones, who used to call her his little wife, and not only gave her many playthings, but spent whole hours in playing with her himself.

Some readers may, perhaps, be pleased with these minute circumstances, in relating of which we follow the example of Plutarch, one of the best of our brother historians; and others, to whom they may appear trivial, will, we hope, at least pardon them, as we are never prolix on such occasions.

Chapter iii.

The arrival of Mr Western, with some matters concerning the paternal authority.

MRS MILLER had not long left the room when Mr Western entered; but not before a small wrangling bout had passed between him and his chairmen; for the fellows, who had taken up their burden at the Hercules Pillars, had conceived no hopes of having any future good customer in the squire ; and they were moreover farther encouraged by his generosity (for he had given them of his own accord sixpence more than their fare) ; they therefore very boldly demanded another shilling, which so provoked the squire, that he not only bestowed many hearty curses on them at the door, but retained his anger after he came into the room ; swearing that all the Londoners were like the court, and thought of nothing but plundering country gentlemen. "D——n me," says he, "if I won't walk in the rain rather than get into one of their hand-barrows again. They have jolted me more in a mile than Brown Bess would in a long fox-chase."

When his wrath on this occasion was a little appeased, he resumed the same passionate tone on another. "There," says he, "there is fine business forwards now. The hounds have changed at last ; and when we imagined we had a fox to deal with, od-rat it, it turns out to be a badger at last! "

"Pray, my good neighbour," said Allworthy, "drop your metaphors, and speak a little plainer." "Why, then," says the squire, "to tell you plainly, we have been all this time afraid of a son of a whore of a bastard of somebody's, I don't know whose, not I. And now here's a confounded son of a whore of a lord, who may be a bastard too for what I know or care, for he shall never have a daughter of mine by my consent. They have beggared the nation, but they shall never beggar me. My land shall never be sent over to Hanover."

"You surprize me much, my good friend," said Allworthy. "Why, zounds! I am surprized myself," answered the squire. "I went to zee sister Western last night, according to her own appointment, and there I was had into a whole room full of women. There was my lady cousin Bellaston, and my Lady Betty, and my Lady Catherine, and my lady I don't know who; d——n me, if ever you catch me among such a kennel of hoop-petticoat b——s! D——n me, I'd rather be run by my own dogs, as one Acton was, that the story-book says was turned into a hare, and his own dogs killed un and eat un. Od-rabbit it, no mortal was ever run in such a manner; if I dodged one way, one had me; if I offered to clap back, another snapped me. 'O! certainly one of the greatest matches in England,' says one cousin (here he attempted to mimic them); 'A very advantageous offer indeed,' cries another cousin (for you must know they be all my cousins, thof I never zeed half o' um before). 'Surely,' says that fat a——se b——, my Lady Bellaston, 'cousin, you must be out of your wits to think of refusing such an offer.'"

"Now I begin to understand," says Allworthy; "some person hath made proposals to Miss Western, which the ladies of the family approve, but is not to your liking."

"My liking!" said Western, "how the devil should it? I tell you it is a lord, and those are always volks whom you know I always resolved to have nothing to do with. Did unt I refuse a matter of vorty years' purchase now for a bit of land, which one o' um had a mind to put into a park, only because I would have no dealings with lords, and dost think I would marry my daughter zu? Besides, ben't I engaged to you, and did I ever go off any bargain when I had promised?"

"As to that point, neighbour," said Allworthy, "I entirely release you from any engagement. No contract can be binding between parties who have not a full power to make it at the time, nor ever afterwards acquire the power of fulfilling it."

"Slud! then," answered Western, "I tell you I have power, and I will fulfil it. Come along with me directly to Doctors' Commons, I will get a licence; and I will go to sister and take away the wench by force, and she shall ha un, or I will lock her up, and keep her upon bread and water as long as she lives."

"Mr Western," said Allworthy, "shall I beg you will hear my full sentiments on this matter?"—"Hear thee; ay, to be sure I will," answered he. "Why, then, sir," cries Allworthy, "I can truly say, without a compliment either to you or the young lady, that when this match was proposed, I embraced it very readily and heartily, from my regard to you both. An alliance between two families so nearly neighbours, and between whom there had always existed so mutual an intercourse and good harmony, I thought a most desirable event; and with regard to the young lady, not only the concurrent opinion of all who knew her, but my own observation assured me that she would be an inestimable treasure to a good husband. I shall say nothing of her personal qualifications, which certainly are admirable; her good nature, her charitable disposition, her modesty, are too well known to need any panegyric: but she hath one quality which existed in a high degree in that best of women, who is now one of the first of angels, which, as it is not of a glaring kind, more commonly escapes observation; so little indeed is it remarked, that I want a word to express it. I must use negatives on this occasion. I never heard anything of pertness, or what is called repartee, out of her mouth; no pretence to wit, much less to that kind of wisdom which is the result only of great learning and experience, the affectation of which, in a young woman, is as absurd as any of the affectations of an ape. No dictatorial sentiments, no judicial opinions, no profound criticisms. Whenever I have seen her in the company of men, she hath been all attention, with the modesty of a learner, not the forwardness of a

teacher. You'll pardon me for it, but I once, to try
her only, desired her opinion on a point which was
controverted between Mr Thwackum and Mr Square.
To which she answered, with much sweetness, 'You
will pardon me, good Mr Allworthy; I am sure
you cannot in earnest think me capable of deciding
any point in which two such gentlemen disagree.'
Thwackum and Square, who both alike thought themselves sure of a favourable decision, seconded my request. She answered with the same good humour, 'I
must absolutely be excused: for I will affront neither
so much as to give my judgment on his side.' Indeed,
she always shewed the highest deference to the understandings of men; a quality absolutely essential to the
making a good wife. I shall only add, that as she is
most apparently void of all affectation, this deference
must be certainly real."

Here Blifil sighed bitterly; upon which Western,
whose eyes were full of tears at the praise of Sophia,
blubbered out, "Don't be chicken-hearted, for shat ha
her, d——n me, shat ha her, if she was twenty times as
good."

"Remember your promise, sir," cried Allworthy,
"I was not to be interrupted." "Well, shat unt,"
answered the squire; "I won't speak another word."

"Now, my good friend," continued Allworthy, "I
have dwelt so long on the merit of this young lady,
partly as I really am in love with her character, and
partly that fortune (for the match in that light is really
advantageous on my nephew's side) might not be imagined to be my principal view in having so eagerly
embraced the proposal. Indeed, I heartily wished to
receive so great a jewel into my family; but though I
may wish for many good things, I would not, therefore,
steal them, or be guilty of any violence or injustice to
possess myself of them. Now to force a woman into

a marriage contrary to her consent or approbation, is an act of such injustice and oppression, that I wish the laws of our country could restrain it; but a good conscience is never lawless in the worst regulated state, and will provide those laws for itself, which the neglect of legislators hath forgotten to supply. This is surely a case of that kind; for, is it not cruel, nay, impious, to force a woman into that state against her will; for her behaviour in which she is to be accountable to the highest and most dreadful court of judicature, and to answer at the peril of her soul? To discharge the matrimonial duties in an adequate manner is no easy task; and shall we lay this burthen upon a woman, while we at the same time deprive her of all that assistance which may enable her to undergo it? Shall we tear her very heart from her, while we enjoin her duties to which a whole heart is scarce equal? I must speak very plainly here. I think parents who act in this manner are accessories to all the guilt which their children afterwards incur, and of course must, before a just judge, expect to partake of their punishment; but if they could avoid this, good heaven! is there a soul who can bear the thought of having contributed to the damnation of his child?

"For these reasons, my best neighbour, as I see the inclinations of this young lady are most unhappily averse to my nephew, I must decline any further thoughts of the honour you intended him, though I assure you I shall always retain the most grateful sense of it."

"Well, sir," said Western (the froth bursting forth from his lips the moment they were uncorked), "you cannot say but I have heard you out, and now I expect you'll hear me; and if I don't answer every word on't, why then I'll consent to gee the matter up. First then, I desire you to answer me one question—— Did not I beget her? did not I beget her? answer me that. They say, indeed, it is a wise father that knows his own child; but I am sure I have the best title to her, for I bred her up. But I believe you will allow me to be her father, and if I be, am I not to govern my own child? I ask you that, am I not to govern my own child? and if I am to govern her in other matters, surely I am to govern her in this, which concerns her most. And what am I desiring all this while? Am I desiring her to do anything for me? to give me anything?—Zu much on t'other side, that I am only desiring her to take away half my estate now, and t'other half when I die. Well, and what is it all vor? Why, is unt it to make her happy? It's enough to make one mad to hear volks talk; if I was going to marry myself, then she would ha reason to cry and to blubber; but, on the contrary, han't I offered to bind down my land in such a manner, that I could not marry if I would, seeing as narro' woman upon earth would ha me. What the devil in hell can I do more? I contribute to her damnation!—Zounds! I'd zee all the world d—n'd bevore her little vinger should be hurt. Indeed, Mr Allworthy, you must excuse me, but I am surprized to hear you talk in zuch a manner, and I must say, take it how you will, that I thought you had more sense."

Allworthy resented this reflection only with a smile; nor could he, if he would have endeavoured it, have conveyed into that smile any mixture of malice or contempt. His smiles at folly were indeed such as we may suppose the angels bestow on the absurdities of mankind.

Blifil now desired to be permitted to speak a few words. "As to using any violence on the young lady, I am sure I shall never consent to it. My conscience will not permit me to use violence on any one, much less on a lady for whom, however cruel she is to me,

I shall always preserve the purest and sincerest affection; but yet I have read that women are seldom proof against perseverance. Why may I not hope then by such perseverance at last to gain those inclinations, in which for the future I shall, perhaps, have no rival; for as for this lord, Mr Western is so kind to prefer me to him; and sure, sir, you will not deny but that a parent hath at least a negative voice in these matters; nay, I have heard this very young lady herself say so more than once, and declare that she thought children inexcusable who married in direct opposition to the will of their parents. Besides, though the other ladies of the family seem to favour the pretensions of my lord, I do not find the lady herself is inclined to give him any countenance; alas! I am too well assured she is not; I am too sensible that wickedest of men remains uppermost in her heart."

"Ay, ay, so he does," cries Western.

"But surely," says Blifil, "when she hears of this murder which he hath committed, if the law should spare his life——"

"What's that?" cries Western. "Murder! hath he committed a murder, and is there any hopes of seeing him hanged?—Tol de rol, tol lol de rol." Here he fell a singing and capering about the room.

"Child," says Allworthy, "this unhappy passion of yours distresses me beyond measure. I heartily pity you, and would do every fair thing to promote your success."

"I desire no more," cries Blifil; "I am convinced my dear uncle hath a better opinion of me than to think that I myself would accept of more."

"Lookee," says Allworthy, "you have my leave to write, to visit, if she will permit it—but I insist on no thoughts of violence. I will have no confinement, nothing of that kind attempted."

"Well, well," cries the squire, "nothing of that kind shall be attempted; we will try a little longer what fair means will effect; and if this fellow be but hanged out of the way—Tol lol de rol! I never heard better news in my life—I warrant everything goes to my mind.—Do, prithee, dear Allworthy, come and dine with me at the Hercules Pillars: I have bespoke a shoulder of mutton roasted, and a spare-rib of pork, and a fowl and egg-sauce. There will be nobody but ourselves, unless we have a mind to have the landlord; for I have sent Parson Supple down to Basingstoke after my tobacco-box, which I left at an inn there, and I would not lose it for the world; for it is an old acquaintance of above twenty years' standing. I can tell you landlord is a vast comical bitch, you will like un hugely."

Mr Allworthy at last agreed to this invitation, and soon after the squire went off, singing and capering at the hopes of seeing the speedy tragical end of poor Jones.

When he was gone, Mr Allworthy resumed the aforesaid subject with much gravity. He told his nephew, "He wished with all his heart he would endeavour to conquer a passion, in which I cannot," says he, "flatter you with any hopes of succeeding. It is certainly a vulgar error, that aversion in a woman may be conquered by perseverance. Indifference may, perhaps, sometimes yield to it; but the usual triumphs gained by perseverance in a lover are over caprice, prudence, affectation, and often an exorbitant degree of levity, which excites women not over-warm in their constitutions to indulge their vanity by prolonging the time of courtship, even when they are well enough pleased with the object, and resolve (if they ever resolve at all) to make him a very pitiful amends in the end. But a fixed dislike, as I am afraid this is, will rather gather strength than be conquered by time. Besides, my dear, I have another apprehension which you must excuse. I am afraid this passion which you have for this fine young creature hath her beautiful person too much for its object, and is unworthy of the name of that love which is the only foundation of matrimonial felicity. To admire, to like, and to long for the possession of a beautiful woman, without any regard to her sentiments towards us, is, I am afraid, too natural; but love, I believe, is the child of love only; at least, I am pretty confident that to love the creature who we are assured hates us is not in human nature. Examine your heart, therefore, thoroughly, my good boy, and if, upon examination, you have but the least suspicion of this kind, I am sure your own virtue and religion will impel you to drive so vicious a passion from your heart, and your good sense will soon enable you to do it without pain."

The reader may pretty well guess Blifil's answer; but, if he should be at a loss, we are not at present at leisure to satisfy him, as our history now hastens on to matters of higher importance, and we can no longer bear to be absent from Sophia.

Chapter iv.

An extraordinary scene between Sophia and her aunt.

THE lowing heifer and the bleating ewe, in herds and flocks, may ramble safe and unregarded through the pastures. These are, indeed, hereafter doomed to be the prey of man; yet many years are they suffered to enjoy their liberty undisturbed. But if a plump doe be discovered to have escaped from the forest, and to repose herself in some field or grove, the whole parish is presently alarmed, every man is ready to set his dogs after her; and, if she is preserved from the rest by the good squire, it is only that he may secure her for his own eating.

I have often considered a very fine young woman of fortune and fashion, when first found strayed from the pale of her nursery, to be in pretty much the same situation with this doe. The town is immediately in an uproar; she is hunted from park to play, from court to assembly, from assembly to her own chamber, and rarely escapes a single season from the jaws of some devourer or other; for, if her friends protect her from some, it is only to deliver her over to one of their own chusing, often more disagreeable to her than any of the rest; while whole herds or flocks of other women securely, and scarce regarded, traverse the park, the play, the opera, and the assembly; and though, for the most part at least, they are at last devoured, yet for a long time do they wanton in liberty, without disturbance or controul.

Of all these paragons none ever tasted more of this persecution than poor Sophia. Her ill stars were not contented with all that she had suffered on account of Blifil, they now raised her another pursuer, who seemed likely to torment her no less than the other had done. For though her aunt was less violent, she was no less assiduous in teizing her, than her father had been before.

The servants were no sooner departed after dinner than Mrs Western, who had opened the matter to Sophia, informed her, "That she expected his lordship that very afternoon, and intended to take the first opportunity of leaving her alone with him." "If you do, madam," answered Sophia, with some spirit, "I shall take the first opportunity of leaving him by him-

self." "How! madam!" cries the aunt; "is this
the return you make me for my kindness in relieving
you from your confinement at your father's?" "You
know, madam," said Sophia, "the cause of that confinement was a refusal to comply with my father in
accepting a man I detested; and will my dear aunt,
who hath relieved me from that distress, involve me
in another equally bad?" "And do you think then,
madam," answered Mrs Western, "that there is no
difference between my Lord Fellamar and Mr Blifil?"
"Very little, in my opinion," cries Sophia; "and,
if I must be condemned to one, I would certainly have
the merit of sacrificing myself to my father's pleasure."
"Then my pleasure, I find," said the aunt, "hath very
little weight with you; but that consideration shall not
move me. I act from nobler motives. The view of
aggrandizing my family, of ennobling yourself, is what
I proceed upon. Have you no sense of ambition?
Are there no charms in the thoughts of having a
coronet on your coach?" "None, upon my honour,"
said Sophia. "A pincushion upon my coach would
please me just as well." "Never mention honour,"
cries the aunt. "It becomes not the mouth of such
a wretch. I am sorry, niece, you force me to use
these words, but I cannot bear your groveling temper;
you have none of the blood of the Westerns in you. But,
however mean and base your own ideas are, you shall
bring no imputation on mine. I will never suffer the
world to say of me that I encouraged you in refusing
one of the best matches in England; a match which,
besides its advantage in fortune, would do honour to
almost any family, and hath, indeed, in title, the advantage of ours." "Surely," says Sophia, "I am born
deficient, and have not the senses with which other
people are blessed; there must be certainly some sense
which can relish the delights of sound and show, which

I have not; for surely mankind would not labour so
much, nor sacrifice so much for the obtaining, nor
would they be so elate and proud with possessing, what
appeared to them, as it doth to me, the most insignifi-
cant of all trifles."

"No, no, miss," cries the aunt; "you are born with
as many senses as other people; but I assure you you
are not born with a sufficient understanding to make a
fool of me, or to expose my conduct to the world; so
I declare this to you, upon my word, and you know,
I believe, how fixed my resolutions are, unless you
agree to see his lordship this afternoon, I will, with
my own hands, deliver you to-morrow morning to my
brother, and will never henceforth interfere with you,
nor see your face again." Sophia stood a few moments
silent after this speech, which was uttered in a most
angry and peremptory tone; and then, bursting into
tears, she cryed, "Do with me, madam, whatever you
please; I am the most miserable undone wretch upon
earth; if my dear aunt forsakes me where shall I look
for a protector?" "My dear niece," cries she, "you
will have a very good protector in his lordship; a
protector whom nothing but a hankering after that vile
fellow Jones can make you decline." "Indeed,
madam," said Sophia, "you wrong me. How can
you imagine, after what you have shewn me, if I had
ever any such thoughts, that I should not banish them for
ever? If it will satisfy you, I will receive the sacra-
ment upon it never to see his face again." "But,
child, dear child," said the aunt, "be reasonable; can
you invent a single objection?" "I have already, I
think, told you a sufficient objection," answered Sophia.
"What?" cries the aunt; "I remember none."
"Sure, madam," said Sophia, "I told you he had
used me in the rudest and vilest manner." "Indeed,
child," answered she, "I never heard you, or did not

understand you :—but what do you mean by this rude, vile manner?" "Indeed, madam," said Sophia, "I am almost ashamed to tell you. He caught me in his arms, pulled me down upon the settee, and thrust his hand into my bosom, and kissed it with such violence that I have the mark upon my left breast at this moment." "Indeed!" said Mrs Western. "Yes, indeed, madam," answered Sophia; "my father luckily came in at that instant, or Heaven knows what rudeness he intended to have proceeded to." "I am astonished and confounded," cries the aunt. "No woman of the name of Western hath been ever treated so since we were a family. I would have torn the eyes of a prince out, if he had attempted such freedoms with me. It is impossible! sure, Sophia, you must invent this to raise my indignation against him." "I hope, madam," said Sophia, "you have too good an opinion of me to imagine me capable of telling an untruth. Upon my soul it is true." "I should have stabbed him to the heart, had I been present," returned the aunt. "Yet surely he could have no dishonourable design; it is impossible! he durst not: besides, his proposals shew he hath not; for they are not only honourable, but generous. I don't know; the age allows too great freedoms. A distant salute is all I would have allowed before the ceremony. I have had lovers formerly, not so long ago neither; several lovers, though I never would consent to marriage, and I never encouraged the least freedom. It is a foolish custom, and what I never would agree to. No man kissed more of me than my cheek. It is as much as one can bring oneself to give lips up to a husband; and, indeed, could I ever have been persuaded to marry, I believe I should not have soon been brought to endure so much." "You will pardon me, dear madam," said Sophia, "if I make one observation: you own you have had many lovers, and the world knows it, even if you should deny it. You refused them all, and, I am convinced, one coronet at least among them." "You say true, dear Sophy," answered she; "I had once the offer of a title." "Why, then," said Sophia, "will you not suffer me to refuse this once?" "It is true, child," said she, "I have refused the offer of a title; but it was not so good an offer; that is, not so very, very good an offer." —"Yes, madam," said Sophia; "but you have had very great proposals from men of vast fortunes. It was not the first, nor the second, nor the third advantageous match that offered itself." "I own it was not," said she. "Well, madam," continued Sophia, "and why may not I expect to have a second, perhaps, better than this? You are now but a young woman, and I am convinced would not promise to yield to the first lover of fortune, nay, or of title too. I am a very young woman, and sure I need not despair." "Well, my dear, dear Sophy," cries the aunt, "what would you have me say?" "Why, I only beg that I may not be left alone, at least this evening; grant me that, and I will submit, if you think, after what is past, I ought to see him in your company." "Well, I will grant it," cries the aunt. "Sophy, you know I love you, and can deny you nothing. You know the easiness of my nature; I have not always been so easy. I have been formerly thought cruel; by the men, I mean. I was called the cruel Parthenissa. I have broke many a window that has had verses to the cruel Parthenissa in it. Sophy, I was never so handsome as you, and yet I had something of you formerly. I am a little altered. Kingdoms and states, as Tully Cicero says in his epistles, undergo alterations, and so must the human form." Thus run she on for near half an hour upon herself, and her conquests, and her cruelty, till the arrival of my lord, who, after a most tedious visit, during which Mrs Western never once offered to leave the room, retired, not much more satisfied with the aunt than with the niece; for Sophia had brought her aunt into so excellent a temper, that she consented to almost everything her niece said; and agreed that a little distant behaviour might not be improper to so forward a lover.

Thus Sophia, by a little well-directed flattery, for which surely none will blame her, obtained a little ease for herself, and, at least, put off the evil day. And now we have seen our heroine in a better situation than she hath been for a long time before, we will look a little after Mr Jones, whom we left in the most deplorable situation that can be well imagined.

Chapter v.

Mrs Miller and Mr Nightingale visit Jones in the prison.

WHEN Mr Allworthy and his nephew went to meet Mr Western, Mrs Miller set forwards to her son-in-law's lodgings, in order to acquaint him with the accident which had befallen his friend Jones; but he had known it long before from Partridge (for Jones, when he left Mrs Miller, had been furnished with a room in the same house with Mr Nightingale). The good woman found her daughter under great affliction on account of Mr Jones, whom having comforted as well as she could, she set forwards to the Gatehouse, where she heard he was, and where Mr Nightingale was arrived before her.

The firmness and constancy of a true friend is a circumstance so extremely delightful to persons in any kind of distress, that the distress itself, if it be only temporary, and admits of relief, is more than compensated by bringing this comfort with it. Nor are instances of this kind so rare as some superficial and inaccurate observers have reported. To say the truth, want of compassion is not to be numbered among our general faults. The black ingredient which fouls our disposition is envy. Hence our eye is seldom, I am afraid, turned upward to those who are manifestly greater, better, wiser, or happier than ourselves, without some degree of malignity; while we commonly look downwards on the mean and miserable with sufficient benevolence and pity. In fact, I have remarked, that most of the defects which have discovered themselves in the friendships within my observation have arisen from envy only: a hellish vice; and yet one from which I have known very few absolutely exempt. But enough of a subject which, if pursued, would lead me too far.

Whether it was that Fortune was apprehensive lest Jones should sink under the weight of his adversity, and that she might thus lose any future opportunity of tormenting him, or whether she really abated somewhat of her severity towards him, she seemed a little to relax her persecution, by sending him the company of two such faithful friends, and what is perhaps more rare, a faithful servant. For Partridge, though he had many imperfections, wanted not fidelity; and though fear would not suffer him to be hanged for his master, yet the world, I believe, could not have bribed him to desert his cause.

While Jones was expressing great satisfaction in the presence of his friends, Partridge brought an account that Mr Fitzpatrick was still alive, though the surgeon declared that he had very little hopes. Upon which, Jones fetching a deep sigh, Nightingale said to him, "My dear Tom, why should you afflict yourself so upon an accident, which, whatever be the consequence, can be attended with no danger to you, and in which your conscience cannot accuse you of having been the least to blame? If the fellow should die, what have you done more than taken away the life of a ruffian in your own defence? So will the coroner's inquest certainly find it; and then you will be easily admitted to bail; and, though you must undergo the form of a trial, yet it is a trial which many men would stand for you for a shilling." "Come, come, Mr Jones," says Mrs Miller, "chear yourself up. I knew you could not be the aggressor, and so I told Mr Allworthy, and so he shall acknowledge too, before I have done with him."

Jones gravely answered, "That whatever might be his fate, he should always lament the having shed the blood of one of his fellow-creatures, as one of the highest misfortunes which could have befallen him. But I have another misfortune of the tenderest kind ——O! Mrs Miller, I have lost what I held most dear upon earth." "That must be a mistress," said Mrs Miller; "but come, come; I know more than you imagine" (for indeed Partridge had blabbed all); "and I have heard more than you know. Matters go better, I promise you, than you think; and I would not give Blifil sixpence for all the chance which he hath of the lady."

"Indeed, my dear friend, indeed," answered Jones, "you are an entire stranger to the cause of my grief. If you was acquainted with the story, you would allow my case admitted of no comfort. I apprehend no danger from Blifil. I have undone myself." "Don't despair," replied Mrs Miller; "you know not what a woman can do; and if anything be in my power, I promise you I will do it to serve you. It is my duty. My son, my dear Mr Nightingale, who is so kind to tell me he hath obligations to you on the same account, knows it is my duty.   Shall I go to the lady myself?   I will say anything to her you would have me say."

"Thou best of women," cries Jones, taking her by the hand, "talk not of obligations to me;——but as you have been so kind to mention it, there is a favour which, perhaps, may be in your power.   I see you are acquainted with the lady (how you came by your information I know not), who sits, indeed, very near my heart.   If you could contrive to deliver this (giving her a paper from his pocket), I shall for ever acknowledge your goodness."

"Give it me," said Mrs Miller.   "If I see it not in her own possession before I sleep, may my next sleep be my last!   Comfort yourself, my good young man! be wise enough to take warning from past follies, and I warrant all shall be well, and I shall yet see you happy with the most charming young lady in the world; for I so hear from every one she is."

"Believe me, madam," said he, "I do not speak the common cant of one in my unhappy situation. Before this dreadful accident happened, I had resolved to quit a life of which I was become sensible of the wickedness as well as folly.   I do assure you, notwithstanding the disturbances I have unfortunately occasioned in your house, for which I heartily ask your pardon, I am not an abandoned profligate. Though I have been hurried into vices, I do not approve a vicious character, nor will I ever, from this moment, deserve it."

Mrs Miller expressed great satisfaction in these declarations, in the sincerity of which she averred she had an entire faith; and now the remainder of the conversation past in the joint attempts of that good woman and Mr Nightingale to cheer the dejected spirits of Mr Jones, in which they so far succeeded as to leave him much better comforted and satisfied than they found him; to which happy alteration nothing so much contributed as the kind undertaking of Mrs Miller to deliver his letter to Sophia, which he despaired of finding any means to accomplish; for when Black George produced the last from Sophia, he informed Partridge that she had strictly charged him, on pain of having it communicated to her father, not to bring her any answer. He was, moreover, not a little pleased to find he had so warm an advocate to Mr Allworthy himself in this good woman, who was, in reality, one of the worthiest creatures in the world.

After about an hour's visit from the lady (for Nightingale had been with him much longer), they both took their leave, promising to return to him soon; during which Mrs Miller said she hoped to bring him some good news from his mistress, and Mr Nightingale promised to enquire into the state of Mr Fitzpatrick's wound, and likewise to find out some of the persons who were present at the rencounter.

The former of these went directly in quest of Sophia, whither we likewise shall now attend her.

<hr />

Chapter vi.

In which Mrs Miller pays a visit to Sophia.

ACCESS to the young lady was by no means difficult; for, as she lived now on a perfect friendly footing with her aunt, she was at full liberty to receive what visitants she pleased.

Sophia was dressing when she was acquainted that there was a gentlewoman below to wait on her. As she was neither afraid, nor ashamed, to see any of her own sex, Mrs Miller was immediately admitted.

Curtsies and the usual ceremonials between women who are strangers to each other, being past, Sophia said, " I have not the pleasure to know you, madam." " No, madam," answered Mrs Miller, " and I must beg pardon for intruding upon you. But when you know what has induced me to give you this trouble, I hope——" " Pray, what is your business, madam?" said Sophia, with a little emotion. " Madam, we are not alone," replied Mrs Miller, in a low voice. " Go out, Betty," said Sophia.

When Betty was departed, Mrs Miller said, " I was desired, madam, by a very unhappy young gentleman, to deliver you this letter." Sophia changed colour when she saw the direction, well knowing the hand, and after some hesitation, said—" I could not conceive, madam, from your appearance, that your business had been of such a nature.—Whomever you brought this letter from, I shall not open it. I should be sorry to entertain an unjust suspicion of any one ; but you are an utter stranger to me."

" If you will have patience, madam," answered Mrs Miller, " I will acquaint you who I am, and how I came by that letter." " I have no curiosity, madam, to know anything," cries Sophia ; " but I must insist on your delivering that letter back to the person who gave it you."

Mrs Miller then fell upon her knees, and in the most passionate terms implored her compassion ; to which Sophia answered : " Sure, madam, it is surprizing you should be so very strongly interested in the behalf of this person. I would not think, madam "——" No, madam," says Mrs Miller, " you shall not think any-thing but the truth. I will tell you all, and you will not wonder that I am interested. He is the best-

natured creature that ever was born."——She then
began and related the story of Mr Anderson.——
After this she cried, "This, madam, this is his goodness; but I have much more tender obligations to him.
He hath preserved my child."——Here, after shed-
ding some tears, she related everything concerning that
fact, suppressing only those circumstances which would
have most reflected on her daughter, and concluded
with saying, "Now, madam, you shall judge whether I
can ever do enough for so kind, so good, so generous a
young man; and sure he is the best and worthiest of all
human beings."

The alterations in the countenance of Sophia had
hitherto been chiefly to her disadvantage, and had inclined her complexion to too great paleness; but she
now waxed redder, if possible, than vermilion, and
cried, "I know not what to say; certainly what arises
from gratitude cannot be blamed——But what service
can my reading this letter do your friend, since I am
resolved never——" Mrs Miller fell again to her
entreaties, and begged to be forgiven, but she could
not, she said, carry it back. "Well, madam," says
Sophia, "I cannot help it, if you will force it upon
me.——Certainly you may leave it whether I will or
no." What Sophia meant, or whether she meant anything, I will not presume to determine; but Mrs
Miller actually understood this as a hint, and presently
laying the letter down on the table, took her leave,
having first begged permission to wait again on Sophia;
which request had neither assent nor denial.

The letter lay upon the table no longer than till Mrs
Miller was out of sight; for then Sophia opened and
read it.

This letter did very little service to his cause; for it
consisted of little more than confessions of his own unworthiness, and bitter lamentations of despair, together

with the most solemn protestations of his unalterable fidelity to Sophia, of which, he said, he hoped to convince her, if he had ever more the honour of being admitted to her presence; and that he could account for the letter to Lady Bellaston in such a manner, that, though it would not entitle him to her forgiveness, he hoped at least to obtain it from her mercy. And concluded with vowing that nothing was ever less in his thoughts than to marry Lady Bellaston.

Though Sophia read the letter twice over with great attention, his meaning still remained a riddle to her; nor could her invention suggest to her any means to excuse Jones. She certainly remained very angry with him, though indeed Lady Bellaston took up so much of her resentment, that her gentle mind had but little left to bestow on any other person.

That lady was most unluckily to dine this very day with her aunt Western, and in the afternoon they were all three, by appointment, to go together to the opera, and thence to Lady Thomas Hatchet's drum. Sophia would have gladly been excused from all, but would not disoblige her aunt; and as to the arts of counterfeiting illness, she was so entirely a stranger to them, that it never once entered into her head. When she was drest, therefore, down she went, resolved to encounter all the horrors of the day, and a most disagreeable one it proved; for Lady Bellaston took every opportunity very civilly and slily to insult her; to all which her dejection of spirits disabled her from making any return; and, indeed, to confess the truth, she was at the very best but an indifferent mistress of repartee.

Another misfortune which befel poor Sophia was the company of Lord Fellamar, whom she met at the opera, and who attended her to the drum. And though both places were too publick to admit of any particularities, and she was farther relieved by the musick at the one place, and by the cards at the other, she could not, however, enjoy herself in his company; for there is something of delicacy in women, which will not suffer them to be even easy in the presence of a man whom they know to have pretensions to them which they are disinclined to favour.

Having in this chapter twice mentioned a drum, a word which our posterity, it is hoped, will not understand in the sense it is here applied, we shall, notwithstanding our present haste, stop a moment to describe the entertainment here meant, and the rather as we can in a moment describe it.

A drum, then, is an assembly of well-dressed persons of both sexes, most of whom play at cards, and the rest do nothing at all; while the mistress of the house performs the part of the landlady at an inn, and like the landlady of an inn prides herself in the number of her guests, though she doth not always, like her, get anything by it.

No wonder then, as so much spirits must be required to support any vivacity in these scenes of dulness, that we hear persons of fashion eternally complaining of the want of them; a complaint confined entirely to upper life. How insupportable must we imagine this round of impertinence to have been to Sophia at this time; how difficult must she have found it to force the appearance of gaiety into her looks, when her mind dictated nothing but the tenderest sorrow, and when every thought was charged with tormenting ideas!

Night, however, at last restored her to her pillow, where we will leave her to soothe her melancholy at least, though incapable we fear of rest, and shall pursue our history, which, something whispers us, is now arrived at the eve of some great event.

Chapter vij.

A pathetic scene between Mr Allworthy and Mrs Miller

MRS MILLER had a long discourse with Mr Allworthy, at his return from dinner, in which
she acquainted him with Jones's having unfortunately lost all which he was pleased to bestow on
him at their separation; and with the distresses to
which that loss had subjected him; of all which she
had received a full account from the faithful retailer
Partridge. She then explained the obligations she had
to Jones; not that she was entirely explicit with regard
to her daughter; for though she had the utmost confidence in Mr Allworthy, and though there could be
no hopes of keeping an affair secret which was unhappily
known to more than half a dozen, yet she could not
prevail with herself to mention those circumstances
which reflected most on the chastity of poor Nancy,
but smothered that part of her evidence as cautiously
as if she had been before a judge, and the girl was now
on her trial for the murder of a bastard.

Allworthy said, there were few characters so absolutely vicious as not to have the least mixture of good
in them. "However," says he, "I cannot deny but
that you have some obligations to the fellow, bad as he
is, and I shall therefore excuse what hath past already,
but must insist you never mention his name to me more;
for, I promise you, it was upon the fullest and plainest
evidence that I resolved to take the measures I have
taken." "Well, sir," says she, "I make not the
least doubt but time will shew all matters in their true
and natural colours, and that you will be convinced this
poor young man deserves better of you than some other
folks that shall be nameless."

"Madam," cries Allworthy, a little ruffled, "I will

not hear any reflections on my nephew; and if ever
you say a word more of that kind, I will depart from
your house that instant. He is the worthiest and best
of men; and I once more repeat it to you, he hath
carried his friendship to this man to a blameable length,
by too long concealing facts of the blackest die. The
ingratitude of the wretch to this good young man is
what I most resent; for, madam, I have the greatest
reason to imagine he had laid a plot to supplant my
nephew in my favour, and to have disinherited him."

"I am sure, sir," answered Mrs Miller, a little
frightened (for, though Mr Allworthy had the utmost
sweetness and benevolence in his smiles, he had great
terror in his frowns), "I shall never speak against any
gentleman you are pleased to think well of. I am
sure, sir, such behaviour would very little become me,
especially when the gentleman is your nearest relation;
but, sir, you must not be angry with me, you must not
indeed, for my good wishes to this poor wretch. Sure
I may call him so now, though once you would have
been angry with me if I had spoke of him with the
least disrespect. How often have I heard you call him
your son? How often have you prattled to me of him
with all the fondness of a parent? Nay, sir, I cannot
forget the many tender expressions, the many good
things you have told me of his beauty, and his parts,
and his virtues; of his good-nature and generosity. I
am sure, sir, I cannot forget them, for I find them all
true. I have experienced them in my own cause.
They have preserved my family. You must pardon
my tears, sir, indeed you must. When I consider the
cruel reverse of fortune which this poor youth, to whom
I am so much obliged, hath suffered; when I consider
the loss of your favour, which I know he valued more
than his life, I must, I must lament him. If you had
a dagger in your hand, ready to plunge into my heart,

I must lament the misery of one whom you have loved, and I shall ever love."

Allworthy was pretty much moved with this speech, but it seemed not to be with anger; for, after a short silence, taking Mrs Miller by the hand, he said very affectionately to her, "Come, madam, let us consider a little about your daughter. I cannot blame you for rejoicing in a match which promises to be advantageous to her, but you know this advantage, in a great measure, depends on the father's reconciliation. I know Mr Nightingale very well, and have formerly had concerns with him; I will make him a visit, and endeavour to serve you in this matter. I believe he is a worldly man; but as this is an only son, and the thing is now irretrievable, perhaps he may in time be brought to reason. I promise you I will do all I can for you."

Many were the acknowledgments which the poor woman made to Allworthy for this kind and generous offer, nor could she refrain from taking this occasion again to express her gratitude towards Jones, "to whom," said she, "I owe the opportunity of giving you, sir, this present trouble." Allworthy gently stopped her; but he was too good a man to be really offended with the effects of so noble a principle as now actuated Mrs Miller; and indeed, had not this new affair inflamed his former anger against Jones, it is possible he might have been a little softened towards him, by the report of an action which malice itself could not have derived from an evil motive.

Mr Allworthy and Mrs Miller had been above an hour together, when their conversation was put an end to by the arrival of Blifil and another person, which other person was no less than Mr Dowling, the attorney, who was now become a great favourite with Mr Blifil, and whom Mr Allworthy, at the desire of his nephew, had made his steward; and had likewise recommended him to Mr Western, from whom the attorney received a promise of being promoted to the same office upon the first vacancy; and, in the meantime, was employed in transacting some affairs which the squire then had in London in relation to a mortgage.

This was the principal affair which then brought Mr Dowling to town; therefore he took the same opportunity to charge himself with some money for Mr Allworthy, and to make a report to him of some other business; in all which, as it was of much too dull a nature to find any place in this history, we will leave the uncle, nephew, and their lawyer concerned, and resort to other matters.

Chapter viii.

Containing various matters.

BEFORE we return to Mr Jones, we will take one more view of Sophia.

Though that young lady had brought her aunt into great good humour by those soothing methods which we have before related, she had not brought her in the least to abate of her zeal for the match with Lord Fellamar. This zeal was now inflamed by Lady Bellaston, who had told her the preceding evening, that she was well satisfied from the conduct of Sophia, and from her carriage to his lordship, that all delays would be dangerous, and that the only way to succeed was to press the match forward with such rapidity that the young lady should have no time to reflect, and be obliged to consent while she scarce knew what she did; in which manner, she said, one-half of the marriages among people of condition were brought about. A fact very probably true, and to which, I suppose, is owing the mutual tenderness which afterwards exists among so many happy couples.

A hint of the same kind was given by the same lady to Lord Fellamar; and both these so readily embraced the advice that the very next day was, at his lordship's request, appointed by Mrs Western for a private interview between the young parties. This was communicated to Sophia by her aunt, and insisted upon in such high terms, that, after having urged everything she possibly could invent against it without the least effect, she at last agreed to give the highest instance of complacence which any young lady can give, and consented to see his lordship.

As conversations of this kind afford no great entertainment, we shall be excused from reciting the whole that past at this interview; in which, after his lordship had made many declarations of the most pure and ardent passion to the silent blushing Sophia, she at last collected all the spirits she could raise, and with a trembling low voice said, " My lord, you must be yourself conscious whether your former behaviour to me hath been consistent with the professions you now make." " Is there," answered he, " no way by which I can atone for madness? what I did I am afraid must have too plainly convinced you, that the violence of love had deprived me of my senses." " Indeed, my lord," said she, " it is in your power to give me a proof of an affection which I much rather wish to encourage, and to which I should think myself more beholden." " Name it, madam," said my lord, very warmly. " My lord," says she, looking down upon her fan, " I know you must be sensible how uneasy this pretended passion of yours hath made me." " Can you be so cruel to call it pretended?" says he. " Yes, my lord," answered Sophia, " all professions of love to those whom we persecute are most insulting pretences. This pursuit of yours is to me a most cruel persecution: nay, it is taking a most ungenerous advantage of my unhappy situation." "Most lovely, most adorable charmer, do not accuse me," cries he, "of taking an ungenerous advantage, while I have no thoughts but what are directed to your honour and interest, and while I have no view, no hope, no ambition, but to throw myself, honour, fortune, everything at your feet." "My lord," says she, "it is that fortune and those honours which gave you the advantage of which I complain. These are the charms which have seduced my relations, but to me they are things indifferent. If your lordship will merit my gratitude, there is but one way." "Pardon me, divine creature," said he, "there can be none. All I can do for you is so much your due, and will give me so much pleasure, that there is no room for your gratitude." "Indeed, my lord," answered she, "you may obtain my gratitude, my good opinion, every kind thought and wish which it is in my power to bestow; nay, you may obtain them with ease, for sure to a generous mind it must be easy to grant my request. Let me beseech you, then, to cease a pursuit in which you can never have any success. For your own sake as well as mine I entreat this favour; for sure you are too noble to have any pleasure in tormenting an unhappy creature. What can your lordship propose but uneasiness to yourself by a perseverance, which, upon my honour, upon my soul, cannot, shall not prevail with me, whatever distresses you may drive me to." Here my lord fetched a deep sigh, and then said—"Is it then, madam, that I am so unhappy to be the object of your dislike and scorn; or will you pardon me if I suspect there is some other?" Here he hesitated, and Sophia answered with some spirit, "My lord, I shall not be accountable to you for the

reasons of my conduct.   I am obliged to your lordship
for the generous offer you have made; I own it is
beyond either my deserts or expectations; yet I hope,
my lord, you will not insist on my reasons, when I
declare I cannot accept it."   Lord Fellamar returned
much to this, which we do not perfectly understand,
and perhaps it could not all be strictly reconciled
either to sense or grammar; but he concluded his
ranting speech with saying, "That if she had pre-
engaged herself to any gentleman, however unhappy
it would make him, he should think himself bound
in honour to desist."   Perhaps my lord laid too much
emphasis on the word gentleman; for we cannot else
well account for the indignation with which he inspired
Sophia, who, in her answer, seemed greatly to resent
some affront he had given her.

While she was speaking, with her voice more raised
than usual, Mrs Western came into the room, the fire
glaring in her cheeks, and the flames bursting from her
eyes.   "I am ashamed," says she, "my lord, of the
reception which you have met with.   I assure your
lordship we are all sensible of the honour done us; and
I must tell you, Miss Western, the family expect a
different behaviour from you."   Here my lord interfered on behalf of the young lady, but to no purpose;
the aunt proceeded till Sophia pulled out her handkerchief, threw herself into a chair, and burst into a violent
fit of tears.

The remainder of the conversation between Mrs
Western and his lordship, till the latter withdrew,
consisted of bitter lamentations on his side, and on
hers of the strongest assurances that her niece should
and would consent to all he wished.   "Indeed, my
lord," says she, "the girl hath had a foolish education,
neither adapted to her fortune nor her family.   Her
father, I am sorry to say it, is to blame for everything.

The girl hath silly country notions of bashfulness. Nothing else, my lord, upon my honour; I am convinced she hath a good understanding at the bottom, and will be brought to reason."

This last speech was made in the absence of Sophia; for she had some time before left the room, with more appearance of passion than she had ever shown on any occasion; and now his lordship, after many expressions of thanks to Mrs Western, many ardent professions of passion which nothing could conquer, and many assurances of perseverance, which Mrs Western highly encouraged, took his leave for this time.

Before we relate what now passed between Mrs Western and Sophia, it may be proper to mention an unfortunate accident which had happened, and which had occasioned the return of Mrs Western with so much fury, as we have seen.

The reader then must know that the maid who at present attended on Sophia was recommended by Lady Bellaston, with whom she had lived for some time in the capacity of a comb-brush: she was a very sensible girl, and had received the strictest instructions to watch her young lady very carefully. These instructions, we are sorry to say, were communicated to her by Mrs Honour, into whose favour Lady Bellaston had now so ingratiated herself, that the violent affection which the good waiting-woman had formerly borne to Sophia was entirely obliterated by that great attachment which she had to her new mistress.

Now, when Mrs Miller was departed, Betty (for that was the name of the girl), returning to her young lady, found her very attentively engaged in reading a long letter, and the visible emotions which she betrayed on that occasion might have well accounted for some suspicions which the girl entertained; but indeed they had yet a stronger foundation, for she had overheard the whole scene which passed between Sophia and Mrs Miller.

Mrs Western was acquainted with all this matter by Betty, who, after receiving many commendations and some rewards for her fidelity, was ordered, that, if the woman who brought the letter came again, she should introduce her to Mrs Western herself.

Unluckily, Mrs Miller returned at the very time when Sophia was engaged with his lordship. Betty, according to order, sent her directly to the aunt; who, being mistress of so many circumstances relating to what had past the day before, easily imposed upon the poor woman to believe that Sophia had communicated the whole affair; and so pumped everything out of her which she knew relating to the letter and relating to Jones.

This poor creature might, indeed, be called simplicity itself. She was one of that order of mortals who are apt to believe everything which is said to them; to whom nature hath neither indulged the offensive nor defensive weapons of deceit, and who are consequently liable to be imposed upon by any one who will only be at the expense of a little falshood for that purpose. Mrs Western, having drained Mrs Miller of all she knew, which, indeed, was but little, but which was sufficient to make the aunt suspect a great deal, dismissed her with assurances that Sophia would not see her, that she would send no answer to the letter, nor ever receive another; nor did she suffer her to depart without a handsome lecture on the merits of an office to which she could afford no better name than that of procuress.—This discovery had greatly discomposed her temper, when, coming into the apartment next to that in which the lovers were, she overheard Sophia very warmly protesting against his lordship's addresses. At which the rage already kindled burst forth, and she

rushed in upon her niece in a most furious manner, as
we have already described, together with what past at
that time till his lordship's departure.

No sooner was Lord Fellamar gone than Mrs
Western returned to Sophia, whom she upbraided in
the most bitter terms for the ill use she had made of
the confidence reposed in her; and for her treachery
in conversing with a man with whom she had offered
but the day before to bind herself in the most solemn
oath never more to have any conversation. Sophia
protested she had maintained no such conversation.
"How, how! Miss Western," said the aunt; "will
you deny your receiving a letter from him yesterday?"
"A letter, madam!" answered Sophia, somewhat surprized. "It is not very well bred, miss," replies the
aunt, "to repeat my words. I say a letter, and I insist
upon your showing it me immediately. "I scorn a
lie, madam," said Sophia; "I did receive a letter,
but it was without my desire, and, indeed, I may say,
against my consent." "Indeed, indeed, miss," cries
the aunt, "you ought to be ashamed of owning you
had received it at all; but where is the letter? for I
will see it."

To this peremptory demand, Sophia paused some
time before she returned an answer; and at last only
excused herself by declaring she had not the letter in
her pocket, which was, indeed, true; upon which her
aunt, losing all manner of patience, asked her niece this
short question, whether she would resolve to marry Lord
Fellamar, or no? to which she received the strongest
negative. Mrs Western then replied with an oath,
or something very like one, that she would early the
next morning deliver her back into her father's hand.

Sophia then began to reason with her aunt in the
following manner:—"Why, madam, must I of necessity be forced to marry at all? Consider how cruel

you would have thought it in your own case, and how much kinder your parents were in leaving you to your liberty. What have I done to forfeit this liberty? I will never marry contrary to my father's consent, nor without asking yours——And when I ask the consent of either improperly, it will be then time enough to force some other marriage upon me." "Can I bear to hear this," cries Mrs Western, "from a girl who hath now a letter from a murderer in her pocket?" "I have no such letter, I promise you," answered Sophia; "and, if he be a murderer, he will soon be in no condition to give you any further disturbance." "How, Miss Western!" said the aunt, "have you the assurance to speak of him in this manner; to own your affection for such a villain to my face?" "Sure, madam," said Sophia, "you put a very strange construction on my words." "Indeed, Miss Western," cries the lady, "I shall not bear this usage; you have learnt of your father this manner of treating me; he hath taught you to give me the lie. He hath totally ruined you by this false system of education; and, please heaven, he shall have the comfort of its fruits; for once more I declare to you, that to-morrow morning I will carry you back. I will withdraw all my forces from the field, and remain henceforth, like the wise king of Prussia, in a state of perfect neutrality. You are both too wise to be regulated by my measures; so prepare yourself, for to-morrow morning you shall evacuate this house."

Sophia remonstrated all she could; but her aunt was deaf to all she said. In this resolution therefore we must at present leave her, as there seems to be no hopes of bringing her to change it.

Chapter ix.

What happened to Mr Jones in the prison.

MR JONES passed about twenty-four melancholy hours by himself, unless when relieved by the company of Partridge, before Mr Nightingale returned; not that this worthy young man had deserted or forgot his friend; for, indeed, he had been much the greatest part of the time employed in his service.

He had heard, upon enquiry, that the only persons who had seen the beginning of the unfortunate rencounter were a crew belonging to a man-of-war which then lay at Deptford. To Deptford therefore he went in search of this crew, where he was informed that the men he sought after were all gone ashore. He then traced them from place to place, till at last he found two of them drinking together, with a third person, at a hedge-tavern near Aldersgate.

Nightingale desired to speak with Jones by himself (for Partridge was in the room when he came in). As soon as they were alone, Nightingale, taking Jones by the hand, cried, "Come, my brave friend, be not too much dejected at what I am going to tell you—— I am sorry I am the messenger of bad news; but I think it my duty to tell you." "I guess already what that bad news is," cries Jones. "The poor gentleman then is dead."——"I hope not," answered Nightingale. "He was alive this morning; though I will not flatter you; I fear, from the accounts I could get, that his wound is mortal. But if the affair be exactly as you told it, your own remorse would be all you would have reason to apprehend, let what would happen; but forgive me, my dear Tom, if I entreat you to make the worst of your story to your friends. If you disguise anything to us, you will only be an enemy to yourself."

"What reason, my dear Jack, have I ever given you," said Jones, "to stab me with so cruel a suspicion?" "Have patience," cries Nightingale, "and I will tell you all. After the most diligent enquiry I could make, I at last met with two of the fellows who were present at this unhappy accident, and I am sorry to say, they do not relate the story so much in your favour as you yourself have told it." "Why, what do they say?" cries Jones. "Indeed what I am sorry to repeat, as I am afraid of the consequence of it to you. They say that they were at too great a distance to overhear any words that passed between you: but they both agree that the first blow was given by you." "Then, upon my soul," answered Jones, "they injure me. He not only struck me first, but struck me without the least provocation. What should induce those villains to accuse me falsely?" "Nay, that I cannot guess," said Nightingale, "and if you yourself, and I, who am so heartily your friend, cannot conceive a reason why they should belie you, what reason will an indifferent court of justice be able to assign why they should not believe them? I repeated the question to them several times, and so did another gentleman who was present, who, I believe, is a seafaring man, and who really acted a very friendly part by you; for he begged them often to consider that there was the life of a man in the case; and asked them over and over, if they were certain; to which they both answered, that they were, and would abide by their evidence upon oath. For heaven's sake, my dear friend, recollect yourself; for, if this should appear to be the fact, it will be your business to think in time of making the best of your interest. I would not shock you; but you know, I believe, the severity

of the law, whatever verbal provocations may have
been given you." "Alas! my friend," cries Jones,
"what interest hath such a wretch as I? Besides,
do you think I would even wish to live with the reputation of a murderer? If I had any friends (as,
alas! I have none), could I have the confidence to
solicit them to speak in the behalf of a man condemned
for the blackest crime in human nature? Believe me,
I have no such hope; but I have some reliance on a
throne still greatly superior; which will, I am certain,
afford me all the protection I merit."

He then concluded with many solemn and vehement
protestations of the truth of what he had at first
asserted.

The faith of Nightingale was now again staggered,
and began to incline to credit his friend, when Mrs
Miller appeared, and made a sorrowful report of the
success of her embassy; which when Jones had heard,
he cried out most heroically, "Well, my friend, I am
now indifferent as to what shall happen, at least with
regard to my life; and if it be the will of Heaven that
I shall make an atonement with that for the blood I
have spilt, I hope the Divine Goodness will one day
suffer my honour to be cleared, and that the words of
a dying man, at least, will be believed, so far as to
justify his character."

A very mournful scene now past between the prisoner and his friends, at which, as few readers would
have been pleased to be present, so few, I believe, will
desire to hear it particularly related. We will, therefore, pass on to the entrance of the turnkey, who
acquainted Jones that there was a lady without who
desired to speak with him when he was at leisure.

Jones declared his surprize at this message. He
said, "He knew no lady in the world whom he could
possibly expect to see there." However, as he saw no

reason to decline seeing any person, Mrs Miller and Mr Nightingale presently took their leave, and he gave orders to have the lady admitted.

If Jones was surprized at the news of a visit from a lady, how greatly was he astonished when he discovered this lady to be no other than Mrs Waters! In this astonishment then we shall leave him awhile, in order to cure the surprize of the reader, who will likewise, probably, not a little wonder at the arrival of this lady.

Who this Mrs Waters was, the reader pretty well knows; what she was, he must be perfectly satisfied. He will therefore be pleased to remember that this lady departed from Upton in the same coach with Mr Fitzpatrick and the other Irish gentleman, and in their company travelled to Bath.

Now there was a certain office in the gift of Mr Fitzpatrick at that time vacant, namely that of a wife: for the lady who had lately filled that office had resigned, or at least deserted her duty. Mr Fitzpatrick therefore, having thoroughly examined Mrs Waters on the road, found her extremely fit for the place, which, on their arrival at Bath, he presently conferred upon her, and she without any scruple accepted. As husband and wife this gentleman and lady continued together all the time they stayed at Bath, and as husband and wife they arrived together in town.

Whether Mr Fitzpatrick was so wise a man as not to part with one good thing till he had secured another, which he had at present only a prospect of regaining; or whether Mrs Waters had so well discharged her office, that he intended still to retain her as principal, and to make his wife (as is often the case) only her deputy, I will not say; but certain it is, he never mentioned his wife to her, never communicated to her the letter given him by Mrs Western, nor ever once hinted his purpose of repossessing his wife; much less did he ever mention the name of Jones. For, though he intended to fight with him wherever he met him, he did not imitate those prudent persons who think a wife, a mother, a sister, or sometimes a whole family, the safest seconds on these occasions. The first account therefore which she had of all this was delivered to her from his lips, after he was brought home from the tavern where his wound had been drest.

As Mr Fitzpatrick, however, had not the clearest way of telling a story at any time, and was now, perhaps, a little more confused than usual, it was some time before she discovered that the gentleman who had given him this wound was the very same person from whom her heart had received a wound, which, though not of a mortal kind, was yet so deep that it had left a considerable scar behind it. But no sooner was she acquainted that Mr Jones himself was the man who had been committed to the Gatehouse for this supposed murder, than she took the first opportunity of committing Mr Fitzpatrick to the care of his nurse, and hastened away to visit the conqueror.

She now entered the room with an air of gaiety, which received an immediate check from the melancholy aspect of poor Jones, who started and blessed himself when he saw her. Upon which she said, "Nay, I do not wonder at your surprize; I believe you did not expect to see me; for few gentlemen are troubled here with visits from any lady, unless a wife. You see the power you have over me, Mr Jones. Indeed, I little thought, when we parted at Upton, that our next meeting would have been in such a place." "Indeed, madam," says Jones, "I must look upon this visit as kind; few will follow the miserable, especially to such dismal habitations." "I protest, Mr Jones," says she, " I can hardly persuade myself you are the same agreeable fellow I saw at Upton. Why, your face is more miserable than any dungeon in the universe. What can be the matter with you?" " I thought, madam," said Jones, " as you knew of my being here, you knew the unhappy reason." " Pugh ! " says she, " you have pinked a man in a duel, that's all." Jones exprest some indignation at this levity, and spoke with the utmost contrition for what had happened. To which she answered, " Well, then, sir, if you take it so much to heart, I will relieve you ; the gentleman is not dead, and, I am pretty confident, is in no danger of dying. The surgeon, indeed, who first dressed him was a young fellow, and seemed desirous of representing his case to be as bad as possible, that he might have the more honour from curing him : but the king's surgeon hath seen him since, and says, unless from a fever, of which there are at present no symptoms, he apprehends not the least danger of life." Jones shewed great satisfaction in his countenance at this report ; upon which she affirmed the truth of it, adding, " By the most extraordinary accident in the world I lodge at the same house ; and have seen the gentleman, and I promise you he doth you justice, and says, whatever be the consequence, that he was entirely the aggressor, and that you was not in the least to blame."

Jones expressed the utmost satisfaction at the account which Mrs Waters brought him. He then informed her of many things which she well knew before, as who Mr Fitzpatrick was, the occasion of his resentment, &c. He likewise told her several facts of which she was ignorant, as the adventure of the muff, and other particulars, concealing only the name of Sophia. He then lamented the follies and vices of which he had been guilty ; every one of which, he said, had been attended with such ill consequences, that he should be unpardonable if he did not take warning, and quit those vicious courses for the future. He lastly concluded with assuring her of his resolution to sin no more, lest a worse thing should happen to him.

Mrs Waters with great pleasantry ridiculed all this, as the effects of low spirits and confinement. She repeated some witticisms about the devil when he was sick, and told him, "She doubted not but shortly to see him at liberty, and as lively a fellow as ever; and then," says she, "I don't question but your conscience will be safely delivered of all these qualms that it is now so sick in breeding."

Many more things of this kind she uttered, some of which it would do her no great honour, in the opinion of some readers, to remember; nor are we quite certain but that the answers made by Jones would be treated with ridicule by others. We shall therefore suppress the rest of this conversation, and only observe that it ended at last with perfect innocence, and much more to the satisfaction of Jones than of the lady; for the former was greatly transported with the news she had brought him; but the latter was not altogether so pleased with the penitential behaviour of a man whom she had, at her first interview, conceived a very different opinion of from what she now entertained of him.

Thus the melancholy occasioned by the report of Mr Nightingale was pretty well effaced; but the dejection into which Mrs Miller had thrown him still continued. The account she gave so well tallied with the words of Sophia herself in her letter, that he made not the least doubt but that she had disclosed his letter to her aunt, and had taken a fixed resolution to abandon him. The torments this thought gave him were to be equalled only by a piece of news which fortune had yet in store for him, and which we shall communicate in the second chapter of the ensuing book.

BOOK XVIII.

Chapter i.

A farewel to the reader.

WE are now, reader, arrived at the last stage of our long journey. As we have, therefore, travelled together through so many pages, let us behave to one another like fellow-travellers in a stage coach, who have passed several days in the company of each other; and who, notwithstanding any bickerings or little animosities which may have occurred on the road, generally make all up at last, and mount, for the last time, into their vehicle with chearfulness and good humour; since after this one stage, it may possibly happen to us, as it commonly happens to them, never to meet more.

As I have here taken up this simile, give me leave to carry it a little farther. I intend, then, in this last book, to imitate the good company I have mentioned in their last journey. Now, it is well known that all jokes and raillery are at this time laid aside; whatever characters any of the passengers have for the jest-sake personated on the road are now thrown off, and the conversation is usually plain and serious.

In the same manner, if I have now and then, in the

course of this work, indulged any pleasantry for thy entertainment, I shall here lay it down. The variety of matter, indeed, which I shall be obliged to cram into this book, will afford no room for any of those ludicrous observations which I have elsewhere made, and which may sometimes, perhaps, have prevented thee from taking a nap when it was beginning to steal upon thee. In this last book thou wilt find nothing (or at most very little) of that nature. All will be plain narrative only; and, indeed, when thou hast perused the many great events which this book will produce, thou wilt think the number of pages contained in it scarce sufficient to tell the story.

And now, my friend, I take this opportunity (as I shall have no other) of heartily wishing thee well. If I have been an entertaining companion to thee, I promise thee it is what I have desired. If in anything I have offended, it was really without any intention. Some things, perhaps, here said, may have hit thee or thy friends; but I do most solemnly declare they were not pointed at thee or them. I question not but thou hast been told, among other stories of me, that thou wast to travel with a very scurrilous fellow; but whoever told thee so did me an injury. No man detests and despises scurrility more than myself; nor hath any man more reason; for none hath ever been treated with more; and what is a very severe fate, I have had some of the abusive writings of those very men fathered upon me, who, in other of their works, have abused me themselves with the utmost virulence.

All these works, however, I am well convinced, will be dead long before this page shall offer itself to thy perusal; for however short the period may be of my own performances, they will most probably outlive their own infirm author, and the weakly productions of his abusive contemporaries.

Chapter ii.

Containing a very tragical incident.

WHILE Jones was employed in those unpleasant meditations, with which we left him tormenting himself, Partridge came stumbling into the room with his face paler than ashes, his eyes fixed in his head, his hair standing an end, and every limb trembling. In short, he looked as he would have done had he seen a spectre, or had he, indeed, been a spectre himself.

Jones, who was little subject to fear, could not avoid being somewhat shocked at this sudden appearance. He did, indeed, himself change colour, and his voice a little faultered while he asked him, What was the matter?

"I hope, sir," said Partridge, "you will not be angry with me. Indeed I did not listen, but I was obliged to stay in the outward room. I am sure I wish I had been a hundred miles off, rather than have heard what I have heard." "Why, what is the matter?" said Jones. "The matter, sir? O good Heaven!" answered Partridge, "was that woman who is just gone out the woman who was with you at Upton?" "She was, Partridge," cried Jones. "And did you really, sir, go to bed with that woman?" said he, trembling.—"I am afraid what past between us is no secret," said Jones.—"Nay, but pray, sir, for Heaven's sake, sir, answer me," cries Partridge. "You know I did," cries Jones. "Why then, the Lord have mercy upon your soul, and forgive you," cries Partridge; "but as sure as I stand here alive, you have been a-bed with your own mother."

Upon these words Jones became in a moment a greater picture of horror than Partridge himself. He was, indeed, for some time struck dumb with amazement,

and both stood staring wildly at each other. At last
his words found way, and in an interrupted voice he
said, "How! how! what's this you tell me?" "Nay,
sir," cries Partridge, "I have not breath enough left
to tell you now, but what I have said is most certainly
true.—That woman who now went out is your own
mother. How unlucky was it for you, sir, that I did
not happen to see her at that time, to have prevented
it! Sure the devil himself must have contrived to
bring about this wickedness."

"Sure," cries Jones, "Fortune will never have done
with me till she hath driven me to distraction. But
why do I blame Fortune? I am myself the cause of
all my misery. All the dreadful mischiefs which have
befallen me are the consequences only of my own folly
and vice. What thou hast told me, Partridge, hath
almost deprived me of my senses! And was Mrs
Waters, then—but why do I ask? for thou must
certainly know her——If thou hast any affection for
me, nay, if thou hast any pity, let me beseech thee to
fetch this miserable woman back again to me. O
good Heavens! incest——with a mother! To what
am I reserved!" He then fell into the most violent
and frantic agonies of grief and despair, in which Partridge declared he would not leave him; but at last,
having vented the first torrent of passion, he came a
little to himself; and then, having acquainted Partridge
that he would find this wretched woman in the same
house where the wounded gentleman was lodged, he
despatched him in quest of her.

If the reader will please to refresh his memory, by
turning to the scene at Upton, in the ninth book, he
will be apt to admire the many strange accidents which
unfortunately prevented any interview between Partridge
and Mrs Waters, when she spent a whole day there
with Mr Jones. Instances of this kind we may

frequently observe in life, where the greatest events are produced by a nice train of little circumstances; and more than one example of this may be discovered by the accurate eye, in this our history.

After a fruitless search of two or three hours, Partridge returned back to his master, without having seen Mrs Waters. Jones, who was in a state of desperation at his delay, was almost raving mad when he brought him his account. He was not long, however, in this condition before he received the following letter:

" Sir,

" Since I left you I have seen a gentleman, from whom I have learned something concerning you which greatly surprizes and affects me; but as I have not at present leisure to communicate a matter of such high importance, you must suspend your curiosity till our next meeting, which shall be the first moment I am able to see you. O, Mr Jones, little did I think, when I past that happy day at Upton, the reflection upon which is like to embitter all my future life, who it was to whom I owed such perfect happiness. Believe me to be ever sincerely your unfortunate

" J. Waters."

" P.S. I would have you comfort yourself as much as possible, for Mr Fitzpatrick is in no manner of danger; so that whatever other grievous crimes you may have to repent of, the guilt of blood is not among the number."

Jones having read the letter, let it drop (for he was unable to hold it, and indeed had scarce the use of any one of his faculties). Partridge took it up, and having received consent by silence, read it likewise; nor had it upon him a less sensible effect. The pencil, and not the pen, should describe the horrors which appeared in both their countenances. While they both remained speechless the turnkey entered the room, and, without taking any notice of what sufficiently discovered itself in the faces of them both, acquainted Jones that a man without desired to speak with him. This person was presently introduced, and was no other than Black George.

As sights of horror were not so usual to George as they were to the turnkey, he instantly saw the great disorder which appeared in the face of Jones. This he imputed to the accident that had happened, which was reported in the very worst light in Mr Western's family; he concluded, therefore, that the gentleman was dead, and that Mr Jones was in a fair way of coming to a shameful end. A thought which gave him much uneasiness; for George was of a compassionate disposition, and notwithstanding a small breach of friendship which he had been over-tempted to commit, was, in the main, not insensible of the obligations he had formerly received from Mr Jones.

The poor fellow, therefore, scarce refrained from a tear at the present sight. He told Jones he was heartily sorry for his misfortunes, and begged him to consider if he could be of any manner of service. "Perhaps, sir," said he, "you may want a little matter of money upon this occasion; if you do, sir, what little I have is heartily at your service."

Jones shook him very heartily by the hand, and gave him many thanks for the kind offer he had made; but answered, "He had not the least want of that kind." Upon which George began to press his services more eagerly than before. Jones again thanked him, with assurances that he wanted nothing which was in the power of any man living to give. "Come, come, my good master," answered George, "do not take the matter so much to heart. Things may end better than

you imagine; to be sure you an't the first gentleman
who hath killed a man, and yet come off." "You
are wide of the matter, George," said Partridge, "the
gentleman is not dead, nor like to die. Don't disturb
my master, at present, for he is troubled about a matter
in which it is not in your power to do him any good."
"You don't know what I may be able to do, Mr Partridge," answered George; "if his concern is about
my young lady, I have some news to tell my master."
"What do you say, Mr George?" cried Jones.
"Hath anything lately happened in which my Sophia
is concerned? My Sophia! how dares such a wretch
as I mention her so profanely." "I hope she will be
yours yet," answered George. "Why yes, sir, I have
something to tell you about her. Madam Western
hath just brought Madam Sophia home, and there hath
been a terrible to do. I could not possibly learn the
very right of it; but my master he hath been in a vast
big passion, and so was Madam Western, and I heard
her say, as she went out of doors into her chair, that
she would never set her foot in master's house again.
I don't know what's the matter, not I, but everything
was very quiet when I came out; but Robin, who
waited at supper, said he had never seen the squire for
a long while in such good humour with young madam;
that he kissed her several times, and swore she should
be her own mistress, and he never would think of confining her any more. I thought this news would please
you, and so I slipped out, though it was so late, to
inform you of it." Mr Jones assured George that it
did greatly please him; for though he should never
more presume to lift his eyes toward that incomparable
creature, nothing could so much relieve his misery as
the satisfaction he should always have in hearing of her
welfare.

The rest of the conversation which passed at the

visit is not important enough to be here related. The reader will, therefore, forgive us this abrupt breaking off, and be pleased to hear how this great good-will of the squire towards his daughter was brought about.

Mrs Western, on her first arrival at her brother's lodging, began to set forth the great honours and advantages which would accrue to the family by the match with Lord Fellamar, which her niece had absolutely refused; in which refusal, when the squire took the part of his daughter, she fell immediately into the most violent passion, and so irritated and provoked the squire, that neither his patience nor his prudence could bear it any longer; upon which there ensued between them both so warm a bout at altercation, that perhaps the regions of Billingsgate never equalled it. In the heat of this scolding Mrs Western departed, and had consequently no leisure to acquaint her brother with the letter which Sophia received, which might have possibly produced ill effects; but, to say truth, I believe it never once occurred to her memory at this time.

When Mrs Western was gone, Sophia, who had been hitherto silent, as well indeed from necessity as inclination, began to return the compliment which her father had made her, in taking her part against her aunt, by taking his likewise against the lady. This was the first time of her so doing, and it was in the highest degree acceptable to the squire. Again, he remembered that Mr Allworthy had insisted on an entire relinquishment of all violent means; and, indeed, as he made no doubt but that Jones would be hanged, he did not in the least question succeeding with his daughter by fair means; he now, therefore, once more gave a loose to his natural fondness for her, which had such an effect on the dutiful, grateful, tender, and affectionate heart of Sophia, that had her honour, given to Jones, and something else, perhaps, in which he was concerned, been removed, I much doubt whether she would not have sacrificed herself to a man she did not like, to have obliged her father. She promised him she would make it the whole business of her life to oblige him, and would never marry any man against his consent; which brought the old man so near to his highest happiness, that he was resolved to take the other step, and went to bed completely drunk.

Chapter iij.

Allworthy visits old Nightingale ; with a strange discovery that he made on that occasion.

THE morning after these things had happened, Mr Allworthy went, according to his promise, to visit old Nightingale, with whom his authority was so great, that, after having sat with him three hours, he at last prevailed with him to consent to see his son.

Here an accident happened of a very extraordinary kind ; one indeed of those strange chances whence very good and grave men have concluded that Providence often interposes in the discovery of the most secret villany, in order to caution men from quitting the paths of honesty, however warily they tread in those of vice.

Mr Allworthy, at his entrance into Mr Nightingale's, saw Black George ; he took no notice of him, nor did Black George imagine he had perceived him.

However, when their conversation on the principal point was over, Allworthy asked Nightingale, Whether he knew one George Seagrim, and upon what business he came to his house ? "Yes," answered Nightingale, "I know him very well, and a most extraordinary fellow he is, who, in these days, hath been able to hoard up £500 from renting a very small estate of £30 a year." "And is this the story which he hath told you?" cries Allworthy. "Nay, it is true, I promise you," said Nightingale, "for I have the money now in my own hands, in five bank-bills, which I am to lay out either in a mortgage, or in some purchase in the north of England." The bank-bills were no sooner produced at Allworthy's desire than he blessed himself at the strangeness of the discovery. He presently told Nightingale that these bank-bills were formerly his, and then acquainted him with the whole affair. As there are no men who complain more of the frauds of business than highwaymen, gamesters, and other thieves of that kind, so there are none who so bitterly exclaim against the frauds of gamesters, &c., as usurers, brokers, and other thieves of this kind; whether it be that the one way of cheating is a discountenance or reflection upon the other, or that money, which is the common mistress of all cheats, makes them regard each other in the light of rivals; but Nightingale no sooner heard the story than he exclaimed against the fellow in terms much severer than the justice and honesty of Allworthy had bestowed on him.

Allworthy desired Nightingale to retain both the money and the secret till he should hear farther from him; and, if he should in the meantime see the fellow, that he would not take the least notice to him of the discovery which he had made. He then returned to his lodgings, where he found Mrs Miller in a very dejected condition, on account of the information she had received from her son-in-law. Mr Allworthy, with great chearfulness, told her that he had much good news to communicate; and, with little further preface, acquainted her that he had brought Mr Nightingale to consent to see his son, and did not in the least doubt to effect a perfect reconciliation between them; though he found the father more sowered by another accident of the same kind which had happened in his family. He then mentioned the running away of the uncle's daughter, which he had been told by the old gentleman, and which Mrs Miller and her son-in-law did not yet know.

The reader may suppose Mrs Miller received this account with great thankfulness, and no less pleasure ; but so uncommon was her friendship to Jones, that I am not certain whether the uneasiness she suffered for his sake did not overbalance her satisfaction at hearing a piece of news tending so much to the happiness of her own family ; nor whether even this very news, as it reminded her of the obligations she had to Jones, did not hurt as well as please her ; when her grateful heart said to her, "While my own family is happy, how miserable is the poor creature to whose generosity we owe the beginning of all this happiness ! "

Allworthy, having left her a little while to chew the cud (if I may use that expression) on these first tidings, told her he had still something more to impart, which he believed would give her pleasure. "I think," said he, "I have discovered a pretty considerable treasure belonging to the young gentleman, your friend ; but perhaps, indeed, his present situation may be such that it will be of no service to him." The latter part of the speech gave Mrs Miller to understand who was meant, and she answered with a sigh, "I hope not, sir." "I hope so too," cries Allworthy, "with all my heart ; but my nephew told me this morning he had heard a very bad account of the affair."———— "Good Heaven ! sir," said she—"Well, I must not speak, and yet it is certainly very hard to be obliged to hold one's tongue when one hears."————"Madam," said Allworthy, "you may say whatever you please, you know me too well to think I have a prejudice

against any one; and as for that young man, I assure
you I should be heartily pleased to find he could acquit
himself of everything, and particularly of this sad affair.
You can testify the affection I have formerly borne
him. The world, I know, censured me for loving
him so much. I did not withdraw that affection from
him without thinking I had the justest cause. Believe
me, Mrs Miller, I should be glad to find I have been
mistaken." Mrs Miller was going eagerly to reply,
when a servant acquainted her that a gentleman without
desired to speak with her immediately. Allworthy
then enquired for his nephew, and was told that he
had been for some time in his room with the gentleman
who used to come to him, and whom Mr Allworthy
guessing rightly to be Mr Dowling, he desired presently
to speak with him.

When Dowling attended, Allworthy put the case
of the bank-notes to him, without mentioning any name,
and asked in what manner such a person might be
punished. To which Dowling answered, "He thought
he might be indicted on the Black Act; but said, as
it was a matter of some nicety, it would be proper to
go to counsel. He said he was to attend counsel
presently upon an affair of Mr Western's, and if Mr
Allworthy pleased he would lay the case before them."
This was agreed to; and then Mrs Miller, opening
the door, cried, "I ask pardon, I did not know you
had company;" but Allworthy desired her to come
in, saying he had finished his business. Upon which
Mr Dowling withdrew, and Mrs Miller introduced
Mr Nightingale the younger, to return thanks for the
great kindness done him by Allworthy: but she had
scarce patience to let the young gentleman finish his
speech before she interrupted him, saying, "O sir!
Mr Nightingale brings great news about poor Mr Jones:
he hath been to see the wounded gentleman, who is

out of all danger of death, and, what is more, declares he fell upon poor Mr Jones himself, and beat him. I am sure, sir, you would not have Mr Jones be a coward. If I was a man myself, I am sure, if any man was to strike me, I should draw my sword. Do pray, my dear, tell Mr Allworthy, tell him all yourself." Nightingale then confirmed what Mrs Miller had said ; and concluded with many handsome things of Jones, who was, he said, one of the best-natured fellows in the world, and not in the least inclined to be quarrelsome. Here Nightingale was going to cease, when Mrs Miller again begged him to relate all the many dutiful expressions he had heard him make use of towards Mr Allworthy. "To say the utmost good of Mr Allworthy," cries Nightingale, "is doing no more than strict justice, and can have no merit in it : but indeed, I must say, no man can be more sensible of the obligations he hath to so good a man than is poor Jones. Indeed, sir, I am convinced the weight of your displeasure is the heaviest burthen he lies under. He hath often lamented it to me, and hath as often protested in the most solemn manner he hath never been intentionally guilty of any offence towards you ; nay, he hath sworn he would rather die a thousand deaths than he would have his conscience upbraid him with one disrespectful, ungrateful, or undutiful thought towards you. But I ask pardon, sir, I am afraid I presume to intermeddle too far in so tender a point." "You have spoke no more than what a Christian ought," cries Mrs Miller. "Indeed, Mr Nightingale," answered Allworthy, "I applaud your generous friendship, and I wish he may merit it of you. I confess I am glad to hear the report you bring from this unfortunate gentleman ; and, if that matter should turn out to be as you represent it (and, indeed, I doubt nothing of what you say), I may, perhaps, in time, be brought to think better than lately I have of this young man ; for this good gentlewoman here, nay, all who know me, can witness that I loved him as dearly as if he had been my own son. Indeed, I have considered him as a child sent by fortune to my care. I still remember the innocent, the helpless situation in which I found him. I feel the tender pressure of his little hands at this moment. He was my darling, indeed he was." At which words he ceased, and the tears stood in his eyes.

As the answer which Mrs Miller made may lead us into fresh matters, we will here stop to account for the visible alteration in Mr Allworthy's mind, and the abatement of his anger to Jones. Revolutions of this kind, it is true, do frequently occur in histories and dramatic writers, for no other reason than because the history or play draws to a conclusion, and are justified by authority of authors ; yet, though we insist upon as much authority as any author whatever, we shall use this power very sparingly, and never but when we are driven to it by necessity, which we do not at present foresee will happen in this work.

This alteration then in the mind of Mr Allworthy was occasioned by a letter he had just received from Mr Square, and which we shall give the reader in the beginning of the next chapter.

Chapter iv.

Containing two letters in very different stiles.

" MY WORTHY FRIEND,—I informed you in my last that I was forbidden the use of the waters, as they were found by experience rather to increase than lessen the symptoms of my distemper. I must now acquaint you with a piece of news, which, I believe, will afflict my friends more than it hath afflicted me. Dr Harrington and Dr Brewster have informed me that there is no hopes of my recovery.

"I have somewhere read, that the great use of philosophy is to learn to die. I will not therefore so far disgrace mine as to shew any surprize at receiving a lesson which I must be thought to have so long studied. Yet, to say the truth, one page of the Gospel teaches this lesson better than all the volumes of antient or modern philosophers. The assurance it gives us of another life is a much stronger support to a good mind than all the consolations that are drawn from the necessity of nature, the emptiness or satiety of our enjoyments here, or any other topic of those declamations which are sometimes capable of arming our minds with a stubborn patience in bearing the thoughts of death, but never of raising them to a real contempt of it, and much less of making us think it is a real good. I would not here be understood to throw the horrid censure of atheism, or even the absolute denial of immortality, on all who are called philosophers. Many of that sect, as well antient as modern, have, from the light of reason, discovered some hopes of a future state; but in reality, that light was so faint and glimmering, and the hopes were so incertain and precarious, that it may be justly doubted on which side their belief turned. Plato himself concludes his Phædon with declaring that his best arguments amount only to raise a probability; and Cicero himself seems rather to profess an inclination to believe, than any actual belief in the doctrines of immortality. As to myself, to be very sincere with you, I never was much in earnest in this faith till I was in earnest a Christian.

"You will perhaps wonder at the latter expression; but I assure you it hath not been till very lately that I could, with truth, call myself so. The pride of philosophy had intoxicated my reason, and the sublimest of all wisdom appeared to me, as it did to the Greeks of old, to be foolishness. God hath, however, been so gracious to shew me my error in time, and to bring me into the way of truth, before I sunk into utter darkness for ever.

"I find myself beginning to grow weak, I shall therefore hasten to the main purpose of this letter.

"When I reflect on the actions of my past life, I know of nothing which sits heavier upon my conscience than the injustice I have been guilty of to that poor wretch your adopted son. I have, indeed, not only connived at the villany of others, but been myself active in injustice towards him. Believe me, my dear friend, when I tell you, on the word of a dying man, he hath been basely injured. As to the principal fact, upon the misrepresentation of which you discarded him, I solemnly assure you he is innocent. When you lay upon your supposed deathbed, he was the only person in the house who testified any real concern ; and what happened afterwards arose from the wildness of his joy on your recovery ; and, I am sorry to say it, from the baseness of another person (but it is my desire to justify the innocent, and to accuse none). Believe me, my friend, this young man hath the noblest generosity of heart, the most perfect capacity for friendship, the highest integrity, and indeed every virtue which can ennoble a man. He hath some faults, but among them is not to be numbered the least want of duty or gratitude towards you. On the contrary, I am satisfied, when you dismissed him from your house, his heart bled for you more than for himself.

"Worldly motives were the wicked and base reasons of my concealing this from you so long: to reveal it now I can have no inducement but the desire of serving the cause of truth, of doing right to the innocent, and of making all the amends in my power for a past offence. I hope this declaration, therefore, will have the effect desired, and will restore this deserving young man to your favour; the hearing of which, while I am yet alive, will afford the utmost consolation to,

Sir,

Your most obliged,

obedient humble servant,

THOMAS SQUARE."

The reader will, after this, scarce wonder at the revolution so visibly appearing in Mr Allworthy, notwithstanding he received from Thwackum, by the same post, another letter of a very different kind, which we shall here add, as it may possibly be the last time we shall have occasion to mention the name of that gentleman.

" SIR,

" I am not at all surprized at hearing from your worthy nephew a fresh instance of the villany of Mr Square the atheist's young pupil. I shall not wonder at any murders he may commit; and I heartily pray that your own blood may not seal up his final commitment to the place of wailing and gnashing of teeth.

" Though you cannot want sufficient calls to repentance for the many unwarrantable weaknesses exemplified in your behaviour to this wretch, so much to the prejudice of your own lawful family, and of your character; I say, though these may sufficiently be supposed to prick and goad your conscience at this season, I should yet be wanting to my duty, if I spared to give you some admonition in order to bring you to a due sense of your errors. I therefore pray you seriously to consider the judgment which is likely to overtake this wicked villain; and let it serve at least as a warning to you, that you may not for the future despise the advice of one who is so indefatigable in his prayers for your welfare.

"Had not my hand been withheld from due correction, I had scourged much of this diabolical spirit out of a boy, of whom from his infancy I discovered the devil had taken such entire possession. But reflections of this kind now come too late.

"I am sorry you have given away the living of Westerton so hastily. I should have applied on that occasion earlier, had I thought you would not have acquainted me previous to the disposition.———Your objection to pluralities is being righteous over-much. If there were any crime in the practice, so many godly men would not agree to it. If the vicar of Aldergrove should die (as we hear he is in a declining way), I hope you will think of me, since I am certain you must be convinced of my most sincere attachment to your highest welfare—a welfare to which all worldly considerations are as trifling as the small tithes mentioned in Scripture are, when compared to the weighty matters of the law.

I am, sir,
Your faithful humble servant,
ROGER THWACKUM."

This was the first time Thwackum ever wrote in this authoritative stile to Allworthy, and of this he had afterwards sufficient reason to repent, as in the case of those who mistake the highest degree of goodness for the lowest degree of weakness. Allworthy had indeed never liked this man. He knew him to be proud and ill-natured; he also knew that his divinity itself was tinctured with his temper, and such as in many respects he himself did by no means approve; but he was at the same time an excellent scholar, and most indefatigable in teaching the two lads. Add to this, the strict severity of his life and manners, an unimpeached honesty, and a most devout attachment to religion. So that, upon the whole, though Allworthy did not esteem nor love the man, yet he could never bring himself to part with a tutor to the boys, who was, both by learning and industry, extremely well qualified for his office; and he hoped, that as they were bred up in his own house, and under his own eye, he should be able to correct whatever was wrong in Thwackum's instructions.

Chapter b.

In which the history is continued.

MR ALLWORTHY, in his last speech, had recollected some tender ideas concerning Jones, which had brought tears into the good man's eyes. This Mrs Miller observing, said, "Yes, yes, sir, your goodness to this poor young man is known, notwithstanding all your care to conceal it; but there is not a single syllable of truth in what those villains said. Mr Nightingale hath now discovered the whole matter. It seems these fellows were employed by a lord, who is a rival of poor Mr Jones, to have pressed him on board a ship.——I assure them I don't know who they will press next. Mr Nightingale here hath seen the officer himself, who is a very pretty gentleman, and hath told him all, and is very sorry for what he undertook, which he would never have done, had he known Mr Jones to have been a gentleman; but he was told that he was a common strolling vagabond."

Allworthy stared at all this, and declared he was a

stranger to every word she said. "Yes, sir," answered she, "I believe you are.——It is a very different story, I believe, from what those fellows told the lawyer."

"What lawyer, madam? what is it you mean?" said Allworthy. "Nay, nay," said she, "this is so like you to deny your own goodness: but Mr Nightingale here saw him." "Saw whom, madam?" answered he. "Why, your lawyer, sir," said she, "that you so kindly sent to enquire into the affair." "I am still in the dark, upon my honour," said Allworthy. "Why then do you tell him, my dear sir," cries she. "Indeed, sir," said Nightingale, "I did see that very lawyer who went from you when I came into the room, at an alehouse in Aldersgate, in company with two of the fellows who were employed by Lord Fellamar to press Mr Jones, and who were by that means present at the unhappy rencounter between him and Mr Fitzpatrick." "I own, sir," said Mrs Miller, "when I saw this gentleman come into the room to you, I told Mr Nightingale that I apprehended you had sent him thither to inquire into the affair." Allworthy shewed marks of astonishment in his countenance at this news, and was indeed for two or three minutes struck dumb by it. At last, addressing himself to Mr Nightingale, he said, "I must confess myself, sir, more surprized at what you tell me than I have ever been before at anything in my whole life. Are you certain this was the gentleman?" "I am most certain," answered Nightingale. "At Aldersgate?" cries Allworthy. "And was you in company with this lawyer and the two fellows?"——"I was, sir," said the other, "very near half an hour." "Well, sir," said Allworthy, "and in what manner did the lawyer behave? did you hear all that past between him and the fellows?" "No, sir," answered Nightingale, "they had been together before I came.—In my presence the lawyer said little; but, after I had several times examined the fellows, who persisted in a story directly contrary to what I had heard from Mr Jones, and which I find by Mr Fitzpatrick was a rank falshood, the lawyer then desired the fellows to say nothing but what was the truth, and seemed to speak so much in favour of Mr Jones, that, when I saw the same person with you, I concluded your goodness had prompted you to send him thither."—" And did you not send him thither?" says Mrs Miller.—"Indeed I did not," answered Allworthy; " nor did I know he had gone on such an errand till this moment."—"I see it all!" said Mrs Miller, " upon my soul, I see it all! No wonder they have been closeted so close lately. Son Nightingale, let me beg you run for these fellows immediately——find them out if they are above-ground. I will go myself"——"Dear madam," said Allworthy, " be patient, and do me the favour to send a servant upstairs to call Mr Dowling hither, if he be in the house, or, if not, Mr Blifil." Mrs Miller went out muttering something to herself, and presently returned with an answer, " That Mr Dowling was gone; but that the t'other," as she called him, " was coming."

Allworthy was of a cooler disposition than the good woman, whose spirits were all up in arms in the cause of her friend. He was not however without some suspicions which were near akin to hers. When Blifil came into the room, he asked him with a very serious countenance, and with a less friendly look than he had ever before given him, " Whether he knew anything of Mr Dowling's having seen any of the persons who were present at the duel between Jones and another gentleman?"

There is nothing so dangerous as a question which comes by surprize on a man whose business it is to conceal truth, or to defend falshood. For which reason those worthy personages, whose noble office it is to save the lives of their fellow-creatures at the Old Bailey, take the utmost care, by frequent previous examination, to divine every question which may be asked their clients on the day of tryal, that they may be supplyed with proper and ready answers, which the most fertile invention cannot supply in an instant. Besides, the sudden and violent impulse on the blood, occasioned by these surprizes, causes frequently such an alteration in the countenance, that the man is obliged to give evidence against himself. And such indeed were the alterations which the countenance of Blifil underwent from this sudden question, that we can scarce blame the eagerness of Mrs Miller, who immediately cryed out, " Guilty, upon my honour ! guilty, upon my soul ! "

Mr Allworthy sharply rebuked her for this impetuosity ; and then turning to Blifil, who seemed sinking into the earth, he said, " Why do you hesitate, sir, at giving me an answer ? You certainly must have employed him ; for he would not, of his own accord, I believe, have undertaken such an errand, and especially without acquainting me."

Blifil then answered, " I own, sir, I have been guilty of an offence, yet may I hope your pardon ? "——— " My pardon," said Allworthy, very angrily.——— " Nay, sir," answered Blifil, " I knew you would be offended ; yet surely my dear uncle will forgive the effects of the most amiable of human weaknesses. Compassion for those who do not deserve it, I own is a crime ; and yet it is a crime from which you yourself are not entirely free. I know I have been guilty of it in more than one instance to this very person ; and I will own I did send Mr Dowling, not on a vain and fruitless enquiry, but to discover the witnesses, and to endeavour to soften their evidence. This, sir, is the truth; which, though I intended to conceal from you, I will not deny."

"I confess," said Nightingale, "this is the light in which it appeared to me from the gentleman's behaviour."

"Now, madam," said Allworthy, "I believe you will once in your life own you have entertained a wrong suspicion, and are not so angry with my nephew as you was."

Mrs Miller was silent; for, though she could not so hastily be pleased with Blifil, whom she looked upon to have been the ruin of Jones, yet in this particular instance he had imposed upon her as well as upon the rest; so entirely had the devil stood his friend. And, indeed, I look upon the vulgar observation, "That the devil often deserts his friends, and leaves them in the lurch," to be a great abuse on that gentleman's character. Perhaps he may sometimes desert those who are only his cup acquaintance; or who, at most, are but half his; but he generally stands by those who are thoroughly his servants, and helps them off in all extremities, till their bargain expires.

As a conquered rebellion strengthens a government, or as health is more perfectly established by recovery from some diseases; so anger, when removed, often gives new life to affection. This was the case of Mr Allworthy; for Blifil having wiped off the greater suspicion, the lesser, which had been raised by Square's letter, sunk of course, and was forgotten; and Thwackum, with whom he was greatly offended, bore alone all the reflections which Square had cast on the enemies of Jones.

As for that young man, the resentment of Mr Allworthy began more and more to abate towards him. He told Blifil, "He did not only forgive the extraordinary efforts of his good-nature, but would give him the pleasure of following his example." Then, turning to Mrs Miller with a smile which would have become an angel, he cryed, "What say you, madam? shall we take a hackney-coach, and all of us together pay a visit to your friend? I promise you it is not the first visit I have made in a prison."

Every reader, I believe, will be able to answer for the worthy woman; but they must have a great deal of good-nature, and be well acquainted with friendship, who can feel what she felt on this occasion. Few, I hope, are capable of feeling what now passed in the mind of Blifil; but those who are will acknowledge that it was impossible for him to raise any objection to this visit. Fortune, however, or the gentleman lately mentioned above, stood his friend, and prevented his undergoing so great a shock; for at the very instant when the coach was sent for, Partridge arrived, and, having called Mrs Miller from the company, acquainted her with the dreadful accident lately come to light; and hearing Mr Allworthy's intention, begged her to find some means of stopping him: "For," says he, "the matter must at all hazards be kept a secret from him; and if he should now go, he will find Mr Jones and his mother, who arrived just as I left him, lamenting over one another the horrid crime they have ignorantly committed."

The poor woman, who was almost deprived of her senses at his dreadful news, was never less capable of invention than at present. However, as women are much readier at this than men, she bethought herself of an excuse, and, returning to Allworthy, said, "I am sure, sir, you will be surprized at hearing any objection from me to the kind proposal you just now made; and yet I am afraid of the consequence of it, if carried immediately into execution. You must imagine, sir, that all the calamities which have lately befallen this poor young fellow must have thrown him into the lowest dejection of spirits; and now, sir, should we all on a sudden fling him into such a violent fit of joy, as I know your presence will occasion, it may, I am afraid, produce some fatal mischief, especially as his servant, who is without, tells me he is very far from being well."

"Is his servant without?" cries Allworthy; "pray call him hither. I will ask him some questions concerning his master."

Partridge was at first afraid to appear before Mr Allworthy; but was at length persuaded, after Mrs Miller, who had often heard his whole story from his own mouth, had promised to introduce him.

Allworthy recollected Partridge the moment he came into the room, though many years had passed since he had seen him. Mrs Miller, therefore, might have spared here a formal oration, in which, indeed, she was something prolix; for the reader, I believe, may have observed already that the good woman, among other things, had a tongue always ready for the service of her friends.

"And are you," said Allworthy to Partridge, "the servant of Mr Jones?" "I can't say, sir," answered he, "that I am regularly a servant, but I live with him, an't please your honour, at present. *Non sum qualis eram*, as your honour very well knows."

Mr Allworthy then asked him many questions concerning Jones, as to his health, and other matters; to all which Partridge answered, without having the least regard to what was, but considered only what he would have things appear; for a strict adherence to truth was not among the articles of this honest fellow's morality or his religion.

During this dialogue Mr Nightingale took his leave, and presently after Mrs Miller left the room, when Allworthy likewise despatched Blifil; for he imagined that Partridge when alone with him would be more explicit than before company. They were no sooner left in private together than Allworthy began, as in the following chapter.

Chapter vi.

In which the history is farther continued.

"SURE, friend," said the good man, "you are the strangest of all human beings. Not only to have suffered as you have formerly for obstinately persisting in a falshood, but to persist in it thus to the last, and to pass thus upon the world for a servant of your own son! What interest can you have in all this? What can be your motive?"

"I see, sir," said Partridge, falling down upon his knees, "that your honour is prepossessed against me, and resolved not to believe anything I say, and, therefore, what signifies my protestations? but yet there is one above who knows that I am not the father of this young man."

"How!" said Allworthy, "will you yet deny what you was formerly convicted of upon such unanswerable, such manifest evidence? Nay, what a confirmation is your being now found with this very man, of all which twenty years ago appeared against you! I thought you had left the country! nay, I thought you had been long since dead.—In what manner did you know anything of this young man? Where did you meet with him, unless you had kept some correspondence together? Do not deny this;

for I promise you it will greatly raise your son in my opinion, to find that he hath such a sense of filial duty as privately to support his father for so many years."

"If your honour will have patience to hear me," said Partridge, "I will tell you all."——Being bid go on, he proceeded thus : "When you honour conceived that displeasure against me, it ended in my ruin soon after ; for I lost my little school ; and the minister, thinking I suppose it would be agreeable to your honour, turned me out from the office of clerk ; so that I had nothing to trust to but the barber's shop, which, in a country place like that, is a poor livelihood ; and when my wife died (for till that time I received a pension of £12 a year from an unknown hand, which indeed I believe was your honour's own, for nobody that ever I heard of doth these things besides)——but, as I was saying, when she died, this pension forsook me ; so that now, as I owed two or three small debts, which began to be troublesome to me, particularly one * which an attorney brought up by law-charges from 15s. to near £30, and as I found all my usual means of living had forsook me, I packed up my little all as well as I could, and went off.

"The first place I came to was Salisbury, where I got into the service of a gentleman belonging to the law, and one of the best gentlemen that ever I knew, for he was not only good to me, but I know a thousand good and charitable acts which he did while I staid

* This is a fact which I knew happen to a poor clergyman in Dorsetshire, by the villany of an attorney who, not contented with the exorbitant costs to which the poor man was put by a single action, brought afterwards another action on the judgment, as it was called. A method frequently used to oppress the poor, and bring money into the pockets of attorneys, to the great scandal of the law, of the nation, of Christianity, and even of human nature itself.

with him; and I have known him often refuse business because it was paultry and oppressive." "You need not be so particular," said Allworthy; "I know this gentleman, and a very worthy man he is, and an honour to his profession."———"Well, sir," continued Partridge, "from hence I removed to Lymington, where I was above three years in the service of another lawyer, who was likewise a very good sort of a man, and to be sure one of the merriest gentlemen in England. Well, sir, at the end of the three years I set up a little school, and was likely to do well again, had it not been for a most unlucky accident. Here I kept a pig; and one day, as ill fortune would have it, this pig broke out, and did a trespass, I think they call it, in a garden belonging to one of my neighbours, who was a proud, revengeful man, and employed a lawyer, one——one——I can't think of his name; but he sent for a writ against me, and had me to size. When I came there, Lord have mercy upon me——to hear what the counsellors said! There was one that told my lord a parcel of the confoundedest lies about me; he said that I used to drive my hogs into other folk's gardens, and a great deal more; and at last he said, he hoped I had at last brought my hogs to a fair market. To be sure, one would have thought that, instead of being owner only of one poor little pig, I had been the greatest hog-merchant in England. Well——" "Pray," said Allworthy, "do not be so particular, I have heard nothing of your son yet." "O it was a great many years," answered Partridge, "before I saw my son, as you are pleased to call him.—— I went over to Ireland after this, and taught school at Cork (for that one suit ruined me again, and I lay seven years in Winchester jail)."———"Well," said Allworthy, "pass that over till your return to England." ——"Then, sir," said he, "it was about half a year ago that I landed at Bristol, where I staid some time, and not finding it do there, and hearing of a place between that and Gloucester where the barber was just dead, I went thither, and there I had been about two months when Mr Jones came thither." He then gave Allworthy a very particular account of their first meeting, and of everything, as well as he could remember, which had happened from that day to this; frequently interlarding his story with panegyrics on Jones, and not forgetting to insinuate the great love and respect which he had for Allworthy. He concluded with saying, "Now, sir, I have told your honour the whole truth." And then repeated a most solemn protestation, "That he was no more the father of Jones than of the Pope of Rome;" and imprecated the most bitter curses on his head, if he did not speak truth.

"What am I to think of this matter?" cries Allworthy. "For what purpose should you so strongly deny a fact which I think it would be rather your interest to own?" "Nay, sir," answered Partridge (for he could hold no longer), "if your honour will not believe me, you are like soon to have satisfaction enough. I wish you had mistaken the mother of this young man, as well as you have his father."—And now being asked what he meant, with all the symptoms of horror, both in his voice and countenance, he told Allworthy the whole story, which he had a little before expressed such desire to Mrs Miller to conceal from him.

Allworthy was almost as much shocked at this discovery as Partridge himself had been while he related it. "Good heavens!" says he, "in what miserable distresses do vice and imprudence involve men! How much beyond our designs are the effects of wickedness sometimes carried!" He had scarce uttered these words, when Mrs Waters came hastily and abruptly into the room. Partridge no sooner saw her than he cried, "Here, sir, here is the very woman herself. This is the unfortunate mother of Mr Jones. I am sure she will acquit me before your honour. Pray, madam——"

Mrs Waters, without paying any regard to what Partridge said, and almost without taking any notice of him, advanced to Mr Allworthy. "I believe, sir, it is so long since I had the honour of seeing you, that you do not recollect me." "Indeed," answered Allworthy, "you are so very much altered, on many accounts, that had not this man already acquainted me who you are, I should not have immediately called you to my remembrance. Have you, madam, any particular business which brings you to me?" Allworthy spoke this with great reserve; for the reader may easily believe he was not well pleased with the conduct of this lady; neither with what he had formerly heard, nor with what Partridge had now delivered.

Mrs Waters answered—"Indeed, sir, I have very particular business with you; and it is such as I can impart only to yourself. I must desire, therefore, the favour of a word with you alone: for I assure you what I have to tell you is of the utmost importance."

Partridge was then ordered to withdraw, but before he went, he begged the lady to satisfy Mr Allworthy that he was perfectly innocent. To which she answered, "You need be under no apprehension, sir; I shall satisfy Mr Allworthy very perfectly of that matter."

Then Partridge withdrew, and that past between Mr Allworthy and Mrs Waters which is written in the next chapter.

Chapter vij.

Continuation of the history.

MRS WATERS remaining a few moments silent, Mr Allworthy could not refrain from saying, " I am sorry, madam, to perceive, by what I have since heard, that you have made so very ill a use——" " Mr Allworthy," says she, interrupting him, " I know I have faults, but ingratitude to you is not one of them. I never can nor shall forget your goodness, which I own I have very little deserved; but be pleased to wave all upbraiding me at present, as I have so important an affair to communicate to you concerning this young man, to whom you have given my maiden name of Jones."

" Have I then," said Allworthy, " ignorantly punished an innocent man, in the person of him who hath just left us? Was he not the father of the child?" " Indeed he was not," said Mrs Waters. " You may be pleased to remember, sir, I formerly told you, you should one day know; and I acknowledge myself to have been guilty of a cruel neglect, in not having discovered it to you before. Indeed, I little knew how necessary it was." " Well, madam," said Allworthy, " be pleased to proceed." " You must remember, sir," said she, " a young fellow, whose name was Summer." " Very well," cries Allworthy, " he was the son of a clergyman of great learning and virtue, for whom I had the highest friendship." " So it appeared, sir," answered she; " for I believe you bred the young man up, and maintained him at the university; where, I think, he had finished his studies, when he came to reside at your house; a finer man, I must say, the sun never shone upon; for, besides the handsomest person I ever saw, he was so genteel, and had so much wit and good breeding." "Poor gentleman," said Allworthy, "he was indeed untimely snatched away; and little did I think he had any sins of this kind to answer for; for I plainly perceive you are going to tell me he was the father of your child."

"Indeed, sir," answered she, "he was not." "How!" said Allworthy, "to what then tends all this preface?" "To a story," said she, "which I am concerned falls to my lot to unfold to you. O, sir! prepare to hear something which will surprize you, will grieve you." "Speak," said Allworthy, "I am conscious of no crime, and cannot be afraid to hear." "Sir," said she, "that Mr Summer, the son of your friend, educated at your expense, who, after living a year in the house as if he had been your own son, died there of the small-pox, was tenderly lamented by you, and buried as if he had been your own; that Summer, sir, was the father of this child." "How!" said Allworthy; "you contradict yourself." "That I do not," answered she; "he was indeed the father of this child, but not by me." "Take care, madam," said Allworthy, "do not, to shun the imputation of any crime, be guilty of falshood. Remember there is One from whom you can conceal nothing, and before whose tribunal falshood will only aggravate your guilt." "Indeed, sir," says she, "I am not his mother; nor would I now think myself so for the world." "I know your reason," said Allworthy, "and shall rejoice as much as you to find it otherwise; yet you must remember, you yourself confest it before me." "So far what I confest," said she, "was true, that these hands conveyed the infant to your bed; conveyed it thither at the command of its mother; at her commands I afterwards owned it, and thought myself, by her generosity, nobly rewarded, both for my secrecy and my shame." "Who could this woman be?" said Allworthy. "Indeed, I tremble to name her," answered Mrs Waters. "By all this preparation I am to guess that she was a relation of mine," cried he. "Indeed she was a near one." At which words Allworthy started, and she continued— "You had a sister, sir." "A sister!" repeated he, looking aghast.—"As there is truth in heaven," cries she, "your sister was the mother of that child you found between your sheets." "Can it be possible?" cries he, "Good heavens!" "Have patience, sir," said Mrs Waters, "and I will unfold to you the whole story. Just after your departure for London, Miss Bridget came one day to the house of my mother. She was pleased to say she had heard an extraordinary character of me, for my learning and superior understanding to all the young women there, so she was pleased to say. She then bid me come to her to the great house; where, when I attended, she employed me to read to her. She expressed great satisfaction in my reading, shewed great kindness to me, and made me many presents. At last she began to catechise me on the subject of secrecy, to which I gave her such satisfactory answers, that, at last, having locked the door of her room, she took me into her closet, and then locking that door likewise, she said she should convince me of the vast reliance she had on my integrity, by communicating a secret in which her honour, and consequently her life, was concerned. She then stopt, and after a silence of a few minutes, during which she often wiped her eyes, she enquired of me if I thought my mother might safely be confided in. I answered, I would stake my life on her fidelity. She then imparted to me the great secret which laboured in her breast, and which, I believe, was delivered with more pains than she afterwards suffered in child-birth. It was then contrived that my mother and myself only should attend at the time, and that Mrs Wilkins should be sent out of the way, as she accordingly was, to the very furthest part of Dorsetshire, to enquire the character of a servant; for the lady had turned away her own maid near three months before; during all which time I officiated about her person upon trial, as she said, though, as she afterwards declared, I was not sufficiently handy for the place. This, and many other such things which she used to say of me, were all thrown out to prevent any suspicion which Wilkins might hereafter have, when I was to own the child; for she thought it could never be believed she would venture to hurt a young woman with whom she had intrusted such a secret. You may be assured, sir, I was well paid for all these affronts, which, together with being informed with the occasion of them, very well contented me. Indeed, the lady had a greater suspicion of Mrs Wilkins than of any other person; not that she had the least aversion to the gentlewoman, but she thought her incapable of keeping a secret, especially from you, sir; for I have often heard Miss Bridget say, that, if Mrs Wilkins had committed a murder, she believed she would acquaint you with it. At last the expected day came, and Mrs Wilkins, who had been kept a week in readiness, and put off from time to time, upon some pretence or other, that she might not return too soon, was dispatched. Then the child was born, in the presence only of myself and my mother, and was by my mother conveyed to her own house, where it was privately kept by her till the evening of your return, when I, by the command of Miss Bridget, conveyed it into the bed where you found it. And all suspicions were afterwards laid asleep by the artful conduct of your sister, in pretending ill-will to

the boy, and that any regard she shewed him was out
of meer complacence to you."

Mrs Waters then made many protestations of the
truth of this story, and concluded by saying, "Thus,
sir, you have at last discovered your nephew; for so
I am sure you will hereafter think him, and I question
not but he will be both an honour and a comfort to
you under that appellation."

"I need not, madam," said Allworthy, "express
my astonishment at what you have told me; and yet
surely you would not, and could not, have put together
so many circumstances to evidence an untruth.   I confess I recollect some passages relating to that Summer,
which formerly gave me a conceit that my sister had
some liking to him.   I mentioned it to her; for I had
such a regard to the young man, as well on his own
account as on his father's, that I should willingly have
consented to a match between them; but she exprest
the highest disdain of my unkind suspicion, as she
called it; so that I never spoke more on the subject.
Good heavens!   Well!   the Lord disposeth all things.
——Yet sure it was a most unjustifiable conduct in my
sister to carry this secret with her out of the world."
"I promise you, sir," said Mrs Waters, "she always
profest a contrary intention, and frequently told me she
intended one day to communicate it to you.   She said,
indeed, she was highly rejoiced that her plot had succeeded so well, and that you had of your own accord
taken such a fancy to the child, that it was yet un-
necessary to make any express declaration.   Oh! sir,
had that lady lived to have seen this poor young man
turned like a vagabond from your house: nay, sir,
could she have lived to hear that you had yourself
employed a lawyer to prosecute him for a murder of
which he was not guilty——Forgive me, Mr Allworthy, I must say it was unkind.—Indeed, you have

been abused, he never deserved it of you." "Indeed, madam," said Allworthy, "I have been abused by the person, whoever he was, that told you so." "Nay, sir," said she, "I would not be mistaken, I did not presume to say you were guilty of any wrong. The gentleman who came to me proposed no such matter; he only said, taking me for Mr Fitzpatrick's wife, that, if Mr Jones had murdered my husband, I should be assisted with any money I wanted to carry on the prosecution, by a very worthy gentleman, who, he said, was well apprized what a villain I had to deal with. It was by this man I found out who Mr Jones was; and this man, whose name is Dowling, Mr Jones tells me is your steward. I discovered his name by a very odd accident; for he himself refused to tell it me; but Partridge, who met him at my lodgings the second time he came, knew him formerly at Salisbury."

"And did this Mr Dowling," says Allworthy, with great astonishment in his countenance, "tell you that I would assist in the prosecution?"——"No, sir," answered she, "I will not charge him wrongfully. He said I should be assisted, but he mentioned no name. Yet you must pardon me, sir, if from circumstances I thought it could be no other."——"Indeed, madam," says Allworthy, "from circumstances I am too well convinced it was another. Good Heaven! by what wonderful means is the blackest and deepest villany sometimes discovered!—Shall I beg you, madam, to stay till the person you have mentioned comes, for I expect him every minute? nay, he may be, perhaps, already in the house."

Allworthy then stept to the door, in order to call a servant, when in came, not Mr Dowling, but the gentleman who will be seen in the next chapter.

Chapter viij.

Further continuation.

THE gentleman who now arrived was no other than Mr Western. He no sooner saw Allworthy, than, without considering in the least the presence of Mrs Waters, he began to vociferate in the following manner: "Fine doings at my house! A rare kettle of fish I have discovered at last! who the devil would be plagued with a daughter?" "What's the matter, neighbour?" said Allworthy. "Matter enough," answered Western: "when I thought she was just a coming to; nay, when she had in a manner promised me to do as I would ha her, and when I was a hoped to have had nothing more to do than to have sent for the lawyer, and finished all; what do you think I have found out? that the little b— hath bin playing tricks with me all the while, and carrying on a correspondence with that bastard of yours. Sister Western, whom I have quarrelled with upon her account, sent me word o't, and I ordered her pockets to be searched when she was asleep, and here I have got un signed with the son of a whore's own name. I have not had patience to read half o't, for 'tis longer than one of parson Supple's sermons; but I find plainly it is all about love; and indeed what should it be else? I have packed her up in chamber again, and to-morrow morning down she goes into the country, unless she consents to be married directly, and there she shall live in a garret upon bread and water all her days; and the sooner such a b— breaks her heart the better, though, d—n her, that I believe is too tough. She will live long enough to plague me." "Mr Western," answered Allworthy, "you know I have always protested against force, and you yourself consented that none should be

used." "Ay," cries he, "that was only upon condition that she would consent without. What the devil
and doctor Faustus! shan't I do what I will with my
own daughter, especially when I desire nothing but her
own good?" "Well, neighbour," answered Allworthy, "if you will give me leave, I will undertake
once to argue with the young lady." "Will you?"
said Western; "why that is kind now, and neigh-
bourly, and mayhap you will do more than I have been
able to do with her; for I promise you she hath a very
good opinion of you." "Well, sir," said Allworthy,
"if you will go home, and release the young lady from
her captivity, I will wait upon her within this half-
hour." "But suppose," said Western, "she should
run away with un in the meantime? For lawyer
Dowling tells me there is no hopes of hanging the
fellow at last; for that the man is alive, and like to do
well, and that he thinks Jones will be out of prison
again presently." "How!" said Allworthy; "what,
did you employ him then to enquire or to do anything
in that matter?" "Not I," answered Western, "he
mentioned it to me just now of his own accord."
"Just now!" cries Allworthy, "why, where did you
see him then? I want much to see Mr Dowling."
"Why, you may see un an you will presently at my
lodgings; for there is to be a meeting of lawyers
there this morning about a mortgage. 'Icod! I shall
lose two or dree thousand pounds, I believe, by that
honest gentleman, Mr Nightingale." "Well, sir,"
said Allworthy, "I will be with you within the half-
hour." "And do for once," cries the squire, "take
a fool's advice; never think of dealing with her by
gentle methods, take my word for it those will never
do. I have tried 'um long enough. She must be
frightened into it, there is no other way. Tell her
I'm her father; and of the horrid sin of disobedience,

and of the dreadful punishment of it in t'other world, and then tell her about being locked up all her life in a garret in this, and being kept only on bread and water." "I will do all I can," said Allworthy; "for I promise you there is nothing I wish for more than an alliance with this amiable creature." "Nay, the girl is well enough for matter o'that," cries the squire; "a man may go farther and meet with worse meat; that I may declare o'her, thof she be my own daughter. And if she will but be obedient to me, there is narrow a father within a hundred miles o' the place, that loves a daughter better than I do; but I see you are busy with the lady here, so I will go huome and expect you; and so your humble servant."

As soon as Mr Western was gone Mrs Waters said, "I see, sir, the squire hath not the least remembrance of my face. I believe, Mr Allworthy, you would not have known me neither. I am very considerably altered since that day when you so kindly gave me that advice, which I had been happy had I followed." "Indeed, madam," cries Allworthy, "it gave me great concern when I first heard the contrary." "Indeed, sir," says she, "I was ruined by a very deep scheme of villany, which if you knew, though I pretend not to think it would justify me in your opinion, it would at least mitigate my offence, and induce you to pity me: you are not now at leisure to hear my whole story; but this I assure you, I was betrayed by the most solemn promises of marriage; nay, in the eye of heaven I was married to him; for, after much reading on the subject, I am convinced that particular ceremonies are only requisite to give a legal sanction to marriage, and have only a worldly use in giving a woman the privileges of a wife; but that she who lives constant to one man, after a solemn private affiance, whatever the world may call her, hath little to charge on her own conscience." "I am sorry, madam," said Allworthy, "you made so ill a use of your learning. Indeed, it would have been well that you had been possessed of much more, or had remained in a state of ignorance. And yet, madam, I am afraid you have more than this sin to answer for." "During his life," answered she, "which was above a dozen years, I most solemnly assure you I had not. And consider, sir, on my behalf, what is in the power of a woman stript of her reputation and left destitute; whether the good-natured world will suffer such a stray sheep to return to the road of virtue, even if she was never so desirous. I protest, then, I would have chose it had it been in my power; but necessity drove me into the arms of Captain Waters, with whom, though still unmarried, I lived as a wife for many years, and went by his name. I parted with this gentleman at Worcester, on his march against the rebels, and it was then I accidentally met with Mr Jones, who rescued me from the hands of a villain. Indeed, he is the worthiest of men. No young gentleman of his age is, I believe, freer from vice, and few have the twentieth part of his virtues; nay, whatever vices he hath had, I am firmly persuaded he hath now taken a resolution to abandon them." "I hope he hath," cries Allworthy, "and I hope he will preserve that resolution. I must say, I have still the same hopes with regard to yourself. The world, I do agree, are apt to be too unmerciful on these occasions; yet time and perseverance will get the better of this their disinclination, as I may call it, to pity; for though they are not, like heaven, ready to receive a penitent sinner; yet a continued repentance will at length obtain mercy even with the world. This you may be assured of, Mrs Waters, that whenever I find you are sincere in such good intentions, you shall want no assistance in my power to make them effectual."

Mrs Waters fell now upon her knees before him, and, in a flood of tears, made him many most passionate acknowledgments of his goodness, which, as she truly said, savoured more of the divine than human nature.

Allworthy raised her up, and spoke in the most tender manner, making use of every expression which his invention could suggest to comfort her, when he was interrupted by the arrival of Mr Dowling, who, upon his first entrance, seeing Mrs Waters, started, and appeared in some confusion; from which he soon recovered himself as well as he could, and then said he was in the utmost haste to attend counsel at Mr Western's lodgings; but, however, thought it his duty to call and acquaint him with the opinion of counsel upon the case which he had before told him, which was that the conversion of the moneys in that case could not be questioned in a criminal cause, but that an action of trover might be brought, and if it appeared to the jury to be the moneys of plaintiff, that plaintiff would recover a verdict for the value.

Allworthy, without making any answer to this, bolted the door, and then, advancing with a stern look to Dowling, he said, "Whatever be your haste, sir, I must first receive an answer to some questions. Do you know this lady?"——"That lady, sir!" answered Dowling, with great hesitation. Allworthy then, with the most solemn voice, said, "Look you, Mr Dowling, as you value my favour, or your continuance a moment longer in my service, do not hesitate nor prevaricate; but answer faithfully and truly to every question I ask.——Do you know this lady?"——"Yes, sir," said Dowling, "I have seen the lady." "Where, sir?" "At her own lodgings."

—"Upon what business did you go thither, sir; and who sent you?" "I went, sir, to enquire, sir, about Mr Jones." "And who sent you to enquire about him?" "Who, sir? why, sir, Mr Blifil sent me." "And what did you say to the lady concerning that matter?" "Nay, sir, it is impossible to recollect every word." "Will you please, madam, to assist the gentleman's memory?" "He told me, sir," said Mrs Waters, "that if Mr Jones had murdered my husband, I should be assisted by any money I wanted to carry on the prosecution, by a very worthy gentleman, who was well apprized what a villain I had to deal with. These, I can safely swear, were the very words he spoke."—"Were these the words, sir?" said Allworthy. "I cannot charge my memory exactly," cries Dowling, "but I believe I did speak to that purpose."—"And did Mr Blifil order you to say so?" "I am sure, sir, I should not have gone on my own accord, nor have willingly exceeded my authority in matters of this kind. If I said so, I must have so understood Mr Blifil's instructions." "Look you, Mr Dowling," said Allworthy; "I promise you before this lady, that whatever you have done in this affair by Mr Blifil's order I will forgive, provided you now tell me strictly the truth; for I believe what you say, that you would not have acted of your own accord and without authority in this matter.——Mr Blifil then likewise sent you to examine the two fellows at Aldersgate?"—"He did, sir." "Well, and what instructions did he then give you? Recollect as well as you can, and tell me, as near as possible, the very words he used."——"Why, sir, Mr Blifil sent me to find out the persons who were eye-witnesses of this fight. He said, he feared they might be tampered with by Mr Jones, or some of his friends. He said, blood required blood; and that not only all who concealed a murderer, but those who omitted anything in their power to bring him to justice, were sharers in his guilt. He said, he found you was very desirous of having the villain brought to justice, though it was not proper you should appear in it." "He did so?" says Allworthy.— "Yes, sir," cries Dowling; "I should not, I am sure, have proceeded such lengths for the sake of any other person living but your worship."—"What lengths, sir?" said Allworthy.—"Nay, sir," cries Dowling, "I would not have your worship think I would, on any account, be guilty of subornation of perjury; but there are two ways of delivering evidence. I told them, therefore, that if any offers should be made them on the other side, they should refuse them, and that they might be assured they should lose nothing by being honest men, and telling the truth. I said, we were told that Mr Jones had assaulted the gentleman first, and that, if that was the truth, they should declare it; and I did give them some hints that they should be no losers."—"I think you went lengths indeed," cries Allworthy.——"Nay, sir," answered Dowling, "I am sure I did not desire them to tell an untruth;—— nor should I have said what I did, unless it had been to oblige you."——"You would not have thought, I believe," says Allworthy, "to have obliged me, had you known that this Mr Jones was my own nephew." ——"I am sure, sir," answered he, "it did not become me to take any notice of what I thought you desired to conceal."—"How!" cries Allworthy, "and did you know it then?"—"Nay, sir," answered Dowling, "if your worship bids me speak the truth, I am sure I shall do it.—Indeed, sir, I did know it; for they were almost the last words which Madam Blifil ever spoke, which she mentioned to me as I stood alone by her bedside, when she delivered me the letter I brought your worship from her."—"What letter?"

cries Allworthy.—"The letter, sir," answered Dowling, "which I brought from Salisbury, and which I delivered into the hands of Mr Blifil."——"O heavens!" cries Allworthy: "Well, and what were the words? What did my sister say to you?"—"She took me by the hand," answered he, "and, as she delivered me the letter, said, 'I scarce know what I have written. Tell my brother, Mr Jones is his nephew—He is my son.—Bless him,' says she, and then fell backward, as if dying away. I presently called in the people, and she never spoke more to me, and died within a few minutes afterwards."—Allworthy stood a minute silent, lifting up his eyes; and then, turning to Dowling, said, "How came you, sir, not to deliver me this message?" "Your worship," answered he, "must remember that you was at that time ill in bed; and, being in a violent hurry, as indeed I always am, I delivered the letter and message to Mr Blifil, who told me he would carry them both to you, which he hath since told me he did, and that your worship, partly out of friendship to Mr Jones, and partly out of regard to your sister, would never have it mentioned, and did intend to conceal it from the world; and therefore, sir, if you had not mentioned it to me first, I am certain I should never have thought it belonged to me to say anything of the matter, either to your worship or any other person."

We have remarked somewhere already, that it is possible for a man to convey a lie in the words of truth; this was the case at present; for Blifil had, in fact, told Dowling what he now related, but had not imposed upon him, nor indeed had imagined he was able so to do. In reality, the promises which Blifil had made to Dowling were the motives which had induced him to secrecy; and, as he now very plainly saw Blifil would not be able to keep them, he thought proper now to make this confession, which the promises of forgiveness, joined to the threats, the voice, the looks of Allworthy, and the discoveries he had made before, extorted from him, who was besides taken unawares, and had no time to consider of evasions.

Allworthy appeared well satisfied with this relation, and, having enjoined on Dowling strict silence as to what had past, conducted that gentleman himself to the door, lest he should see Blifil, who was returned to his chamber, where he exulted in the thoughts of his last deceit on his uncle, and little suspected what had since passed below-stairs.

As Allworthy was returning to his room he met Mrs Miller in the entry, who, with a face all pale and full of terror, said to him, "O! sir, I find this wicked woman hath been with you, and you know all; yet do not on this account abandon the poor young man. Consider, sir, he was ignorant it was his own mother; and the discovery itself will most probably break his heart, without your unkindness."

"Madam," says Allworthy, "I am under such an astonishment at what I have heard, that I am really unable to satisfy you; but come with me into my room. Indeed, Mrs Miller, I have made surprizing discoveries, and you shall soon know them."

The poor woman followed him trembling; and now Allworthy, going up to Mrs Waters, took her by the hand, and then, turning to Mrs Miller, said, "What reward shall I bestow upon this gentlewoman, for the services she hath done me?—O! Mrs Miller, you have a thousand times heard me call the young man to whom you are so faithful a friend, my son. Little did I then think he was indeed related to me at all.—Your friend, madam, is my nephew; he is the brother of that wicked viper which I have so long nourished in my bosom.—She will herself tell you the whole story, and how the youth came to pass for her son. Indeed, Mrs Miller, I am convinced that he hath been wronged, and that I have been abused; abused by one whom you too justly suspected of being a villain. He is, in truth, the worst of villains."

The joy which Mrs Miller now felt bereft her of the power of speech, and might perhaps have deprived her of her senses, if not of life, had not a friendly shower of tears come seasonably to her relief. At length, recovering so far from her transport as to be able to speak, she cried, "And is my dear Mr Jones then your nephew, sir, and not the son of this lady? And are your eyes opened to him at last? And shall I live to see him as happy as he deserves?" "He certainly is my nephew," says Allworthy, "and I hope all the rest."—"And is this the dear good woman, the person," cries she, "to whom all this discovery is owing?"—"She is indeed," says Allworthy.—"Why, then," cried Mrs Miller, upon her knees, "may Heaven shower down its choicest blessings upon her head, and for this one good action forgive her all her sins, be they never so many!"

Mrs Waters then informed them that she believed Jones would very shortly be released; for that the surgeon was gone, in company with a nobleman, to the justice who committed him, in order to certify that Mr Fitzpatrick was out of all manner of danger, and to procure his prisoner his liberty.

Allworthy said he should be glad to find his nephew there at his return home; but that he was then obliged to go on some business of consequence. He then called to a servant to fetch him a chair, and presently left the two ladies together.

Mr Blifil, hearing the chair ordered, came downstairs to attend upon his uncle; for he never was deficient in such acts of duty. He asked his uncle if he was going out, which is a civil way of asking a man whither he is going: to which the other making no answer, he again desired to know when he would be pleased to return?—Allworthy made no answer to this neither, till he was just going into his chair, and then, turning about, he said—"Harkee, sir, do you find out, before my return, the letter which your mother sent me on her death-bed." Allworthy then departed, and left Blifil in a situation to be envied only by a man who is just going to be hanged.

Chapter ix.

A further continuation.

ALLWORTHY took an opportunity, whilst he was in the chair, of reading the letter from Jones to Sophia, which Western delivered him; and there were some expressions in it concerning himself which drew tears from his eyes. At length he arrived at Mr Western's, and was introduced to Sophia.

When the first ceremonies were past, and the gentleman and lady had taken their chairs, a silence of some minutes ensued; during which the latter, who had been prepared for the visit by her father, sat playing with her fan, and had every mark of confusion both in her countenance and behaviour. At length Allworthy, who was himself a little disconcerted, began thus: "I am afraid, Miss Western, my family hath been the occasion of giving you some uneasiness; to which, I fear, I have innocently become more instrumental than I intended. Be assured, madam, had I at first known how disagreeable the proposals had been, I should not have suffered you to have been so long persecuted. I hope, therefore, you will not think the design of this visit is to trouble you with any further solicitations of that kind, but entirely to relieve you from them."

"Sir," said Sophia, with a little modest hesitation, "this behaviour is most kind and generous, and such as I could expect only from Mr Allworthy; but as you have been so kind to mention this matter, you will pardon me for saying it hath, indeed, given me great uneasiness, and hath been the occasion of my suffering much cruel treatment from a father who was, till that unhappy affair, the tenderest and fondest of all parents. I am convinced, sir, you are too good and generous to resent my refusal of your nephew. Our inclinations are not in our own power; and whatever may be his merit, I cannot force them in his favour." "I assure you, most amiable young lady," said Allworthy, "I am capable of no such resentment, had the person been my own son, and had I entertained the highest esteem for him. For you say truly, madam, we cannot force our inclinations, much less can they be directed by another." "Oh! sir," answered Sophia, "every word you speak proves you deserve that good, that great, that benevolent character the whole world allows you. I assure you, sir, nothing less than the certain prospect of future misery could have made me resist the commands of my father." "I sincerely believe you, madam," replied Allworthy, "and I heartily congratulate you on your prudent foresight, since by so justifiable a resistance you have avoided misery indeed!" "You speak now, Mr Allworthy," cries she, "with a delicacy which few men are capable of feeling! but surely, in my opinion, to lead our lives with one to whom we are indifferent must be a state of wretchedness.—Perhaps that wretchedness would be even increased by a sense of the merits of an object to whom we cannot give our affections. If I had married Mr Blifil——" "Pardon my interrupting you, madam," answered Allworthy, "but I cannot bear the supposition.——Believe me, Miss Western, I rejoice from my heart, I rejoice in your escape.——I have discovered the wretch for whom you have suffered all this cruel violence from your father to be a villain." "How, sir!" cries Sophia—"you must believe this surprizes me."——"It hath surprized me, madam," answered Allworthy, "and so it will the world.——But I have acquainted you with the real truth." "Nothing but truth," says Sophia, "can, I am convinced, come from the lips of Mr Allworthy.——Yet, sir, such sudden, such unexpected news.——Discovered, you say—— may villany be ever so!"——"You will soon enough hear the story," cries Allworthy;—"at present let us not mention so detested a name.—I have another matter of a very serious nature to propose.—O! Miss Western, I know your vast worth, nor can I so easily part with the ambition of being allied to it.—I have a near relation, madam, a young man whose character is, I am convinced, the very opposite to that of this wretch, and whose fortune I will make equal to what his was to have been. Could I, madam, hope you would admit a visit from him?" Sophia, after a minute's silence, answered, "I will deal with the utmost sincerity with Mr Allworthy. His character, and the obligation I have just received from him, demand it. I have determined at present to listen to no such proposals from any person. My only desire is to be restored to the affection of my father, and to be again the mistress of his family. This, sir, I hope to owe to your good offices. Let me beseech you, let me conjure you, by all the goodness which I, and all who know you, have experienced, do not, the very moment when you have released me from one persecution, do not engage me in another as miserable and as fruitless." "Indeed, Miss Western," replied Allworthy, "I am capable of no such conduct; and if this be your resolution, he must submit to the disappointment, whatever torments he may suffer under it." "I must smile now, Mr Allworthy," answered Sophia, "when you mention the torments of a man whom I do not know, and who can consequently have so little acquaintance with me." "Pardon me, dear young lady," cries Allworthy, "I begin now to be afraid he hath had too much acquaintance for the repose of his future days; since, if ever man was capable of a sincere, violent, and noble passion, such, I am convinced, is my unhappy nephew's for Miss Western." "A nephew of your's, Mr Allworthy!" answered Sophia. "It is surely strange. I never heard of him before." "Indeed, madam," cries Allworthy, "it is only the circumstance of his being my nephew to which you are a stranger, and which, till this day, was a secret to me.—Mr Jones, who has long loved you, he! he is my nephew!" "Mr Jones your nephew, sir!" cries Sophia, "can it be possible?"—"He is, indeed, madam," answered Allworthy; "he is my own sister's son—as such I shall always own him; nor am I ashamed of owning him. I am much more ashamed of my past behaviour to him; but I was as ignorant of his merit as of his birth. Indeed, Miss Western, I have used him cruelly——Indeed I have."——Here the good man wiped his eyes, and after a short pause proceeded —"I never shall be able to reward him for his sufferings without your assistance.——Believe me, most amiable young lady, I must have a great esteem of that offering which I make to your worth. I know he hath been guilty of faults; but there is great goodness of heart at the bottom. Believe me, madam, there is." Here he stopped, seeming to expect an answer, which he presently received from Sophia, after she had a little recovered herself from the hurry of spirits into which so strange and sudden information had thrown her: "I sincerely wish you joy, sir, of a discovery in which you seem to have such satisfaction. I doubt not but you will have all the comfort you can promise yourself from it. The young gentleman hath certainly a thousand good qualities, which makes it impossible he should not behave well to such an uncle."—"I hope, madam," said Allworthy, "he hath those good qualities which must make him a good husband.—He must, I am sure, be of all men the most abandoned, if a lady of your merit should condescend——" "You must pardon me, Mr Allworthy," answered Sophia; "I cannot listen to a proposal of this kind. Mr Jones, I am convinced, hath much merit; but I shall never receive Mr Jones as one who is to be my husband—Upon my honour I never will."—"Pardon me, madam," cries Allworthy, "if I am a little surprized, after what I have heard from Mr Western——I hope the unhappy young man hath done nothing to forfeit your good opinion, if he had ever the honour to enjoy it.— Perhaps, he may have been misrepresented to you, as he was to me. The same villany may have injured him everywhere.—He is no murderer, I assure you; as he hath been called."—"Mr Allworthy," answered Sophia, "I have told you my resolution. I wonder not at what my father hath told you; but, whatever his apprehensions or fears have been, if I know my heart, I have given no occasion for them; since it hath always been a fixed principle with me, never to have married without his consent. This is, I think, the duty of a child to a parent; and this, I hope, nothing could ever have prevailed with me to swerve from. I do not indeed conceive that the authority of any parent can oblige us to marry in direct opposition to our inclinations. To avoid a force of this kind, which I had reason to suspect, I left my father's house, and sought protection elsewhere. This is the truth of my story; and if the world, or my father, carry my intentions any farther, my own conscience will acquit me." "I hear you, Miss Western," cries Allworthy, "with admiration. I admire the justness of your sentiments; but surely there is more in this. I am cautious of offending you, young lady; but am I to look on all which I have hitherto heard or seen as a dream only? And have you suffered so much cruelty from your father on the account of a man to whom you have been always absolutely indifferent?" "I beg, Mr Allworthy," answered Sophia, "you will not insist on my reasons;—yes, I have suffered indeed; I will not, Mr Allworthy, conceal——I will be very sincere with you—I own I had a great opinion of Mr Jones—I believe—I know I have suffered for my opinion—I have been treated cruelly by my aunt, as well as by my father; but that is now past—I beg I may not be farther pressed; for, whatever hath been, my resolution is now fixed. Your nephew, sir, hath many virtues—he hath great virtues, Mr Allworthy. I question not but he will do you honour in the world, and make you happy."—"I wish I could make him so, madam," replied Allworthy; "but that I am convinced is only in your power. It is that conviction which hath made me so earnest a solicitor in his favour." "You are deceived indeed, sir; you are deceived," said Sophia. "I hope not by him. It is sufficient to have deceived me. Mr Allworthy, I must insist on being pressed no farther on this subject. I should be sorry—nay, I will not injure him in your favour. I wish Mr Jones very well. I sincerely wish him well; and I repeat it again to you, whatever demerit he may have to me, I am certain he hath many good qualities. I do not disown my former thoughts; but nothing can ever recal them. At present there is not a man upon earth whom I would more resolutely reject than Mr Jones; nor would the addresses of Mr Blifil himself be less agreeable to me."

Western had been long impatient for the event of this conference, and was just now arrived at the door to listen; when, having heard the last sentiments of his daughter's heart, he lost all temper, and, bursting open the door in a rage, cried out—"It is a lie! It is a d—n'd lie! It is all owing to that d—n'd rascal Jones; and if she could get at un, she'd ha un any hour of the day." Here Allworthy interposed, and addressing himself to the squire with some anger in his look, he said, "Mr Western, you have not kept your word with me. You promised to abstain from all violence."—"Why, so I did," cries Western, "as long as it was possible; but to hear a wench telling such confounded lies——Zounds! doth she think, if she can make vools of other volk, she can make one of me?——No, no, I know her better than thee dost." "I am sorry to tell you, sir," answered Allworthy, "it doth not appear, by your behaviour to this young lady, that you know her at all. I ask pardon for what I say: but I think our intimacy, your own desires, and the occasion justify me. She is your daughter, Mr Western, and I think she doth honour to your name. If I was capable of envy, I should sooner envy you on this account than any other man whatever."—"Odrabbit it!" cries the squire, "I wish she was thine, with all my heart—wouldst soon be glad to be rid of the trouble o' her." "Indeed, my good friend," answered Allworthy, "you yourself are the cause of all the trouble you complain of. Place that confidence in the young lady which she so well deserves, and I am certain you will be the happiest father on earth."——"I confidence in her?" cries the squire. "'Sblood! what confidence can I place in her, when she won't do as I would ha' her? Let her gi' but her consent to marry as I would ha' her, and I'll place as much confidence in her as wouldst ha' me."——"You have no right, neighbour," answered Allworthy, "to insist on any such consent. A negative voice your daughter allows you, and God and nature have thought proper to allow you no more."——"A negative voice!" cries the squire, "Ay! ay! I'll show you what a negative voice I ha.—Go along, go into your chamber, go, you stubborn——." "Indeed, Mr Western," said Allworthy, "indeed you use her cruelly—I cannot bear to see this—you shall, you must behave to her in a kinder manner. She deserves the best of treatment." "Yes, yes," said the squire, "I know what she deserves: now she's gone, I'll shew you what she deserves. See here, sir, here is a letter from my cousin, my Lady Bellaston, in which she is so kind to gi' me to understand that the fellow is got out of prison again; and here she advises me to take all the care I can o' the wench. Odzookers! neighbour Allworthy, you don't know what it is to govern a daughter."

The squire ended his speech with some compliments to his own sagacity; and then Allworthy, after a formal preface, acquainted him with the whole discovery which he had made concerning Jones, with his anger to Blifil, and with every particular which hath been disclosed to the reader in the preceding chapters.

Men over-violent in their dispositions are, for the most part, as changeable in them. No sooner then was Western informed of Mr Allworthy's intention to make Jones his heir, than he joined heartily with the uncle in every commendation of the nephew, and became as eager for her marriage with Jones as he had before been to couple her to Blifil.

Here Mr Allworthy was again forced to interpose, and to relate what had passed between him and Sophia, at which he testified great surprize.

The squire was silent a moment, and looked wild with astonishment at this account.—At last he cried out, "Why, what can be the meaning of this, neighbour Allworthy? Vond o' un she was, that I'll be sworn to.——Odzookers! I have hit o't. As sure as a gun I have hit o' the very right o't. It's all along o' zister. The girl hath got a hankering after this son of a whore of a lord. I vound 'em together at my cousin my Lady Bellaston's. He hath turned the head o' her, that's certain—but d—n me if he shall ha her—I'll ha no lords nor courtiers in my vamily."

Allworthy now made a long speech, in which he repeated his resolution to avoid all violent measures, and very earnestly recommended gentle methods to Mr Western, as those by which he might be assured of succeeding best with his daughter. He then took his leave, and returned back to Mrs Miller, but was forced to comply with the earnest entreaties of the squire, in promising to bring Mr Jones to visit him that afternoon, that he might, as he said, "make all matters up with the young gentleman." At Mr Allworthy's departure, Western promised to follow his advice in his behaviour to Sophia, saying, "I don't know how 'tis, but d—n me, Allworthy, if you don't make me always do just as you please; and yet I have as good an esteate as you, and am in the commission of the peace as well as yourself."

Chapter x.

Wherein the history begins to draw towards a conclusion.

WHEN Allworthy returned to his lodgings, he heard Mr Jones was just arrived before him. He hurried therefore instantly into an empty chamber, whither he ordered Mr Jones to be brought to him alone.

It is impossible to conceive a more tender or moving scene than the meeting between the uncle and nephew (for Mrs Waters, as the reader may well suppose, had at her last visit discovered to him the secret of his birth). The first agonies of joy which were felt on both sides are indeed beyond my power to describe: I shall not therefore attempt it. After Allworthy had raised Jones from his feet, where he had prostrated himself, and received him into his arms, "O my child!" he cried, "how have I been to blame! how have I injured you! What amends can I ever make you for those unkind, those unjust suspicions which I have entertained, and for all the sufferings they have occasioned to you?" "Am I not now made amends?" cries Jones. "Would not my sufferings, if they had been ten times greater, have been now richly repaid? O my dear uncle, this goodness, this tenderness overpowers, unmans, destroys me. I cannot bear the transports which flow so fast upon me. To be again restored to your presence, to your favour; to be once more thus kindly received by my great, my noble, my generous benefactor."—"Indeed, child," cries Allworthy, "I have used you cruelly."——He then explained to him all the treachery of Blifil, and again repeated expressions of the utmost concern, for having been induced by that treachery to use him so ill. "O, talk not so!" answered Jones; "indeed, sir, you have used me nobly. The wisest man might be deceived as you were; and, under such a deception, the best must have acted just as you did. Your goodness displayed itself in the midst of your anger, just as it then seemed. I owe everything to that goodness, of which I have been most unworthy. Do not put me on self-accusation, by carrying your generous sentiments too far. Alas! sir, I have not been punished more than I have deserved; and it shall be the whole business of my future life to deserve that happiness you now bestow on me; for, believe me, my dear uncle, my punishment hath not been thrown away upon me: though I have been a great, I am not a hardened sinner; I thank Heaven, I have had time to reflect on my past life, where, though I cannot charge myself with any gross villany, yet I can discern follies and vices more than enough to repent and to be ashamed of; follies which have been attended with dreadful consequences to myself, and have brought me to the brink of destruction." "I am rejoiced, my dear child," answered Allworthy, "to hear you talk thus sensibly; for as I am convinced hypocrisy (good Heaven! how have I been imposed on by it in others!) was never among your faults, so I can readily believe all you say. You now see, Tom, to what dangers imprudence alone may subject virtue (for virtue, I am now convinced, you love in a great degree). Prudence is indeed the duty which we owe to ourselves; and if we will be so much our own enemies as to neglect it, we are not to wonder if the world is deficient in discharging their duty to us; for when a man lays the foundation of his own ruin, others will, I am afraid, be too apt to build upon it. You say, however, you have seen your errors, and will reform them. I firmly believe you, my dear child; and therefore, from this moment, you shall never be reminded of them by me.

Remember them only yourself so far as for the future to teach you the better to avoid them; but still remember, for your comfort, that there is this great difference between those faults which candor may construe into imprudence, and those which can be deduced from villany only. The former, perhaps, are even more apt to subject a man to ruin; but if he reform, his character will, at length, be totally retrieved; the world, though not immediately, will in time be reconciled to him; and he may reflect, not without some mixture of pleasure, on the dangers he hath escaped; but villany, my boy, when once discovered is irretrievable; the stains which this leaves behind, no time will wash away. The censures of mankind will pursue the wretch, their scorn will abash him in publick; and if shame drives him into retirement, he will go to it with all those terrors with which a weary child, who is afraid of hobgoblins, retreats from company to go to bed alone. Here his murdered conscience will haunt him.—Repose, like a false friend, will fly from him. Wherever he turns his eyes, horror presents itself; if he looks backward, unavailable repentance treads on his heels; if forward, incurable despair stares him in the face, till, like a condemned prisoner confined in a dungeon, he detests his present condition, and yet dreads the consequence of that hour which is to relieve him from it. Comfort yourself, I say, my child, that this is not your case; and rejoice with thankfulness to him who hath suffered you to see your errors, before they have brought on you that destruction to which a persistance in even those errors must have led you. You have deserted them; and the prospect now before you is such, that happiness seems in your own power." At these words Jones fetched a deep sigh; upon which, when Allworthy remonstrated, he said, " Sir, I will conceal nothing from you : I fear there is one consequence of my vices I shall never be able to retrieve. O, my dear uncle! I have lost a treasure." "You need say no more," answered Allworthy; "I will be explicit with you; I know what you lament; I have seen the young lady, and have discoursed with her concerning you. This I must insist on, as an earnest of your sincerity in all you have said, and of the stedfastness of your resolution, that you obey me in one instance. To abide intirely by the determination of the young lady, whether it shall be in your favour or no. She hath already suffered enough from solicitations which I hate to think of; she shall owe no further constraint to my family : I know her father will be as ready to torment her now on your account as he hath formerly been on another's ; but I am determined she shall suffer no more confinement, no more violence, no more uneasy hours." "O, my dear uncle!" answered Jones, "lay, I beseech you, some command on me, in which I shall have some merit in obedience. Believe me, sir, the only instance in which I could disobey you would be to give an uneasy moment to my Sophia. No, sir, if I am so miserable to have incurred her displeasure beyond all hope of forgiveness, that alone, with the dreadful reflection of causing her misery, will be sufficient to overpower me. To call Sophia mine is the greatest, and now the only additional blessing which heaven can bestow ; but it is a blessing which I must owe to her alone." "I will not flatter you, child," cries Allworthy; "I fear your case is desperate : I never saw stronger marks of an unalterable resolution in any person than appeared in her vehement declarations against receiving your addresses ; for which, perhaps, you can account better than myself." "Oh, sir ! I can account too well," answered Jones ; "I have sinned against her beyond all hope of pardon ; and guilty as I am, my guilt unfortunately appears to her in ten times blacker than the real colours. O, my dear uncle! I find my follies are irretrievable; and all your goodness cannot save me from perdition."

A servant now acquainted them that Mr Western was below-stairs; for his eagerness to see Jones could not wait till the afternoon. Upon which Jones, whose eyes were full of tears, begged his uncle to entertain Western a few minutes, till he a little recovered himself; to which the good man consented, and, having ordered Mr Western to be shewn into a parlour, went down to him.

Mrs Miller no sooner heard that Jones was alone (for she had not yet seen him since his release from prison) than she came eagerly into the room, and, advancing towards Jones, wished him heartily joy of his new-found uncle and his happy reconciliation; adding, "I wish I could give you joy on another account, my dear child; but anything so inexorable I never saw."

Jones, with some appearance of surprize, asked her what she meant. "Why then," says she, "I have been with your young lady, and have explained all matters to her, as they were told to me by my son Nightingale. She can have no longer any doubt about the letter; of that I am certain; for I told her my son Nightingale was ready to take his oath, if she pleased, that it was all his own invention, and the letter of his inditing. I told her the very reason of sending the letter ought to recommend you to her the more, as it was all upon her account, and a plain proof that you was resolved to quit all your profligacy for the future; that you had never been guilty of a single instance of infidelity to her since your seeing her in town: I am afraid I went too far there; but Heaven forgive me! I hope your future behaviour will be my justification.

I am sure I have said all I can ; but all to no purpose. She remains inflexible. She says, she had forgiven many faults on account of youth ; but expressed such detestation of the character of a libertine, that she absolutely silenced me. I often attempted to excuse you ; but the justness of her accusation flew in my face. Upon my honour, she is a lovely woman, and one of the sweetest and most sensible creatures I ever saw. I could have almost kissed her for one expression she made use of. It was a sentiment worthy of Seneca, or of a bishop. 'I once fancied, madam,' said she, 'I had discovered great goodness of heart in Mr Jones ; and for that I own I had a sincere esteem ; but an entire profligacy of manners will corrupt the best heart in the world ; and all which a good-natured libertine can expect is, that we should mix some grains of pity with our contempt and abhorrence.' She is an angelic creature, that is the truth on't." "O, Mrs Miller !" answered Jones, "can I bear to think I have lost such an angel?" "Lost! no," cries Mrs Miller ; "I hope you have not lost her yet. Resolve to leave such vicious courses, and you may yet have hopes ; nay, if she should remain inexorable, there is another young lady, a sweet pretty young lady, and a swinging fortune, who is absolutely dying for love of you. I heard of it this very morning, and I told it to Miss Western ; nay, I went a little beyond the truth again ; for I told her you had refused her ; but indeed I knew you would refuse her. And here I must give you a little comfort ; when I mentioned the young lady's name, who is no other than the pretty widow Hunt, I thought she turned pale ; but when I said you had refused her, I will be sworn her face was all over scarlet in an instant ; and these were her very words : 'I will not deny but that I believe he has some affection for me.'"

Here the conversation was interrupted by the arrival of Western, who could no longer be kept out of the room even by the authority of Allworthy himself; though this, as we have often seen, had a wonderful power over him.

Western immediately went up to Jones, crying out, "My old friend Tom, I am glad to see thee with all my heart! all past must be forgotten; I could not intend any affront to thee, because, as Allworthy here knows, nay, dost know it thyself, I took thee for another person; and where a body means no harm, what signifies a hasty word or two? One Christian must forget and forgive another." "I hope, sir," said Jones, "I shall never forget the many obligations I have had to you; but as for any offence towards me, I declare I am an utter stranger." "A't," says Western, "then give me thy fist; a't as hearty an honest cock as any in the kingdom. Come along with me; I'll carry thee to thy mistress this moment." Here Allworthy interposed; and the squire being unable to prevail either with the uncle or nephew, was, after some litigation, obliged to consent to delay introducing Jones to Sophia till the afternoon; at which time Allworthy, as well in compassion to Jones as in compliance with the eager desires of Western, was prevailed upon to promise to attend at the tea-table.

The conversation which now ensued was pleasant enough; and with which, had it happened earlier in our history, we would have entertained our reader; but as we have now leisure only to attend to what is very material, it shall suffice to say that matters being entirely adjusted as to the afternoon visit Mr Western again returned home.

Chapter xi.

The history draws nearer to a conclusion.

WHEN Mr Western was departed, Jones began to inform Mr Allworthy and Mrs Miller that his liberty had been procured by two noble lords, who, together with two surgeons and a friend of Mr Nightingale's, had attended the magistrate by whom he had been committed, and by whom, on the surgeons' oaths, that the wounded person was out of all manner of danger from his wound, he was discharged.

One only of these lords, he said, he had ever seen before, and that no more than once; but the other had greatly surprized him by asking his pardon for an offence he had been guilty of towards him, occasioned, he said, entirely by his ignorance who he was.

Now the reality of the case, with which Jones was not acquainted till afterwards, was this:—The lieutenant whom Lord Fellamar had employed, according to the advice of Lady Bellaston, to press Jones as a vagabond into the sea-service, when he came to report to his lordship the event which we have before seen, spoke very favourably of the behaviour of Mr Jones on all accounts, and strongly assured that lord that he must have mistaken the person, for that Jones was certainly a gentleman; insomuch that his lordship, who was strictly a man of honour, and would by no means have been guilty of an action which the world in general would have condemned, began to be much concerned for the advice which he had taken.

Within a day or two after this, Lord Fellamar happened to dine with the Irish peer, who, in a conversation upon the duel, acquainted his company with the character of Fitzpatrick; to which, indeed, he did not do strict justice, especially in what related to his lady. He said she was the most innocent, the most injured woman alive, and that from compassion alone he had undertaken her cause. He then declared an intention of going the next morning to Fitzpatrick's lodgings, in order to prevail with him, if possible, to consent to a separation from his wife, who, the peer said, was in apprehensions for her life, if she should ever return to be under the power of her husband. Lord Fellamar agreed to go with him, that he might satisfy himself more concerning Jones and the circumstances of the duel; for he was by no means easy concerning the part he had acted. The moment his lordship gave a hint of his readiness to assist in the delivery of the lady, it was eagerly embraced by the other nobleman, who depended much on the authority of Lord Fellamar, as he thought it would greatly contribute to awe Fitzpatrick into a compliance; and perhaps he was in the right; for the poor Irishman no sooner saw these noble peers had undertaken the cause of his wife than he submitted, and articles of separation were soon drawn up and signed between the parties.

Fitzpatrick, who had been so well satisfied by Mrs Waters concerning the innocence of his wife with Jones at Upton, or perhaps, from some other reasons, was now become so indifferent to that matter, that he spoke highly in favour of Jones to Lord Fellamar, took all the blame upon himself, and said the other had behaved very much like a gentleman and a man of honour; and upon that lord's further enquiry concerning Mr Jones, Fitzpatrick told him he was nephew to a gentleman of very great fashion and fortune, which was the account he had just received from Mrs Waters after her interview with Dowling.

Lord Fellamar now thought it behoved him to do everything in his power to make satisfaction to a gentleman whom he had so grossly injured, and without any consideration of rivalship (for he had now given over all thoughts of Sophia), determined to procure Mr Jones's liberty, being satisfied, as well from Fitzpatrick as his surgeon, that the wound was not mortal.   He therefore prevailed with the Irish peer to accompany him to the place where Jones was confined, to whom he behaved as we have already related.

When Allworthy returned to his lodgings, he immediately carried Jones into his room, and then acquainted him with the whole matter, as well what he had heard from Mrs Waters as what he had discovered from Mr Dowling.

Jones expressed great astonishment and no less concern at this account, but without making any comment or observation upon it.   And now a message was brought from Mr Blifil, desiring to know if his uncle was at leisure that he might wait upon him.   Allworthy started and turned pale, and then in a more passionate tone than I believe he had ever used before, bid the servant tell Blifil he knew him not.   "Consider, dear sir," cries Jones, in a trembling voice.   "I have considered," answered Allworthy, "and you yourself shall carry my message to the villain.   No one can carry him the sentence of his own ruin so properly as the man whose ruin he hath so villanously contrived."   "Pardon me, dear sir," said Jones; "a moment's reflection will, I am sure, convince you of the contrary. What might perhaps be but justice from another tongue, would from mine be insult; and to whom?—my own brother and your nephew.   Nor did he use me so barbarously—indeed, that would have been more inexcusable than anything he hath done.   Fortune may tempt men of no very bad dispositions to injustice; but insults proceed only from black and rancorous minds, and have no temptations to excuse them.   Let me beseech you, sir, to do nothing by him in the present height of your anger. Consider, my dear uncle, I was not myself condemned unheard." Allworthy stood silent a moment, and then, embracing Jones, he said, with tears gushing from his eyes, "O my child! to what goodness have I been so long blind!"

Mrs Miller entering the room at that moment, after a gentle rap which was not perceived, and seeing Jones in the arms of his uncle, the poor woman in an agony of joy fell upon her knees, and burst forth into the most ecstatic thanksgivings to heaven for what had happened; then, running to Jones, she embraced him eagerly, crying, "My dearest friend, I wish you joy a thousand and a thousand times of this blest day." And next Mr Allworthy himself received the same congratulations. To which he answered, "Indeed, indeed, Mrs Miller, I am beyond expression happy." Some few more raptures having passed on all sides, Mrs Miller desired them both to walk down to dinner in the parlour, where she said there were a very happy set of people assembled—being indeed no other than Mr Nightingale and his bride, and his cousin Harriet with her bridegroom.

Allworthy excused himself from dining with the company, saying he had ordered some little thing for him and his nephew in his own apartment, for that they had much private business to discourse of; but would not resist promising the good woman that both he and Jones would make part of her society at supper.

Mrs Miller then asked what was to be done with Blifil? "for indeed," says she, "I cannot be easy while such a villain is in my house."—Allworthy answered, "He was as uneasy as herself on the same account." "Oh!" cries she, "if that be the case, leave the matter to me, I'll soon show him the outside out of my doors, I warrant you. Here are two or three lusty fellows below-stairs." "There will be no need of any violence," cries Allworthy; "if you will carry him a message from me, he will, I am convinced, depart of his own accord." "Will I?" said Mrs Miller; "I never did anything in my life with a better will." Here Jones interfered, and said, "He had considered the matter better, and would, if Mr Allworthy pleased, be himself the messenger. I know," says he, "already enough of your pleasure, sir, and I beg leave to acquaint him with it by my own words. Let me beseech you, sir," added he, "to reflect on the dreadful consequences of driving him to violent and sudden despair. How unfit, alas! is this poor man to die in his present situation." This suggestion had not the least effect on Mrs Miller. She left the room, crying, "You are too good, Mr Jones, infinitely too good to live in this world." But it made a deeper impression on Allworthy. "My good child," said he, "I am equally astonished at the goodness of your heart, and the quickness of your understanding. Heaven indeed forbid that this wretch should be deprived of any means or time for repentance! That would be a shocking consideration indeed. Go to him, therefore, and use your own discretion; yet do not flatter him with any hopes of my forgiveness; for I shall never forgive villany farther than my religion obliges me, and that extends not either to our bounty or our conversation."

Jones went up to Blifil's room, whom he found in a situation which moved his pity, though it would have raised a less amiable passion in many beholders. He cast himself on his bed, where he lay abandoning himself to despair, and drowned in tears; not in such tears as flow from contrition, and wash away guilt from minds which have been seduced or surprized into it un-awares, against the bent of their natural dispositions, as

will sometimes happen from human frailty, even to the
good; no, these tears were such as the frighted thief
sheds in his cart, and are indeed the effects of that
concern which the most savage natures are seldom
deficient in feeling for themselves.

It would be unpleasant and tedious to paint this
scene in full length. Let it suffice to say, that the
behaviour of Jones was kind to excess. He omitted
nothing which his invention could supply, to raise and
comfort the drooping spirits of Blifil, before he communicated to him the resolution of his uncle that he
must quit the house that evening. He offered to
furnish him with any money he wanted, assured him of
his hearty forgiveness of all he had done against him,
that he would endeavour to live with him hereafter as
a brother, and would leave nothing unattempted to
effectuate a reconciliation with his uncle.

Blifil was at first sullen and silent, balancing in his
mind whether he should yet deny all; but, finding at
last the evidence too strong against him, he betook
himself at last to confession. He then asked pardon
of his brother in the most vehement manner, prostrated
himself on the ground, and kissed his feet; in short he
was now as remarkably mean as he had been before
remarkably wicked.

Jones could not so far check his disdain, but that it
a little discovered itself in his countenance at this
extreme servility. He raised his brother the moment
he could from the ground, and advised him to bear his
afflictions more like a man; repeating, at the same
time, his promises, that he would do all in his power
to lessen them; for which Blifil, making many professions of his unworthiness, poured forth a profusion
of thanks; and then, he having declared he would
immediately depart to another lodging, Jones returned
to his uncle.

Among other matters, Allworthy now acquainted Jones with the discovery which he had made concerning the £500 bank-notes. "I have," said he, "already consulted a lawyer, who tells me, to my great astonishment, that there is no punishment for a fraud of this kind. Indeed, when I consider the black ingratitude of this fellow toward you, I think a highwayman, compared to him, is an innocent person."

"Good Heaven!" says Jones, "is it possible?—I am shocked beyond measure at this news. I thought there was not an honester fellow in the world.——— The temptation of such a sum was too great for him to withstand; for smaller matters have come safe to me through his hand. Indeed, my dear uncle, you must suffer me to call it weakness rather than ingratitude; for I am convinced the poor fellow loves me, and hath done me some kindnesses, which I can never forget; nay, I believe he hath repented of this very act; for it is not above a day or two ago, when my affairs seemed in the most desperate situation, that he visited me in my confinement, and offered me any money I wanted. Consider, sir, what a temptation to a man who hath tasted such bitter distress, it must be, to have a sum in his possession which must put him and his family beyond any future possiiblity of suffering the like."

"Child," cries Allworthy, "you carry this forgiving temper too far. Such mistaken mercy is not only weakness, but borders on injustice, and is very pernicious to society, as it encourages vice. The dishonesty of this fellow I might, perhaps, have pardoned, but never his ingratitude. And give me leave to say, when we suffer any temptation to atone for dishonesty itself, we are as candid and merciful as we ought to be; and so far I confess I have gone; for I have often pitied the fate of a highwayman, when I have been on the grand jury; and have more than once applied to

the judge on the behalf of such as have had any mitigat-
ing circumstances in their case; but when dishonesty
is attended with any blacker crime, such as cruelty,
murder, ingratitude, or the like, compassion and forgiveness then become faults. I am convinced the fellow
is a villain, and he shall be punished; at least as far as
I can punish him."

This was spoken with so stern a voice, that Jones
did not think proper to make any reply; besides, the
hour appointed by Mr Western now drew so near, that
he had barely time left to dress himself. Here therefore ended the present dialogue, and Jones retired to
another room, where Partridge attended, according to
order, with his cloaths.

Partridge had scarce seen his master since the happy
discovery. The poor fellow was unable either to contain or express his transports. He behaved like one
frantic, and made almost as many mistakes while he
was dressing Jones as I have seen made by Harlequin
in dressing himself on the stage.

His memory, however, was not in the least deficient.
He recollected now many omens and presages of this
happy event, some of which he had remarked at the
time, but many more he now remembered; nor did he
omit the dreams he had dreamt the evening before his
meeting with Jones; and concluded with saying, " I
always told your honour something boded in my mind
that you would one time or other have it in your power
to make my fortune." Jones assured him that this
boding should as certainly be verified with regard to
him as all the other omens had been to himself; which
did not a little add to all the raptures which the
poor fellow had already conceived on account of his
master.

Chapter rij.

Approaching still nearer to the end.

JONES, being now completely dressed, attended his uncle to Mr Western's. He was, indeed, one of the finest figures ever beheld, and his person alone would have charmed the greater part of womankind; but we hope it hath already appeared in this history that Nature, when she formed him, did not totally rely, as she sometimes doth, on this merit only, to recommend her work.

Sophia, who, angry as she was, was likewise set forth to the best advantage, for which I leave my female readers to account, appeared so extremely beautiful, that even Allworthy, when he saw her, could not forbear whispering Western, that he believed she was the finest creature in the world. To which Western answered, in a whisper, overheard by all present, "So much the better for Tom;—for d—n me if he shan't ha the tousling her." Sophia was all over scarlet at these words, while Tom's countenance was altogether as pale, and he was almost ready to sink from his chair.

The tea-table was scarce removed before Western lugged Allworthy out of the room, telling him he had business of consequence to impart, and must speak to him that instant in private, before he forgot it.

The lovers were now alone, and it will, I question not, appear strange to many readers, that those who had so much to say to one another when danger and difficulty attended their conversation, and who seemed so eager to rush into each other's arms when so many bars lay in their way, now that with safety they were at liberty to say or do whatever they pleased, should both remain for some time silent and motionless; insomuch that a stranger of moderate sagacity might have well concluded they were mutually indifferent; but so it was, however strange it may seem; both sat with their eyes cast downwards on the ground, and for some minutes continued in perfect silence.

Mr Jones during this interval attempted once or twice to speak, but was absolutely incapable, muttering only, or rather sighing out, some broken words; when Sophia at length, partly out of pity to him, and partly to turn the discourse from the subject which she knew well enough he was endeavouring to open, said—

"Sure, sir, you are the most fortunate man in the world in this discovery." "And can you really, madam, think me so fortunate," said Jones, sighing, "while I have incurred your displeasure?"—"Nay, sir," says she, "as to that you best know whether you have deserved it." "Indeed, madam," answered he, "you yourself are as well apprized of all my demerits. Mrs Miller hath acquainted you with the whole truth. O! my Sophia, am I never to hope for forgiveness?" —"I think, Mr Jones," said she, "I may almost depend on your own justice, and leave it to yourself to pass sentence on your own conduct."—"Alas! madam," answered he, "it is mercy, and not justice, which I implore at your hands. Justice I know must condemn me.—Yet not for the letter I sent to Lady Bellaston. Of that I most solemnly declare you have had a true account." He then insisted much on the security given him by Nightingale of a fair pretence for breaking off, if, contrary to their expectations, her ladyship should have accepted his offer; but confest that he had been guilty of a great indiscretion to put such a letter as that into her power, "which," said he, "I have dearly paid for, in the effect it has upon you." "I do not, I cannot," says she, "believe otherwise of that letter than you would have me. My conduct, I think, shews you clearly I do not believe there is much in that. And yet, Mr Jones, have I not enough to resent? After what past at Upton, so soon to engage in a new amour with another woman, while I fancied, and you pretended, your heart was bleeding for me? Indeed, you have acted strangely. Can I believe the passion you have profest to me to be sincere? Or, if I can, what happiness can I assure myself of with a man capable of so much inconstancy?" "O! my Sophia," cries he, "do not doubt the sincerity of the purest passion that ever inflamed a human breast. Think, most adorable creature, of my unhappy situation, of my despair. Could I, my Sophia, have flattered myself with the most distant hopes of being ever permitted to throw myself at your feet in the manner I do now, it would not have been in the power of any other woman to have inspired a thought which the severest chastity could have condemned. Inconstancy to you! O Sophia! if you can have goodness enough to pardon what is past, do not let any cruel future apprehensions shut your mercy against me. No repentance was ever more sincere. O! let it reconcile me to my heaven in this dear bosom." "Sincere repentance, Mr Jones," answered she, "will obtain the pardon of a sinner, but it is from one who is a perfect judge of that sincerity. A human mind may be imposed on; nor is there any infallible method to prevent it. You must expect, however, that if I can be prevailed on by your repentance to pardon you, I will at least insist on the strongest proof of its sincerity." "Name any proof in my power," answered Jones eagerly. "Time," replied she; "time alone, Mr Jones, can convince me that you are a true penitent, and have resolved to abandon these vicious courses, which I should detest you for, if I imagined you capable of persevering in them." "Do not imagine it," cries Jones. "On my knees I intreat,

1 implore your confidence, a confidence which it shall be the business of my life to deserve." "Let it then," said she, "be the business of some part of your life to shew me you deserve it. I think I have been explicit enough in assuring you, that, when I see you merit my confidence, you will obtain it. After what is past, sir, can you expect I should take you upon your word?"

He replied, "Don't believe me upon my word; I have a better security, a pledge for my constancy, which it is impossible to see and to doubt." "What is that?" said Sophia, a little surprized. "I will show you, my charming angel," cried Jones, seizing her hand and carrying her to the glass. "There, behold it there in that lovely figure, in that face, that shape, those eyes, that mind which shines through these eyes; can the man who shall be in possession of these be inconstant? Impossible! my Sophia; they would fix a Dorimant, a Lord Rochester. You could not doubt it, if you could see yourself with any eyes but your own." Sophia blushed and half smiled; but, forcing again her brow into a frown—"If I am to judge," said she, "of the future by the past, my image will no more remain in your heart when I am out of your sight, than it will in this glass when I am out of the room." "By heaven, by all that is sacred!" said Jones, "it never was out of my heart. The delicacy of your sex cannot conceive the grossness of ours, nor how little one sort of amour has to do with the heart." "I will never marry a man," replied Sophia, very gravely, "who shall not learn refinement enough to be as incapable as I am myself of making such a distinction." "I will learn it," said Jones. "I have learnt it already. The first moment of hope that my Sophia might be my wife taught it me at once; and all the rest of her sex from that moment became as little the objects of desire to my sense as of passion to my heart." "Well," says Sophia, "the proof of this must be from time. Your situation, Mr Jones, is now altered, and I assure you I have great satisfaction in the alteration. You will now want no opportunity of being near me, and convincing me that your mind is altered too." "O! my angel," cries Jones, "how shall I thank thy goodness! And are you so good to own that you have a satisfaction in my prosperity?—— Believe me, believe me, madam, it is you alone have given a relish to that prosperity, since I owe to it the dear hope——O! my Sophia, let it not be a distant one.—I will be all obedience to your commands. I will not dare to press anything further than you permit me. Yet let me intreat you to appoint a short trial. O! tell me when I may expect you will be convinced of what is most solemnly true." "When I have gone voluntarily thus far, Mr Jones," said she, "I expect not to be pressed. Nay, I will not."—"O! don't look unkindly thus, my Sophia," cries he. "I do not, I dare not press you.—Yet permit me at least once more to beg you would fix the period. O! consider the impatience of love."——"A twelvemonth, perhaps," said she. "O! my Sophia," cries he, "you have named an eternity."—"Perhaps it may be something sooner," says she; "I will not be teazed. If your passion for me be what I would have it, I think you may now be easy."—"Easy! Sophia, call not such an exulting happiness as mine by so cold a name.—— O! transporting thought! am I not assured that the blessed day will come, when I shall call you mine; when fears shall be no more; when I shall have that dear, that vast, that exquisite, ecstatic delight of making my Sophia happy?"——"Indeed, sir," said she, "that day is in your own power."——"O! my dear, my divine angel," cried he, "these words have made me mad with joy.——But I must, I will thank those dear lips which have so sweetly pronounced my bliss." He then caught her in his arms, and kissed her with an ardour he had never ventured before.

At this instant Western, who had stood some time listening, burst into the room, and, with his hunting voice and phrase, cried out, "To her, boy, to her, go to her.——That's it, little honeys, O that's it ! Well ! what, is it all over ? Hath she appointed the day, boy ? What, shall it be to-morrow or next day ? It shan't be put off a minute longer than next day, I am resolved." " Let me beseech you, sir," says Jones, " don't let me be the occasion "——" Beseech mine a——," cries Western. " I thought thou hadst been a lad of higher mettle than to give way to a parcel of maidenish tricks. ——I tell thee 'tis all flimflam. Zoodikers ! she'd have the wedding to-night with all her heart. Would'st not, Sophy ? Come, confess, and be an honest girl for once. What, art dumb ? Why dost not speak ? " " Why should I confess, sir," says Sophia, " since it seems you are so well acquainted with my thoughts ? " ——" That's a good girl," cries he, " and dost consent then ? "   " No, indeed, sir," says Sophia, " I have given no such consent."——" And wunt not ha un then to-morrow, nor next day ? " says Western.—— " Indeed, sir," says she, " I have no such intention." " But I can tell thee," replied he, " why hast nut ; only because thou dost love to be disobedient, and to plague and vex thy father."   " Pray, sir," said Jones, interfering——" I tell thee thou art a puppy," cries he. " When I vorbid her, then it was all nothing but sighing and whining, and languishing and writing ; now I am vor thee, she is against thee. All the spirit of contrary, that's all. She is above being guided and governed by her father, that is the whole truth on't. It is only to disoblige and contradict me."   " What would my papa have me do ? " cries Sophia.   " What would I ha thee do?" says he, "why, gi' un thy hand this moment."———"Well, sir," says Sophia, "I will obey you.—There is my hand, Mr Jones." "Well, and will you consent to ha un to-morrow morning?" says Western.———"I will be obedient to you, sir," cries she.———"Why then to-morrow morning be the day," cries he. "Why then to-morrow morning shall be the day, papa, since you will have it so," says Sophia. Jones then fell upon his knees, and kissed her hand in an agony of joy, while Western began to caper and dance about the room, presently crying out—"Where the devil is Allworthy? He is without now, a talking with that d———d lawyer Dowling, when he should be minding other matters." He then sallied out in quest of him, and very opportunely left the lovers to enjoy a few tender minutes alone.

But he soon returned with Allworthy, saying, "If you won't believe me, you may ask her yourself. Hast nut gin thy consent, Sophy, to be married to-morrow?" "Such are your commands, sir," cries Sophia, "and I dare not be guilty of disobedience." "I hope, madam," cries Allworthy, "my nephew will merit so much goodness, and will be always as sensible as myself of the great honour you have done my family. An alliance with so charming and so excellent a young lady would indeed be an honour to the greatest in England." "Yes," cries Western, "but if I had suffered her to stand shill I shall I, dilly dally, you might not have had that honour yet a while; I was forced to use a little fatherly authority to bring her to." "I hope not, sir," cries Allworthy, "I hope there is not the least constraint." "Why, there," cries Western, "you may bid her unsay all again if you will. Dost repent heartily of thy promise, dost not, Sophia?" "Indeed, papa," cries she, "I do not repent, nor do I believe I ever shall, of any

promise in favour of Mr Jones."   "Then, nephew,"
cries Allworthy, "I felicitate you most heartily; for
I think you are the happiest of men.   And, madam,
you will give me leave to congratulate you on this
joyful occasion: indeed, I am convinced you have
bestowed yourself on one who will be sensible of
your great merit, and who will at least use his best
endeavours to deserve it."   "His best endeavours!"
cries Western, "that he will, I warrant un.——Harkee,
Allworthy, I'll bet thee five pounds to a crown we
have a boy to-morrow nine months; but prithee tell
me what wut ha!   Wut ha Burgundy, Champaigne,
or what? for, please Jupiter, we'll make a night on't."
"Indeed, sir," said Allworthy, "you must excuse me;
both my nephew and I were engaged before I suspected
this near approach of his happiness."——"Engaged!"
quoth the squire, "never tell me.——I won't part with
thee to-night upon any occasion.   Shalt sup here,
please the lord Harry."   "You must pardon me, my
dear neighbour!" answered Allworthy; "I have given
a solemn promise, and that you know I never break."
"Why, prithee, who art engaged to?" cries the
squire.——Allworthy then informed him, as likewise
of the company.——"Odzookers!" answered the
squire, "I will go with thee, and so shall Sophy!
for I won't part with thee to-night; and it would
be barbarous to part Tom and the girl."   This offer
was presently embraced by Allworthy, and Sophia
consented, having first obtained a private promise from
her father that he would not mention a syllable concerning her marriage.

Chapter the last.

In which the history is concluded.

YOUNG Nightingale had been that afternoon, by appointment, to wait on his father, who received him much more kindly than he expected. There likewise he met his uncle, who was returned to town in quest of his new-married daughter.

This marriage was the luckiest incident which could have happened to the young gentleman; for these brothers lived in a constant state of contention about the government of their children, both heartily despising the method which each other took. Each of them therefore now endeavoured, as much as he could, to palliate the offence which his own child had committed, and to aggravate the match of the other. This desire of triumphing over his brother, added to the many arguments which Allworthy had used, so strongly operated on the old gentleman that he met his son with a smiling countenance, and actually agreed to sup with him that evening at Mrs Miller's.

As for the other, who really loved his daughter with the most immoderate affection, there was little difficulty in inclining him to a reconciliation. He was no sooner informed by his nephew where his daughter and her husband were, than he declared he would instantly go to her. And when he arrived there he scarce suffered her to fall upon her knees before he took her up, and embraced her with a tenderness which affected all who saw him; and in less than a quarter of an hour was as well reconciled to both her and her husband as if he had himself joined their hands.

In this situation were affairs when Mr Allworthy and his company arrived to complete the happiness of Mrs Miller, who no sooner saw Sophia than she guessed everything that had happened; and so great was her friendship to Jones, that it added not a few transports to those she felt on the happiness of her own daughter.

There have not, I believe, been many instances of a number of people met together, where every one was so perfectly happy as in this company. Amongst whom the father of young Nightingale enjoyed the least perfect content; for, notwithstanding his affection for his son, notwithstanding the authority and the arguments of Allworthy, together with the other motive mentioned before, he could not so entirely be satisfied with his son's choice; and, perhaps, the presence of Sophia herself tended a little to aggravate and heighten his concern, as a thought now and then suggested itself that his son might have had that lady, or some other such. Not that any of the charms which adorned either the person or mind of Sophia created the uneasiness; it was the contents of her father's coffers which set his heart a longing. These were the charms which he could not bear to think his son had sacrificed to the daughter of Mrs Miller.

The brides were both very pretty women; but so totally were they eclipsed by the beauty of Sophia, that, had they not been two of the best-tempered girls in the world, it would have raised some envy in their breasts; for neither of their husbands could long keep his eyes from Sophia, who sat at the table like a queen receiving homage, or, rather, like a superior being receiving adoration from all around her. But it was an adoration which they gave, not which she exacted; for she was as much distinguished by her modesty and affability as by all her other perfections.

The evening was spent in much true mirth. All were happy, but those the most who had been most unhappy before. Their former sufferings and fears gave such a relish to their felicity as even love and fortune, in their fullest flow, could not have given without the advantage of such a comparison. Yet, as great joy, especially after a sudden change and revolution of circumstances, is apt to be silent, and dwells rather in the heart than on the tongue, Jones and Sophia appeared the least merry of the whole company; which Western observed with great impatience, often crying out to them, "Why dost not talk, boy? Why dost look so grave? Hast lost thy tongue, girl? Drink another glass of wine; sha't drink another glass." And, the more to enliven her, he would sometimes sing a merry song, which bore some relation to matrimony and the loss of a maidenhead. Nay, he would have proceeded so far on that topic as to have driven her out of the room, if Mr Allworthy had not checkt him, sometimes by looks, and once or twice by a "Fie! Mr Western!" He began, indeed, once to debate the matter, and assert his right to talk to his own daughter as he thought fit; but, as nobody seconded him, he was soon reduced to order.

Notwithstanding this little restraint, he was so pleased with the chearfulness and good-humour of the company, that he insisted on their meeting the next day at his lodgings. They all did so; and the lovely Sophia, who was now in private become a bride too, officiated as the mistress of the ceremonies, or, in the polite phrase, did the honours of the table. She had that morning given her hand to Jones, in the chapel at Doctors'-Commons, where Mr Allworthy, Mr Western, and Mrs Miller, were the only persons present.

Sophia had earnestly desired her father that no others of the company, who were that day to dine with him, should be acquainted with her marriage. The same secrecy was enjoined to Mrs Miller, and Jones undertook for Allworthy. This somewhat reconciled the delicacy of Sophia to the public entertainment which, in compliance with her father's will, she was obliged to go to, greatly against her own inclinations. In confidence of this secrecy she went through the day pretty well, till the squire, who was now advanced into the second bottle, could contain his joy no longer, but, filling out a bumper, drank a health to the bride. The health was immediately pledged by all present, to the great confusion of our poor blushing Sophia, and the great concern of Jones upon her account. To say truth, there was not a person present made wiser by this discovery; for Mrs Miller had whispered it to her daughter, her daughter to her husband, her husband to his sister, and she to all the rest.

Sophia now took the first opportunity of withdrawing with the ladies, and the squire sat in to his cups, in which he was, by degrees, deserted by all the company except the uncle of young Nightingale, who loved his bottle as well as Western himself. These two, therefore, sat stoutly to it during the whole evening, and long after that happy hour which had surrendered the charming Sophia to the eager arms of her enraptured Jones.

Thus, reader, we have at length brought our history to a conclusion, in which, to our great pleasure, though contrary, perhaps, to thy expectation, Mr Jones appears to be the happiest of all humankind; for what happiness this world affords equal to the possession of such a woman as Sophia, I sincerely own I have never yet discovered.

As to the other persons who have made any considerable figure in this history, as some may desire to know a little more concerning them, we will proceed. in as few words as possible, to satisfy their curiosity.

Allworthy hath never yet been prevailed upon to see Blifil, but he hath yielded to the importunity of Jones, backed by Sophia, to settle £200 a-year upon him; to which Jones hath privately added a third.

Upon this income he lives in one of the northern counties, about 200 miles distant from London, and lays up £200 a-year out of it, in order to purchase a seat in the next parliament from a neighbouring borough, which he has bargained for with an attorney there. He is also lately turned Methodist, in hopes of marrying a very rich widow of that sect, whose estate lies in that part of the kingdom.

Square died soon after he writ the before-mentioned letter; and as to Thwackum, he continues at his vicarage. He hath made many fruitless attempts to regain the confidence of Allworthy, or to ingratiate himself with Jones, both of whom he flatters to their faces, and abuses behind their backs. But in his stead, Mr Allworthy hath lately taken Mr Abraham Adams into his house, of whom Sophia is grown immoderately fond, and declares he shall have the tuition of her children.

Mrs Fitzpatrick is separated from her husband, and retains the little remains of her fortune. She lives in reputation at the polite end of the town, and is so good an economist, that she spends three times the income of her fortune, without running in debt. She maintains a perfect intimacy with the lady of the Irish peer; and in acts of friendship to her repays all the obligations she owes to her husband.

Mrs Western was soon reconciled to her niece Sophia, and hath spent two months together with her in the country. Lady Bellaston made the latter a formal visit at her return to town, where she behaved to Jones as to a perfect stranger, and, with great civility, wished him joy on his marriage.

Mr Nightingale hath purchased an estate for his son in the neighbourhood of Jones, where the young gentleman, his lady, Mrs Miller, and her little daughter reside, and the most agreeable intercourse subsists between the two families.

As to those of lower account, Mrs Waters returned into the country, had a pension of £60 a-year settled upon her by Mr Allworthy, and is married to Parson Supple, on whom, at the instance of Sophia, Western hath bestowed a considerable living.

Black George, hearing the discovery that had been made, ran away, and was never since heard of; and Jones bestowed the money on his family, but not in equal proportions, for Molly had much the greatest share.

As for Partridge, Jones hath settled £50 a-year on him; and he hath again set up a school, in which he meets with much better encouragement than formerly, and there is now a treaty of marriage on foot between him and Miss Molly Seagrim, which, through the mediation of Sophia, is likely to take effect.

We now return to take leave of Mr Jones and Sophia, who, within two days after their marriage, attended Mr Western and Mr Allworthy into the country. Western hath resigned his family seat, and the greater part of his estate, to his son-in-law, and hath retired to a lesser house of his in another part of the country, which is better for hunting. Indeed, he is often as a visitant with Mr Jones, who, as well as his daughter, hath an infinite delight in doing everything in their power to please him. And this desire of theirs is attended with such success, that the old gentleman declares he was never happy in his life till now. He hath here a parlour and ante-chamber to himself; where he gets drunk with whom he pleases: and his daughter is still as ready as formerly to play to him whenever he desires it; for Jones hath assured her that, as, next to pleasing her, one of his highest satisfactions is to contribute to the happiness of the old man; so, the great duty which she expresses and performs to her father, renders her almost equally dear to him with the love which she bestows on himself.

Sophia hath already produced him two fine children, a boy and a girl, of whom the old gentleman is so fond, that he spends much of his time in the nursery, where he declares the tattling of his little grand-daughter, who is above a year and a half old, is sweeter music than the finest cry of dogs in England.

Allworthy was likewise greatly liberal to Jones on the marriage, and hath omitted no instance of shewing his affection to him and his lady, who love him as a father. Whatever in the nature of Jones had a tendency to vice, has been corrected by continual conversation with this good man, and by his union with the lovely and virtuous Sophia. He hath also, by reflection on his past follies, acquired a discretion and prudence very uncommon in one of his lively parts.

To conclude, as there are not to be found a worthier man and woman, than this fond couple, so neither can any be imagined more happy. They preserve the purest and tenderest affection for each other, an affection daily encreased and confirmed by mutual endearments and mutual esteem. Nor is their conduct towards their relations and friends less amiable than towards one another. And such is their condescension, their indulgence, and their beneficence to those below them, that there is not a neighbour, a tenant, or a servant, who doth not most gratefully bless the day when Mr Jones was married to his Sophia.

THE END.

THE TEMPLE PRESS, PRINTERS, LETCHWORTH.